The Triumphant Tale of
# PIPPA NORTH

ALSO BY **TEMRE BELTZ**

The Tragical Tale of Birdie Bloom

# The Triumphant Tale of
# PIPPA NORTH

# TEMRE BELTZ

**HARPER**

*An Imprint of HarperCollinsPublishers*

Library of Congress Control Number: 2019947152
ISBN 978-0-06-283586-4

Typography by Torborg Davern
20 21 22 23 24  PC/LSCH  10 9 8 7 6 5 4 3 2 1

First Edition

*For Mom and Dad*

CROWN
STADIUM

PEABODY'S ACADEMY
FOR THE TRIUMPHANT

EMERALD HILLS

TRIUMPH
MOUNTAIN

CAPITAL
WANDERLY SQUARE

DEAD TREE
FOREST

SWINGING SWAMP

SAPPHIRE SEA

FORGOTTEN FOREST

FOULWEATHER'S HOME FOR THE TRAGICAL

TRAGIC MOUNTAIN

SLEEPING GIANTS MOUNTAIN RANGE

BEASTLY VALLEY

CASTLE MATILDA

BLACK SEA

MERRY MEADOW

SNAGGLETOOTH ISLES

DEEPEST, DARKEST BOG

PIGGLESTICKS

# CONTENTS

# Salutations.[1]

---

1. This is merely a fancy way of saying "hello." Certainly I could have just said "hello," but perhaps you didn't notice the title on my front cover? This is a *Triumphant* tale, and "hello" is somewhat of an ordinary word, don't you think?

I hail from the kingdom of Wanderly, and in the kingdom of Wanderly, there is no tale quite so beloved as a Triumphant one.[2]

Indeed, those books lucky enough to be selected for the telling of a Triumphant tale enjoy a great deal of fanfare, glowing reviews, and all-around gushing while being adoringly passed from household to household and village to village.

I have chosen a wildly different path.

I have left behind the grand comforts of my position in Wanderly and braved an indescribably exhausting trip—traveling all the way to the shores of your somewhat perplexing kingdom, simply to sit here on this shelf and wait for you.

IT'S ABOUT TIME.

Oh dear. Was that rude? You must forgive me. Triumphants in Wanderly have grown used to not waiting for a single thing. But, then again, perhaps that is one of our problems.

Problems, you ask?

Problems for *Triumphants*?

---

2. Yes, I know the word "Triumphant" is nearly as big as "salutations," but fear not, it is just as easily understood. Triumphants in Wanderly can best be equated with "heroes." Triumphants are the ones who always win, who always come out ahead, and who always get a happy ending.

Ha! If there weren't any problems, do you think I would bother prattling on in such an undignified manner? I don't know how the books in your kingdom typically behave, but in Wanderly we prefer to let our stories speak for themselves.

This worked out fine and well at one time, but things have changed.

As a storybook kingdom, Wanderly is filled with capable writers—we call them "scribes"—who string together an astonishing slew of words with admirable prowess. But you and I both know that all the words in the world do not equal a good story if they are lacking in one crucial element: truth.[3]

The trouble is, the scribes seem to have rejected that guiding principle. Or perhaps they have merely grown so accustomed to hearing the Chancellor's version of things that the difference between truth and outlandish fabrication has become dangerously blurry.

This simply can't be allowed to go on.

Especially with a story like this one.

And so, here I am.

Based on what I shared about Wanderly's Triumphants you are likely settling in for a story with bravado, celebratory trumpets,

---

3. Do not look surprised. I knew the moment you picked me up what sort of a reader you are. An excellent one, that's what! And do not bother protesting because then you will be questioning my judgment, which, if you haven't already deduced, is similarly excellent.

spouts of shimmering confetti, and perhaps even a trophy or some sort of prized blue ribbon.

Please take a moment to adjust your expectations.

Ahem, maybe even dial them down a *bit* more.

Yes, that should do. Of course, I'll do my best to ease you into things. For now I won't mention any wily, scheming magicians or the creatures that slink and slither through their hopelessly muggy swamp. We needn't spend even a minute mulling over conniving bullies named Bernard Benedict Bumble V (it's never a good sign when a numeral appears at the end of a bully's name, is it?) or bemoaning getting singed by a magical, flaming horse whose kind many deem a legend but are as real as the handsome nose on your face.

Yes, we shall have a much cheerier start in a gloomy little pocket of Wanderly known as Ink Hollow, where a girl named Pippa North looked desperately out the doorway on an impossibly rainy day while a mysterious stranger wearing a more mysterious hat slunk nearer and nearer and *nearer*—

Um, on second thought, that doesn't sound very cheery at all, does it? Nevertheless, these are precisely the sorts of ominous details the scribes in Wanderly would have left out, and I have pledged to tell you the *whole* story.

Alas, a story must begin where it begins . . . shall we proceed?

# ONE

# A SOGGY INVITATION

$\mathcal{P}$ippa North stood in the doorway of her family's tiny two-bedroom cottage and took a small (very small) step backward. She was certain she'd never seen so much rain in all of her eleven years. It was falling from the sky by the bucketful.

Pippa glanced down at her black-buckled shoes. Other than a few scuffs to be expected from a pair of hand-me-downs, they were in excellent shape. They looked especially smart when paired with her favorite nearly white socks—the ones with the dainty lace cuff. But regrettably, Pippa's shoes and socks were not at all well-suited for the rain.

A pounding even louder than the rain erupted on the steep, narrow staircase to Pippa's left. It was her four-year-old triplet brothers, Artie, Miles, and Finn, streaking past. Miles and Finn had her two older sisters' fanciest (and only) plumed feather hats perched on their sweaty little heads with Artie leading the charge.

Pippa sighed. She waited one, two, three—

"MOTHER!" cried her fifteen-year-old sister, Jane.

"Oh, Mommy, they've done it *again*!" shrieked her thirteen-year-old sister, Louisa.

At a mere eight months, the smallest North, Rose, was cradled safely in her mother's arms, but even she offered up her own plaintive little "WAHHH!"

The "WAHHH" grew a bit louder when Pippa's mother emerged from the tiny pocket of a kitchen, waving a pancake spatula about in her free hand as if it were a magic wand.[4] When she spied Pippa standing by the door, her eyes lit up. She bustled across the room (a mere three steps), tucked Rose into Pippa's arms with a breathless "Thank you, dear," and then turned on the triplets. She plucked them up by the collars of their flannel pajamas (Miles and Finn in one hand and Artie in the other because he was just a smidge taller) and let them dangle in the air for a half moment before setting them gently down.

*"Boys,"* she said in that mysterious way mothers have of condensing an entire list of arguments into one aptly spoken word.

---

4. The spatula wasn't actually magical. If you find this stop a bit annoying because you have never encountered a single spatula that was magical, well, then you have never spent much time in Wanderly. The kingdom of Wanderly positively *crackles* with magic, which is why it is always wise to be very precise in one's descriptions. Also, as a book, I cannot help being a bit fussy with words.

The triplets' shoulders slumped. At a nod from Artie, the pouty-faced Miles and Finn slipped the prized hats off and into Mrs. North's waiting hands. Without bothering to look, Mrs. North expertly tossed the two hats over her shoulder, where Jane and Louisa snatched them up and pranced back up the stairs to resume their Very Important Business, which typically meant trying out a new hairstyle they'd seen in the pages of the *Wanderly Whistle*.

Mrs. North handily plucked Rose out of Pippa's arms. She bustled back toward the kitchen, presumably to resume her pancake making before the triplets could involve themselves in yet another shenanigan, when she caught sight of Pippa and froze. "Pippa, what are you still doing here? Have you forgotten that it's—it's . . . *Wednesday*?"

But Pippa merely closed the front door, which, up until then, had been hanging wide open. The drumming rain had blended rather seamlessly into the typical morning chaos of the North family cottage, but it hadn't at all been a part of Pippa's plans. She sighed and glanced down at the lunch sack she'd carefully prepared side by side with her father earlier that morning. It seemed to have lost its jaunty tilt and now slouched hopelessly against her ankle.

"I suppose I'll be staying home today. Just this once, I guess," she said.

"Staying home?" Pippa's mother echoed, aghast.

A door upstairs flew open. "Staying home?" Pippa's sisters cried in unison.

"Pippa, home?" the triplets chimed in with their eyes wide.

"Goo-goo?" Rose queried.

Because if Rose enjoyed a good cry, if the triplets craved mischief, if Jane and Louisa appreciated beautiful things, and if the oldest North child, Charlie, enjoyed trekking off with Mr. North—not necessarily to assist with his book peddling but to attend to the cogs, wheels, and fastenings of his cart—there was one thing that everyone knew about Pippa. Pippa loved school.

In the town of Ink Hollow, commoner children were allowed to attend school one day of the week and one day of the week only. Pippa's scheduled day of attendance was Wednesday. And since first beginning school at the age of five, she had never once—no, not even once—missed a single day of instruction. But the town of Ink Hollow had also never seen such a rainstorm. Indeed, it had blown in on a most peculiar wind mere moments after Pippa's father and oldest brother had walked out the door.

A wind so peculiar that when Pippa first heard it she had almost—*almost*—considered whether it was the Winds of Wanderly come to visit. But then, very quickly, she came to her senses. Though the kingdom of Wanderly was full of a great many magical things, the Winds of Wanderly were set apart somehow. Grand. Powerful. *Maybe even more powerful,* some dared to whisper, *than the Chancellor himself.* And so, if all of that were true, Pippa could come to no other conclusion except the Winds of Wanderly could never be bothered with a town as ordinary as Ink Hollow.

So she'd pushed the matter out of her head entirely.

Mrs. North chopped her hands through the air. "No, no," she said. "This simply won't do. You shall don some of my things—" At this, Louisa went sprinting toward their mother and father's bedroom and emerged with Mrs. North's faded yellow rain galoshes and a moth-eaten cloak. Jane took the steps three at a time and bounced to a stop in front of her mother, the bow on her half-finished hairstyle flopping madly about. She held her arms out expectantly for baby Rose.

"I'll take Rose and finish the pancakes, Mother. You tend to Pippa," Jane said.

The triplets, caught up in the shift in momentum, drew up to their knees and began chanting, "Go, Pippa, go! Go, Pippa, go!"

Pippa couldn't help the smile that spread across her face. Because of all the very many elements of daily life that Pippa liked to plan and measure out, her family was the one thing that—on occasion—caught her by surprise.

Living in a family of eight children was not without its challenges, but Pippa couldn't imagine there existed any family that wasn't. And, certainly, the one thing that didn't exist anywhere else in all the kingdom was another Mother and another Father, another Charlie, Louisa, Jane, Artie, Miles, Finn, and Rose. The North family. They were hers, and she was theirs.

With Mrs. North's help, Pippa was nearly armed and ready for the rain when a loud pounding suddenly exploded from the other side of the front door.

Pippa instinctively jumped backward. In a town as tightly knit as Ink Hollow, children skipped up to neighbors' doors laughing and chattering, adults politely lifted their hands for a genteel knock or called out warmly, "Halloo? Anybody home?"

But no one, ever, not once, *pounded*.

Though Pippa saw a quick flicker of concern in her mother's eyes, Mrs. North nevertheless swept toward the door while smoothing the front of her apron. "Excuse me, dear," she said to Pippa with a tight smile. "In a storm such as this, someone might be in need of some real help."

Of all the children in the North home, however, none were more well-read than Pippa. And in a storybook kingdom, this came in quite handy considering all of Wanderly's citizens were required to adhere to their Chancellor-assigned roles. Roles that were intended to build the great story lines of the kingdom and that were spelled out in minute detail in the Chancellor's authorized storybooks (the only sort available in Wanderly). These roles ranged all the way from ordinary commoners, like Pippa's family, to celebrated heroes like Triumphants and even included magical citizens such as wizards and fairy godmothers. In regards to commoners, however, one thing was made very clear throughout all of the Chancellor's stories: they were *not*, by any means, guaranteed a happy ending. In fact, at least half of the commoners were destined to receive an unhappy ending, and it was hard for Pippa to imagine that anything good could follow on the heels of an ominous knock at the door in the midst of a dark and stormy morning. Maybe it was even something as terrible as a witch, maybe—

"Mother, WAIT!" Pippa cried out.

But it was too late.

Mrs. North swung the door open.

There was a man standing on the front porch.

A very tall, very skinny man wearing a very tall, very skinny hat. And before either Pippa or her mother could breathe a word, the man brought his very long, very skinny fingers to the brim of his hat and *disappeared*.

The triplets exploded into a round of delighted applause. Pippa and her mother, together, breathlessly slammed the door shut. Louisa, who was poised halfway down the stairs, stood pale-faced with her jaw agape. Jane, who had taken over the pancakes, poked her head out from the kitchen and asked breezily, "Everything all right in there?"

Reader, it was not.

Certainly four solid walls and a locked door are adequate forms of shelter in many kingdoms, but Wanderly is a magical kingdom—composed, at least in part, of people who can perform said magic.

And so, the tall, skinny man with the tall, skinny hat *reap*peared smack-dab in the center of the North family's cottage, perched, of all places, on top of the worn and splintered coffee table like it was a stage.

"Ta-da!" he exclaimed, as rainwater rolled right off his very fine but very mud-splattered clothing and *plip-plopp*ed onto the floor.

Pippa's heart pounded. The man who had found his way inside their home was most definitely not a witch: he was a magician.[5] There was no mistaking the magical hat, the fancy clothes, and the penchant for performance.

Pippa dutifully lifted her hands in the air and began to applaud. She cast a pointed look in her mother's direction until her mother followed suit. The man's expression softened a hair. His lips spread into a toothy grin. "Thank you, thank you," he said, bowing profusely, and entirely missing Mrs. North's erratic motion for the triplets to get up off the floor and scurry behind her.

Mrs. North greeted the man as if it wasn't one bit unusual to

---

5. If you have fond memories of attending a birthday party where a magician pulled a rabbit out of his hat much to the delight of an adoring audience, you must toss this nonsense out of your head immediately. Despite the belittling things the Chancellor loved to say about them, the magicians in Wanderly were no small thing. Is that a warning? Perhaps.

magically pop into someone's home without an invitation and drip rainwater all over their furnishings. "What brings you to Ink Hollow this morning, sir?" she asked.

The magician's grin disappeared. He crossed his arms against his chest the way the triplets did when their mother announced bedtime. "Is the weather always this foul here? I have swept through the entire village and seen not one other soul! Indeed, the only living thing I came across were chickens. Wet, scraggly chickens that haven't an ounce of appreciation for magic."

Though Pippa could hear her knees knocking, Mrs. North's voice was smooth and steady. "So are you on a magical tour, then?" she asked.

A dark shadow crossed over the magician's face. "I should be, shouldn't I? But alas, I am not." He reached beneath the lapel of his jacket and pulled out a shiny gold badge. Even though Pippa had never seen one in person, she recognized it immediately as a Council badge. The magician sighed and continued, "I'm here, instead, on official Council business. You shall call me Council member Slickabee. I am the magicians' representative on the Council, and today as you all must know is—"

"The examination for admittance to Peabody's Academy for the Triumphant!" Louisa burst out from her position on the stairs. "Every year, on the day of the exam, Council members travel far and wide to select suitable examinees. That's why you've come to Ink Hollow, isn't it?" With all eyes in the room fixed on her, Louisa's cheeks flushed pink. "I—I only know because Jane and I were just looking through the *Wanderly Whistle*. There was an advertisement about it."

The magician, or rather Council member Slickabee, looked long and hard at Louisa before regrettably shaking his head. With his lips set in a thin, determined line, he crossed closer to Jane, who was still caught in the kitchen doorway and clinging protectively to baby Rose. Council member Slickabee eyed the adorable, angel-faced baby—whom everyone in the North family readily agreed was by far the most extraordinary North of them all—and promptly wrinkled his nose. "Ugh! She smells like . . . old milk!"

"Yes, sir," Jane replied, letting out a small sigh of relief. "No matter what we do, the smell insists on lingering."

"Pity," Council member Slickabee said before *click-clack*ing his boots to where the triplets bounced eagerly up and down behind Mrs. North. Upon peering more closely at the boys, however, Council member Slickabee let out a croaking gasp and leaped backward.

"They all have the same face!" he exclaimed. He cast a suspicious glance in Mrs. North's direction. "Why?"

Mrs. North tried her best not to look annoyed, but she wasn't entirely successful. "They are triplets."

Though Council member Slickabee's eyes looked hopelessly dim, he forced his head into a knowing nod. "Triplets," he mused.

"Yes, I've heard of the place. Quite far away though, isn't it?"

And that was the last ridiculous thing he said before his gaze came to rest on Pippa.

It lingered for a moment or two before he suddenly clasped his hands together in delight and cried, "You!"

Pippa looked immediately over her shoulder. But nobody else was there.

"Me?" she said, turning back around with a quizzical expression on her face.

"Her?" Louisa said, shoulders sagging just a hint.

"Yes!" the magician said, striding toward Pippa and gesturing wildly at her galoshes. "She is so . . . so . . . so *prepared*! Haven't you ever heard how the early bunny gets the worm?"

"What?" Mrs. North cried.

Pippa, a devoted champion of facts, couldn't help lifting her finger in the air, regardless of how shaky her voice was. "I'm afraid that's a bird, sir. The early bird gets the worm."

"And smart, too!" the magician said. "Not a single Council member will suspect this is the one and only house I managed to find in such a miserable downpour, and I won't even face a reprimand. Nope, not this week!" He lifted his soggy hat off his head, thrust his arm deep inside, and pulled forth a brilliant purple cloak. It was the primary means by which all the Chancellor's Council members traveled in Wanderly, and, in person, it was exquisite.

The magician swung the cloak around his shoulders and

impatiently wriggled his fingers in Pippa's direction. "Come, come! What are you waiting for? I fear we may already be late."

Pippa's heart began to thump harder. Council member Slickabee couldn't actually be serious, could he? He didn't actually mean to whisk her out of the North family cottage and away from her family, did he? What business did Pippa have in a roomful of potential Triumphants? Pippa was, well, *Pippa*. All she had wanted when she awoke that morning was to go sit on Ms. Pinch's ratty sofa cushion with the other Wednesday students in Ink Hollow and learn how to spell such delightfully obscure words as "narwhal."[6] Pippa cast a frantic look in Mrs. North's direction. Without hesitation, Mrs. North stepped firmly in front of her.

"Sir, I'm afraid my daughter is not available to travel with you," Mrs. North said.

But the magician merely smoothed out the folds of his cloak and reached past Mrs. North to wrap his long, skinny hand around Pippa's wrist.

"Yes, well, selection to sit for the exam is not exactly optional," he said. "If you don't like it—ha!—take it up with the Chancellor. In the meantime, let us not forget your daughter is being considered for a guaranteed happy ending. That's certainly

---

6. Sometimes Pippa even went so far as to pretend that narwhals were actually *real*, but it never lasted long. Out of all the fantastical creatures that existed in Wanderly, the idea of a unicornish whale frolicking about in the sea was just a bit too fanciful, don't you think?

nothing for a commoner to sniff at, is it?"

Mrs. North's face clouded over. The triplets continued to bob up and down while Artie shouted, "Pippa, hero!" Jane let out a dreamy sigh and gushed, "A happy ending, Pippa! A real one! Oh, can you even imagine?"

But Pippa didn't have time to imagine, or even to say goodbye. Indeed, in less than the blink of an eye, Council member Slickabee swirled his cloak through the air and everything—including her beloved family—disappeared right before her eyes.

Pippa was most grateful to feel her galoshes touch down on solid ground but was finding it hard to breathe as she took in her surroundings. Council member Slickabee was hardly any help. Indeed, without so much as a word, he released his grip on her wrist and shoved his way toward the back of the room, where a gaggle of grown-ups clad in similar purple Council cloaks were clustered together, including one who—judging by her stringy, green hair, enormous nose, and noticeably long, black tooth—had to be a witch.

Pippa gulped. She looked out at the collection of desks. Most of them were already filled with other children looking from side to side with similarly wide eyes. Despite the merry fire that crackled in the oversize fireplace just behind Pippa, goose bumps erupted on her arms. Enormous candlelit chandeliers flickered overhead, lush green hills rolled outside the picturesque windows dressing up the walls, and ornate, hand-lettered posters were cheerily positioned all around the expansive room. Posters that said such things as: *Your Happy Ending Is Just a Step Away! Be Adored—Be a Triumphant! Be a Triumphant and Have It All!*

Pippa tried to still her trembling hands. Based on the thrilling sorts of things Triumphants did in storybooks, she wouldn't have been at all surprised if Council member Slickabee swept her away to a forest where a dragon from the Snaggletooth Isles awaited, preparing to launch fireballs at her. Even though Pippa had never once missed a Wednesday school lesson back in Ink Hollow, Ms. Pinch's idea of physical education was stringing buttons on a dreadfully long line of thread. Certainly that wouldn't be a bit of help fending off something as ferocious as a dragon. But, at least for the time being, it seemed the exam would begin with a written portion, and Pippa was quite adept with a pencil.

As Pippa slid into one of the empty seats, one as far away from the witch as possible, she was surprised to feel a slight tingle of excitement. Certainly she didn't entertain any *real* desire to be selected for Peabody's Academy for the Triumphant, but that didn't mean she couldn't return home with some wildly fantastic stories to share over the North family dinner table. Maybe even stories they would tell for years to come. Pippa was just beginning to imagine what those stories might be when she jumped at the sound of a distressed "WAH!"

She looked to her right and was astonished to see a baby seated beside her. The baby was wrapped in a pink polkadot blanket and tucked into a wicker basket resting—quite precariously—on the seat of a chair. Coming from a family of eight children, if there was one thing Pippa knew, it was how to care for a baby. Without hesitation, Pippa swept the baby up and into her arms and patted her gently on the back until a series of irresistible coos gurgled forth.

"If you have any cinch at all, you'll get rid of that baby!" a voice insisted.

Tightening her grip on the baby, Pippa turned to her left. A boy who looked to be about nine glared fiercely at her. He wore a bright green blazer with a large, gold *B* embroidered on the front. The blazer was without a single wrinkle and looked to be very stiff, judging by the boy's awkward posture.

"Any *cinch*?" Pippa asked, checking to be sure that the waistband of her pants was indeed tightly fastened. "Did you mean to say 'sense'? And why would anyone 'get rid' of a baby?"

The boy scowled at Pippa's correction and barreled on. "Babies are the worst! In the history of entrance examinations for Peabody's, babies have been chosen seventy-one percent of the time! And probably even more when they make noises like that."

Before Pippa could answer, a blare of trumpets sounded. The opulent curtains lining the windows began to wriggle and sway with anticipation. The air itself began to *snap*, *crackle*, and *pop* with electricity. The Council members in the back straightened to attention. And Pippa wondered if, after years of living beneath the shadow of his name, today would be the day that she met the Chancellor face-to-face. Though the Chancellor was notoriously elusive, out of all the storybook roles in Wanderly, the Triumphants were the apple of his eye.

Pippa held her breath.

The knob on the door twisted.

The Chancellor was not the one who burst through. Instead, it was a woman. A woman with small, dark eyes and a crown of tight ringlets framing her face. She was clad in bright orange cropped trousers and a pressed button shirt with a rounded collar, and had a brilliant turquoise parrot perched on her shoulder.

"Hello," the woman said, her gaze sweeping across the room.

Pippa blinked. Next to the Chancellor, no one had graced the front page of the *Wanderly Whistle* more than Triumphant Yolanda Bravo and her loyal companion, Dynamite.[7] Most of the *Wanderly Whistle*'s reports tended to be about a Triumphant's latest parade or honorary award, but the stories about Ms. Bravo always involved giants. Now, as far as giants go, the ones in Wanderly were far more reasonable than the Fee-Fi-Fo-Fum variety that enjoyed snacking on a kingdom's citizens—but the giants in Wanderly did have one troublesome attribute: they were terribly grumpy when woken up.

---

7. Take heed: "loyal companion" is an official term and not merely a complimentary one. What story have you ever read where the hero is not aided by at least one loyal companion? As such, upon admittance to Peabody's Academy for the Triumphant, every Triumphant is presented with his or her own furry, finned, scaled, or feathered companion who they remain bound to for life.

A grumpy giant can do a staggering amount of damage in a matter of minutes.

But not with Yolanda Bravo around. Yolanda Bravo wasn't just any Triumphant, she was *the* Triumphant, not to mention one of the most senior members of the Chancellor's Council.

Unfortunately, Ms. Bravo also happened to be marching right up to Pippa. "Who is that you're holding? Is that your sister?" she demanded. Ms. Bravo's gaze flickered toward the back of the room, where the Council members stood. "Did someone forget the rule about no sibling examinees in the same year?"

"Oh, rabbit's feet," Pippa heard Council member Slickabee mumble as he slipped his tall, skinny hat off his head to wipe the sweat from his brow. Pippa's toes curled anxiously inside her mother's roomy galoshes. The boy sitting beside her in the stiff, green blazer leaned back in his seat and snickered.

"This isn't my sister, ma'am," Pippa finally managed to say. "I only picked her up because she was crying and . . ." Pippa hesitated.

"And what?" Ms. Bravo pressed.

Pippa wanted to report that the baby had been left in a very precarious position, and perhaps a baby shouldn't be expected to take such an exam, much less be left unsupervised so near to three very sharp pencils, but all of that seemed a bit critical. And in Wanderly, Pippa had never once seen a Triumphant criticized for anything. She didn't even know if it was allowed.

"And I just, well, I suppose she needed some help," Pippa finished weakly. But at the word "help" Ms. Bravo's eyes lit up.

She whipped a clipboard out from under her arm. She reached for a pencil tucked behind her ear and beneath her curls. She fixed her gaze on Pippa.

"What is your name?" she asked.

"Pippa North."

Ms. Bravo quickly scribbled something down on her paper and then reached for the baby. "I shall be the one to hold her from now on. You will need your hands free for the exam, hmm?"

As Ms. Bravo strode back up the aisle, the boy in the green blazer leaned over and whispered, "I warned you, didn't I? You can never trust a baby, and that one just took your spot for sure!"

But that was fine by Pippa. Indeed, she'd already determined there existed no such spot for her to begin with. Sure, Pippa loved reading stories about thrilling adventures, but she was better suited for the sort of adventures she could have at home—ones that involved teaching her sisters how to save their money instead of spending it all in one fell swoop, designing a new layout for her mother's failing vegetable garden to yield three times as many vegetables, or spending an entire summer teaching the triplets how to float on their backs in the nearby creek. Certainly none of those even hinted at heroic.[8]

---

8. A few years back, I probably would have snorted (yes, books can do such a thing from time to time) and haughtily declared, "You think?" But—and this is enormously difficult for me to admit—I would have been wrong. Because, as with many things, a heroic act doesn't just spontaneously manifest itself. It must be learned; it must be practiced; it must start small before it can become big, and sometimes it is the small things that are the most heroic of all.

At the front of the room, Ms. Bravo cleared her throat. "It is no accident that you are here, children. Indeed, each and every one of you was brought here today because one of our esteemed Council members saw something exemplary in you."

Pippa wondered whether being "prepared," as Council member Slickabee had called her, really belonged under the umbrella of "exemplary," when the boy in the green jacket nudged her elbow and whispered smugly, "Being exemplary runs in my family. Did you notice the *B* on my jacket? If you haven't already guessed, I am a *Bumble*. Bernard Benedict Bumble the Fifth, that is. In my family there are seven Triumphants."

Even though Pippa hadn't a clue who the Bumbles were, and her older sister Louisa—who tended to keep up on those sorts of things—wasn't nearby to fill her in on the details, Pippa tried to smile politely, if only to keep the boy from prattling on, so that she could pay attention.

Unfortunately, boys like Bernard weren't that easy to get rid of.

"My cousin Bettina Bumble is sitting over there," he said, gesturing at a girl with wheat-colored hair and an expression as friendly as a rattlesnake. She was dressed in a nearly identical stiff blazer with a large, gold *B*, only her blazer was purple instead of green. When she saw Pippa and Bernard staring at her, she stuck out her tongue. "After today," Bernard continued, "you'll be able to say that you've met *both* of Wanderly's newest Triumphants."

Pippa thought that was a very odd thing to say, but she was more disappointed that Ms. Bravo had finished making her important declarations, and she had missed them. Indeed, Ms. Bravo's loyal companion, Dynamite, was already busy passing out the exam booklets. When one landed on Pippa's desk, her eyes fell on the first page, and she gasped.

She blinked.

She peered closer.

And something astonishing happened. For the first time in all of Pippa's six years of dedicated test taking, she looked on a question and didn't have the foggiest idea how to answer it.

What's that? You suppose *you* might be able to do better? Very well, then. Have a go at it:

*Circle the letter of the answer that best completes the question.*

*Sixteen orangutans square-dance squirrels*

_____ *glue?*

*a. sticky*

*b. tacky*

*c. glitter*

*d. white*

*e. school*

Though Pippa was certainly expecting something challenging—it was an examination for admittance to Peabody's

Academy for the Triumphant, after all—she was not expecting something this nonsensical. Indeed, how could questions like this—and yes, every single one after it was just as bad—provide any sort of useful decision-making information? Indeed, if this was the sort of examination Triumphants took, perhaps it was no wonder some of those Bumbles had been chosen, because what could this test have to do with being exemplary? Surely the selection of something as significant as the kingdom's Triumphants couldn't be handled so cavalierly, could it?

Despite the wild thumping of her heart, Pippa lifted one shaky hand in the air. A few of the children turned to stare at her. Even Bernard Bumble looked surprised. Pippa couldn't imagine questions were welcomed during the exam, and maybe they were an automatic means for dismissal. This gave Pippa a slight pause because even if she wasn't about to become a Triumphant, that was no reason to get reprimanded. Indeed, Pippa typically took great pleasure in adhering to the rules. Still, what she had to say seemed important enough to risk it.

Ms. Bravo's loyal companion saw her hand first. He swirled near until he came to land on her desk, his talons *click-clack*ing around the perimeter. Ms. Bravo was not far behind.

"What is it this time, Pippa North?" Ms. Bravo asked. Pippa thought she could detect a small smile playing at the corner of Ms. Bravo's lips, but she couldn't imagine why.

"Um, only that I'm afraid there may have been a mistake with the examinations, ma'am. I—I just didn't know if it would be wise to continue on without bringing it to your attention."

"A *mistake*?" Ms. Bravo asked. "A mistake?" she repeated, raising her voice. She looked wildly around the room, but every single one of the other children remained still and frozen. No one uttered a word. "Why, of course there is a mistake! There isn't a single rational question on this whole exam. It's all nonsense, and I know because I'm the one who wrote it!"

Though Ms. Bravo seemed strangely jubilant, Pippa felt her knees turn to mush. Had she just insulted a Triumphant? "I-I'm so sorry. I didn't mean—or rather, what I should have said was—"

"CONGRATULATIONS!" Ms. Bravo burst out.

"Congratulations?" Pippa echoed, while beside her Bernard growled, and in the back of the room the rest of the Council members began whispering furiously back and forth.

Ms. Bravo spun in a small circle. "Ring the bell, Ludwig! We've got our first selection! Ring the bell!"

But Ludwig must not have been paying attention, because no bells rang. A short, round woman leaped up instead. She had the rosiest cheeks Pippa had ever seen. She bustled down the aisle with her Council cloak hiked up over her ankles, one finger wiggling in the air, and her eyebrows twisted with worry.

"Oh, Yolanda, dear?" she said in a voice that sounded like tinkling bells. Pippa assumed she must be a fairy godmother. "Let's wait just a moment, shall we? Remember, the first selection is never ever made until at least the fifth round of examinations.

We're, um, not currently finished with the first. Not to mention, I don't believe you were given permission to write your own exam—and what about the *envelope*? You know, the one with the N-A-M-E-S?"

For a moment, Ms. Bravo's shoulders slumped, but just as quickly she tilted her jaw high in the air and repeated, "Ring the bell, Ludwig! Ring that bell!"

A broad-shouldered man in the back corner, presumably Ludwig, rose to his feet. With a solemn nod of his head, he reached for a thick, braided rope. The rope was attached to a large silver bell at the top of the building, and he gave it a mighty yank. As the sound rolled away, it seemed to grow louder and louder and louder still, as if determined to be heard by every citizen in the kingdom of Wanderly.

"Oh dear," the round woman said, shaking her head and twisting her hands together. "This ought to be a doozy."

"Fairy Goodwell," Ms. Bravo said calmly to the woman, "you needn't worry. The Chancellor placed me in charge of the examinations this year, I must assume for good reason. This child"—Ms. Bravo gestured at a gaping Pippa—"wasn't afraid to question the status quo—she showed confidence, she showed bravery, she showed a dedication to truth!"

Pippa took a tentative step forward. "H-honestly, ma'am, I just like tests. That's all. They're sort of a hobby," she said, wondering now if education was perhaps the riskiest hobby one could ever engage in. Her gaze flickered down to her wooden pencil as if it might have morphed into a tiny sword.

Ms. Bravo barreled on. "Now, Fairy Goodwell, I trust you know what needs to be done next, hmm?"

"I . . . oh . . . well." Fairy Goodwell gulped. "I suppose the Chancellor did put you in charge, Yolanda." She pulled her wand out from beneath her cloak and gave it a few practice swishes. She turned toward Pippa and said, "Go ahead and stand up, child. Please do try to smile a bit. It's not every day your destiny is changed for the good. And you needn't worry one bit about anything going awry. I'm a *registered* fairy godmother."

Pippa felt the room spinning all around her. She was certain she was hearing things. It simply wasn't possible that Ms. Bravo had chosen *her* for Peabody's Academy for the Triumphant and that a fairy godmother was preparing to officially change her destiny right that instant!

Pippa knew she should be grateful, she knew this was the sort of thing that citizens of Wanderly wished endlessly for, but the only awful thought that rolled through her mind was whether the Chancellor's version of a "happy" ending would rob her of the one she was certain she already had. Namely, what about her family?

Pippa couldn't imagine a single good ending that didn't include them.

But with the merest flick of Fairy Goodwell's wrist, an array of dazzling sparks burst forth from her wand. Shades of purple, pink, and blue showered down all around Pippa. The other children (except, of course, for the oh-so-lovely Bumbles) oohed and aahed, and the floor directly beneath Pippa's oversize galoshes began to glow.

Fairy Goodwell slowly lowered her wand. She looked apprehensively in Ms. Bravo's direction. "It's done," she said. "For better or worse, it's done."

And poor Pippa did what no other entrant to Peabody's Academy for the Triumphant had ever done before. She did not whoop; she did not holler. She did not sprint about or execute a series of high-flying joyful leaps. She did not demand an instant interview with a reporter from the *Wanderly Whistle*.

No, Pippa stood, with her eyes fixed on the toe of her mother's galoshes, trying desperately not to cry.

Huzzah?

# TWO

# THE BOY WITHOUT A HAT

Far, far away from Pippa, near the southernmost edge of Wanderly, in the remote and muggy "home" of the magicians known as the Swinging Swamp, eleven-year-old Oliver Dash crept through the dark and twisty hallways of Razzle's School for Meddlesome Boys.

Oliver was not creeping about for any sinister sort of reason. He was merely devoted to practicing the fine art of *subtlety*—a hallmark of the most esteemed magicians—at every opportunity he could find. If you are thinking Oliver seems to be as devoted a student as Pippa, I'm afraid you would be wrong.

There is a stark difference between being a devoted student and being a desperate one, and for the past four years, Oliver had borne the weight of a most unenviable title. Oliver was the oldest boy in the Swinging Swamp not to have received his magician's hat.

In Wanderly a magician's hat was a matter of great mystery. One could not simply stop off at Wanderly's beloved marketplace, Pigglesticks, and pluck a handsome one off the rack. Absolutely not! A magician's hat was nontransferable, and attempting to use a bought, borrowed, or even stolen hat brought about the unhappy, and very final, consequence of being turned into stone.[9] In the normal course of things, a magician's hat simply *arrived* (always unannounced and usually in the dead of night), and along with it came a magician's ability to perform magic. Indeed, all of a magician's powers originated from his hat, and without a hat—without magic—it was questionable whether a magician could be considered a magician at all.

Oliver drew to a halt in front of a door with a shiny gold handle and a shiny gold nameplate. At least, they were supposed to be shiny, but as with most things in the Swinging Swamp, they were instead dusted with a furry coating of the green moss the magicians had long since given up on sloughing away. Indeed, with a steady temperature of absolutely awful, oodles of voracious sinkholes, and nearly three inches of water submerging every exterior pathway, the Swinging Swamp was a most formidable foe.

The magicians, of course, had as much choice in settling in the swamp as they had in the unalterable amendment of their

---

9. If a curse of petrification for attempting to commandeer the magic from another magician's hat in such a way seems harsh to you, I wholeheartedly agree. Alas, I am not the one to make up the rules; it is merely my job to report them.

school's name from Razzle's School for *Magical* Boys to Razzle's School for *Meddlesome* Boys. Both were curses ordered by the Chancellor, who remained aggravatingly unimpressed with the magicians' prowess for performance and was instead bound, set, and determined to demote them from a properly villainous role to that of "nuisance." Certain there could be no more insignificant role than "nuisance," the magicians had spent the past three decades trying to slog their way—quite literally—out of this sordid fate, but alas there they still were.

"Open the door, Oliver! I heard you clunking around a whole two hallways ago!" Headmaster Razzle's voice rang out.

Oliver swallowed. He straightened the collar of the ridiculously short cape that fluttered a whole inch above his waistline. Of course, every other boy Oliver's age had a suave black cape that flowed down to his calves, but every other boy Oliver's age also had his magician's hat. They simply didn't make novice-level capes in Oliver's size.

Oliver pushed open the door of Headmaster Razzle's office and prepared to exclaim in as bright and cheery a voice as he could muster, "Good morning, Headmaster Razzle!" because being called into the headmaster's office didn't *have* to mean he was in a boatload of trouble. Instead he blurted out, "Wh-where did everything go?"

Because Headmaster Razzle's office, which had once been filled to overflowing with a lifetime of carefully collected and catalogued trinkets, was empty. Or rather, nearly empty. His desk remained, and he seemed to be sitting on some semblance of a chair, though it certainly wasn't his beloved jewel-encrusted throne (which everyone secretly agreed was a retired stage prop). The walls, however, were nothing more than an empty vessel for old nails, save for the lone painting that hung just above Headmaster Razzle's head.

Oliver squinted at the painting. "Is that the—"

"Sapphire Sea that laps at the base of Triumph Mountain?" Headmaster Razzle said with a dreamy sigh. "Why, yes, it is. It's hard to imagine even a spit of water not tainted in *green*, but it's not that way everywhere in Wanderly, is it, Oliver?"

Though Oliver got the sense Headmaster Razzle wanted him to nod his head in agreement, he instead just stood there awkwardly. Like most of the students at Razzle's School for Meddlesome Boys, Oliver had never set foot outside the Swinging Swamp. From what Oliver could gather from the school's meager library, it seemed as if there were a great many places in Wanderly that weren't one bit swamp-like, but he couldn't know for sure.

Oliver cleared his throat. "Are you . . . switching offices, sir? Is that why you called me in this morning? You need some help moving?"

At most academic institutions this would be an odd assumption to make, but Oliver was more than used to it. As the oldest student without a hat, he was reminded quite often about what a perpetual drain his presence was on all. So, every extra chore was immediately handed off to Oliver. While the other boys his age practiced magic, he pretended that slaving away was no big deal and that he didn't fall asleep every single night asking the same burning question: *Why me?*

The jaunty tilt of Headmaster Razzle's jaw dipped slightly. For a moment, he almost looked as if he felt sorry for Oliver. But that moment passed very quickly.

"I did not call you in here to discuss my circumstances, Oliver, but rather to discuss yours." Headmaster Razzle looked long and hard at Oliver. "How long do you think this can go on? How long do you think you should stay at this academic institution? Oliver, what if your hat never comes at all?"

Oliver had wondered the same thing more times than he cared to admit, but it didn't seem wise to let Headmaster Razzle know that. "It will come, sir. Perhaps it shall come this week? Tomorrow? Or maybe even tonight? I—I know it shall be soon."

"I'm afraid that's not enough, Oliver. Your predictions are nothing more than wishful thinking, and the other magicians have grown . . . tired of waiting." Headmaster Razzle lifted his eyebrow in Oliver's direction as if that was supposed to mean something, but it didn't. Not to Oliver. It wasn't like he had any control over the arrival of his hat. If he had, he would have made sure it arrived years ago.

After a moment or two of silence, Headmaster Razzle let out a long, rattling breath. "Oliver, they want you to leave. They want you to be expelled from Razzle's School for Meddlesome

Boys. And frankly, I don't see why I should stop it."

Oliver's jaw gaped. "But where would I go? I-I've lived here since I was a baby. Since you found me at the edge of the swamp and carried me here yourself.[10] Headmaster Razzle, this is my home."

Headmaster Razzle's voice was hollow. "A home is a place where you belong, Oliver. And you"—his gaze flickered up to Oliver's woefully bare head—"quite obviously don't."

"I just need a little more time." Oliver's voice tumbled out quickly. "Please, sir. We've already waited this long. I know it will—"

"No!" Headmaster Razzle barked. "There is no more time, Oliver. Change is upon us. Soon, the Chancellor is going to witness the performance of our lives and nothing will ever be the same. Our role is about to change, Oliver. No longer will magicians be seen as merely a sidekick nuisance. Finally, we'll be placed in the spotlight, where we should have been from the very start. But in order for this to happen, everyone"—he paused and looked pointedly at Oliver—"and I mean *everyone*, must be in top form."

Oliver frowned. The only performances he knew about were

---

10. This sounds like a very sad beginning, but it was the same beginning shared by all magician boys. In Wanderly, the Swinging Swamp borders the notoriously witchy abode known as the Dead Tree Forest. Though witches were typically willing to raise their girls for a few years, they wanted nothing to do with their boys. So, they routinely dropped them off at the foot of the Swinging Swamp without so much as a backward glance—they were wicked witches, after all.

the somewhat depressing showcases the magicians performed every month in the Swinging Swamp. They weren't lacking in effort, but they were severely lacking in audience. In fact, no one outside the Swinging Swamp had ever once bothered to attend, and most especially not the Chancellor. Oliver had heard rumors that the magicians were planning a *second* showcase for this month, something they'd never done before, but he hadn't any idea why that should appeal to the Chancellor. Before Oliver had a chance to inquire, however, Headmaster Razzle's face grew deathly pale. He gripped the brim of his hat.

"Incoming!" he cried. *"Incoming!"*

As wonderful and coveted as a magician's hat was, it was not without its flaws. For instance, though nearly anything that could fit comfortably inside a magician's hat (no squishing allowed!) could be made to disappear, the objects didn't actually cease to exist.

Instead, they went *elsewhere.*

As in, whenever an object disappeared inside one magician's hat, it promptly reappeared inside another unrelated magician's hat with little more than a slight bobble as a warning. This wasn't too terrible in the case of tasty snacks like apples, useful items such as pencils, or soft and fuzzy creatures like rabbits, but not all magicians possessed the same sensibilities and sometimes such reprehensible objects as snakes, beetles, and mud balls went hurtling through the space-magic continuum instead.

Headmaster Razzle wrung his hands together. The sheen of

sweat that lined his forehead manifested itself into big, rolling drops. "Ohhhh, I daresay I never will get used to these obnoxious intrusions! What will it be? What will it—AHHHH!" he screamed and promptly began to flail about his office.

Oliver didn't have to wait long to see what it was. Headmaster Razzle's famously tall hat flew into the air, and there sitting atop his head was a wide-eyed, shivering, and very slimy baby octopus. Oliver took an immediate liking to it, although its tentacles did not seem to be sitting well with Headmaster Razzle. Every time Headmaster Razzle managed to pry one off and move to the next, the former clamped right back on.

"Help! Help! HELP!" Headmaster Razzle roared.

Though Oliver tended to be helpful by nature and had been trained to be even more so as a result of his dismal position at school, in this instance, he did *not* jump to Headmaster Razzle's assistance. Instead, he waited. He wondered if perhaps the baby octopus was exactly the help he was in need of; if maybe not all magic in Wanderly was against him.

By that time, Headmaster Razzle had bent fully over with his head pointed toward the floor. He tugged on the baby octopus with all his might, but his hands kept slipping off the octopus's squishy, pink body.

Oliver tried to think of something terrifying to say. He thought back through every book he'd ever come across that mentioned octopuses and then—

"Hurry, sir! Before it inks you!"

"Inks me?" Headmaster Razzle cried, aghast. "What happens if it inks me?"

Bull's-eye! Oliver bounced on his toes as if trying to get a better glimpse of the octopus. "Well, I can't exactly tell what type of octopus it is, but I think in most cases the resulting blindness is only temporary. Maybe a year or so."

"*Blind?* I can't go blind! I have showcases to perform! A school to run! We're finally preparing to turn over a new page, and I refuse to let a slimy invertebrate rip it to shreds!" Headmaster Razzle straightened up. He temporarily stopped his flailing and looked Oliver in the eye. "Get this thing off me, Oliver."

Oliver's heart pounded. This was it. This was the chance he'd been hoping for. "You mean you want me to *help* you? But I thought I was going to be expelled?"

"Of course I want you to help me! Why wouldn't I want you to help me? Why . . ." Headmaster Razzle's voice trailed off. Ever so slowly he began to nod his head, which made it look like the baby octopus was nodding its head, which all would have been quite funny if Oliver's very existence didn't feel as if it were dangling at the end of an extraordinarily thin string. "All right, fine, Oliver. If you get this octopus off my head, you can have one extra week; one extra week to receive your hat and prove you're a proper magician—"

"Thirty days," Oliver said.

"Thirty days? But that's—we might be—ugh!" Headmaster Razzle let out a howl as the octopus removed one particularly adhesive sucker from his forehead, leaving behind an angry red welt. "Fine, thirty days it is! But you're only prolonging the inevitable. If you haven't received your hat by now, all the days in the world won't make a difference."

Headmaster Razzle bent his head toward Oliver, and Oliver began gently trying to pry the octopus free.

"I know I'm a magician, sir," Oliver said. "It's the only thing I know how to be. And I know, because I learned it from you."

"Yes, well, even grown-ups make mistakes, Oliver. And mistakes like you must be done away with."

Oliver's jaw dropped. The baby octopus finally popped free of Headmaster Razzle's head and slid contentedly into Oliver's hands. But all Oliver could hear was the word "mistake," and it pierced so deeply into his heart that it became very difficult to breathe.

Mistakes were wrong answers on a math exam, showing up ten minutes late to an appointment, or putting on someone else's cape.

But people—people—were never mistakes.

People simply couldn't be mistakes.

Could they?

Headmaster Razzle furiously tried to smooth his mussed-up hair. He scooped his fallen hat off the ground and reached for the baby octopus. But Oliver took a step backward.

"Give me that wretched creature so I can send it scuttling off to some other sap," Headmaster Razzle said.

"That's all right," Oliver said, shaking his head. "No need to bother another magician. I know a place where I can take it."

Before Headmaster Razzle could respond, Oliver scurried quickly out of his office. Angry tears pricked at the corners of his eyes.

Oliver didn't actually have a clue what he should do with a baby octopus, but he couldn't stand the thought of watching it disappear; of watching it be sent away; of knowing it didn't have any real place to belong.

A place like Wanderly wasn't well suited for those who didn't fit in. In fact, when every role was painstakingly defined, and adherence to that role was required by the Chancellor, belonging was as necessary as breathing.

Oliver set his jaw. There was simply no other way around it. He didn't have a choice. No matter what anybody said, the Swinging Swamp *was* his home, and he had thirty days to prove it.

THREE

# Dear Fairy Godmother

Way up high on Triumph Mountain, beneath a blue sky full of perfectly puffed marshmallow clouds, Pippa North and Bernard Benedict Bumble V tumbled out from beneath Ms. Bravo's purple Council cloak.

No, this is not a dream sequence. I am not a fan of such gimmicks in books, unless they are absolutely necessary. This—and by "this," I mean *Bernard*—was a very real turn of bad luck. To be fair, Ms. Bravo hadn't wanted to choose Bernard for Peabody's Academy for the Triumphant. Indeed, she argued tooth and nail against the other Council members' repeated insistence on resorting to the "envelope" Fairy Goodwell had referred to when Pippa was selected. Ms. Bravo must have known what was in that envelope—i.e., the Chancellor's "strong recommendations" as to who should be selected[11]—but after five grueling rounds of examination, wailing babies, wan children, and the raised eyebrows of nearly every Council member, Ms. Bravo relented.

Pippa rose slowly to her feet. She squished her toes anxiously inside her mother's galoshes. She resolved not to think on how a fairy godmother had purportedly changed her destiny forever, and instead focused on soaking up every detail of life on Triumph Mountain. One day soon everyone would realize this was all a giant mistake, and when she returned to her family, at the very least she could have a fantastic story to share. Yes, that's what this was—a story-building experience.

"Is Castle Cressida very far, Ms. Bravo?" Pippa asked, referring to the famed home of Peabody's Academy for the Triumphant.

"Very far?" Bernard piped up. "Are you a dimwig? Castle Cressida is right there!"

Pippa was about to inform Bernard that her ponytail was most definitely not a wig, until she realized that he likely meant to say "dimwit." Not wanting to bolster his arsenal of insults, she kept mum and turned instead in the direction he was pointing.

But Bernard's skills of identification seemed to be as skewed as his vocabulary. The structure looming ahead of them was

---

11. Isn't this shameful? I haven't a clue how many years such an "envelope" has been in place, but it does suggest that, as of late, Wanderly's Triumphants had not been selected entirely on the basis of merit.

certainly large enough to be considered a castle, but it was covered nearly head to toe in thick, unrelenting ropes of ivy. There looked to be three spires pointing up at the blue sky, but one of them was cockeyed and another had lost nearly all of its roof shingles. The window boxes were full of nothing but rocks, and the entire structure, if a building could do such a thing, was slouching. Pippa was about to tell Bernard as much, when her eyes fell upon the staircase at the very front of the building.

It was painted in gold. It was chipped, flaking, and peeling, to be sure, but when the sun shifted, it appeared to be trying its best to . . . sparkle. Though the Chancellor never conducted such a thing as public tours of Castle Cressida, he had certainly slapped up enough murals, tapestries, and portraits of it all over Wanderly. Everyone from the ages of zero to one hundred could recognize those stairs. They were a symbol of what life as a Triumphant was supposed to be like: a golden staircase leading all the way to the very top.

Pippa didn't bother to hide her disappointment. Her shoulders slumped. Ms. Bravo seemed to be watching her very, very carefully. "Is this the way Castle Cressida has always looked?" Pippa finally asked.

But before anyone could answer, the large double doors of the building burst open. A middle-aged woman with shimmering silver hair sashayed down the steps with her arms held gingerly at her sides. She was dressed head to toe in light, frothy layers of pink chiffon, and her feet were clad in sparkling, high-heeled dancing shoes. Pippa gulped. It was one thing to hear stories about Mistress Griselda Peabody, Wanderly's finest waltzer and headmistress of Peabody's Academy for the Triumphant, but it was another thing to be confronted by such a powerhouse of grace and elegance in person.[12]

Just behind Mistress Peabody, the Triumphant students filed dutifully out the door and into a perfectly symmetrical formation. They were clad in very formal royal blue and gold uniforms complete with a striped gold and blue tie and a smart royal blue cape. The students positioned on the outermost edges carried the Triumphant flag, which displayed a sword for courage, a heart for devotion to the kingdom, and the flaming silhouette of a fire horse for . . . well—

Pippa frowned. She couldn't exactly remember *what* the fire horse was supposed to symbolize. All she knew was that as long as there had been Triumphants, there had been fire horses. Indeed, fire horses were the original loyal companions, though there was nothing tame about them. They roamed wild and free, but when danger presented itself they fought alongside the Triumphants, setting their manes and tails ablaze.

But those days, unfortunately, were over. At least that's what

---

12. If Mistress Peabody's entrance has aroused your suspicion, because who has ever heard of waltzing being worthy of hero status, let me gently inform you that a great many battles have been won by a swift kick and a leap across a seemingly insurmountable divide. But if Mistress Peabody's entrance has aroused your suspicion for some other reason, carry on.

everybody said. Fire horses had even slipped off the pages of the kingdom's most recent storybooks, and Pippa feared it was only a matter of time before they were forgotten completely. Seeing their image emblazoned on the Triumphant flag, however, made Pippa's heart quicken, and she snuck a glance toward the dense forest as if maybe she might catch a glimpse of one.

As if maybe such a thing were possible.

Mistress Peabody clapped her hands against her chest. She smiled the dazzling sort of smile that seemed to be a hallmark of the Triumphants pictured in the *Wanderly Whistle*. Pippa ran her tongue across her slightly crooked teeth and wondered if that alone might be reason enough to get sent home.

"Oh, welcome! Welcome to Peabody's Academy for the Triumphant! We have been awaiting your arrival with great and momentous anticipation," Mistress Peabody gushed. She gestured at the Triumphant students behind her, but most of them were fiddling with the hems of their capes, staring at their shoes, or gazing off in the distance with glassy-eyed stares. Well, all except for one girl, who looked, curiously, madder than a hornet, and one boy who kept blinking his eyes and sliding his glasses along the bridge of his nose as if he didn't quite believe what he was seeing. Pippa wondered if it was the galoshes. She bet no one had ever shown up on the glittering gold steps of Castle Cressida wearing galoshes.

Mistress Peabody nodded first at Bernard and then Pippa. "Bernard, Bettina . . . welcome to your new home!"

"That's not Bettina!" the mad-as-a-hornet girl burst out from the staircase. "That girl's not even a *Bumble*!"

The Triumphants on the stairs stopped their fiddling. They peered closely at Pippa and then began looking at one another. A few even began whispering back and forth, and Pippa couldn't be sure, but a girl of about seven with her hair twisted up into two buns and a spattering of freckles across her nose may have cast a shy smile in Pippa's direction.

Mistress Peabody, however, was clearly flustered. "Nonsense, Prudence! Certainly you'd recognize your own sister. Of *course* this is Bettina." She cast a questioning look in Ms. Bravo's direction. "Who else could it possibly be?"

As if things couldn't get any more awkward, Ms. Bravo's loyal companion, Dynamite, sprang suddenly off her shoulder and began flying in low circles over the formation of Triumphants squawking gleefully, "PIPPA! WELCOME, PIPPA! PIPPA!"

Ms. Bravo drew up alongside Pippa and placed a reassuring hand on her shoulder. "Lovely to see you again, Griselda," Ms. Bravo said, in a way that Pippa couldn't help but compare to how one might greet a bowl full of broccoli at a dessert buffet. "It is my pleasure to introduce to you Bernard Benedict Bumble the Fifth and . . . Pippa North. These are the two candidates that I selected based on the authority the Chancellor gave to *me* as the Council member in charge of this year's examination."

Mistress Peabody's eye began to twitch. "And why did he do that again?"

Ms. Bravo's eyes flickered briefly toward the surrounding students. "Suffice it to say," she said, "that it is in direct response to the little . . . shall we say . . . *rendezvous* at Beastly Valley."

"Oh, that little thing?" Mistress Peabody said with a wave of her hand. "But that's clear on the other coast of Wanderly. There's nothing of note over there."

"As Triumphants we have sworn an oath to protect Wanderly. All of it," Ms. Bravo said firmly.

"Oh, fiddlesticks. You needn't be so *serious*, Yolanda. Anyhow, who is this P-P-P-P—"

"Pippa?" Ms. Bravo said with a sigh.

"Yes, that's right." Mistress Peabody turned to face Pippa. She tried in vain to recover her radiant smile. "And where does your family reside?"

"In the village of Ink Hollow, ma'am."

"Oh!" Mistress Peabody exclaimed as if someone had dumped a very cold bucket of water on her head. "How very, very. . . quaint! I'm quite certain no one of significance has ever come out of *that* village."

Pippa felt her own eyebrow twitch. Though she was standing on top of the most famous mountain in all of Wanderly in the presence of not one but two Triumphants, she simply could not overlook the offense of terrible manners. "I suppose that depends on your definition of 'significance,' ma'am."

Beside Pippa, Ms. Bravo guffawed. The boy whose glasses kept slipping down his nose noticeably straightened up. But

Mistress Peabody's eyes narrowed, if only for a moment.

"I can tell already that Pippa is going to be a much-needed addition to this academy," Ms. Bravo said as Dynamite landed on her shoulder. "I shall leave you now so that you all may get better acquainted, but please do expect to see me again soon. With this being my first year in charge of the examinations, I would like to drop in and gauge Pippa's and Bernard's progress from time to time."

Mistress Peabody's head snapped up. "Oh, no need for that, Yolanda. I would be more than happy to send you regular updates."

Ms. Bravo, however, let her gaze wander pointedly toward the sagging exterior of Castle Cressida. Pippa couldn't help but notice two flaming circles burn on Mistress Peabody's cheeks.

"Thank you, Griselda, but some things I would prefer to see for myself." With that, Ms. Bravo swirled her purple Council cloak through the air and disappeared in a puff of smoke. Pippa felt suddenly, terribly alone. Though Ms. Bravo was arguably the one to blame for her astonishing predicament, her presence had made Pippa feel . . . safe, in a way that Mistress Peabody's did not.

"Well then," Mistress Peabody said, "regardless of the little mix-up, we really are very glad to see you, Bettina, oh! Um, er—"

"Pippa," the boy with glasses called out from the stairs with a little nod in Pippa's direction. Despite the trauma of the day, she nodded back and wondered if maybe not all Triumphants were as bad as the Bumbles.

"Yes, that's right! Pippa is what I meant to say, unless"—Mistress Peabody looked at Pippa with wide, questioning eyes—"it's just as easy to call you Bettina? Bettina is a nice name, don't you think, and it would certainly make things easier with the Chancellor, hmm?" Upon seeing Pippa's bewildered expression, Mistress Peabody laughed a hair too loudly. "Oh, come on now; it was just a joke. You didn't think I was serious, did you?" But Pippa had the strangest feeling that if she had agreed, Mistress Peabody would have gladly made the switch, however superficial it was.

"Anyhow," Mistress Peabody continued, "we ought to make our way inside now. A reporter from the *Wanderly Whistle* is dying to interview you both, and we wouldn't want to keep your families waiting, now, would we?"

Pippa's stomach flip-flopped. Suddenly Castle Cressida seemed like the grandest place in the world, suffocating green ivy and all. "Our families are waiting for us? Inside there?" she asked, dashing nearly halfway up the steps.

But Mistress Peabody frowned. "Certainly not, but they are waiting to talk to you via magic mirror. I daresay you are probably the first Triumphant in your family and congratulations are in order, isn't that right, Pippa?"

Pippa's heart sank down to the bottom of her mother's

galoshes. "I'm afraid my family doesn't have a magic mirror," she said quietly.

Right away, Bernard piped up, "Oh pity. We only have *four* in our mansion."

Even Mistress Peabody looked slightly annoyed with him. "That's no matter, Pippa. You're a Triumphant now. The moment you were chosen, arrangements were already being made. Your family may not have had a magic mirror when you left them, but certainly now they do." Seeing Pippa's shocked expression, Mistress Peabody continued, "For champion's sake, stop gaping. Don't you know anything about being a Triumphant?"

Pippa was beginning to wonder if she did, but Mistress Peabody was already rushing ahead of the Triumphant students, *click-clack*ing a snappy rhythm along the castle's marble floor. Though the marble was riddled with a panoply of unsightly cracks, it wasn't hard to imagine how beautiful it had once been. Most of the children plodded along behind Mistress Peabody, though a few kept looking over their shoulders to peek curiously at Pippa. Bernard made a beeline for fellow Bumble, Prudence, and the boy with glasses lingered behind as if something fascinating had suddenly occurred with his shoelace.

As soon as Pippa drew near, however, he popped up like a jack-in-the-box.

"Hello there," he said.

"Is everything all right with your shoe?" Pippa asked.

"My shoe? Oh, right, my shoe! Yes. I mean, no. I mean, it's fine now, thanks for asking."

"Sure," Pippa said. And then she continued on, mulling over what exactly she was going to say to her family through the magic mirror. *Guess what, everybody. I'm a new Triumphant!* Or maybe something more playful like, *Wondering who the new Triumphant is? You're looking at her!* Of course, she could always opt for the truth, which would have sounded something more like, *Please rescue me and don't ever make me come back here*, but wouldn't that be terribly ungrateful?

Pippa pressed her eyes shut and thought back to Louisa's disappointment when Council member Slickabee passed her by. Pippa had never realized Louisa was dreaming of such a fate— why couldn't this have happened to *her*?

"Ms. Bravo's loyal companion, Dynamite, is something else, isn't he?" the boy continued, darting after her. "Have you ever seen a shade of blue like that? Not me. I mean, it's not like I'd ever want any companion other than my goat, Leonardo—hey, did you know goats can skip?" he said, interrupting himself. But when the boy saw Pippa's blank expression, he gulped. "The first day here isn't always easy, is it? Well, the Bumbles don't seem to mind, but for everyone else it's kind of . . . a lot."

Pippa nodded. And then she said softly, "So how often do kids make it back home?"

Behind his glasses, the boy's eyes widened. "Um, never. They can't, actually. Once you've been changed by a fairy godmother, only a fairy godmother can change you back. Otherwise you'd be acting outside of your role, and you could get in big trouble for that."

"Do you think a fairy godmother would ever do such a thing?" Pippa asked quickly. "I mean, change a Triumphant back to what they were before?"

The boy shook his head warily. "I don't think anyone's ever tried. And certainly not through normal wishing channels—fairy godmothers aren't allowed to grant a Triumphant's wishes because we've already got a happy ending. Your letter would get tossed out in the first round of sorting. But anyhow, I think you're sort of missing the point. Getting chosen for Peabody's Academy for the Triumphant is supposed to be an honor."

Pippa sighed. "I know," she said. And then, "What's your name, by the way?"

The boy's eyes lit up. "I'm Ernest. I'm sort of an old-timer. I've been here since I was three, which is lucky for me because I was adorable back then."

"Oh, uh . . . you were?" Pippa said a bit uncertainly.

Ernest nodded vigorously. "I'm not trying to brag; it's actually common knowledge. Back then, all you had to do was open the latest issue of the *Wanderly Whistle*, and there I was in an advertisement for toothpaste, winter hats, everything. Wanderly's most charming toddler ever. Mum said I was a shoo-in for a Triumphant, and she was right. It is sort of weird to reach your peak at age three, though. In fact, I wouldn't really recommend it. If Triumphant appointments weren't for life, I bet Mistress Peabody would have kicked me out at age seven. That's the year I got these charmers," he said, pointing at his glasses. "I think it all went downhill from there."

Pippa raised her eyebrow. "You mean that's the year you were given the gift of perfect eyesight?" she said.

Ernest grinned. "That too, I guess. I never really thought of it that way. Um, Pippa," Ernest said, shuffling a bit faster in order to keep up with her, "I hope you'll give us a chance. I mean, I know you're stuck here, but maybe you'll find that you actually like it here. Maybe you're here for a reason."

But before Pippa could answer, she heard a familiar, warm voice.

"Pippa? Is—is she there? Is this thing working?"

"Mother!" Pippa cried out, and though she hardly meant to, she pushed Ernest out of the way and barreled down the hallway. She swung around a corner and skidded to a halt in front of a very ornate-looking mirror with a smoky facade. Certainly she'd heard about magic mirrors before, and one had even made its way to the general store in Ink Hollow, where everyone oohed and aahed over it for weeks, but she'd never actually used one.

Her mother's face slowly came into focus along with bits and pieces of the rest of her family members. They were all trying in vain to fit inside the mirror frame, which meant they were a tangled mess of limbs—only Artie's chin could be seen from where he was positioned on top of Charlie's shoulders, one half of Jane's face didn't quite make the cut, and Miles was blocking her father entirely except for the very tip of his forehead. Even still, Pippa was sure she'd never seen a lovelier image in all her life. Tears sprang immediately to her eyes.

"Oh, how precious. She's crying tears of joy *again*!" Mistress Peabody interjected. Pippa heard the sound of scribbling and noticed for the first time the reporter from the *Wanderly Whistle* perched just behind Mistress Peabody with a pencil gripped firmly in hand. Mistress Peabody continued, "There really is no moment like the one when a new Triumphant is congratulated by their loved ones."

And that was all it took for Pippa's family to burst into celebratory praise.

"I always knew you had it in you, little sis," Pippa's oldest brother, Charlie, said with a proud flash of his dimples.

"I can't think of a greater destiny for you than this." Her father beamed, peeking out from behind Miles.

Jane leaned down and pressed her right eye against the mirror as if trying to get a better look at Pippa's surroundings. "Is everything beautiful? Is everything absolutely wonderful?" she asked delightedly.

Louisa smiled weakly. "Congratulations, Pippa," she said, but her voice was swiftly drowned out by the triplets' energetic and rising chant of, "Dra-gons! Dra-gons! Dra-gons!"

Mistress Peabody clapped her hands together and let out

a little squeal. "If it's dragons they want, perhaps it's dragons they'll get! Maybe you'll be our next Crowne Stadium champion, Pippa. Imagine that!" She bent her head near to the still scribbling reporter and whispered, "No, no, dear . . . it's Crowne *Stadium* not *gymnasium*."

Pippa, meanwhile, felt like she'd swallowed a rock. She hadn't expected her family to be anything less than supportive, but a part of her just wanted them to cry and wail and beg her to come home.

Was she the only one in all of Wanderly—well, other than the Bumbles, perhaps—who thought her admittance to Peabody's Academy for the Triumphant was the worst mistake ever?

Through her tears, she was just about to ask her family as much, but Mistress Peabody said beneath her breath, "Don't be selfish, Pippa. This moment's as much for them as it is for you. You wouldn't want to deny them that joy, would you?"

Pippa licked her lips. She looked at her family, blinking anxiously at her, pressed as close to the mirror as they possibly could. And Pippa knew Mistress Peabody was wrong. Regardless of how everyone else in Wanderly revered Triumphants, her family would never want her to stay in a place where she was unhappy. Still, considering what she'd learned from Ernest, she didn't want to make her family worry unnecessarily. At least not until she could come up with a plan to get home that wouldn't involve putting them at risk of violating any of the Chancellor's rules too.

Pippa forced a bright smile onto her face. "Thank you,

everybody," she said. "I—I never imagined such a thing could happen. It really is exciting, isn't it?"

And though the approving gleam in Mistress Peabody's eye sent chills down Pippa's spine, and the *scritch-scratch* of the *Wanderly Whistle* reporter's pencil grated on her ears, Pippa took great comfort in placing her hand in her pocket. Inside was a folded-up sheet of paper that her mother insisted Pippa and all her siblings carry with them in case of an emergency.[13] Pippa had never thought she would ever have to put the paper to use, but she was already imagining scrawling out the words: "Dear Fairy Godmother." Because if Ernest was right, if only a fairy godmother had the power to make her a commoner again, then surely somewhere in Wanderly there had to be at least one who was willing to help her.

Wasn't that what fairy godmothers were all about?

---

13. If you are wondering why Pippa's mother did not distribute something more useful, such as a bit of spare change, a map, or possibly even a potion, you mustn't forget that Wanderly is a storybook kingdom. And in a storybook kingdom, the right words at the right time and in the hands of the right person could change, quite simply, everything.

FOUR

# A SNAKE NAMED DELILAH

Deep down in the heart of the Swinging Swamp, Oliver Dash awoke to the sound of voices, and his heart immediately began to pound. Oliver always made it a point to rise long before any of the other students in the dormitory stirred awake. Oliver faced enough ridicule during the waking hours, and he'd learned the hard way that sound sleeping left him far too vulnerable.

Oliver cautiously blinked one eye open. Save for the three youngest, who were still sound asleep—one of whom was small enough to require the use of a crib—most of the other boys were gathered around seven-year-old Theodore's bed. And there, in Theodore's hands, was a hat.

Oliver bolted upright. His chest tightened.

His gaze swept toward the window that—despite the putrid

swamp air—was always left open to allow for a hat's mysterious delivery. And last night it had happened again. A new hat had arrived. But, as always, it had swept right past Oliver and on to someone else.

Oliver was only three days closer to Headmaster Razzle's deadline, but it felt like a terrible blow. A small part of him had hoped that, in the face of such dire need, his hat would take pity on him, make up for all those miserable years of waiting, and hurry up already! Alas, things never seemed to go Oliver's way.

Theodore bounced up and down, tossing his hat into the air and loosely catching it on the tip of his thumb. Oliver's fingers strained at his sides, and all he could think was: *What if he drops it?* But it wasn't Oliver's hat to care for.

"Tell us again how you found it," a five-year-old boy, Herbert, said, touching a hand to his bare head as if his own magician's hat might pop out of thin air at any moment.

"I crushed it. I was sleeping real good, rolled over onto my stomach, and then—splat! There it was," Theodore said with a grin.

The rest of the boys erupted into laughter, while Oliver tried not to gasp at the thought of a squished hat.

One of the older boys, Frederick, who remained lounging on his own bed, called out lazily, "You better believe we'll never hear the end of this from Von Hollow. After choosing you as his assistant for last night's showcase, he'll take full credit for sure."

Despite Frederick's casual tone, the name Von Hollow rippled throughout the room. Master Von Hollow was the Swinging Swamp's nastiest magician. His main source of income was the acceptance of bribes, and he loved nothing more than a "good deal." He was ruthless, cunning, and unquestionably skilled. And while most magicians sent objects they disappeared jetting willy-nilly around the space-magic continuum, Master Von Hollow was the one and only magician who could make something disappear *and* guarantee its destination.

Theodore stopped bouncing. In typical magician fashion, he adamantly refused to give a single bit of credit to anyone other than himself. "No way! My hat must have already been on its way before the showcase. Just watch this!" he cried.

He brought his small fingers to the brim of his hat. Though Frederick and a few of the older boys snickered, everyone else grew quiet, watching and waiting. Oliver leaned as far forward as he dared, eager to see what Theodore could do, wondering what *he* might do if the hat had been his, but the miniature mushroom that popped into view was rather disappointing.

Frederick howled with laughter. Theodore glared angrily at him. "At least I conjured an illusion on my first try," he protested.

Of the three powers that a magician's hat bestowed—personal travel by vanishing, making objects disappear, and illusions—illusions were the magicians' favorite. Despite the fact that the objects the magicians conjured were precisely as their name implied, i.e., completely fake, illusions were the one trick that garnered a moderate amount of fear and respect from the citizens of Wanderly. Ironically, this fear was borne of the same habit most magicians found so annoying about their hats: the sudden, startling reappearance of other magicians' disappeared objects—you didn't forget about that pink baby octopus, did you? Of course, the magicians didn't actually create those objects from nothing, but they weren't about to set the record straight and instead played up the misconception to its absolute fullest.

If you asked Oliver, fake or not, it was still entirely unsettling to turn the corner at Razzle's School for Meddlesome Boys, never knowing whether you might happen upon an illusion of a snarling tiger, a three-headed monster, or an army of spiders.

Oliver wasn't thinking about spiders in this moment, however. Oliver was thinking about something Frederick had said. Something he'd never once considered. Had Master Von Hollow really had something to do with the arrival of Theodore's hat? Master Von Hollow was an exceptionally fearsome magician; was it possible that a bit of his prowess had managed to somehow rub off on Theodore during the showcase? Certainly a magician's skills weren't transferrable during the ordinary course of a day, but maybe there was something special about what happened onstage—maybe there was something special about the connection between a magician and his assistant.

Oliver looked slowly around the room. Beginning at age six, every student became eligible to participate in a showcase as a magician's assistant. Not surprisingly, every student over the age of six had done exactly that. Everyone, that is, except Oliver.

Alas, we have come to another one of those moments in the story where the circumstances are almost too cruel to mention. I said from the beginning, however, that I traveled here for the sole purpose of telling the whole truth, and so here it is. Do come a bit closer, though, as we needn't shout it from the rooftops.

Oliver—who had spent a lifetime trying to find his place among a group of applause-seeking showmen—suffered from a severe case of *stage fright*.

Indeed, it was so bad that when Oliver last auditioned to be a magician's assistant three years ago, his nervous clumsiness had led to the magician in question spraining his ankle, tearing a hole in his hat, and plunging headfirst into the moat surrounding Razzle's School for Meddlesome Boys.[14] After that, Headmaster Razzle decreed that, for the safety and preservation of all, Oliver should never be allowed to set foot onstage again; a decision that even Oliver had agreed with.

But what if that decision had been the start of all his problems? What if the one thing standing between Oliver and

---

14. Did I mention the moat surrounding Razzle's School for Meddlesome Boys was routinely patrolled by an ancient gang of gargantuan crocodiles? Of course, the crocodiles could have likely wiped out the entire population of magicians years ago, but lucky for the magicians—ha!—the crocodiles' appetite for torment was higher than their appetite for prey. In short, they kept the magicians around merely to toy with them.

proving he belonged here was . . . the stage? Would he really do anything it took to avoid getting kicked out of the Swinging Swamp?

*Yes.*

Oliver's pulse began to race; his palms began to sweat. If Oliver remembered correctly, Master Von Hollow was the magician scheduled for one more showcase before Oliver's deadline. Oliver would have much preferred to work with, well, any other magician besides Master Von Hollow, but perhaps it was for the best. Perhaps Master Von Hollow had more skill to spare than anybody. It certainly had seemed to be enough for Theodore, who, despite Frederick's pestering, was now surrounded by an entire collection of tiny mushrooms. Of course, all of that was assuming Master Von Hollow would actually *choose* Oliver as his assistant, but Oliver had an idea about that too.

Oliver slid down the sandy hill that Razzle's School for Meddlesome Boys was built on, sprinted past the snoring gang of ancient crocodiles, and ducked into the creaky boathouse where the school's pack of rowboats swayed eagerly back and forth.

The names of the rowboats—*Jack, Sue, Rocky, Pearl, Syd,* and *Cecelia*—were painted on the sides in bright, bold letters, not as a matter of sentimentality but as a matter of necessity. The rowboats weren't ordinary rowboats but enchanted rowboats obtained from the magicians' next-door neighbors in the Dead Tree Forest, i.e., the witches. Each rowboat had a wildly divergent personality and strong opinions to boot. This did not bode well for an eleven-year-old boy with a ridiculously short cape and no hat, but so far the rowboat known as *Syd* didn't seem to mind much, and maybe even not at all. Fortunately for Oliver, he saw no sign of *Rocky*, the rowboat that had the greatest disdain for him and tended to spray him with swamp goo at every opportunity.

Oliver drew near to *Syd* and swung his legs inside. "Hello there," Oliver said. He delivered three short pats to *Syd*'s hull, and *Syd* pulled obediently away from the dock. *Syd* plowed through the murky green water and past the clusters of catfish that turned their whiskered faces up at Oliver and mewed pitifully.

Once Oliver and *Syd* made their way out of the deepest, darkest parts of the moat, they eased onto the flats, where a network of shallow channels—some no more than six inches deep—branched off in a dozen different directions. In the center of it all was a crude, mud-splattered wooden sign that read in drippy red paint: "The Carousel." And, just in case that wasn't creepy enough, the sign also had a rudimentary picture of a skull drawn on it.

*Syd* shivered and attempted to turn around, but Oliver stuck his oar in the mud. He looked over his shoulder in the direction of the comparatively cheery main channels of the swamp and then back to the Carousel. He swiped his arm across his forehead, which was damp with perspiration. Oliver had heard stories of the Carousel. Stories of magicians rowing in and never rowing back out. The Carousel teemed with slithering things, the Carousel was laden with jumbo-size sinkholes, but the Carousel was also renowned for its fine collection of exotic and rare plants. A collection of exotic and rare plants that included the one thing Oliver was certain would cure his stage fright: worm root.

At Razzle's School for Meddlesome Boys, when the topic of worm root came up (which was almost never) it was met with little more than a series of yawns. Mostly because the effect of a worm root plant, if consumed, was to provide a massive dose of confidence—something most magicians were already over-flowing with and not one bit interested in acquiring more of. Oliver, however, could recite even the most obscure of Head-master Razzle's lessons in his sleep. He wasn't in possession of an exceptional memory but was merely a victim of Headmaster Razzle's burdensome request to take copious notes for everyone else, while they spent the class period toying around with magic.

If this sounds terribly unfair to you, *it was*. But sometimes even terribly unfair things harbor a bit of good. In this case, the cornucopia of magicianly terms and concepts that constantly bounced around Oliver's head was the source of his one and only idea for curing his stage fright.

Oliver set his jaw. He gave *Syd* a reassuring pat. "This shouldn't take long, *Syd*. I know exactly what I'm looking for."

Though *Syd* let out a weighty sigh, he nevertheless inched

forward. But the deeper they went into the Carousel, the darker it got. The trees in the Carousel were curiously large. Their great, big trunks jutted out of the swamp goo with leafy canopies so dense that not even a glimmer of sunlight could eke through. Oliver gulped. If the Carousel was this dark during the day, what would it be like to be here at night? What would—

*HISSSSS.* An ominous sound slithered near, and Oliver froze.

He sucked up a breath, looking carefully from left to right. But other than the constant gurgle and pop of the water, everything was still.

Oliver wasn't afraid of any mere snake. At Razzle's School for Meddlesome Boys, being situated on a sand hill and surrounded by a moat, snakes wriggled down the hallways like common house spiders. Sometimes Oliver even pulled them out from underneath his pillow at night. But those snakes did not hiss loud enough to make the trees shake, and of all the beasts rumored to live within the depths of the Carousel, there was one that was whispered about more than any other: *Delilah.*

Oliver set his jaw and urged *Syd* toward the gooey banks of a mudflat. He swung his legs over the edge and planted his feet in a heap of squishy mud. He told himself that Delilah was nothing more than a tall tale and that even a place like the Swinging Swamp couldn't hide a creature of those staggering proportions. At a rumored forty feet long and six feet around, Delilah would measure bigger even than one of the Carousel's enormous trees.

*HISSSSSSSSSSS*. The bothersome sound erupted again, much closer and much louder.

Oliver straightened up, wondering if perhaps he and Syd should come back another day, when a giant mud ball whirred through the air and smacked him in the back of the head.

"Ouch!" Oliver cried, but before he could duck, two more oozing mud balls made their mark. One splattered against his cheek, and the other pelted his too-short cape.

The laughter followed. And Oliver's heart sank when two students from Razzle's School for Meddlesome Boys leaped out from behind a cluster of trees.

"Gee, I'm sorry, Oliver. Did that mud ball *hit* you?" Nicholas Snark said with mock sincerity. He strutted in front of the other boy, Duncan, and swirled his calf-length cape through the air with panache. After tipping his hat in Oliver's direction, he continued, "Without a hat on, you're almost impossible to see! But I bet you hear that a lot, don't you?"

"Not really," Oliver muttered, but he kept his eyes low. Most everyone agreed that Nicholas Snark was the Swinging Swamp's next Master Von Hollow. His skills at illusion were the best—or worst, depending on your standing with him—and even grown-up magicians loitered on the sandy banks of Razzle's School for Meddlesome Boys to ask him for some tips from time to time.

"Well, you're lucky Duncan and I found you. Don't you

know that students aren't allowed in the Carousel? That it's dangerous?" Nicholas said.

Oliver crossed his arms against his chest, though it was very hard to look dignified with mud dripping down his cheek. "And you two aren't students?"

"Sure, we are," Duncan piped up. "But we're here on a *special* assignment. Headmaster Razzle sent us here to practice our illusions. But you wouldn't know anything about that because—"

"I know, I know. I don't have a hat," Oliver finished for him, which certainly took a bit of wind out of Duncan's bully sails. Oliver went on, "Why can't you practice your illusions at Razzle's? Why would the headmaster send you all the way out here?"

"Because Headmaster Razzle wants us to think big," Nicholas said with a gleam in his eye.

Oliver frowned. Why would anyone need an illusion that big? Did it have anything to do with Headmaster Razzle's insistence that soon the Chancellor would acknowledge the magicians in a way that he never had before?

*HISSSSSSS*. The sound was very nearly upon them, this time accompanied by a noisy rustle, as if something was slithering through the grass. Nicholas and Duncan exchanged glances with one another, and a wave of relief washed over Oliver.

*Big* illusions.

Of course! Nicholas and Duncan were trying to conjure an illusion of Delilah. Oliver couldn't imagine why Headmaster

Razzle would want such a thing, but it took the edge off the shivers rippling up and down Oliver's spine; at least he would be able to continue his search for worm root without worrying about getting eaten by a real anaconda.

Duncan's and Nicholas's eyes suddenly widened. Their faces paled, and they stumbled backward, all while jabbing their fingers in the air at something behind Oliver. But Oliver wasn't about to give Nicholas and Duncan the satisfaction of being scared. When they went back to Razzle's and bragged to the other students about their illusion of Delilah, they wouldn't get to say Oliver had been fooled.

And so, Oliver forced a smile on his face. He turned slowly around and wasn't one bit surprised to find himself face-to-face with what really was an impressive representation of Delilah. Her eyes were perfectly cold and calculating, her forked tongue flicked in and out of her mouth in an unnerving fashion, and she looked even bigger than six feet around.

Oliver reminded himself that—giant anaconda or not—all magicians' illusions were powered by fear and could be made to disappear by the touch of an unafraid observer. He just had to get close enough to Delilah, reach out his hand, and then, *poof*, everything would return to normal: hot, sticky, and muddy as ever, but minus a giant snake.

Oliver marched right up to the giant anaconda. He heard some muffled gasps, the pounding of feet, and then a crash of the underbrush as if Nicholas and Duncan had run away. They certainly seemed committed to maintaining the charade—but Oliver was just as committed to turning over a new page. He was a magician, he belonged in the Swinging Swamp, and soon everyone else would see it too.

With all that energy pulsing through Oliver, he felt nearly invincible. Oliver had enough real obstacles in his life. He wasn't about to let an imaginary one stand in his way. He reached out and laid a firm hand on Delilah.

But Delilah did not disappear.

To the contrary, she *wriggled*.

Not to mention, her skin was an awful combination of cold, clammy, and scaly. Oliver's knees began to quiver. He knew illusions were supposed to look real, but he didn't know they could feel real too.

Reader, I suspect you and I both saw it coming. Even still it is hard to put into words the feeling of dread that arises when one discovers they have just picked a fight with a legendary anaconda. It is somewhere between realizing that one has agreed to walk barefoot over a field of molten lava and that one has agreed to go skydiving and inconveniently forgotten to pack a parachute.

And, as one tends to do in moments of sheer and utter desperation, Oliver let out a loud and panicked cry. He spun madly around searching for something, anything, that might be of help, and his eyes landed on the closest thing he had to a friend in the Swinging Swamp: *Syd*.

*Syd* hadn't left!

*Syd* was still waiting faithfully, albeit anxiously, at the end of the muddy bank. Though Oliver was fairly certain Delilah knew how to swim, if the school's enchanted rowboats kept the students safe from the ancient gang of crocodiles, perhaps they might do the same with anacondas? At the very least, *Syd* was loads faster than Oliver, and if they were lucky, maybe Delilah would get tired of chasing them. The only problem was, Delilah's hissing was becoming more insistent, and her giant coils stood between Oliver and *Syd* like an insurmountable mountain.

Oliver looked up, down, and around. He zeroed in on something swaying gently from up above. It was a clump of swinging vines—the very same vines the Swinging Swamp was named for. They hovered all over the swamp. Most times they merely got tangled around the magicians' hats or dripped swamp slime onto their fancy clothes, but Oliver had never been happier to see them.

Oliver took a deep breath. He'd never actually tried to swing from the swamp's vines, though he'd seen a few of the more daring students cross over the school's moat while the crocodile gang launched themselves out of the water, snapping wildly at their capes. He could do this. He actually *had* to do this. Well, either that or make his home inside Delilah's belly, and that really wasn't what he'd meant when he said he wanted to stay in the Swinging Swamp.

Oliver bent his knees. He sprang up from the squishy mud and wrapped his arms and legs around the thickest of the vines. He shimmied up and began to swing back and forth for momentum. Delilah was beside herself. Her tongue flicked in and out furiously as her meal dangled enticingly in front of her. Finally, Oliver leaped away from the vine. His heart caught in his throat, but as he sailed clear over Delilah's head, he knew it was enough.

"Yes!" Oliver cried out triumphantly as he plopped into the mud. He scrambled onto his hands and knees and half ran, half crawled toward *Syd*. *Syd* was at the ready. As soon as Oliver tumbled inside, they zoomed out of the Carousel, leaving behind one very disappointed anaconda.

When *Syd* finally slowed down, Oliver bent over the boat's side. "Thanks for saving my life, buddy," he whispered. And though it pained him to say it because he didn't have anything near to a plan B, he added, "And don't worry. Worm root or no worm root, we're never going back inside that Carousel again."

But *Syd* appeared to be only half listening. He veered suddenly to the left, and then to the right, and then back again to the left. Oliver squinted. There, fluttering a few feet ahead, was the largest monarch butterfly Oliver had ever seen, or rather the only one he'd ever seen. Monarch butterflies weren't really a native species of the swamp.

"Are you . . . chasing that butterfly, *Syd*?" Oliver asked.

As he spoke, a sudden gust of wind sent the butterfly swirling closer. But that was very odd. Indeed, the Swinging Swamp was so utterly devoid of any sort of breeze that the magicians often daydreamed about constructing great big fans to cool the entire place down.

Of course, in the kingdom of Wanderly, anytime one considered the wind, one could not help but think of the Winds of Wanderly. The magicians claimed to be wholly unimpressed by the Winds, but sometimes late at night, and perhaps especially when he was feeling his loneliest, Oliver couldn't keep from *wondering*.

The monarch butterfly fluttered down and alighted on Oliver's finger. It pumped its wings once, twice, and then, without any warning at all, exploded into a cloud of sparkling gold dust. Oliver's jaw dropped. He watched as the wind rolled near and swirled the dust into a sheet of paper, which came to rest on the toe of Oliver's muddy boot.

Oliver blinked, because certainly it *had* to be the Winds of Wanderly; certainly only the Winds of Wanderly could do that.

Oliver quickly swept the paper up. It appeared to be . . . a letter. Oliver couldn't imagine who would want to send him a letter, but he drew it near and read aloud:

> Dear Fairy Godmother,
> My name is Pippa. I am eleven years old. I am sorry I didn't use the standard channels for wish delivery, but this is not a

standard wish. I'm not in need of an invitation to some fancy ball, a shopping spree at Pigglesticks, or even my very own pony (though any of those would be excellent). In fact, I'm not asking for anything new at all, but rather a return to how things used to be.

Fairy Godmother, I'll get straight to the point: you have to help me get home. There are nine people waiting there for me, and I simply can't live without them.

If you're wondering how I ended up away from home, I didn't do anything ridiculous like try to run away or wander off in the wrong direction because I got distracted eating berries. No, my problem is much more complicated than that. I was sent away by magic, which means the only way I can return is by magic.

I wish I had my own magic; I wish I didn't have to bother you (to be clear, I'm not actually submitting these wishes, just the one about going home). Honestly, after seeing the mounds of letters villagers in my town send your way and not one of them answered, I'm a little bit skeptical about you. But I don't think now is the time to be doubtful. I think now, more than ever, I've got to find something to believe in. For better or worse, I'm picking you.

So please help me, Fairy Godmother. Your response can't come soon enough. I don't know if you've ever experienced something like sadness (fairy godmothers are always so cheery in storybooks), but it feels like my heart's been replaced with a rock, and that's a whole lot to carry around.

Very truly yours,

Pippa North

PS: Being new to all this, I'm not sure how wishes in Wanderly normally work. Are they free? Is there an IOU system? Do I need to fill out a satisfaction survey and submit it to the Council? Please advise.

PPS: Don't forget to send your reply via the Winds of Wanderly—that probably seems risky to you, but if the Winds aren't on our side, I doubt we'll pull this off anyways.

Oliver blinked. If the Winds of Wanderly really had delivered the letter, maybe they weren't as mighty as everyone believed. The Merry Meadow, where the fairy godmothers lived, was an entire riverbank away and then some. Ha! If the Winds of Wanderly had dropped this Pippa's letter even a hint to the east, it would have wound up in the hands of a wicked witch, perhaps the only fate worse than finding its way to Oliver.

Not only was Oliver *not* a fairy godmother, he was a boy magician without a hat. On a magical scale of one to ten, Oliver rang in at a big, fat zero. And the girl sounded so desperate. Almost as desperate as Oliver. Why wouldn't the Winds of Wanderly want to help her?

With a sigh, Oliver glanced back down at the letter. His eyes came to rest on the line about whether wishes were free. Were wishes free? Oliver hadn't a clue. Absent a Council directive, fairy godmothers were forbidden from helping anyone other than commoners, so Oliver had never bothered to find out more. But certainly, it wouldn't be unusual to expect some form of payment, would it?

In a sudden rush of exhilaration, Oliver came to a startling conclusion. What if the Winds of Wanderly hadn't made a mistake after all? What if the girl's letter had been delivered to Oliver not in order to help *her* but to help *him*?

Oliver would have never considered pocketing a total stranger's money before, but without the worm root, he was going to need something. In all of the Swinging Swamp no one loved money more than Master Von Hollow. Perhaps a pouch full of grubins would be the exact incentive Oliver needed. Perhaps Oliver could still be chosen as an assistant for the magician's showcase and receive his hat before Headmaster Razzle's deadline!

Though it hardly seemed fair that Oliver should secure his home at the expense of keeping this girl away from hers, who was he to stand in the way of the Winds of Wanderly? At least that's what Oliver told himself as he bit his lip and tried very hard not to think about the rest of the girl's words.

About how she said her heart felt like it had been replaced with a rock.

Oliver had always assumed he was the only one who felt that way. He never imagined there could be someone else out there too. Someone who might understand. And though at one time Oliver would have jumped at the chance for a friend, what he needed now, what his very survival depended on, was a hat.

Decided, Oliver reached beneath the fold of his muddy cape. He fished out a pencil and a piece of paper. He bent his head low and wrote: ***Dear Pippa, This is your fairy godmother . . .***

# FIVE

# A Toothless Witch

Life on Triumph Mountain, so far, was nothing like Pippa expected.

Though there were very many reasons why she was desperate to get away from Peabody's Academy for the Triumphant, the one bright spot was the promise of what fascinating things she might learn during her (hopefully) brief stay.

Triumphants had the best of everything, didn't they? Surely not a single corner would be cut in providing them with the best education in the entire kingdom. And, at the very least, it had to be far superior to what she'd experienced in Ms. Pinch's leaky classroom back in Ink Hollow.

Of course, all of that depended on having an instructor. So far, despite the daily A+ grades distributed to the students, Mistress Peabody hadn't bothered to show up for a single lesson or hand out a single assignment.[15] Based on the other Triumphants' shoulder-shrugging, blasé reactions, Mistress Peabody's absence must not have been anything new, but in Pippa's opinion it was very un-Triumphant-like.

Pippa might not have found the dismal state of their classroom affairs so devastating had she received a letter back from her fairy godmother, but despite lingering by every open window in case the Winds of Wanderly should drop by, she'd received nothing. Not a single word.

With the castle's magic mirror stowed behind a hopelessly locked door, Pippa had never felt so terribly alone, and in the quietest of moments, she was beginning to wonder if she would ever see her family again.

And so, quite peculiarly, as she made her way to the dining hall, Pippa's hope rested on a most astonishing banner the castle staff hung the night prior, the one that read: "Welcome, Witch Bonecrusher."

At first Pippa thought it was a joke. What did witches have to do with Triumphants? And if the general public wasn't invited for tours of Castle Cressida, why would anyone allow a witch to go traipsing about? But the seven-year-old girl with the two buns on the sides of her head, the one who smiled shyly at

---

15. Are you wondering how it is possible to receive a grade for classwork that was never even begun? I am beginning to wonder such things myself. Not to mention how many *other* things Triumphants may have received but didn't do a single thing to earn. . . .

Pippa on the day of her arrival and whose name was Anastasia, had informed her that every year at least one villain visited the Triumphants' classroom as an essential part of the students' training.

Pippa knew this should have terrified her, that her glimpse of a witch at the examination should have been enough to last her the next fifty years at least, but it had been a very awful few days. And if the arrival of a witch meant the return of their school lessons—assuming the witch was coming as a guest and not a substitute teacher—Pippa was willing to risk it. Not to mention, this was the first real sign that the academy was committed to turning out heroes as real as the kingdom's villains.

Pippa turned the corner and sucked up a breath when she saw a broken curtain rod languishing on the floor and awash in a sea of burgundy velvet. She hurried near and gently gathered the fabric in her arms, tucking it discreetly against the wall. Pippa wasn't nearly so put off by Castle Cressida's broken-down appearance as when she had first arrived. Partly because the castle seemed so apologetic about it all, as if it weren't *trying* to crumble to bits but that it was merely a symptom of a larger problem.

When Pippa entered the dining hall, she was surprised to find that it was empty. Apparently the other Triumphants did not believe in eating a breakfast of champions or they didn't think a witch was all that noteworthy of a visitor. Pippa shivered. She couldn't imagine ever underestimating a witch. As she moved toward the buffet table, her eyes roved across the room and up to the ceiling. A row of tapestries lined the perimeter of the dining hall, but they were rolled up tight like secrets.

Pippa couldn't help wondering what was on them—and what other secrets Castle Cressida might be keeping—but her step quickened when she spied a heaping platter of cinnamon rolls. As far as Pippa was concerned, the castle's sweet treats were the first thing that lived up to the Triumphant name and then some. But as delicious as the goodies tasted, what was most fascinating were the unusual ways they made Pippa feel. Last night's chocolate chip cookies had almost made her feel . . . brave. Maybe even a little bit Triumphant, if you will. Pippa had never met another chocolate chip cookie that could do that.

Cinnamon roll in hand, Pippa plopped into one of the two dozen golden thrones arranged at the large table. She plunged her fork into the soft dough and—

"Oh!" A small gasp rang out in the quiet.

Pippa looked up in time to see someone dive beneath the tablecloth. Pippa carefully lifted a corner of the fine silk fabric and peered beneath. There, crouched on all fours, was a girl who looked to be no more than a year or two older than Pippa. She had the most voluminous hair Pippa had ever seen and was wearing an apron. The girl scrunched her eyes shut as if that might make her invisible.

"Um, hello there," Pippa said.

The girl's eyes popped open. She looked from left to right and whispered, "The staff and the students aren't supposed to talk to each other. Mistress Peabody's orders, but"—the girl tilted her head curiously to the side—"since you started it, I've gotta ask, are you her? Are you Pippa North? Pardon my saying so, but are you the one who saved us from another Bumble?"

"I, well, I . . . perhaps," Pippa said, feeling suddenly self-conscious. "What's your name?"

The girl finally crawled out from beneath the table and onto her feet. She executed a short curtsy, but when her eyes fell down across the fabric of her apron covered in bits of sugar, frosting, jam, and a heap of other things, she cringed.

Pippa's eyes lit up. "Are you the one who makes all the amazing goodies?" she asked.

"Gee, how could you tell? I'm a regular mess, aren't I?"

"My mother always says you can tell a genius by looking at their mess," Pippa said with a nod.

The girl's expression brightened. "It must be nice to have a mother like that."

"Yes," Pippa said softly, "it is. You still didn't tell me your name though?"

"I'm Maisy. I'm in charge of all the baking, even if Mistress Peabody refuses to acknowledge it. Mistress Peabody refuses to acknowledge a lot of things though so I—whoops!" Maisy clapped a hand over her mouth. "Oh, I said too much. I always say too much."

Before Pippa could respond, the curtains hanging near the

windows began to flutter. A breeze blew into the room, soft at first, but then it began to swirl faster. So fast that even the crystal glasses on the table began to bobble wildly.

Pippa and Maisy exchanged glances. The name hung silently on both of their lips, the only name it could possibly be: *the Winds of Wanderly*.

And there, suddenly, soaring on the Winds' coattails, came a metallic green dragonfly. It buzzed and whirred and spun about the room. It touched lightly down on Pippa's head and then Maisy's, and Maisy dashed after it with open hands.

"Be careful!" Pippa called out. "Do you think it's safe?"

Maisy looked over her shoulder. "I'm not sure if the Winds of Wanderly are ever safe, but they're always good."

Suddenly the dragonfly spun and flew full speed in Pippa's direction. She threw her hands over her face and braced herself for a bite or a sting or whatever it was that angry dragonflies did, but nothing happened. And when she lowered her hands all she saw on the ground was a pile of slimy, green goo. Her jaw dropped.

"Did I do that?" she said. "Was that my fault?"

Maisy's eyes were wide. "No, it—it just exploded. It . . ." Her voice trailed off. The Winds began rippling over the goo, spinning it in the air until it transformed into a sheet of paper.

A cry of delight escaped Pippa's lips, and she snatched the paper out of the air. It had to be a letter from her fairy godmother. Pippa couldn't believe she had written back! She couldn't believe that maybe, just maybe, her life was about to get back to normal.

But Maisy took a small, very small, step forward. "Are you, um, sure that's for you?" she asked.

Pippa's heart raced. She had almost forgotten she wasn't alone. She had intended to keep her fairy godmother plan a secret from everybody, but how was she going to do that now?

"Yes, I've been . . . waiting for this letter. See it, um, says my name right here," Pippa said, pointing to her name while carefully concealing the rest of the letter's contents with her other hand.

Maisy's face fell. "Oh, yes, I do see. And I'm sorry, I—I should have left you to your thoughts a long time ago."

Maisy turned to leave.

Pippa, however, had been spending more than enough time alone with her thoughts. What Pippa really missed was the constant clatter and bustle of living in a tiny two-bedroom cottage with nine other people and never having enough elbow room. Even with the other students around, everything about Peabody's Academy for the Triumphant felt so vast and so lonely. In a family of ten, Pippa had never really had a need for a friend, but perhaps that was exactly what she needed now.

Pippa took a deep breath. "Maisy," she called out. "Are you good at keeping secrets?" Maisy nodded vigorously, and Pippa continued, "This might sound crazy, but this is a letter from my fairy godmother. I asked her—and this is what you can't say a word about—if she would help me get home."

Maisy's eyes went wide. "And what did she say?" she whispered.

Pippa brought the letter near and read aloud:

> *Dear Pippa,*
>
> *This is your fairy godmother, Olivanderella Dash. I'm glad you chose to write to me. Even though I'm exactly as cheery as every storybook you've ever read (rosy-cheeked too!), if I try hard I can imagine what it might feel like to have a rock heart, and it's awful. I'm sorry for that.*
>
> *You're right that your wish isn't like any I've ever seen, and I'm pretty sure the pony would have been easier. You sure I can't sway you in that direction? In my experience animals, or even rowboats, tend to be better company than most people, and you mentioned, what was it, NINE people at your house? That's a lot.*
>
> *Still, there's no place like home, is there? And in that case, I'll just have to see what I can do. It would be helpful if you could let me know whose magic sent you away in the first place? If you haven't noticed, there's sort of a magical hierarchy in Wanderly, and it makes a difference whether you tangled with a witch or a magician or were reprimanded by a Council member.*
>
> *As for payment, it would only be fair, right? And for*

*an unusual wish like this one, especially considering the additional effort of utilizing the Winds of Wanderly, I'm going to open the bidding at one hundred grubins (paid up front, of course). Though it would warm my heart to do it all for free, the kingdom of Wanderly can't run on nothing.*

> *Sparkles and Smiles,*
> *Fairy Dash*

Pippa tried to swallow. But the knot in her throat was simply too big. Almost as big as the term "one hundred grubins." Pippa didn't think her father earned that much for six months' worth of work as a book peddler, and it sure didn't seem like there were many money-earning opportunities on Triumph Mountain.

Maisy frowned. "I'm not trying to be critical—honestly, I'm not—but did that letter seem a bit . . . odd to you? I mean, not all fairy godmothers are really rosy-cheeked, are they?" she asked, her hand grazing across her own cheeks.

"I was a bit more concerned about the 'one hundred grubins' part," Pippa said with a sigh. "I had no idea how expensive wishes were. I might not have bothered to write if I did."

"Yeah, about that—" Maisy began, but she was very rudely interrupted by a high-pitched, shrieking *cackle*.

"The witch!" Pippa cried, whirling about. "Oh, the witch! She must have arrived! She must be here right now! Doesn't the castle have an alarm system or something?"

"An alarm system?" Maisy echoed. She thought for a moment and then shook her head. She dipped her hand into her apron pocket and whipped out a large wooden spoon. "I've got this though. Think that'll help?"

"Well, considering that witch likely arrived on an entire broomstick, a wooden spoon doesn't seem like much, but it's better than the nothing I've got." Pippa reached out and linked arms with Maisy. "Are you ready?"

But Maisy shook her head. She pulled gently away from Pippa's grasp. "That's awfully kind of you, Pippa, but I'd get in big trouble from Mistress Peabody," she said.

"For helping me?"

"That's not how she'd see it. She'd say you were helping me."

Pippa frowned. She couldn't imagine how Triumphants could be called on to save the entire kingdom if they weren't allowed to help the person standing right next to them. "But isn't helping others the whole point of being a Triumphant?"

Maisy looked genuinely confused. "Is it? Anyhow, don't worry about me. I'll slip out through the back hallway, and if this witch is anything like the last one who visited, trust me, you'll be just fine."

But when a second unnerving cackle rolled near, Pippa's pulse began to race.

"If you say so," Pippa said. "And please remember not to say anything about—"

"About what?" Maisy grinned, and with her spoon held high, she scurried away.

Pippa moved toward the dining hall's main entrance and opened the door the merest crack. She froze at the sound of voices before realizing they weren't at all witchy, but young and girlish. Swinging the door wider, she saw seven-year-old Anastasia walking hand in hand with three-year-old Viola.

"Come on," Anastasia urged the little girl. "We're almost there, and if we hurry we might get a seat up front."

*A seat up front?* Pippa couldn't fathom why that would be desirable, especially for the smallest Triumphant of all, but she rushed to catch up with the girls nevertheless. Traveling in numbers seemed to be the wisest thing to do when a cackling witch was afoot.

When the girls reached the classroom, Pippa's heart soared. Mistress Peabody was back just as Pippa had hoped! She was posted at the front entrance and armed with her dazzling smile. She was dressed head to toe in shades of green complete with a small veiled hat that Pippa assumed was the latest fashion even if it looked like a giant spinach leaf poised on her head. Mistress Peabody didn't say a word about her frustrating absenteeism, but maybe she planned to make up for it with a spectacular lesson. She ushered the girls in while exclaiming in a breathy voice, "Welcome, welcome, girls! Seats are first come, first served, and I wouldn't linger. They're filling up quickly!"

Pippa peeked over the heads of the other Triumphants and

gasped. The witch was actually *inside* the classroom! She was seated on a chair positioned at the front of the room, wearing a whole mess of black: a black cardigan with ratty sleeves and a whopping mud stain; a black blouse with buttons made of bone; five layers of wrinkled and rustling black skirts; black tights riddled with holes; and high-heeled black witchy boots missing a few brass hooks. Her hair was a deep shade of midnight blue and her nose, as Pippa had expected, was very, very large.

The witch's gaze flickered up. She seemed to look right at Pippa. She lifted her hands; she cracked her knobby knuckles. Pippa was certain she was about to shout out some horrible curse, but instead she just . . . yawned.

Anastasia looked over her shoulder to see if Pippa was following along, but when the two girls took their seats in the front row, Pippa vehemently shook her head. She plopped into the last row of seats beside the boy with the glasses, Ernest.

Ernest's eyes brightened. "Oh, hey there," he said. He nodded in the witch's direction. "Looks like it's going to be a *wicked* day of instruction, doesn't it?"

As if on cue, the witch counted out one-two-three on her bony fingers. She sucked up a deep breath, let loose yet another impeccably bone-chilling cackle, and promptly folded her hands in her lap, waiting. *Patiently.*

Pippa was horrified. "What is wrong with her?" she whispered in Ernest's direction.

"Wrong with her?" Ernest repeated as if he didn't quite

understand the question. But as he surveyed the witch, he gave a little nod. "I suppose her clothing is a bit disheveled, but I think that's only to be expected coming from a place like the Dead Tree Forest." He shivered. "I've heard it's terribly dusty there, and—"

"Not her clothes, Ernest. Her clothes may be the only thing that makes sense. I'm talking about the way she's acting. She's sitting. Patiently. In a chair. In a classroom filling up with juicy children—"

"Ugh! That's disgusting, Pippa," Ernest said, wrinkling his nose.

"Of course it is. Haven't you ever heard those child-eating witch stories? Witches are the worst!"

Unfortunately, Mistress Peabody chose that moment to shut the classroom door. Everyone grew still and quiet and Pippa's words echoed loudly back and forth like a bouncy ball. She cringed, expecting Mistress Peabody to scold her for speaking so rudely, but instead Mistress Peabody turned her dazzling smile up a shade brighter.

"You are right, Bettina, witches are certainly the worst. Without the Triumphants of Wanderly to protect the helpless citizens, our kingdom would be one of chaos and strife. It is imperative that we carry on the traditions of the heroes who came before us, and that is why today we will be practicing on the real thing."

Bettina?!

Pippa's hand immediately shot straight up in the air. Though she was miles away from home, saddled with an unwanted destiny, beneath the care of an unreliable Triumphant, and in the presence of a peculiar witch, she did find herself in a classroom. And in a classroom, Pippa knew precisely what to do. There were rules and structure and clearly defined channels for fixing such harrowing problems as repeated misidentification.

"Oops!" Mistress Peabody said with a knowing smile and a pointed nod at Pippa's outstretched hand. "In a Triumphant classroom we're all leaders, Bettina. There shall be no raised hands, or any rules at all, in this classroom."

Pippa felt as if she'd been stung. She slowly lowered her hand. She sat forcibly on top of it. The raising of hands was a fundamental of every classroom, and this was going to be a hard habit to break.

Of course, then Prudence Bumble unhelpfully piped up, "Real Triumphants don't need such things as rules. Rules are for simpletons, *Bettina*." She stifled a giggle and exchanged smug glances with Bernard.

At the front of the classroom, three-year-old Viola almost fell out of her seat pointing in Pippa's direction. "That's not Bettina!" she insisted.

"Of course it's Bettina, dear," Mistress Peabody answered sweetly without bothering to look her way.

Pippa sucked up a breath. She spoke loudly and boldly out

of turn though she didn't relish it one bit. "I told you already, I'm *Pippa*."

The witch at the front of the room snickered. Like she found the whole snafu amusing. But, just as quickly, she changed her expression back to one of boredom.

"Well, then, I suppose Pippa it is," Mistress Peabody said tightly. "Now," she went on, "it's not every day that we have a real, live wicked witch in the classroom. Thank you for joining us today, Ms. Bonecrusher." Mistress Peabody arched her eyebrow expectantly at the students, and they all chimed in monotonously, "Thank you for joining us today, Ms. Bonecrusher."

Ms. Bonecrusher, however, was busy flossing her teeth with what appeared to be a midnight blue hair she had plucked from her head. She pulled the hair out repeatedly to examine the contents.[16]

Mistress Peabody cleared her throat. Loudly. When Ms. Bonecrusher finally looked up, she tossed the hair over her shoulder and dutifully rolled out another cackle.

"Who would like to be the first student to subdue Ms. Bonecrusher this morning?" Mistress Peabody asked brightly.

No one popped out of their seat.

"Come on, children, don't be shy," Mistress Peabody coaxed.

---

16. For the record, I take absolutely no joy in relaying these foul details. I never did have the spine to be a purely witchy book, but if you find you're into that sort of thing, I'd be happy to suggest a few titles.

"You are Triumphants, after all."

Pippa thought she heard the witch snort at the word "Triumphants," but there was so much nervous shuffling going on among the students that it was a bit hard to tell. Finally, however, Prudence rose ceremoniously from her seat. She inched slowly down the aisle as if wanting to ensure that every single pair of eyes was on her. When Prudence drew up in front of Ms. Bonecrusher, she struck a grandiose pose only to have Ms. Bonecrusher speak first.

"Hello, *Bettina*," she said with a devious snicker.

A look of indignation flashed across Prudence's face. "No one ever said *I* was Bettina. I'm Prudence Bumble. Weren't you paying any attention at all?"

But judging by the gleam in the witch's eye, it was clear she had been paying attention and was very much enjoying irking Prudence.

Prudence thrust her fists at her sides and stomped her foot on the ground.

She whirled in Mistress Peabody's direction. "That—that witch—is mocking me!" she shrieked.

Mistress Peabody, hands trembling, pulled a crinkled piece of paper from the pocket of her dancing skirt. She tried in vain to smooth out the edges. "No, no, that can't be," she said, shaking her head. "Mocking is definitely not on today's agenda."

Prudence rolled her eyes and turned her attention back to Ms. Bonecrusher, who seemed to be growing more invigorated by the second. "Apologize, witch!" Prudence insisted.

"Apologize, witch!" Ms. Bonecrusher mimicked back in a hilariously identical tone.

The students gasped. Prudence's cheeks flamed. Pippa gulped and leaned in to Ernest. "Is this the way villainous visits usually tend to go?" she whispered.

Mistress Peabody, meanwhile, sashayed anxiously toward Ms. Bonecrusher. She waved the crinkled agenda beneath her nose. "Yoo-hoo, Ms. Bonecrusher! You must not have reviewed this very carefully. Please do take a minute to—"

Ms. Bonecrusher wrenched the agenda out of Mistress Peabody's hands. She smiled a gruesome witchy smile and ripped the agenda right down the middle. "Sometimes plans change," she hissed.

The classroom erupted into chaos. Mistress Peabody sprinted toward her desk and began frantically tossing things over her shoulder while mumbling something about "emergency restraints" and "proper screening, my pointed toe." Prudence, losing every ounce of her prior bravado, tried to dash away, but Ms. Bonecrusher yanked her backward by the hem of her cape.

With Prudence gripped tight in one hand, Ms. Bonecrusher turned to face the class. "Are there any other Bettinas in the room?" she boomed.

Prudence jabbed her finger in Pippa's direction. "Over there!" she said in between great, heaving wails. "She's the one that started all this!"

Pippa's stomach dropped. She sank a bit lower in her chair. "But I'm not even a Bumble!" she cried.

To which Bernard blurted out a few desks away, "Bumble? Who said anything about a Bumble? My last name's *Rumble*," and pulled his cape entirely over his head as if that were a sufficient hiding spot.

"Bernard!" Prudence admonished.

Beside Pippa, Ernest leaped suddenly to his feet. His face was ghastly pale and beads of sweat rolled down his forehead. "STOP!" he shouted.

Ms. Bonecrusher's eyes flashed. "What did you say?" she asked, eyeing Ernest as if he were a small bug.

"What are you doing, Ernest?" Pippa whispered fervently.

"W-what we've been trained to do," he said, sliding his glasses up along the bridge of his nose.

Pippa was terribly worried about Ernest, but she couldn't help marveling at his bravery. She waited to see what he would do. The witch waited to see what he would do. Even the walls of Castle Cressida sucked up a dusty breath and waited to see what he would do, but after a full ten seconds of waiting, and with all eyes on him, it appeared that Ernest had already *done* what he was going to do.

"Mistress Peabody taught us that 'stop' is the most powerful word in Wanderly . . . if it comes from a Triumphant, that is," Ernest explained rather weakly.

Apparently Ms. Bonecrusher didn't agree because she slapped

her knee and howled with laughter. The Triumphants all turned to Mistress Peabody for an explanation, but she was still furiously tossing items out from her desk, standing in a heap of rubble, and mumbling distractedly to herself. Thankfully, Castle Cressida hadn't stopped paying attention. In one big creaking, moaning, groaning display of effort, it dipped into its pool of ailing resources and did what it could; i.e., it managed to throw off an entire sheet of ultra-sticky, ultra-tacky wallpaper aimed straight for Ms. Bonecrusher.[17]

The witch never had a chance. Wallpaper, as it turns out, is a surprising foe. She threw her hands over her head for protection, Prudence wriggled away to freedom, and the wallpaper wrapped cleanly around Ms. Bonecrusher like a witchy burrito. She teetered and bobbled about, but with her arms pinned against her sides, she toppled helplessly onto the floor. Rolling to and fro, Ms. Bonecrusher worked herself into a proper rage, hissing and spitting and cursing and doing all the witchy things Pippa had expected from her at the start. The witch, it seemed, had a well-defined set of teeth after all.

What Pippa couldn't understand was why Ms. Bonecrusher had ever bothered to act otherwise. Mistress Peabody seemed to think it had to do with that agenda she was waving about, but if the details of a villainous visit were worked out beforehand,

---

17. I'm not about to pretend a rogue sheet of wallpaper wins any awards for most glamorous rescue, but perhaps it was the most resourceful. And a rescue *is* still a rescue, after all.

what was so heroic about that?

Mistress Peabody cleared her throat. She lifted her gauzy green skirts and leaped gracefully over the wallpapered, and still hollering, witch. Though her eyes were a bit glazed over, she exclaimed, "Excellent job, Ernest! You performed just as we practiced. Why don't you visit the Chest of Unnecessaries for a well-deserved prize, hmm?"

Pippa was stunned. Mistress Peabody acted as if it was all fun and games and the class hadn't been one breath away from being cursed by a wicked witch. Still, Pippa couldn't keep her eyes from following Ernest as he stepped to the front of the room and kneeled beside a plain wooden chest. Pippa noticed Prudence watching him too. She looked positively pea-green, as if she thought Mistress Peabody should have given *her* credit for subduing Ms. Bonecrusher, when really the true hero among them was Castle Cressida.

Ernest reached into the chest and carefully pulled something forth. He was still a bit pale-faced, but he grinned broadly when he held the shiny, new baseball bat over his head like a trophy. The rest of the Triumphants clapped politely, while Ernest exclaimed, "Just what I always wanted, my sixth baseball bat!"

Pippa didn't know how something could be what you always wanted when you already had five of them, but perhaps the Chest of Unnecessaries was used to piling heaps of rewards on the Triumphants.

Suddenly, Pippa's heart thumped.

If the Chest of Unnecessaries liked extravagant gift giving, maybe there was still hope. Maybe the Chest of Unnecessaries could give her the grubins she needed to pay her fairy godmother and return home. Once she did, Pippa would be all too glad to put the business of heroes—if there even was such a thing—far, far behind her. Now she just had to wait for the perfect opportunity.

SIX

# Magician's Assistant, Anyone?

**O**n the southernmost fringe of the Swinging Swamp, standing in a field of impossibly tall, marshy grass buzzing with gnats, Oliver tilted his head up and eyed the gloomy, three-story exterior of Master Von Hollow's mansion. He was tempted to wheel around and sprint right back in the direction he came from, thank you very much, but that certainly wouldn't bring him any closer to his hat. Nor would it silence Master Von Hollow's tattling murder of crows that had already gotten a good look at him.

There was no guarantee that paying Master Von Hollow a visit would further Oliver's desperate mission, but at least it was something more than sitting around at Razzle's School for Meddlesome Boys and waiting for a letter from a girl.

At the time, the venture of letter writing had seemed so

promising. Genius, even! Not to mention, every time Oliver thought back to how the Winds of Wanderly—*the* Winds of Wanderly—had swept into the depths of the swamp and took notice of him, he stopped in his tracks and marveled.

He only hoped the Winds of Wanderly hadn't taken offense to his plan to pretend to be a fairy godmother, but now he wasn't so sure. Five whole days had passed since he'd replied to the girl's letter, and he hadn't heard a single word in response. Soon Master Von Hollow would hold auditions for the coveted role of his assistant, and with no grubins and no worm root, the only trick Oliver had up his sleeve was good old-fashioned flattery.

Oliver squished determinedly through the mud, climbed onto Master Von Hollow's creaky front porch, and lifted the brass door knocker in the shape of a hat. He brought it down three times against the door and waited. When Master Von Hollow didn't answer, Oliver crept a hair closer and pressed his ear against the door.

He heard footsteps! Heavy, plodding footsteps as if someone was coming down the stairs. Hurriedly, he reached up and brought the door knocker down three more times. A loud crash ensued, followed by an outburst of angry grumbling. Finally the knob on Master Von Hollow's door began to twist open. Oliver frantically mussed up his hair. He was certain a little height made the absence of his hat less noticeable—it didn't— plastered a friendly smile on his face, and pretended his heart wasn't banging like a drum.

When Master Von Hollow appeared, he was not smiling. Indeed, that sort of nasty lip curl was best described as a snarl. Despite the fearsome look in Master Von Hollow's eyes, and the dust that covered a whole half side of his face and made him look eerily like a ghost, Oliver's gaze went straight to Master Von Hollow's hat. He had never been so close to it before. And it was *marvelous*. It wasn't as tall as Headmaster Razzle's, though, really, Headmaster Razzle's was a bit too tall and was always causing him to knock into doorframes and such. Nor was it as crusted with gemstones or studded with bright, colorful feathers like the other hats Oliver had seen, but it veritably hummed with magic.

Master Von Hollow huffed. "Close your mouth, you ridiculous boy! If you had any sense about you, you'd never set foot on my porch! I thought Razzle ended his ridiculous school fund-raising campaign months ago, but just so we're clear, I do not want, nor will I ever want, anything as ridiculous as gift wrapping paper. Indeed, it's quite presumptuous to assume a belief in such a senseless activity as gift giving, don't you think?"

"Um, I beg your pardon, sir," Oliver said, wiping the sweat off his brow, "but I'm not here for fund-raising or anything like that. You, um, are just the most famous magician in the swamp—"

"Yes," Master Von Hollow agreed as if Oliver were discussing something as uncontroversial as the weather.

"And, well, over at Razzle's we all want to be like you—"

"Do you now?" Master Von Hollow asked, sounding just a bit more interested.

"So it only seems natural to do something nice for you." Oliver forced his hands to his sides and tried to stop jittering. "To express our thanks. For being so . . . great. Anyhow, if there's anything that you might need help with today, perhaps I can *assist* you?" Oliver held his breath. He had determined to use the word "assist" or, better yet, "assistant" as many times during his visit as possible in hopes that, when the time came for Master Von Hollow to choose an assistant for his showcase, he couldn't help but think of Oliver.

"Headmaster Razzle really sent you here for that?" Master Von Hollow asked with an arc of his eyebrow.

Oliver gulped. Headmaster Razzle, of course, would be horrified to know what Oliver was up to, but he'd been so busy lately packing things into boxes, staring endlessly at his lone Sapphire Sea painting, and sending Nicholas and his sidekick Duncan away for more "special assignments" that it wasn't very hard to slip away.

Discreetly avoiding the question, Oliver executed a little bow. "At your service, sir."

"Hmm, well, there is something that needs to be done. Perhaps something that you could be of use for . . ." Master Von Hollow's voice trailed off, and Oliver made the innocent mistake of peering behind Master Von Hollow and into his mansion.

There at the bottom of the winding and dusty staircase was

a large box, presumably the cause of the loud crash. Its contents had spilled out all over the floor and rolled up against three stacks of similar sealed boxes. Like Headmaster Razzle's office, Master Von Hollow's mansion was peculiarly . . . empty.

Master Von Hollow's eyes flashed. He stepped outside his mansion and slammed the door behind him. The murder of crows that were spying from the porch rail began to anxiously flap their wings. Master Von Hollow loomed over Oliver. "Get your eyes off my property, you little miscreant! I don't know what information Razzle has been blabbing to you boys, but I'll not have you meddling in my business, you hear?"

Oliver bobbed his head vigorously up and down, but he froze when Master Von Hollow reached out and clamped a hand on his shoulder. Despite the perpetually muggy conditions of the Swinging Swamp, Master Von Hollow's touch felt like ice. He wrenched Oliver closer and furrowed his brow as if noticing something. With a sinking feeling, Oliver knew exactly what was coming.

"Where is your hat?" Master Von Hollow said through gritted teeth.

There was no real avoiding this question, and Oliver feared a clever response would earn him a solid thump on the head or worse. In his desperation for a hat, he couldn't forget precisely what sort of magician he was dealing with (an unscrupulous one, that's what).

"I don't have one yet, sir," Oliver said miserably.

Master Von Hollow sucked in a breath. "You're the boy without a hat? You're the oldest boy in the Swinging Swamp never to have received his hat?"

As if Oliver needed reminding. "Yes, sir, that's me," Oliver said, reluctantly claiming the loathsome title.

"Well, then, that's absolutely . . . perfect!" Master Von Hollow exclaimed. He released his grip from Oliver's shoulder and lightly brushed the wrinkles off his too-short cape.

"It—it is?" Oliver asked, wide-eyed. Oliver was certain the word "perfect" had never once been used in association with him. He couldn't believe his good luck! Perhaps Oliver had never needed the grubins or worm root to begin with; perhaps he (along with everyone else) was wrong about Master Von Hollow; and maybe, finally, Oliver was going to get the mentor he always hoped for.

"Yes! Of all the boys in the Swinging Swamp, you are the one who will be missed the least. If something terrible befalls you, not even Headmaster Razzle will get on my case. This really is a matter of the right help at the right time, isn't it?" Master Von Hollow asked with a bright smile plastered on his face. He brushed past Oliver and began striding toward the thick wall of trees that lined his mansion on either side. He shoved a clump of branches out of the way and looked in Oliver's direction. "Come along, then! Let's not dillydally. For where you're going, you'll need to use my rowboat."

With that, Master Von Hollow dove in, and the wall of trees

swallowed him up completely. Trying not to think of what a terrible turn his visit had taken, and whether he might still find a way to use the word "assistant" at least once more, Oliver brought his hand up to the place where Master Von Hollow disappeared and pushed against it. The wall of trees pushed *back*. But finally, with an uneasy rustle and a groan, it relented, and Oliver tumbled through headfirst.

"Ouch!" he cried, landing with a heavy thud. He blinked his eyes. It was much darker than he anticipated. It wasn't just a wall of trees that lined Master Von Hollow's mansion; it was more like a thick overhead tunnel of trees. Oliver felt suddenly very alone.

"Master Von Hollow?" Oliver called out. He crept carefully through the dense foliage and kept his gaze fixed on the ground in avoidance of sinkholes. Sinkholes were always a risk in the Swinging Swamp, but you could typically count on someone being near enough to help pull you out if need be. Oliver had the sense that if he tumbled into a sinkhole on Master Von Hollow's property, that might be the end of him.

Seeing a looming figure a few feet ahead, Oliver breathed a small sigh of relief. "Master Von Hollow?" he called out. He picked up his pace, but when he came upon the man, a feeling of dread washed over him.

It was *not* Master Von Hollow. It wasn't even a magician at all, at least not anymore.

Oliver reached his shaking fingers out toward the stone statue but stopped short. This was what happened if you tried to use another magician's hat.

Oliver had been warned about such a fate, and if ever there was a place to stumble across a petrified magician, it was at Master Von Hollow's home. In light of Master Von Hollow's skill and position, it was rumored that his hat had been the object of attempted robbery on at least six different occasions.

Oliver shivered. Six lives . . . gone. As far as he knew, there was no remedy for petrification.

Oliver tried not to look at the expression on the stone magician's face, but he couldn't help it. It was so full of sadness and regret. It made Oliver feel empty inside. And scared. Surely the magician had known the consequences of using another magician's hat. How could he have done it anyways? Was it really so easy to be blinded? To become so focused on pursuing one thing that everything else could be lost in return? The hair on the back of Oliver's neck prickled with unease. That wasn't what *he* was doing, was it? He wanted a hat, certainly, but only so that he could fit in, so that he could belong, so that he could have a home. But was there a cost he hadn't considered?

"Do you like my sculpture, boy?" Master Von Hollow whispered, creeping up behind Oliver. "I have more like it, if you're interested in taking a peek. Some of the poor saps even have real hats on their heads. I keep a collection of dead magicians' hats just for fun, and wouldn't you know, you can't even harness the magic in those hats without turning into stone! Of course . . ."

He paused and slipped his hat off his head. He held it out toward Oliver, eyes gleaming. "You're always welcome to try my hat on for size, hmm?"

"No, thank you," Oliver said, taking a step—all right, more like a leap—backward. "With all due respect, sir, I-I'm sure my hat is already on its way."

Master Von Hollow shrugged. He placed his hat back on his head and continued walking along. Oliver hurried after him. "According to Razzle, your case is practically hopeless, but suit yourself. Now, are you ready to hear the details of your assignment?"

Oliver nodded bleakly at the same time that a horse let out a shrill whinny. He readied himself for—wait, a *horse* let out a shrill whinny?

In case I have not made it clear by now, the Swinging Swamp is a haven for slinking, slithering things; for foul, smelly things; for things with razor-sharp teeth and venomous stingers; for the cast-out, shoved-aside, perhaps-we-can-forget-them things. Horses, as I am sure you are well aware, do not fit onto this list. Horses, in Oliver's experience, or at least based on everything he'd ever overheard, which was actually quite a lot because when no one wants to talk to you, you do plenty of listening, had never once been spotted in the Swinging Swamp.

Without thinking, Oliver ran curiously toward the sound. He made a sharp right and nearly somersaulted down a steep slope. Master Von Hollow bellowed at him to "STOP!" but it was too late. Oliver had already seen it. There, situated at the foot of the hill and enclosed by a crude-looking fence, was an entire herd of horses. At least Oliver thought they were horses. They didn't much look like the strong, majestic creatures he'd seen in storybooks, but they did have four hooves, manes, tails (however patchy), and long, mud-splattered snouts they were using to graze among the swamp moss. That moss, however, must not have been very nourishing considering Oliver could count every single bone in the horses' bodies. He shivered. Maybe there was a good reason horses didn't typically make their home in the Swinging Swamp.

Still, Oliver didn't want to be insulting.

"They certainly are something," he finally said.

Master Von Hollow snorted. "If by 'something' you mean 'pitiful,' then yes, they certainly are."

"Oh," Oliver said, frowning. "I assumed the horses belonged to you. This . . . is still your land, isn't it?"

"Of course it's my land! I'm the richest magician in the Swinging Swamp! And these creatures do belong to me, but that doesn't mean I *like* them. Indeed, there are lots of reasons for keeping things, boy, the very least of those being affection."

Remembering how big and bold Master Von Hollow's show-cases tended to be, Oliver wondered if he planned to somehow incorporate the horses as part of the show. Even in this woeful state, a horse was still a horse—certainly far more impressive than something like a rabbit. Of course, there was no way

Master Von Hollow could make a whole horse disappear; there was no way one would fit inside his hat. But he had to be planning something, and Oliver almost grinned, thinking that out of all the times to be chosen as Master Von Hollow's assistant, this might be the most exciting of all.

"I, um, am very experienced with horses," Oliver piped up. "W-would you like to see?"

Considering Oliver didn't have one bit of experience with horses, he really hoped Master Von Hollow would *not* want to see, but he figured he had to at least make the offer.

"I'm much more interested in how much experience you have in minding your own business, and if you are always this impossibly nosy!" Master Von Hollow hissed, and perhaps to be sure Oliver didn't go running off again, he grabbed hold of Oliver's wrist. He yanked Oliver back up the hill. As they climbed, Oliver felt a sudden and startling wave of heat wash over him. He dabbed at the beads of perspiration on his forehead and looked over his shoulder in the direction of the horses. But they weren't paying him any attention. They still had their noses to the ground, futilely shuffling through layer after layer of mud.

When they reached the top of the hill, Master Von Hollow pointed in the direction of a lone rowboat swaying gently in the mud stream. He dipped his hand into his pocket and pulled out a piece of paper, which he thrust beneath Oliver's nose.

"This is the person you will be meeting with. You will be picking something up on my behalf. Something *important*."

Oliver blinked at the name written on the paper. He slowly shook his head. "I-I've never ventured out of the Swinging Swamp before. I don't know if Headmaster Razzle would allow it."

"Well, don't get cold feet now, boy. Headmaster Razzle does what I tell him to, and who said anything about going outside the Swinging Swamp?"

Oliver gestured at the paper. "This is a girl's name. There aren't any girls that live in the Swinging Swamp."

"Yes, I know. But Helga Hookeye is a witch," Master Von Hollow said.

That didn't make Oliver feel better at all, especially considering Master Von Hollow's earlier comment about Oliver not being missed if something terrible happened to him. Countless terrible things could happen anytime a witch was involved. Though the witches crept in and out of the Swinging Swamp on a fairly regular basis, they almost never dropped by Razzle's School for Meddlesome Boys, and Oliver was happy to stay away from them. Still, if he managed to complete such a horrific task, Master Von Hollow would *have* to consider him for the role of his assistant, wouldn't he?

"Um, what am I picking up exactly, sir?" Oliver asked.

"Helga knows what to give you."

"Yes, but she's a witch, sir. What if she tries to give me the wrong thing?"

Master Von Hollow frowned. He pursed his lips. "That is not

a completely irrelevant point. All right, fine. You'll be picking up a VIP."

"I—I . . ." Oliver took a deep breath. "Is it safe for me to handle a Very Important Potion?" Oliver had heard of VIPs before, but they weren't the sort of thing one typically encountered in the Swinging Swamp. Magicians didn't often attempt to dabble beyond their hat magic, and when a witchy enchantment was necessary, the witches typically came and performed the spell themselves.

"I don't know, is it?" Master Von Hollow snapped, clearly annoyed. "You will tell her that Master *Whom* sent you—do NOT use my real name—and you will give her this in return." Master Von Hollow stuffed three bundles of magician's thread into Oliver's arms.

Oliver's jaw gaped. Magician's thread was in high demand in Wanderly. Other than dabbling in bribery, it was the primary means by which Master Von Hollow had made his fortune and was perhaps the one and only valuable thing even the Chancellor agreed the magicians had to offer. Magician's thread was light, thin, translucent, unbreakable (except by the person who put it in place), and an excellent, if somewhat fickle, conductor of magic. The thread was taken directly from a magician's hat, which shed only small bits at a time; this made the harvesting process frustratingly slow and tedious. Oliver couldn't possibly imagine how badly Master Von Hollow wanted that VIP to be willing to part with such a quantity.

Master Von Hollow hiked up his elegant-looking trousers and sloshed toward the rowboat. "I really do hate this miserable swamp," he muttered before swinging his leg back and delivering a hefty kick to the rowboat. Oliver winced at the sound of the loud *crack* as the rowboat snapped to attention. Unlike the rowboats at Razzle's, this one had no name painted brightly on the side.

"There now, this rowboat will get you safely to the Creeping Corridor—"

"The Creeping Corridor?" Oliver interrupted.

Master Von Hollow shut his eyes. "*Don't* tell me that you don't know if you're allowed to go to the Creeping Corridor."

That was easy enough for Oliver. The Creeping Corridor was the Swinging Swamp's shadowy version of an outdoor mall. It drew sinister types from all over who were looking to deal in dark wares or hard-to-find ingredients or merely to meet up for a bit of foul company over a popping cauldron. No, Oliver didn't wonder if he was allowed to go to such a place; he already knew he wasn't allowed to go to such a place.

Master Von Hollow cracked one eye open. "As I was saying, after you arrive at the Creeping Corridor . . . well, Helga is Helga. No one can possibly predict how she will react to you so I can't guarantee how or if you will make it back. Just remember, I didn't go looking for you, you came and knocked on my door. Now you have no choice but to do what I tell you."

And with a dramatic spin that swirled the edges of his long

cape, Master Von Hollow vanished into the trees. Oliver climbed into the rowboat in pursuit of a—*gulp*—witch. Surely nothing could go wrong. Surely nothing at—

Oh, I can't even stand to utter such nonsense. Certainly by now you know how legitimately awful the witches in Wanderly are, but Helga Hookeye was in an extra-special class. She ranked among the top five worst witches in the entire kingdom alongside the likes of Council member Rudey Longtooth, broomstick-racing champion Irma Scram, and number one curmudgeon Agnes Prunella Crunch.[18]

And so, as we leave Oliver behind, perhaps the best thing to be hoped for is that whatever happened to go wrong, it wouldn't be completely and utterly disastrous.

---

18. Disclaimer: witches are highly unstable, and this list can fluctuate wildly. For example, I vaguely recall hearing a rumor about that last witch—Agnes Prunella Crunch—being suspected of an act of *friendship*. Although, come to think of it, maybe it was that other witch Maggie Pruneface Bunch? Anyhow, the only thing that really matters is that it's always wise to double-check your sources even when dealing with a diligent book.

# SEVEN

# A Sizzling Companion

In the wee hours of the morning before the rising sun began to paint the sky a perfectly rosy shade of pink, Pippa North tiptoed through the dark hallways of Castle Cressida. Despite the fact that a wicked witch had nearly taken the entire castle hostage the day before, and there was merely the flicker of a few candlelit wall sconces to light her way, Pippa wasn't afraid; she was motivated.

This motivation was only fueled by Mistress Peabody's astonishing announcement at last night's dinner table that Peabody's two newest students, Bernard and Pippa, would be receiving their loyal companion assignments on the very next day. Though all the students had cheered—and Bernard had bragged that he'd probably get matched with a lion because lions were the king of all—Pippa thought she was going to be sick in her silk napkin.

The pairing of a loyal companion and a Triumphant was a *huge* deal. Indeed, what was Ms. Bravo without her turquoise macaw, Dynamite? And when a match was made, it was supposed to be for life. Pippa, on the other hand, was doing everything she could to find a way out of Peabody's Academy and back home with the hope of never having to return again. She could only imagine the sort of complications that could arise if she got stuck with a loyal companion. Or if a loyal companion got stuck with her.

First, there was the logistical issue of space. If she brought a loyal companion back home with her to Ink Hollow, could her family really fit one more living creature inside their teensy two-bedroom cottage? Not to mention her mother's long-standing, adamant rule about no pets.[19] And beyond that, would a loyal companion really be satisfied if its most thrilling challenge was picking food out of the triplets' hair after an epic food fight or haggling over spinach prices at the grocer's cart? There was, of course, much more to life as a commoner, especially in the North family, but would a *Triumphant* loyal companion ever see it that way?

Pippa didn't think so, and so she was on her way to the Triumphants' classroom to visit the Chest of Unnecessaries and

---

19. This rule had much more to do with the triplets than Mrs. North. The triplets' pockets were surprisingly deep, and if she had said yes to every toad, lizard, slug, and snail that accompanied them home, the North family's cottage would have been overrun long ago.

secure those one hundred grubins for her fairy godmother, Olivanderella Dash.

"Pippa?" a voice whispered from behind her.

Pippa skidded to a halt. She whirled around and found herself eye to eye with a pair of round spectacles. "Ernest!" she exclaimed. "I'm so glad it's you."

Ernest's eyes lit up. "Really? Not many people say that around here. But what are you doing up so early?"

Pippa hesitated. "I, um, well . . . what are *you* doing up so early?" she finished weakly.

Ernest looked up and down the hallway. Then he leaned closer and whispered, "*Lemon bars*. I can't resist them! They were on the dessert menu last night, and I was hoping one or two might be left over on last night's platter. You know, just for a little snack."

Before Pippa could answer, a door cracked open a few feet away and a girl poked her head out. Even in the dim lighting, Pippa recognized Maisy. "I didn't know that was you, Pippa!" Maisy said. "I was just on my way to the dining hall to check on the breakfast croissants when I heard the word 'snack,' clear as day. It's sort of a code word among bakers. Are you hungry?"

Ernest's eyes grew wide. He turned to Pippa. "You know the baker?" he said. "The one who makes the lemon bars?"

"Yes," Pippa said with a smile. "And no matter what Mistress Peabody says, after years of living under the same roof, it's about time you got to know her too. Ernest, this is Maisy; Maisy, this is Ernest."

Maisy executed a little curtsy. Ernest's cheeks flushed a deep shade of pink. "Your lemon bars are the best things I've ever tasted," he gushed.

"I—oh—wow, really?" Maisy said, a grin lighting up her face. When Ernest nodded, she continued, "Then I'll definitely try to get those on the menu more often."

"How about tonight?" Ernest said. "After all, we should do something to celebrate Pippa's big day."

Maisy's eyes lit up. "Pippa's big day?" she echoed. "Oh, Pippa, does that mean you found a way to get the grubins after all? Is your fairy godmother coming here today, to grant your wish?"

Behind Ernest, Pippa was frantically shaking her head and trying to get Maisy to stop, but it was too late. "Fairy who-mother? Grubins?" Ernest cried, whirling around to face her. "Pippa, what is Maisy talking about?"

Maisy's shoulders slumped. "Oh no," she said quietly. "Ernest didn't know about any of that, did he? Oh, Pippa, I'm so sorry, I just . . ."

"It's all right. I was just about to tell Ernest," Pippa said. But she felt a twinge of guilt. She didn't actually know if she *was* going to tell Ernest, but seeing the disappointment in his eyes, remembering that he was the one who gave her the idea to write to a fairy godmother in the first place, it was what she wanted to be true.

Ernest slowly shook his head. "I know your first day here was rough, but I thought things were starting to get better. I thought Peabody's was starting to . . . grow on you. I didn't know you were working with a fairy godmother all this time."

"'Working' is sort of a strong word," Pippa said, thinking back on the one letter she'd received. "And until I come up with one hundred grubins, it doesn't sound like there's much she can do."

Ernest's jaw dropped. "One hundred grubins! But, Pippa, that's—"

"A ton? I know. But, Ernest, I don't belong here. I miss my family. I miss them so much sometimes it's hard to breathe. Castle Cressida isn't anything like what the Chancellor's made it out to be, and yesterday a witch came to visit who I am pretty sure no one had an ounce of control over—including Mistress Peabody. Today I'm supposed to be paired with my loyal companion for life who's going to assist me on quests that I never wanted to go on in the first place. I'm not cut out to be a hero, and I was already happy with my ending!" Pippa swiped at the tears that she hadn't realized were falling. Maisy took a small step in her direction and rested a comforting hand on Pippa's shoulder.

Ernest stared down at his royal blue slipper socks. "Just because you belong with your family doesn't mean you can't belong here too." But when Pippa didn't say anything, Ernest asked, "Do you really think you'll be able to come up with one hundred grubins?"

"I do," Pippa said firmly. "And that's the real reason why I'm up so early. I'm on my way to the classroom, and I'm going to see if the Chest of Unnecessaries will give me the grubins."

Ernest's jaw gaped. "Mistress Peabody's prize box?" he said. "Pippa, there are some things you've got to know about that box—"

"I know Prudence Bumble bragged about asking it for a ball gown," Pippa said, "and it gave her the most beautiful—"

"Yes," Ernest countered, "but only because she didn't have any place to wear it to—"

"And I know Viola asked it for a train set, and it gave her three of them—"

"Yes," Ernest agreed, "but only because she already had four—"

"And Anastasia told me that Mistress Peabody sometimes asks it for her fancy outfits—"

"Yes, but only because nobody needs that many ruffles," Ernest said. Pippa opened her mouth to offer yet another example, but Ernest cried out, "Pippa, please! You've got to listen. The Chest of Unnecessaries is just like it sounds. It's only useful for things that you *don't* need. In fact, if you ask it for something you do need, bad things happen."

So that was why Ernest got his *sixth* baseball bat. The Chest of Unnecessaries didn't give extravagant gifts; it gave useless ones. But maybe it didn't have to work that way; maybe trying was worth the risk, especially because Pippa couldn't think of a single other option.

"When you say 'bad things happen,'" Pippa began slowly, "how bad do you mean, exactly?"

Maisy's hand flew to her mouth. "Wait! Is that why Mistress Peabody's hair turned green last winter? Because of a tangle with the Chest of Unnecessaries?" Ernest nodded, and Maisy explained to Pippa, "She wore a wig for months, but it wasn't a very good one. The staff placed bets on whether it was an unlucky visit to the hair salon or a mild curse. I never imagined it was the result of that wooden box."

Pippa combed her fingers through the ends of her ponytail with a thoughtful expression on her face. "You know, I've never really been that particular about my hair, and there are certainly worse things than green." She nodded her head determinedly. "All right, then."

"All right, then?" Ernest exclaimed. "Pippa, there's no guarantee you'll get green hair. You'll probably get something different. You might get something worse. Maybe even Tragic End worse."

"I—really?" Pippa said. She wasn't in need of the Chancellor's version of a happy ending, but that didn't mean she wanted a tragical ending, either. Of all the roles in Wanderly, the Tragicals had the very worst of it. Though it was true that in a storybook kingdom not everyone could get a happy ending, the Chancellor sought to optimize this process by assigning bad endings to those who—according to him—were already marked for doom, i.e., the kingdom's orphans. And so the Tragicals were shuttled off to the easternmost peninsula of Wanderly, atop the crooked and crumbling peak of Tragic Mountain, where, at Foulweather's Home for the Tragical, they spent their days learning about all the horrible ways in which they were likely to die and how to cheerfully accept such a fate.[20]

Pippa's chest was tight. She was having difficulty breathing. Finally, she said, "So, you're saying that asking the Chest of Unnecessaries for one hundred grubins is . . . hopeless?"

"No," Ernest said, swallowing hard. He took a deep breath and squared his shoulders. "I'm saying that I think I should be the one to do it, because I'm not the one who needs it. And I think we should probably do it fast before I lose my nerve."

Without waiting for a response, Ernest walked determinedly past Pippa and Maisy and through the door of the Triumphants' classroom. By the time Pippa and Maisy caught up with him, he was already kneeling in front of the Chest of Unnecessaries.

"Ernest, you really don't have to do this," Pippa said.

Ernest lifted his head. He paused for a moment. "I know I don't have to do this," he said. "But I think maybe that's the very reason why I want to, if that makes any sense?"

Pippa smiled. "I think it makes perfect sense for a hero."

---

20. If you find this infuriating and it makes you want to throw tomatoes at the Chancellor, then I knew there was a reason I liked you! You are also, unfortunately, miles ahead of the majority of Wanderly's Triumphants (a numbing fact of which I am not at all proud), who tended to go along with the idea that such a barbaric practice was "sad but necessary." Bah!

At the word "hero," Ernest's eyes lit up. He took a deep breath, he cleared his throat, and he called out in a loud, clear voice, "Give me one hundred grubins!"

Beside Pippa, Maisy whispered, "Do you think it would have been better to say 'please'?"

"I don't think so," Pippa whispered back. "I've been learning that Triumphants don't have nice manners. They don't even raise their hands in class."

Manners aside, the Chest of Unnecessaries didn't react one bit to Ernest's request. It just sat there, doing absolutely nothing.

"Is it . . . broken?" Maisy asked.

Ernest frowned. "It can't be. It gave me my sixth baseball bat yesterday. Maybe I'm doing something wrong."

"Try again, but a little louder," Pippa said.

Ernest rolled up his sleeves. "Give me one hundred grubins!" he nearly shouted.

The Chest of Unnecessaries began to glow. It began to glow a bright and ominous shade of *green*.

It rattled and banged and clanged against the floor.

It shimmied and twisted and even growled a bit.

Finally, in a puff of green smoke, the lid burst wide open.

"Is my hair green?" Ernest blurted out. "Did it turn my hair green?"

Maisy and Pippa vigorously shook their heads, and Ernest blew out a little sigh of relief. "Maybe it actually worked, then," he said, taking a step closer to the Chest of Unnecessaries. "Maybe the grubins are inside the chest!"

*Hissssss*. A merry sound rang out.

Ernest froze. "Was that one of you?" he asked, looking from Maisy to Pippa and back again. "Please tell me that was one of you."

But the sound was unmistakably coming from within the Chest of Unnecessaries. Ernest, Maisy, and Pippa inched closer to it, and something black and shiny with incredibly long antennae inched its way out to greet them.

"Oh!" Maisy exclaimed, clasping her hands against her chest, "it's just a cockroach! Poor little bug must have accidentally fallen inside. And here I was worried we might have a snake problem on our hands!"

But then *another* pair of antennae popped out. And another, and soon dozens of cockroaches—hissing cockroaches, no less—were sliding down the edge of the Chest of Unnecessaries and sashaying into every nook and cranny of the classroom.

Ernest's eyes bulged. He hopped from one foot to the next as three cockroaches scurried toward him. "Um, does anyone have any ideas about what we should do? Because I'm pretty sure even Mistress Peabody's not going to be able to ignore these guys."

Pippa gawked at the ever-growing parade of cockroaches. She hung her head. "It must have given us one hundred hissing cockroaches instead of one hundred grubins. Oh, what a terrible mess!"

Pippa slipped off her royal blue cape and began using it to gently herd the cockroaches back toward the Chest of Unnecessaries.

Maisy leaped up. "Great idea, Pippa!" she said. She reached into her apron pocket and whipped out her wooden cooking spoon. She whirled it through the air and prepared to sweep it across the floor. "Come on, Ernest! If we work together, maybe we can corral them all." And though Ernest was looking a bit glum (and slightly squeamish), he perked up considerably at the irresistible scent of lemon bars wafting off Maisy's cooking spoon.

"Oh!" he said, taking a deep sniff. "It smells just like those lemon bars! I can almost taste them! It almost makes me feel like everything's going to be . . . okay."

Apparently, the hissing cockroaches couldn't have agreed more. They all turned on a dime. They scurried in Maisy's direction as fast as their six legs could carry them. They hissed a perfectly synchronized and merry tune as they followed the scent of Maisy's lemon bars and marched back toward the Chest of Unnecessaries. Every last one of them hopped gleefully inside and Maisy closed the lid finally shut.

She brushed her hands off with a satisfied grin on her face and plunked her spoon back in her apron pocket.

Pippa shook her head in awe. "Maisy, you did it! Don't let me forget to get that recipe from you before I go home." A shadow crossed over Pippa's face. "I mean, if I go home. Or when I go home, or—"

"You *will* find a way home, Pippa," Maisy said softly. "The Chest of Unnecessaries didn't work, but something will. I know it."

"And in the meantime, I think we ought to get you ready to meet your loyal companion," Ernest said. "Who knows, if yours is anything like my goat, Leonardo, maybe it'll make you feel differently about being a Triumphant. Maybe it will even make you want to stay. I couldn't imagine a day away from Leonardo."

Pippa, however, thought the odds of that happening were one in one million.

Later that morning, Pippa stood on the famed glittering gold steps of Castle Cressida. Though she could have been wrong, the steps looked slightly less peely and perhaps a hint more sparkly than the day she first arrived. Pippa, unfortunately, was dressed from head to toe in a suit of armor. It was maybe the only thing she'd ever worn that was even more uncomfortable than the stiff, royal blue Triumphant uniforms, and getting into it had caused her to be ten minutes late. When Mistress Peabody caught sight of Pippa, she executed a little two-step and rushed closer.

"You look fabulous!" Mistress Peabody exclaimed. "It really is all about looking the part, isn't it? Come along," she said, gesturing at the festive red and white tent that had been set up on Castle Cressida's front lawn. "Bernard is already seated at the inquisition table, and the other students can barely stand the suspense! We even have a few Council members present!"

Pippa clunked after Mistress Peabody as quickly as her chain-mail suit would allow. When Mistress Peabody pulled back the curtain, the entire crowd burst into enthusiastic applause. Pippa felt her cheeks grow warm. She felt her insides grow warm too. She'd never had anyone greet her in such a way. It became suddenly easy to see how this was the sort of thing Triumphants not only got used to but craved. And maybe even at the expense of other more important things.

"Pippa, please take your seat," Mistress Peabody said, directing her attention to the front of the room, where two thrones sat before a long wooden table. Bernard, also clad in a chain-mail suit of armor, was already seated at one of the thrones. He didn't bother to turn his head even the slightest bit in Pippa's direction.

As Pippa clanked noisily along, she spotted Ms. Bravo seated in the front row with Dynamite perched on her shoulder. Ms. Bravo gave her one of those dazzling "front page of the *Wanderly Whistle*" smiles, but unlike Mistress Peabody's, hers actually seemed genuine. Way in the back, Pippa thought she saw the tall magician's hat that belonged to Council member Slickabee, but it was hard to tell because he kept ducking and bobbing and weaving and was furiously scribbling onto a notepad. He also looked quite a bit different when he wasn't completely soaked with rainwater.

By far the best thing, however, was that the rest of the Triumphants were accompanied by their own loyal companions. Pippa had heard so much about the loyal companions—well, at least a lot about Ernest's—but she hadn't yet gotten a tour of the Loyal Companions' Barn, where they were all kept (except for Mistress Peabody's goldfish, which she kept in a fishbowl in her bedchambers but sometimes toted around the castle).

Ernest waved his hands in the air at Pippa and pointed proudly down at the goat beside him. "Leonardo!" he mouthed. "This is Leonardo!" Leonardo had uneven horns, a black ring of fur around each eye as if he were wearing spectacles of his own, a few long, wispy hairs beneath his chin, and blocky teeth that stuck out so far, he looked to be constantly grinning. Pippa couldn't help grinning back because Ernest was right, Leonardo was pretty perfect.

Beside Ernest, Prudence Bumble kept huffing and wriggling her fingers in front of her nose as if either Leonardo or Ernest or probably both were emitting a gag-inducing smell. Perched on her shoulders was a raccoon that kept shifting its gaze around the room and finding new people to hiss and snarl at.

Pippa finally slid into her seat at the front of the tent and gulped when she saw the two large cages looming in front of her and Bernard. Each one was draped in a large swath of red velvet fabric. Mistress Peabody lifted her fully ruffled arms in the air until the room began to quiet down.

"Thank you for coming today, ladies and gentlemen. We are gathered here to celebrate one of the longest standing traditions for the kingdom's Triumphants, the bestowing of a loyal companion! Today I will be asking our newest students Bernard and . . . and . . . and *Pippa* a series of questions. Based on their answers to these questions, Bernard's and Pippa's loyal companions will appear inside these two enchanted cages. Is everyone ready to begin?"

Pippa heaved a sigh of relief. She was still terrified about what having a loyal companion would mean for her plans, but when Mistress Peabody had ordered that she and Bernard dress in chain-mail suits, she'd worried they were about to be sent off on their first quest and that she'd have to wrangle a loyal companion with her bare hands! A series of questions—the equivalent of a test, really—was certainly something Pippa could handle. Maybe she'd even end up with a loyal companion she would actually be compatible with.

Mistress Peabody reached for a sealed envelope on top of the table. She opened it up, selected the top two sheets of paper, and held them high for all to see. On one paper was written the word "big" and on the other paper was written the word "small."

"Please state your preference," Mistress Peabody said solemnly.

"Big," Bernard said with a smug smile. He was probably imagining looking down on everyone from the back of an elephant or some other enormous creature.

"Small," Pippa said with equal certainty. If she was going to be stuck hauling her loyal companion home, it really would help if it were chipmunk-size.

As soon as the word came out of Pippa's mouth, the curtain covering the large cage in front of her wriggled.

Pippa jumped and Bernard snickered.

Mistress Peabody quickly explained, "It's only the cages, dear. They are listening. That is how they come up with your perfect match."

"Unless you don't have a match because you're an impostu—" Bernard hissed under his breath.

Certain that her posture was just fine, thank you very much, Pippa quietly corrected him. "I believe the word you are looking for is 'imposter.'"

Mistress Peabody held up two new sheets of paper. On one was the word "low" and on the other, the word "high."

"High," Bernard said with a sniff, as if he found the choice insulting.

"Low," Pippa said, because she already didn't fit in at Peabody's Academy for the Triumphant, and the last thing she needed was a loyal companion with an attitude problem.

The curtains covering the cages wriggled a second time, a bit more vigorously.

As Pippa waited for the next round of questions, she was surprised to find that it was almost maybe a little bit fun. This time the two sheets Mistress Peabody lifted in the air read "captivating" or "camouflaged." Though Pippa couldn't deny the appeal of a loyal companion as beautiful as Ms. Bravo's turquoise macaw, Dynamite, she also couldn't forget that she might be requiring her loyal companion to move back to a town where the most unusual pet was a rooster. For the sake of her future loyal companion, Pippa dutifully said, "Camouflaged," while Bernard, who probably wasn't convinced the Triumphant uniforms were glitzy enough, answered predictably, "Captivating."

Mistress Peabody waited for the red velvet to wriggle, and then she dipped her hand into the envelope one last time. "This is it," she said with a slight tremble to her voice. "This is the final question that will determine who your loyal companion will be. Choose wisely, Triumphants!"

Pippa snuck one last glance at the audience behind her. Ernest and his goat, Leonardo, were both anxiously chewing on a strand of grass. Viola and her beaver, Choo-Choo, were bouncing up and down; Anastasia and her marmoset, Whisper, were holding tightly to one another; and Ms. Bravo's turquoise macaw, Dynamite, soared around the room squawking, "BIG NEWS! GET READY! BIG NEWS!"

Mistress Peabody thrust the final papers high in the air, and Pippa sucked in a deep breath.

All the other comparisons had been so easy; Pippa hadn't even needed to think about them really, but this one was different. Pippa looked from the paper that read "Peas" to the one that read "Carrots." It wasn't that it was a difficult question; it was just that Pippa liked them both. And she also didn't see how preferring one vegetable over the other had anything at all to do with a loyal companion. Still, she had seen enough peculiar things at Peabody's Academy for the Triumphant that questioning it seemed like more trouble than it was worth.

"Carrots," Pippa finally decided.

"Peas," Bernard said. He shot a knowing look in Pippa's direction and leaned over to whisper, "My father made me study every loyal companion pairing from the past decade. And the last time someone chose carrots, they got *that*." Bernard glanced distastefully in Leonardo's direction, where Ernest was giving Pippa a cheery thumbs-up sign.

Pippa didn't bother answering. Her eyes were fixed on the red velvet fabric hanging over the cages, which was now not only rippling but billowing wildly. A hush fell over the entire room and—with a loud *BANG*—Pippa knew in an instant that the cages were no longer empty. Their loyal companions had arrived. Without missing a beat, Mistress Peabody reached up and swept the velvet curtain away from the cage containing Bernard's loyal companion.

Someone gasped. At least a few people giggled. And Bernard's face turned a bright shade of red. Prancing around in the cage was the largest peacock Pippa had ever seen. It opened its mouth and let loose a deafening scream. Everyone in the crowd groaned, some placing their hands over their ears. Bernard's loyal companion was beautiful, sure, but Pippa guessed it wasn't exactly receiving the reception he had in mind. Bernard crossed his arms against his chest and stubbornly tilted his chin away from his loyal companion. He fixed his eyes on the cage in front of Pippa as if the only thing that might make him feel better was Pippa being assigned a termite.

"Congratulations, Bernard," Mistress Peabody said, a bit uneasily. "Your loyal companion is large among its kind, flies high, is captivating in color, and is a PEAcock. Let's all give Bernard and his new loyal companion a round of applause." The crowd complied, but then everyone hurriedly turned their gazes in Pippa's direction. Mistress Peabody, obviously delighting in the crowd's interest, struck a dramatic pose before sweeping the red velvet curtain away and revealing a—

"Donkey! Ha! Pippa got a *donkey*! That's not even a proper horse. Talk about embarrassing. And it's ugly too!" Bernard shouted with a smug look on his face.

Pippa's chest tightened. The creature in the cage looked terrified. Its head hung low, and its large, pointed ears swiveled back and forth as if trying to make sense of where it was and what had just happened. Bernard was right that it was a bit small for a horse, but Pippa was certain it wasn't a donkey.

Bernard continued to blab on, "How is that donkey going to help anyone? It doesn't even look like it can walk without tipping over!" As if in agreement, Bernard's peacock let out another ear-piercing scream.

Pippa rose from her throne and walked closer to the horse. She wrapped her hands gently around the golden bars of the cage. "Don't be afraid," she whispered. "Everything will be all right. You can't possibly be as lost as I am, can you?"

As if it understood her words, the horse managed to lift its head. It looked right into Pippa's eyes, and then, miraculously, a single spark ignited on its mane.

Pippa felt an immediate rush of panic. She didn't think ordinary horses were supposed to light up like candles, but from the front row of the audience, Ms. Bravo gasped out loud. She jumped on top of her seat in a wholly undignified but wholly ecstatic manner. She pumped her hand wildly in the air. "That's not a donkey, that's a fire horse!" she exclaimed.

Pippa shook her head in disbelief. "A f-f-fire horse? But it's so small. And dirty. It looks so hungry. And isn't the *whole* mane and tail supposed to catch fire, not just one strand?"

Ms. Bravo shot a glance in Mistress Peabody's direction.

"Yes, well, like many things on Triumph Mountain, this fire horse is hardly in its best shape. But"—Ms. Bravo's expression softened—"that doesn't mean it can't be restored."

Dynamite squawked jubilantly, "BIG NEWS! FIRE HORSE! BIG NEWS!"

"Don't forget about the peacock!" Bernard shouted. "The peacock is really, really . . ." He paused as if trying to find something good to say. He must have got tired of thinking, however, because all he came up with was *"Blue!"* And then he shot the peacock a look of disgust, as if it were the peacock's fault that it wasn't a fire horse.

But nobody was listening to Bernard. Mistress Peabody—probably dreaming of all the delicious publicity the fire horse would garner—flapped her ruffled arms in a tizzy of delight. The other students followed Ms. Bravo's lead, the shorter ones jumping on top of their chairs in order to get a better glimpse of the beloved creature they'd only read about in storybooks. And at the center of it all stood Pippa and her fire horse, blinking dubiously and looking as if they'd prefer to be anywhere else in all of Wanderly.

At least they had something in common.

EIGHT

# PIGNAPPED!

Oliver Dash pulled off the main channel of the Swinging
Swamp's swirling green river and drew Master Von Hollow's
reticent rowboat onto a sandy bank. He carefully tucked the
three bundles of magician's thread beneath his cape and slipped
onto the Creeping Corridor's wooden deck. The deck ran along
the side of the river and was filled with two tiers of shops and a
haphazard sprinkling of cart vendors.

Oliver could hardly believe he was there to see a witch. A
witch named Helga Hookeye, no less. Oliver had been to the
Creeping Corridor only once before, on an ill-fated school field
trip that resulted in (1) a few of the boys getting lost (as in, they
didn't resurface for two whole days), (2) several of them turning
into buzzing mosquitoes after sampling a potion at the Hole in

the Wall,[21] and (3) the rest getting terribly sick to their stomachs from a jumbo pack of fried frog legs. Accordingly, Headmaster Razzle vowed never to repeat the trip, and he had, so far, been true to his word.

Oliver took a deep breath and merged into the moderate-size crowd. Though he wasn't nearly as conspicuous as when he'd been one of a gaggle of clamoring boys following behind Headmaster Razzle's extraordinarily tall hat, he hardly felt safe. He kept his eyes low and his hair mussed. A few feet ahead, Oliver spied a sign that read, "Twisted Goblet 'Atta Way," and a shiver rippled down his spine. The Twisted Goblet was a notoriously witchy hangout—the sort of place most people tried to block out of their minds—but potentially the best chance Oliver had for finding Helga. Even though the sign pointed down a dark and narrow alley, Oliver was relieved to get off the main walkway before anyone happened to notice that he was rather old not to be in possession of a hat or that his cape was three sizes too small.

Oliver squeezed down the alley, trying very hard not to think about what might be slithering alongside him. Finally, the alley opened onto a log cabin illuminated by candlelight, flickering

---

21. At the Creeping Corridor there was an actual hole in the wall where the witches placed their latest potions for sale. If you think it strange that a witch should rely on an honor-system policy for payment, bravo! The *real* purpose of the Hole in the Wall was to test out their new potions for free. Sometimes the potions worked . . . sometimes they didn't.

from within and shining through the cracks. A low din of raspy voices and the occasional cackle pealed out. Lined up noncha-lantly beside the door, and as if they weren't one of Wanderly's most magical (and shiver-inducing) objects, were a dozen and a half broomsticks. Oliver hurried by them as quickly as he could and pushed through the door of the Twisted Goblet.

Oliver didn't have to worry about being noticed. The cabin was so full of witches, and twice as many flitting shadows, that it was easy enough to slink toward the counter, where a weary magician wearing a clown suit and a big red nose was refilling a bowl of peanuts. The witches, of course, weren't eating the pea-nuts, but launching them at one another from across the room and aiming, especially, for the eyes. Oliver didn't even bother to ask the magician about the clown suit. Trying to make a living while being surrounded by witches couldn't be easy, and he'd probably had far worse hexes placed on him than that.

"Excuse me, sir," Oliver said. "Can you please tell me where I can find Helga Hookeye?"

The magician's eyes bulged. His hand jerked and peanuts went rolling along the countertop. Oliver couldn't imagine this was a good sign. "You sure?" the magician finally choked out.

Oliver's hand went straight to his head. The way it often did without him meaning for it to. As if maybe, one time, a hat would just happen to be there. As if the moment he'd been waiting for, hoping for, yearning for, would have come and gone without him even noticing. He was, of course, still utterly hatless. Soon, he would be homeless too.

"I'm sure, sir," Oliver said, trying to make his voice steady.

The magician lifted his hand and gestured toward a table in the far corner of the cabin. A witch with fiery red hair was sitting there all by herself. Her boots, propped up on the table, were dripping with swamp goo. She was licking something off the tips of her fingers. Oddly enough, despite how crowded it was, a radius of empty tables surrounded her.

Oliver adjusted the hem of his short cape and set off in the witch's direction. When he drew near to her table, she didn't bother moving her witchy boots or even lifting the brim of her saucily tilted hat so that he could meet her eyes. Instead, she grunted and said beneath her breath, "Git!"

Oliver would have liked nothing more than to "git." Indeed, witches are uniquely equipped to make every citizen in their right mind want to "git." But those who "git" don't get magician's hats, and so Oliver said, "I'm looking for a witch named Helga Hookeye. Have I found her?"

Helga stopped licking her fingers. "Depends on who's askin'," she said.

"Master Whom," Oliver said quickly.

"Master *Who*?" she barked.

"Whom," Oliver repeated. "Master *Whom*."

"That's what I'm askin', you little flea!"

Oliver tugged at the collar of his cape. The conversation was getting heated, and heated conversations with witches usually didn't end well. Oliver wished Master Von Hollow hadn't forbidden him from using his real name, or that Master Von Hollow had put a little more thought into his fake one. Oliver, oh pity, tried to *reason* with Helga. "No, you see, the name of the person who sent me actually *is* Whom. W-H-O-M—"

But Helga was over it. She let out an unnerving shriek (which caused three other witches to shriek back just for funsies). She yanked her witch's hat off her head and tossed it angrily in the air. She slammed her gooey boots on the ground and leaned all the way across the table. Oliver gasped at the sight of a large question-marked-shaped scar that hung over her right eye. She reached out and grabbed ahold of Oliver's wrist. Oliver felt his knees turn to jelly.

"Don't even think about giving me a grammar lesson! The only word I care about spelling is W-I-K-K-E-D, what do you think about that?" she hissed. "Now tell me what you're here for, and I'll decide whether or not I'm going to turn you into a toad."

Contemplating how highly inconvenient *that* would be, Oliver determined it was time to show Helga Hookeye the one thing she wouldn't be able to resist. He carefully lifted the corner of his cape to reveal one of the bundles of magician's thread. Helga's eyes gleamed. Oliver hated to think of all the mischief a wicked witch could get into with not one but *three* bundles of magician's thread, but he supposed he'd just have to trust Master Von Hollow that the Very Important Potion—whatever it was—was absolutely worth it.

"In return for this," Oliver said, "I was told that you would have a VIP to give me. May I have it please?"

The corner of Helga's lip curled. "Of course I have a VIP. I'm Helga Hookeye! I'm armed with an entire arsenal of VIPs! What you really oughta ask is whether I'm willing to give you one, and guess what? I've made up my mind. I am definitely NOT . . . going to turn you into a toad!"

Oliver, who had hastily positioned a chair in between him and Helga, as if a little wood might be enough to repel magic, began to breathe again. "I sure am glad to hear that. I think we got off on the wrong—"

Helga exploded into a fit of wild cackling. Her cackles were punctuated by a few unbecoming snorts, and her eyes even looked to be glistening with tears. She smacked her hand repeatedly against the table.

"I, uh," Oliver began, scratching his hatless head. "Um, did I miss something?"

"I said I'm not," she said between heaving breaths, "going to turn you into a toad—because I'd rather turn you into . . . a PIG!"

The magic swirled off Helga's fingertips before Oliver had time to blink. He opened his mouth to scream, protest, or just do something, but all that came out was a frantic "Oink, oink!" He watched helplessly as Helga crouched down beside him. The three bundles of magician's thread had tumbled out of his arms and spilled onto the ground. Helga swept all three of them up with a greedy smile, while Oliver *click-clack*ed furiously about on his four little hooves.

"Oh, quit yer fussin'," she said. "I'm not about to whip up a perfectly good pig and then turn it loose in the swamp! You are a bit *small* for my taste"—she paused and narrowed her eyes at Oliver as if he'd had anything to do with the transformation—"but not small enough that I'll be starvin' in the morning!"

Piglet hearts, apparently, can thump just as fast as human hearts. Not only had Oliver not gotten the VIP that Master Von Hollow sent him for, not only had he gotten turned into a piglet, but now a wicked witch was planning to eat him for dinner. Everything that Oliver had been working toward—Headmaster Razzle's awful thirty-day deadline, snagging a role as Master Von Hollow's assistant, finally getting his magician's hat and never once having to worry about fitting in again—was over, done for, kaput! This was the end for Oliver and, if you asked him, it really seemed quite tragical. He didn't know much about those orphan kids stuck up on Tragic Mountain, but maybe that's why he had never fit in as a magician. Maybe all this time he'd been a Tragical, and his destiny, or rather his doom, was finally catching up to him.

Though Oliver hadn't realized it, his complete and total despair had translated into a fit of piggy wailing. But he snapped to attention when he felt a prick of sharp fingernails in the soft pink skin of his underbelly. The ground tumbled away as Helga roughly stashed him beneath her armpit. She smelled like old earth, crushed pine needles, and rotten eggs. All of it made Oliver's head spin, and it was almost tempting to just give in to the "oink, oink" and pretend he had never been an eleven-year-old wannabe magician in the first place. It had all been very hard, and for what? What had come of it?

Helga bent her head low. Her knotty hair swept over his eyes and her breath was hot in his ears. "Quit yer squealin', you hear? You're in a room full of witches, and not one of them cares what I did to a pip-squeak like you!"

Oliver turned his wet snout from one end of the dark and shadowy cabin to the other. Helga was right. Everywhere he looked there was raucous and naughty behavior. Three witches beside him were standing on top of a table and using the heels of their witchy boots to grind the peanuts into a very messy layer of peanut butter. A few tables to the left, two witches were playing a heated round of Go Snitch and snarling over a platter of—*gulp*—enchanted betting bones at stake between them. Just beyond that, two witches were caught in the throes of an evil glaring contest that, judging by their disheveled appearance, very well may have begun a whole two days ago. Frankly, Oliver wondered how he had ever had the nerve to walk into such a place.

Helga, with Oliver firmly secured, replaced her jaunty hat,

now bulging with the magician's thread, on top of her head, and stomped out of the Twisted Goblet. She paused just outside the door and surveyed the row of broomsticks. She impatiently tapped her foot.

"For cryin' out loud, why do you all have to look so much alike?" she screeched.

Oliver wanted to point out that back at Razzle's School for Meddlesome Boys he could look down at the boat dock and pick *Syd* out all the way from his dormitory window, but since he was a pig the only thing that came out was a hearty "Snort!"

"Shut up!" Helga barked.

"Oh," a voice crooned from behind. "Having a bad day?"

"Oink, oink, oink!" Oliver screamed in agreement. In response, Helga's fingernails dug harder into his belly, but when she wheeled around to face the mysterious voice, Oliver's heart soared. There, standing in front of them, was Council member Slickabee! Oliver was certain he'd never been so happy to see another magician in his life, even if Headmaster Razzle did always complain that Council member Slickabee had a "big head" from his years of work on the Chancellor's Council. Big head or not, he still fit into a magician's hat and that was good enough for Oliver.

"Oh, it's you," Helga Hookeye said with about as much enthusiasm as one greets an old banana peel. But Oliver, pressed tight against Helga's side, could feel the chilling race of her small, witchy heart. "Whaddya want, Slickabee?"

Council member Slickabee raised his finger in the air. "That's *Council member* Slickabee, don't forget. And"—he reached beneath the lapel of his jacket and pulled forth an envelope— "I'd expect you would be happier to see me. Or maybe you forgot about your little petition to the Council?"

A low growl erupted from Helga. Oliver felt her body tense before she sprang forward and snatched the envelope right out of Slickabee's hand. But Helga just stared at it. Indeed, it is very hard to open an envelope with one hand, and Oliver wasn't about to make it any easier. He let out a shrill squeal; he pummeled his tiny hooves into her side and wound up tangled in the raggedy fabric of her black sweater.

Council member Slickabee cleared his throat. "Why don't you just set your pig on the ground?" he asked.

"Ha! If you were going to be someone's dinner, do you think you'd sit around and wait to be tossed in the pot?" Helga said. "But since you're so interested in bein' helpful, how's about you hold him?"

Helga didn't wait for an answer. She thrust Oliver into Council member Slickabee's arms and began clawing at the envelope. Oliver tried desperately to think of how he could somehow convey to Council member Slickabee that he wasn't actually a piglet but a student at Razzle's School for Meddlesome Boys. Considering that his vocabulary merely consisted of "Oink" and

"Oink, Oink," he was having great difficulty.

"Helga," Council member Slickabee began, his voice suddenly tense.

"Shut yer trap!" Helga said, not bothering to look up. "Can't you see I'm reading a letter?"

"Yes, but this piglet, it's—ah, well, it seems to be wearing a cape. Do you always dress up your dinner before you eat it?"

"For goblin's sake, of course I—" Helga cursorily glanced up from her letter. Her jaw dropped. Though the rest of Oliver's clothes were sitting in a useless pile on the floor of the Twisted Goblet, Council member Slickabee was right. Oliver was wearing a cape. It had shrunk right along with him and was finally the perfect size! Though Oliver hadn't turned out to be much of a magician, he had somehow managed to be the most heroic-looking pig in the entire kingdom of Wanderly.

"As I was saying, I certainly . . . *do* get a kick out of dressing up my dinner. Doesn't every witch?" Helga finished with an anxious glint in her eye.

Council member Slickabee lifted Oliver up so they were nearly nose to snout.

"Oink, oink, oink, oink!" Oliver squealed.

Council member Slickabee frowned. "You know, Helga, if I'm not mistaken, I think this piglet is trying to talk to me."

"Heh, I think that says more about you than the pig," Helga said with a nod of her head. She turned the letter in her hands upside down and dangled it by its tip. "There're too many words on this blasted thing! Just tell me what it says, why don't you?"

Council member Slickabee lowered Oliver just a bit. "Fair enough," he said. "That letter was written to inform you that your petition to engage in an officially monitored Triumphant encounter for a nice reward is denied."

"WHAAA?" Helga said, her face turning bright red. "You—you—you came lookin' for me to deliver that garbage? This is my twenty-first petition!"

Council member Slickabee didn't seem at all sympathetic. "And your twenty-first denial. It didn't help you much that a witch went rogue during last week's demonstration at Castle Cressida. That required a lot of damage control, let me tell you. The Chancellor was hardly motivated to open up the gates to a witch as demonstrably wicked as you."

"But I thought that's what witches were supposed to be!" Helga roared.

"Yes, but some witches are simply too wicked to be trusted with the kingdom's Triumphants. Consider it a compliment."

Helga fumed. "I'll consider it a compliment when someone fills my pocket with grubins! Now give me back my piglet," she said in a low voice. She yanked Oliver so hard out of Council member Slickabee's hands that she left behind a small piece of Oliver's cape.

"Oh no. You've gone and torn his handsome little cape. That's a shame," Council member Slickabee said. But when he looked at the piece of fabric still sitting on his palm, his eyes narrowed in on something. He brought the fabric closer for examination, and Oliver's piglet heart soared. "What's this writing?" he said. And then he tried to read it aloud. "Rooster's . . . no . . . Riddle's . . . no, that's not it, either . . . Raz—" Council member Slickabee gasped. His hands balled up into fists at his sides, and his eyes caught fire. "That's not a pig at all, is it, Helga? That's a boy! That's a magician! You were planning to—to—to *eat* a student from Razzle's School for Meddlesome Boys! What were you thinking?!"

Was there anything so wonderful as the truth? Oliver didn't think so, and despite the fact that he was still caught in Helga's crooked embrace, he was plenty content to sit and let her and Council member Slickabee hash it out because, at the very least, Oliver was certain he would no longer be cooked that night.

"Quit yer finger pointin'!" Helga cried.

"Finger pointing? I hardly have to finger point! You are holding a piglet in your arm that is wearing a cape, and you told me yourself he was dinner."

"But he was buggin' me! He wouldn't leave me alone. Came in demanding I hand over a VIP—"

"A VIP?" Council member Slickabee said. "And what did he have in return?"

Helga licked her lips. "Nothin'!" she said. "Absolutely nothin'!"

Council member Slickabee crossed his arms. He drummed his fingertips against his elbow. "May I see your hat, please?" he asked.

"Why, you don't like yours anymore?" Helga said with a sneer.

"No, I am a Council member, and I would like to see your hat!"

Helga reached up with one hand. She carefully lifted her hat an inch or two above her head. "Happy?"

"Turn it over so I can see *inside* it," Council member Slickabee commanded.

When Helga reluctantly passed it his way, the three bundles of magician's thread shone in the dim light. "Nothing, hmm?" Council member Slickabee said. "And I suppose you'd have me believe that this thread came from your own wicked hat? Now, I would like you to hand me the pig, along with the VIP, otherwise I will be keeping the magician's thread and reporting you to the Council."

Oliver had never seen a defeated witch before. He certainly hadn't expected such a display from a witch like Helga Hookeye. But apparently not even someone as magical as a witch got everything she wanted. She plopped Oliver into Council member Slickabee's hands and yanked on the strap of a black knapsack secured over her shoulder. With a snort she rummaged about, sifting through what sounded to be a heap of clinking vials, until she finally emerged with the blackest potion Oliver had ever seen.[22] She slipped it into Council member Slickabee's pocket with an incendiary glare and then stomped toward the row of broomsticks, rudely kicking each one awake until she located her own.

Council member Slickabee shook out the folds of his brilliant purple Council cloak and clutched Oliver a bit tighter beneath his arm. "Come along, then, piglet," he said. "I have business to attend to at Razzle's, and I'm sure you are more than ready to go home."

Though Council member Slickabee hadn't a clue what those words meant to Oliver, Oliver's piglet heart thumped.

*Home.*

Yes, he was more than ready to go home.

He only wished it were as easy as that.

In a whirling, twirling blink of an eye, Council member Slickabee and Oliver tumbled into Headmaster Razzle's office. When Oliver shook loose from Council member Slickabee's purple Council cloak he was disappointed to find that he was still a piglet. Headmaster Razzle seemed less than enthused by it too.

---

22. RSA (Reader Service Announcement): If you ever happen to stumble upon a witch's knapsack, don't sample ANYTHING. In fact, it's often the pink, sparkly, and frothy potions that get people into the worst kind of predicaments.

"Council member Slickabee," he said, while seated at his desk, "why have you brought a *pig* into my office?"

Council member Slickabee tipped his hat. "Good afternoon, Razzle. And this is no ordinary pig. He's one of yours."

Headmaster Razzle sniffed. "I do not keep pigs, Gulliver."

"No, not one of your *pigs*, one of your *students*. I rescued him out of Helga Hookeye's curly fingernails."

"Helga Hookeye?" Headmaster Razzle said with a raised eyebrow and an ill-concealed shiver. He nodded in Oliver's direction. "Consider yourself lucky, hmm? Now, I wonder which boy you are. I sent Nicholas and Duncan off this morning to work on their super-super-size illusions, but neither one of them is foolish enough to fall into the lap of a witch."

Headmaster Razzle drew a sudden sharp breath. "Oh no," he said with a groan.

"What is it?" Council member Slickabee said, leaning in closer.

"I see quite clearly this pig has on a ridiculous cape, but did you notice a hat? If he was wearing a hat, his hat should have shrunk with him too. The essential apparel is bound to him."

Council member Slickabee frowned. "I don't remember having seen a hat. Do you think Helga would have stolen it?"

"Because she's short on magic and particularly eager to turn to stone?" Headmaster Razzle asked with a roll of his eyes. "Of course she didn't steal it. This pig never had a hat to begin with! This is Oliver Dash, and Oliver Dash's days here are already numbered! Isn't that right, Oliver?" Headmaster Razzle bent down to look at Oliver.

Oliver felt like he had swallowed a rock. Deadline aside, messing up Master Von Hollow's transaction and requiring rescue by a Council member could only hasten his expulsion. Oliver decided that he would just have to use his porcine image to his advantage. He would feign total oblivion. And no one would be able to prove a thing until he had regained his human shape.

Oliver blinked. "Oink!" he squealed.

"I should say so!" Headmaster Razzle said.

"Oink, oink!" Oliver chimed in.

"You got that right—"

"Um, Headmaster Razzle, pardon the interruption, but are you quite certain the pig understands you?"

Headmaster Razzle froze. "He doesn't?"

"I don't know—"

"He does?"

Council member Slickabee sighed.

"Oink, oink, oink!" Oliver threw in for good measure.

Headmaster Razzle crossed his arms against his chest. "Hmmm, I suppose it is a bit hard to know for sure, isn't it?"

"Why don't you just allow him to stay on here until Helga's curse wears off?" Council member Slickabee said. "We're certainly busy enough without the addition of a delinquent boy to trifle with. In any case, I didn't just come here to drop off a pig. I came because I have *news*."

A slow smile spread across Headmaster Razzle's face. "Now that is far, far more interesting than a pig. Do tell what you've learned, Gulliver!"

"For starters, the invitations have been sent out. The venue for Master Von Hollow's showcase is secured, and it is precisely the night we hoped: September thirtieth! It will be, by far, the largest audience—"

"And the most *important*," Headmaster Razzle interjected.

"And the most important audience we've had since the Chancellor first shoved us off into the Swinging Swamp and forgot all about how extraordinary we are," Council member Slickabee finished with a flourish.

"Honestly, Gulliver, it's a wonder to me how you've managed to last on the Council for so long. The Chancellor's list of suggested 'nuisance' duties alone is enough to make me heave."

"Yes, but if I hadn't managed to control my temper all these years, would we find ourselves at last drawing near to the precipice of change? I think not!"

Headmaster Razzle lifted his eyebrow. "Maybe. But I dare say Master Von Hollow would have something to say about *his* role in the matter."

"Hmph," Council member Slickabee said with a pout. "Master Von Hollow can't even figure out how to pick up his own

VIP order. That's what the boy was doing there, by the way. Master Von Hollow sent him to pick up the . . . oh, what's that one called again? The one that helps him do that hat trick?" Council member Slickabee tapped the tip of his fingernail on his tooth, deep in thought. "Well, I suppose they're *all* hat tricks, but the special one that extends the brim of his hat?"

"The Black Wreath?" Headmaster Razzle choked out. "He sent *Oliver* to pick up a potion like the Black Wreath? Why would he do such a thing?"

Council member Slickabee shrugged. "My best guess is that he was trying to avoid questions. No one uses the amount of Black Wreath that Von Hollow's used over the years without being up to something. If Helga ever realizes all those orders are from the *same* person, you'd better believe she'd use it to her advantage. She certainly needs points with the Council. Anyhow, because I intercepted her, there was no real harm done—"

Headmaster Razzle coughed and thrust his finger in Oliver's direction. "No real harm done? Gulliver, he's a pig!"

"Well, not for forever. He'll probably be back to normal in one to seven days."

Considering Oliver wasn't supposed to understand a word of what was going on, he tried very, very hard not to run around the room squealing. True, it was still better than being roasted for dinner, but seven days? He couldn't be a pig for seven days. The audition to be the assistant in Master Von Hollow's showcase was in *five* days. What if he missed it? What hope would he possibly have left then?

Headmaster Razzle sighed. "Yes, but when he does return to normal that simply must be the end for Oliver."

Oliver shivered from the tip of his snout down to his curly pink tail.

"Hmmmm," Council member Slickabee mused.

"Don't tell me you're being soft-hearted, Gulliver? We've been working toward this moment for decades! Master Von Hollow has orchestrated the showcase of a lifetime. We finally have a hope, a decent hope, of getting out of this disgusting swamp and having the citizens of Wanderly see us for the marvels that we are. I know it's harsh, but we're going to need all the help we can get, *not* the involvement of a boy that is an utter disaster."

"Oh, did you think I was feeling badly for the boy?" Council member Slickabee asked. "To the contrary, I was simply remembering that I forgot to eat lunch, and I'm actually quite hungry."

"Oh, how thoughtless of me! Do say you'll stay for lunch?" Council member Slickabee nodded, and Headmaster Razzle continued, with a gleam in his eye, "I'll escort you to the dining room myself, but first may I have a copy of the invitation? You did bring one for me, didn't you?"

Council member Slickabee shrugged. "Suit yourself," he said. "I figure you ought to keep this too. I certainly don't want to be caught with it while wandering around the Capital. I'd never explain my way out of that."

He plunked the large vial of the Black Wreath down on Headmaster Razzle's desk, while Headmaster Razzle carefully tucked the invitation into his top desk drawer. Without meaning to, Oliver craned his piggy head. He really, *really* wanted to see what was written on that invitation. Headmaster Razzle had mentioned something about a venue, but every performance Oliver had ever seen had been held right there in the swamp. Were magicians even allowed to hold a showcase outside the Swinging Swamp? And what was Master Von Hollow using that VIP for? The name alone—the Black Wreath—made Oliver shiver. It couldn't be a special effect just for the upcoming showcase, because Council member Slickabee had said that Master Von Hollow had been using it for years.

Lately, Oliver had been so consumed by his quest to receive a hat that he hadn't fully considered the weight of Headmaster Razzle's words or what he'd meant when he said that the magicians' roles were about to change. Nothing ever changed in Wanderly, except by decree of the Council. Had the magicians found a way around that? How—and at what cost?

But before Oliver could think on it any longer, Headmaster Razzle stooped down and swept Oliver into his arms. He wrinkled his nose. "Do you mind if we drop him in the dungeon on our way? I don't want him running among the students and stirring up bothersome questions."

"But don't you think the other students will notice the boy is missing?" Council member Slickabee asked.

"Oh, don't worry about that. Nobody notices Oliver. Nobody ever has, and nobody ever will."

And though it was a terrible, awful thing to say, deep down in the secret places of his heart, Oliver worried that it was true. He worried that he would never be accepted by the rest of the magicians. And for the first time since determining to get his hat at all costs, Oliver wondered if a hat would be enough.

NINE

# A Hater of Hats

Pippa and Ernest pushed through the double doors of Castle Cressida on their way to the Loyal Companions' Barn. Pippa had already visited with her loyal companion a few times in the five days since the Loyal Companions "fiasco,"[23] but it hadn't really gone the way she'd expected. Her fire horse spent most of the time hanging his head, snuffling discontentedly, and doing a very good job of showing Pippa his backside. Today, however, would be their first official training session, and Pippa was glad for the help.

But Pippa and Ernest didn't get very far. They hopped off the

---

23. This is Pippa's term and not my own. I frankly saw it coming. Bernard and Prudence Bumble, however, had spent their entire lifetimes being fed a steady diet of baloney (I am not talking about the lunch meat) and remained adamant that if anyone should have received a fire horse, it should have been a Bumble.

final golden step and promptly drew to a skidding halt. Lying on the ground in front of them was an enormous, messy tangle of ivy. The same suffocating ivy that grew back within hours every time Mistress Peabody ordered it cut down from Castle Cressida's exterior.

The ivy lying on the ground, however, was brown and withered; it looked done for. And when Pippa looked up over her shoulder, Castle Cressida proudly glistened back.

"Ernest," Pippa began, "have you noticed anything different about Castle Cressida lately?"

Ernest slid his glasses up along the bridge of his nose. "Well, other than this ivy, I guess there is something. . . . I mean, it's sort of a weird something and a small something, but you asked if I'd noticed *anything* and so—"

"What is it, Ernest?" Pippa interrupted. She wasn't trying to be impatient, but she also loathed being tardy. Not to mention, she'd heard rumors that Ms. Bravo would be dropping in, and Pippa was hoping to ask her at least some of the questions she didn't trust Mistress Peabody to answer correctly.

"Lately, the boys' bathroom has smelled like"—Ernest looked from left to right as if to be sure nobody was listening, then he lowered his voice to a whisper—"*strawberries*."

"Strawberries?" Pippa repeated. "Interesting. And what did it used to smell like?"

An immediate look of disgust erupted on Ernest's face. "Let's just say *not* strawberries. Why do you ask?"

"I was just trying to figure out whether Castle Cressida is improving. Getting stronger, somehow."

"Huh," Ernest said with a shrug. "I hadn't thought about it, but that sure would be a nice change." He paused, looking carefully in Pippa's direction. "I mean, if Castle Cressida *really* got spiffed up, I wonder if it's even the sort of place you'd never want to leave. Just saying. . . ."

Pippa sighed. "It's nice of you to say, Ernest. Really it is. But that's not what makes a home, is it? At least that hasn't been the case for me."

"Oh, I was just thinking that maybe you were starting to feel differently. I mean, out of all the loyal companions in Wanderly, you were matched with a fire horse. The last time that happened was decades ago!"

"Ernest, have you looked at that fire horse?" Pippa asked. "Closely, I mean? He's kind of a mess."

Oddly enough, a slow smile spread across Ernest's face. Pippa put her hands on her hips. "Why are you smiling like that?"

"No reason," Ernest said, moving past Pippa with a slight spring in his step.

Pippa hurried to catch up with him. "Come on, what did I say?"

"Well, I might be wrong, but it almost sounded like you were *worried* about—uh, what was his name again?"

"Ferdinand," Pippa said without thinking.

Ernest pumped his fist in the air. "You named him too? I

knew it! You and Ferdinand have already bonded. And now for the rest of your life—"

"Whoa! Hold your horses there, Ernest," Pippa said.

But Ernest's grin only deepened. "I think you mean hold *your* horse."

"You know, you really are a little bit stubborn," Pippa said, brushing past him.

"Yes, and you're moving very quickly for someone who's not at all excited to see their loyal companion."

As Pippa and Ernest continued to make their way down the gently sloping hill and into the lush green valley with the meandering stream, the red planks of the Loyal Companions' Barn came into view. They were worn and weathered and perfectly inviting. The barn was bordered by three separate paddocks—one of which contained a melancholy-looking Ferdinand—and big bales of golden hay were stacked so high on one side they almost touched the roof. At the front of the barn, Ms. Bravo, with Dynamite perched on her shoulder, stood alongside Mistress Peabody. In Mistress Peabody's arms was the glass bowl containing her loyal companion goldfish, Dixie.

Most of the other Triumphants were spread across the field, already working with their loyal companions. Pippa spotted Viola and her beaver, Choo-Choo, building a fort together out of a bundle of sticks, while not too far away Anastasia and her marmoset, Whisper, were practicing sneaking up on one of the other Triumphant boys and his goose (considering the honking racket they were making, that wasn't going to be too hard of a task). Prudence and her raccoon were busy using their nimble fingers to pick the locks on the paddock gates. Bernard, however, was standing all alone, a short distance away, and glaring at Pippa.

"Took you long enough," Bernard said once Pippa and Ernest got closer. "Ms. Bravo wouldn't let me do anything with Bob until you got here.[24] And why are you always hanging out with *him*? He smells like a goat."

"You say that like it's a bad thing," Ernest said with a bewildered expression. "Speaking of which, Leonardo is probably wondering where I am. Good luck on your first lesson, Pippa!" he said, before running off toward the barn's large double doors.

Pippa drew in a shaky breath and glanced in Ferdinand's direction. Although Ferdinand was one of Wanderly's most legendary creatures, she tried to remind herself that (1) he was much smaller than she'd imagined, (2) a single spark was way more manageable than an entire flaming mane and tail, and (3) he wasn't exactly brave and bold but instead undeniably glum.

Bernard followed her gaze and smirked. "Too bad your

---

24. If Bob seems like an outrageously ordinary name for a creature as nuanced as a peacock, you are 100 percent right. Bernard, determined not to be upstaged, specifically chose such a name to keep his loyal companion "in his place." But perhaps "Bob" meant something different in peacock, because Bob's antics hadn't slowed down one bit.

loyal companion's broken, Pippa. It was almost a monudental achievement."

Certain that Bernard had no interest in paying a compliment to her teeth, Pippa sighed. "'Monumental,' you mean?"

"That's what I said," Bernard insisted, jutting his chin out. "But I bet that's why we never see fire horses anymore. They're no longer worthy of Triumphants. And now that a fire horse has been paired with you, no one will ever doubt that again."

"Yeah, well, broken things don't have to stay broken, Bernard. Sometimes they get fixed." And something inside Pippa's heart seemed to click into place. Because if it was true of a fire horse, couldn't it be true of her too? That no matter how bad things looked, there was still a reason to hope that she'd find her way home?

"And you think *you're* going to fix him?" Bernard said, crossing his arms against his chest.

"I don't know. But I don't think heroes—real ones, anyways—," she said with a sideways look in Bernard's direction, "give up easily."

Bernard waved his hand in the air. "That's old-school stuff. Nowadays there's one thing and only one thing that matters: a hero always wins."

"That's ridiculous, Bernard. No one can win all the time."

"In Wanderly they can. In fact, the Chancellor's guaranteed it. And the Chancellor's never wrong."

Pippa pressed her lips together. She thought the Chancellor was wrong about a great many things. For starters, he didn't seem to have a complete handle on happy endings, otherwise Pippa wouldn't have been dying to go back home to her common life with her common family. But standing next to two Council members didn't really seem to be the right place to bring that up.

"Pippa, Bernard," Ms. Bravo called out. "Please come closer." Ms. Bravo paused before continuing, "First of all, congratulations. I'm sure I don't need to explain to you that the relationship you share with your loyal companion is one of a kind." On her shoulder, Dynamite squawked enthusiastically. "In fact, in all of Wanderly, perhaps nothing will serve to grow, sharpen, and challenge you more than your loyal companion. Wouldn't you agree, Mistress Peabody?"

"Oh, certainly," Mistress Peabody said. "It's hard to know where I'd be without Dixie." She lifted Dixie's bowl so high in the air that a bit of water sloshed out the side. Mistress Peabody stifled a shriek as it splashed first on her cheek and then on the toe of her satin dancing slipper. Dixie, meanwhile, trembled inside the pink plastic castle at the bottom of her bowl.

Pippa frowned. Whatever wisdom Dixie had to impart, it didn't seem like Mistress Peabody had learned all that much. But maybe that wasn't necessarily Mistress Peabody's fault— Dixie was a *fish* after all.

"Ms. Bravo," Pippa asked, "how are we supposed to learn all that from our loyal companions when none of our loyal companions talk?"

Ms. Bravo beamed. "That's part of the *fun*, Pippa. The learning process is different for everyone. It would hardly be satisfying if I told you outright."

To the contrary, Pippa thought that would be very satisfying. She liked answers and certainty. Especially when those answers involved a creature capable of spontaneously bursting into flames. Ms. Bravo, however, seemed quite adamant, so Pippa continued, "And it's hard not to notice how very different all of our loyal companions are. Why not just assign everyone the same sort of creature? Then we could all learn together, couldn't we?"

Ms. Bravo nodded. "That is an excellent question, Pippa. And a timely one. The loyal companions are different because all of you are different, and despite what others say, it's these differences that allow heroes to do their best work. One of a loyal companion's most important functions is to serve as a mirror. Your loyal companion is meant to reflect the good in you"—she paused, and her voice grew a bit more serious—"and also the bad. A wise Triumphant learns to heed both."

The weight of Ms. Bravo's words—and the fact that he was paired with a brash, overconfident peacock—didn't seem to register with Bernard. Instead, he said in a casual tone, "So are there ever any take backs?"

"Excuse me—take backs?" Ms. Bravo repeated.

For once, Bernard's words made Pippa pause, and not because he needed correction. Was it possible that there were also take backs for such a thing as fairy godmothers? She could certainly use a less expensive one than Fairy Dash.

"Yeah, you know, like an exchange." Bernard continued. "What if you don't like your loyal companion? What if you think you were assigned the wrong one?"

Mistress Peabody glanced suddenly down at Dixie. She pursed her lips, as if considering whether she actually liked Dixie as much as she claimed to.

Ms. Bravo frowned. "There are no wrong assignments, Bernard. And a loyal companion isn't like a coat you have lost interest in. If you find there are characteristics about your loyal companion that you don't like, well, perhaps that is where your work should begin. On yourself, of course."

A look of indignation flashed across Bernard's face. "May we begin our practice now?" he asked through gritted teeth.

Ms. Bravo held his gaze a moment longer and then nodded her head. Bernard stomped off toward the paddock where his peacock, Bob, stood with his feathers fully fanned out and bowing profusely to an audience of absolutely no one. Pippa turned to leave as well, but Ms. Bravo stopped her.

"Pippa, I know the timing is a bit unfortunate, but Mistress Peabody has arranged for a reporter from the *Wanderly Whistle* to observe you and Ferdinand today. Now, everyone knows this is your first training session. This is not meant to put any pressure on you, but for once I can't say I disagree with Mistress Peabody. Pippa, the discovery of a fire horse on Triumph Mountain, one that has returned to become a Triumphant's loyal companion no less, will infuse this kingdom with some much-needed hope. Who are we to deny them that?"

Pippa frowned. "But, Ms. Bravo, I can't take any credit for Ferdinand. I didn't do anything special to get him. I honestly don't know why it happened."

What Pippa really wanted to confess, however, was that if giving Ferdinand back meant escaping Triumph Mountain and going home to her family, she would have done it in an instant.

For the first time since arriving at Castle Cressida, Pippa wondered if her attitude was a bit selfish. Ferdinand hardly looked to be in a good place. What if he'd come to Pippa specifically looking for help? If she didn't help him, could she be certain that someone else would?

Ms. Bravo smiled kindly. "Perhaps that's exactly the reason why the fire horse was chosen for you. Perhaps anyone else would have used the situation for their own gain. I daresay yours is a refreshing attitude these days, Pippa."

"Oh? And what attitude is that exactly?" Mistress Peabody piped up.

"It's called 'humble,' Griselda. Ever heard of it?" But before Mistress Peabody could answer, Ms. Bravo turned back to Pippa. "Now, if there's anything you need, just give a holler.

And remember, go slow. Regardless of how he looks right now, back in the day, a herd of fire horses could take down any opponent."

"Um, yes, about that," Pippa said. "If I were to touch Ferdinand's flames or even brush up against them accidentally, would they . . . burn me?"

"Absolutely," Ms. Bravo said. "But only until you have gained his trust. After that, you can ride on his back while he's fully engulfed in flames and never feel a single thing. At least that's what the old stories say."

Pippa tried to tell herself that was good news; that it was nice to know there would come a time when she didn't have to worry about being burned to a crisp, but considering that time wasn't likely now, when she made her way over to Ferdinand, her knees were knocking.

"Hello there, Ferdinand," Pippa said softly.

If Ferdinand heard her, he didn't show it. His head hung as low as it ever had, and a few flies buzzed noisily around his ears. Pippa had given him a bath the day after the Loyal Companions Ceremony, which had actually consisted of nothing more than lobbing a few buckets full of water at him from the other side of the fence. Still, it was a small improvement. In particular, with the caked-on coating of mud washed away, Ferdinand's soft, golden Palomino shade would no longer be mistaken for dull brown. The knotty mess of his mane and tail, however, were a different story. Pippa knew horses didn't do things like brush their hair, but Ferdinand's mane and tail were interwoven with a multitude of branches, berries, and dead leaves, as if he'd been wandering all over Triumph Mountain, searching desperately for something. Sort of like the way Pippa was searching desperately for a way *off* Triumph Mountain.

Pippa frowned. "I don't understand, Ferdinand. You're already home. What is it that you could possibly be looking for?"

Pippa dug her hand into the pocket of her cape and pulled forth the sugar cubes Maisy had given her just that morning. Maisy, first-rate baker that she was, had assured Pippa they weren't just any old sugar cubes, but a very special and secret blend she'd whipped up specifically for this purpose. When Pippa asked her if that purpose was I Will Not Singe My Triumphant Companion, Maisy had laughed, but not enough to wash away the worry in her eyes.

"Come on, Ferdinand," Pippa coaxed. "If you like these sugar cubes anywhere near as much as Ernest likes Maisy's lemon bars, then you're in for a special treat." At the word "treat," Ferdinand's ears twisted toward her. Pippa felt her heart thump. She stretched her arm so far through the railing that her cheek squished up against the wood. "That's it, Ferdinand. I have a treat. Just for you. But you'll have to come over here and get it. Come on, now. You can do it."

Miraculously, Ferdinand took a few shuffling steps toward her, and then a few more. He stopped just short of her outstretched hand and looked at her as if to say, "Now what?"

"Now you come here. You have to get closer. I can't reach you."

Ferdinand suddenly tossed his head. Pippa was so frightened by the movement that her hand jerked upward and all the sugar cubes rolled right off and plopped into the grass. Ferdinand stared after them for a moment, sighed, and then turned back around in the direction from which he'd come.

Pippa had come so close! She was certain that if she'd had just another minute or two, Ferdinand would have gotten curious enough to investigate, and who knew what sort of magic one of Maisy's decadent creations would work? Pippa set her jaw. She didn't like staring a solution in the face and having it evade her. She knew the Triumphants were supposed to take it slow with their loyal companions, that trust was built over time, but it wasn't like Ferdinand seemed agitated. And Pippa was fast. She could be in and out of Ferdinand's paddock before Ferdinand lifted his mopey head.

Pippa slid fully through the wood slats and crept toward the spot where the sugar cubes had fallen. Ferdinand continued to graze in the far corner of the paddock, with no other movement but the occasional swishing of his knotty tail. Pippa had picked up nearly half the sugar cubes when a small voice cried out, "Pippa, fire horsey?" Pippa looked up and saw Viola and Choo-Choo leaning against the gate.

"It's okay, Viola," Pippa said in as soft a voice as she could manage. "Just go back to what you were building with Choo-Choo." Pippa's voice was not, however, soft enough. Ferdinand jerked his head up. He whirled around to face Pippa, and though he didn't move, his nostrils flared. Pippa's heart began to race. Standing there, in the paddock, with nothing between her and Ferdinand, he suddenly seemed a lot more mighty than mopey.

*Snap, pop, boom, boom!*

Pippa cringed at the bright flashing of a camera. It was the reporter from the *Wanderly Whistle*, and her photographer was having a field day.

"Please," Pippa whispered loudly. "Please just wait a moment. You'll frighten him."

The reporter, Ms. Dottie Banks, whom Pippa recognized from her first day on Triumph Mountain at the magic mirror visit with her family, bobbed her head eagerly up and down. She clasped her hands against her chest. "Did we come at an exciting moment? Oh, how thrilling this is for the citizens of Wanderly! What are you doing in there, by the way, dear? Practicing a very special trick, I presume?"

"Not really, ma'am," Pippa said. She watched nervously as Ferdinand began to paw at the ground. Pippa began to back away very, very slowly, holding her breath as she moved closer to the fence and closer to safety.

Ms. Banks tossed her head toward the sky and squinted. "Timmy?" she called out to the photographer. "Can you fetch my hat? I suppose the sun really does shine brighter atop Triumph Mountain," she said with a grin. Timmy dove immediately into one of the seven or eight bags he was toting around. He emerged with the tallest hat Pippa had ever seen, which likely required its own separate bag, and was made even taller by Ms. Banks's advanced height. It was a handsome hat, to be sure. A deep violet shade replete with daisies whose petals were brushed with glitter. It had a little rhinestone veil coming off the front of it and looked like it had probably been displayed in the front window of one of the fanciest shoppes at Pigglesticks. Ms. Banks smiled as she set the hat atop her head.

Unfortunately, Ferdinand chose that moment to go absolutely berserk. His pawing at the ground transformed into a full-fledged rearing up on his hind legs. He let out a whinny so shrill and so deafening that Pippa pressed her hands against her ears. The worst part of all was that he exploded into motion, racing around and around and around the paddock in a blur, leaving Pippa with no other alternative but to stumble toward the middle of the paddock like a bull's-eye target.

"Pippa!" Viola's shout quickly turned into a wail of tears.

A short distance away, Ms. Bravo's head snapped up. She was working with Prudence Bumble and her loyal companion raccoon, but she sprinted immediately in Pippa's direction, leaving Prudence to trudge sullenly along after her.

Without missing a beat, Ms. Bravo hopped onto the fence's wood slats. She grabbed a nearby lead rope, circled it into a lasso, and began sweeping it through the air, trying to catch Ferdinand as he whipped by. Though Ms. Bravo wasn't having a bit of luck, Pippa was just grateful not to be alone.

Standing behind Ms. Bravo, Ms. Banks wrung her hands. She took a few nervous steps backward, causing her hat to sway through the air. Curiously enough, Ferdinand began to race *faster*. "Oh dear, no one said anything about the fire horse being dangerous. Is—is this normal?" Ms. Banks said.

Mistress Peabody sashayed over at record speed and linked her arm through Ms. Banks's. "How lovely to see you, Dottie!" she gushed. "And did I overhear you asking if this fire horse is dangerous? Of course it's not *dangerous*! It's exactly like every other fire horse you've ever read about. Its only goal is to protect, defend, and promote Triumphants! Isn't that grand?"

Ms. Banks nodded a bit uncertainly. Her hat bobbled so far forward that it almost tipped right off her head. Mistress Peabody steadied it with a pink-polished fingernail. "Is this a juvenile fire horse?" Ms. Banks said. "Indeed, it is quite a bit smaller than I was expecting and, um—does it always just have one flame like that or is it warming up?"

Still stuck at the center of the arena, Pippa studied Ferdinand carefully. Every time she thought he was about to calm down, he would ramp right back up and it always seemed to be in response to Ms. Banks. Maybe it was something about her voice. Or maybe it was the way she moved. Or maybe it was—

"Your hat!" Pippa cried out from the center of the arena. "Ms. Banks, I think Ferdinand's afraid of your hat! If you don't mind, can you please remove it?"

Ms. Banks's cheeks flushed. "My hat?" she exclaimed. "But this hat is the latest fashion. It's brand-new this season!"

"Ms. Banks, I didn't say it wasn't a lovely hat, only that I think it's scaring Ferdinand. Please, Ms. Banks!" Pippa said.

Though Ms. Banks hardly appeared happy about it, Ms. Bravo looked to be one centimeter away from plucking it off herself, and after a moment, Ms. Banks obliged. She reluctantly untied the strings of her hat and set it down where it was no longer visible. Ferdinand skidded to an instant halt. Pippa sprinted toward the fence, where Ms. Bravo's hands wrapped securely around her arms and helped pull her all the way through.

Pippa stumbled to her feet—just in time to see the barn doors burst wide open and Leonardo come charging out, Ernest racing behind him at full speed and shouting, "STOP! LEONARDO, NOOOO!"

Ms. Banks gathered up her skirts in her hands as if preparing to make a fast getaway. "This must be another creature that's not dangerous, hmm?" she said, her voice shaking the slightest bit. "I sure am glad to be surrounded by Triumphants at a time like this."

Recognizing the determined glint in Leonardo's eye, all the Triumphant students ran for cover. Every single one, that is, except for Prudence Bumble, who, presumably in an attempt to drown out the commotion surrounding Pippa, had wrapped her raccoon's tail around her head like a set of fuzzy earmuffs and was oblivious to Ernest's frantic warning.

Leonardo lowered his head, and his horns followed suit. Pippa could barely stand to watch as he crashed right into Prudence's backside, knocking her off balance, and causing her to plummet into a pile of "mud."[25] She lay there long enough for Ernest to secure a jubilant Leonardo and exclaim in between breaths, "I'm so sorry, Prudence. I didn't mean for it to happen. Leonardo's learning, really he is. He's a bit feisty is all, but he'd never really hurt anybody."

The only answer, however, was a *snap, pop, boom, boom* as the photographer caught every detail of Prudence's disheveled appearance on camera. While Ernest miserably led Leonardo away, Pippa glanced sheepishly in Ms. Banks's direction. Pippa couldn't imagine a more sour end to her first official training session with Ferdinand, but perhaps that was her fault for

---

25. Triumphant books don't usually dabble in crude humor, but if *you* would like to consider what else Prudence might have tumbled into considering the number of animals running about, be my guest.

expecting anything different. She should have known that even with a creature as magnificent as a fire horse by her side, it couldn't possibly be enough to render her stay at Peabody's Academy for the Triumphant anything other than what it had been from the very beginning: a giant mistake.

# CROWS RUIN EVERYTHING

In the kingdom of Wanderly, perhaps the only place more miserable than the Swinging Swamp was a dungeon located inside the Swinging Swamp and, more specifically, the dungeon inside Razzle's School for Meddlesome Boys.

Ironically enough, the dungeon was as awful as it was because no one ever used it. Headmaster Razzle considered himself far too grown-up to delve into the sticky affairs of children. He found discipline exhausting and, frankly, he didn't see how things like nice manners and sharing made much difference. And so, when the boys had an argument, when the boys did something egregious to one another, he simply waved his hand in the air and said, "Carry on, carry on," and no one was ever once punished.

And so, the dungeon sat and sat.

The dungeon sat some more.

And then one day it became the temporary home of a piglet.

That piglet, of course, was poor Oliver.

Oliver, as you may well remember, didn't shy away from hard work. Up until Headmaster Razzle's terrible thirty-day deadline, he had tried to prove his worth by doing every chore that no one else wanted to do. But piglets do not have helpful things like hands and fingers. They have hooves. Hooves that can accomplish little if any cleaning, and so for the past five days, Oliver had been forced to live in the dungeon's squalor. Squalor for a piglet is not such a big deal, but squalor for a boy turned into a piglet was awful.

Oliver couldn't believe the staying force of Helga's magic. When Council member Slickabee had said transformation could take anywhere from one to seven days, Oliver hadn't actually thought it would take that long. And yesterday when his feet spontaneously returned, he was certain the rest of him would follow quickly after. But it hadn't. It was only now, five whole days since he'd made the mistake of slinking into the Twisted Goblet, that Oliver was able to slide back into his normal clothes and let himself out of the dungeon—never mind the curly pig tail and the pair of soft, floppy ears that still remained.

The first thing Oliver noticed once he climbed the drippy dungeon steps and peeked into the hallway was the quiet. Oliver knew exactly where everyone must be. He had heard the boys chattering about it; he had heard several of them bragging about it; today was the day that Oliver had pinned every hope on for securing a hat and his place in the Swinging Swamp: the auditions for the role of Master Von Hollow's assistant.

Oliver couldn't believe he had missed it.

Granted, even if he hadn't been transformed into a piglet, the odds of Oliver being chosen were far worse than he'd originally planned. Despite his best efforts, Oliver hadn't managed to snag the worm root for stellar confidence. Despite going so far as to pose as a fairy godmother and even tamper with a girl's wish, Oliver didn't have any grubins to make his audition more attractive. And despite stepping fully outside his comfort zone and offering up his services to Master Von Hollow, even going so far as to negotiate with a *witch*, Oliver had managed to make a disaster out of that too!

Oliver's eyes welled up with tears. He looked up and down the tunnel-like school hallway with the flickering candlelit sconces and the paintings hanging on the wall; the very same paintings he had looked at every day for as long as he could remember. Oliver had never thought seeing those ugly old paintings was something to be glad about, but he wondered now if he would ever see them again.

With his head hanging, Oliver watched a snake slither by. He marveled at how it moved with such purpose, seeming to know precisely where it was going. Feeling a bit envious, Oliver followed it. He followed it all the way to the kitchen, but a snake's needs, as it turns out, aren't that complicated, and it was simply looking to warm itself by the fire.

Oliver sighed. He turned in the direction of the boys' dormitory but found himself positioned, of all places, in front of Headmaster Razzle's office. And suddenly he remembered. He remembered Council member Slickabee talking about securing a venue for Master Von Hollow's showcase; he remembered Headmaster Razzle talking about change—real change—and the most important audience in the entire kingdom. And all of that very important, top secret information was written down on an invitation. An invitation Headmaster Razzle had secured in his top desk drawer.

Did he dare sneak into Headmaster Razzle's office to look at the invitation for himself?

Oliver had never done such a thing before.

But now that he'd missed the auditions, now that there was no way for Oliver to be selected as Master Von Hollow's assistant, now that Oliver was no longer in piglet form, what was to stop Headmaster Razzle from throwing Oliver out upon his return to the school that very night?

If that invitation was so important to Headmaster Razzle, maybe there was something on it that would be useful to Oliver as well. It was worth a try, anyways, and Oliver certainly didn't have anything to lose.

Oliver placed his sweaty hand on the doorknob and twisted. It opened with an ominous creak. He quickly slipped inside and shut the door behind him in case any magicians came back from the auditions early.

It felt strange to be in Headmaster Razzle's office all alone. The desk chair where Headmaster Razzle usually sat seemed to eye Oliver disapprovingly, as if it knew he had no business being there. Try as he might, Oliver couldn't avoid its glare because Headmaster Razzle's office was even *emptier* than it had been five days ago. Other than the desk and chair, there was nothing more than a few lingering dust bunnies, an empty hat rack, and that painting on the wall where the Sapphire Sea sparkled and glistened and gleamed as if inviting him to come for a swim, as if even someone like Oliver would be welcomed there.

Oliver turned from the painting and slid open Headmaster Razzle's desk drawer. The invitation was lying on top. His hand trembled as he slipped it free, and his eyes pored over the fancy handwriting.

*Hear Ye! Hear Ye! You are formally invited to celebrate Wanderly's finest at the Annual Fall Picnic Extravaganza! Don't miss a chance to catch a glimpse of your favorite young hero and cheer them on as they win medal after medal and trophy after trophy! Guest* accommodations will be provided in the famed Castle Cressida. Gourmet meals will be served. The entire event is complimentary for the families of our beloved Triumphant students, with the understanding that all will boast appropriately about their unforgettable experience on Triumph Mountain. Long live Wanderly's Triumphants!

All hail to the Chancellor!

Date: September 30-October 1

Arrival Time: Sunset

Location: Triumph Mountain

Mood: Happily Ever After

Oliver's jaw dropped. Triumph Mountain? That was the proposed venue for Master Von Hollow's showcase? The Chancellor had stuck the magicians in the most undesirable place in all of Wanderly—a place where they would have no hope of attracting even an audience full of commoners—and the magicians thought the Chancellor would allow them to conduct a showcase on Triumph Mountain? In front of Triumphants and their families? It didn't make any sense!

Unless, of course, the Chancellor didn't *know* that's what the magicians planned to do. But Oliver couldn't imagine what good could come of that. Even if Master Von Hollow completed every last trick—which was questionable considering the audience would be full of heroes trained to defend Wanderly—surely the Chancellor would punish the magicians for their treasonous behavior when it was all over.

Headmaster Razzle said the magicians' roles were about to change, but he couldn't have meant by getting in trouble with the Chancellor; that would be far worse even than life in the Swinging Swamp. A shiver went down Oliver's spine. Unless the magicians had determined that the only way to kick their humiliating role of "nuisance" was to prove they were as villainous as the witches, in a way that no one, not even the Chancellor, could deny.

Oliver's breath came in short bursts. He looked anxiously around the room. He'd thought the invitation would provide him with answers, but all he had now were more questions. In particular, were the magicians really considering the unthinkable—an *attack* on the kingdom's Triumphants?

Oliver gulped. He'd never personally known a Triumphant, but he did know that attacking one was seriously off-limits. And he was sort of glad about that. As burdensome (to put it mildly) as the Chancellor's roles were, it was nice to live in a kingdom where there would always be heroes to count on. But what if, with this showcase, the magicians turned everything on its head? Based on how the magicians ran things in the Swinging Swamp, Oliver couldn't imagine this would mean good things ahead for Wanderly.

But what was a boy without a hat supposed to do about it?

Oliver sighed and glanced back down at the invitation. His eyes scanned to and fro, looking for something that might be of help, and then he zeroed in on the word "annual." That was it! The Triumphants' picnic happened only once a year! If Oliver somehow managed to sabotage Master Von Hollow's showcase, if the magicians' plan depended on an audience of Triumphants and their families, the magicians might be forced to postpone their plans until next year.

If the magicians had to wait a whole year for their new role, Headmaster Razzle might keep Oliver around simply for purposes of swampy labor. That would mean three hundred and sixty-five more chances to get his hat! And maybe, for the sake of Wanderly, a year would even give the magicians time to reconsider what Oliver suspected was a nefarious plan.

Yes, Oliver couldn't think of a single reason why sabotaging Master Von Hollow's showcase wasn't a good idea.

Suddenly, the heavy front door of Razzle's School for Meddlesome Boys crashed open. A flow of excited chatter tumbled down the hallway and slipped beneath the door of Headmaster Razzle's office.

Oliver froze. The auditions must have been over. Everyone had returned to school. Trying not to panic, Oliver told himself he would simply wait until the boys had moved past Headmaster Razzle's office, and then he would discreetly slip out. Oliver was good at being quiet; Headmaster Razzle himself said no one ever noticed Oliver; the hallways were dark and shadowy . . . for once, all that might work in his favor.

Of course, that was before Oliver heard Headmaster Razzle's footsteps. He was headed right for his office and singing jovially at the top of his lungs, "LA-DEE-DOO-DA-DA-DEE!"

Oliver could only imagine how quickly Headmaster Razzle's tune would change when he saw Oliver rummaging through his desk drawer. Oliver looked wildly for a place to hide, but Headmaster Razzle's office was so empty. There wasn't a single coat on the coatrack he could wrap himself in, no sofa full of pillow cushions he could pile on top of himself, and no furniture other than the desk that he could crouch behind. Oliver wished he could jump into that painting of the Sapphire Sea, but that was impossible. The only option he really had was to shimmy through the little window above Headmaster Razzle's desk and make a run for it.

"LA-DEE-DOOBY-DOOBY-DOO!" Headmaster Razzle's voice tumbled closer.

Oliver hopped on top of Headmaster Razzle's desk. He popped the window open and braced himself against the gust of smelly, humid swamp air that poured in. He sprang up from the desk and tried to grab onto the windowsill, but he kept falling short. He bent his knees deeper and this time, when he jumped up, he caught enough air to hook his elbows on the sill. With a grunt, he pulled himself up and thrust his head and shoulders through the opening. Unfortunately, the first thing Oliver glimpsed below was an enormous pair of wide-open jaws. A member of the ancient crocodile gang was sleeping right outside the window!

Headmaster Razzle's footsteps halted. He was just outside the office door. Any minute now he would turn the handle only to discover Oliver's backside hanging from the windowsill and still sporting a curly pig tail that spilled over the waistband of his pants! But if Oliver pushed himself all the way out, he'd land right in the jaws of a crocodile.

"Pssst! Pssst!" he whispered as loudly as he dared.

The crocodile, however, didn't shift an inch. With his feet helplessly dangling and his hands gripped tight on the sill, Oliver realized he had only one option left. He thought of every good and decadent thing he'd ever eaten, and when he was sure his mouth had never been so full of saliva, he arched back his head and spat right in the crocodile's one open eye.[26]

Bull's-eye! Or rather, croc's eye!

The crocodile jerked awake. It clacked its jaws shut. It swung its head from left to right, but never did look up. The bewildered crocodile scurried off through the green sludge, and Oliver shoved himself finally through the window. Oliver didn't stop to catch his breath but sprinted for the safety of the thick tangle of swinging vines before Headmaster Razzle could stop to wonder why his office window was open, and perhaps even

---

26. If you have never experienced the peculiar trauma of witnessing a crocodile sleeping with one eye open—especially a gargantuan one—consider yourself (very) lucky.

get curious enough to peek out of it. Unfortunately, what Oliver didn't realize was that the bottoms of his shoes were covered in dungeon muck. Dungeon muck that Oliver had inadvertently smeared all over Headmaster Razzle's desk and was bound to raise *questions*.

As Oliver sloshed through the Swinging Swamp, he could hardly believe he was headed toward Master Von Hollow's mansion by choice. But as he reviewed all the jumbled-up bits and pieces of information he hadn't fully realized he was collecting over the past two weeks—the grown-up magicians' mysterious moving boxes, Headmaster Razzle's "super-size" illusion assignments for Nicholas and Duncan, Master Von Hollow's hoarding of Helga's Black Wreath potion—Oliver kept coming back to Master Von Hollow's secret herd of horses.

Horses were not the sort of props magicians typically used in a showcase, which led Oliver to believe that Master Von Hollow was keeping them precisely to wow the Triumphants, their families, and maybe even the Chancellor himself. If Oliver was right, if he managed to set the horses free, that might be just the act of sabotage he was looking for.

Ever since first laying eyes on those horses, Oliver hadn't been able to forget about them. Something about them seemed so sad, and so lost, somehow. The effect could have come about wholly as a result of living with Master Von Hollow, but Oliver had a feeling there was more to it than that.

Oliver moved so swiftly that he didn't notice the Winds were blowing until he drew to a halt at the top of the hill leading down to the horse paddock.

*Swoosh.* The Winds of Wanderly dove deep into the Swinging Swamp and swirled toward Oliver.

*Swish.* The Winds of Wanderly lifted up the folds of his cape.

And then, tumbling near, a bright, cheery red beetle—a *lady*bug, if you will—landed square on the tip of Oliver's nose. Oliver's jaw dropped.

The Winds of Wanderly had found Oliver for a second time, and surely this was the response to the letter Oliver had been waiting for. The letter from the girl with the stony heart like his. The girl who was supposed to supply the grubins Oliver had planned to use to "enhance" his audition for Master Von Hollow.

Only now, the auditions were over.

Oliver might have felt a bit miffed considering the letter's untimely delivery, but it wasn't like Oliver could have auditioned with pig ears and a curly tail anyways.

Oliver touched his fingertip gently to his nose, and the ladybug exploded in a cloud of sparkling golden dust that arranged itself into a letter. Oliver read aloud:

Dear Fairy Dash,
First off, I want to say thank you. It's hard to describe how

I felt when your letter came soaring through the window, and that's not just because it flew in as a dragonfly, which was surprising (and a bit scary), to say the least! What mattered most of all was knowing I wasn't in this by myself. That even though I'm far away from home, that doesn't mean I have to be alone. It also doesn't hurt that you're a real live fairy godmother, and even if you fairy godmothers do hardly answer any wishes, maybe that's just because you're saving up all your magic for the ones that matter the most. Thank you for putting my wish in this category.

All that being said, I have one small request regarding the payment for my wish. In short, I don't see how I can possibly come up with that many grubins. I'm not trying to undervalue your magic, and I'm not afraid of a little elbow grease—remember, I come from a family of TEN—but where I'm stuck, there aren't many working opportunities available. The one thing I did try backfired so badly that I wound up with one hundred hissing cockroaches instead of one hundred grubins! I bet you're glad I didn't include any of those with my letter, huh?

Anyhow, is there ANY other way I can pay for my wish? Maybe there's a monthly payment plan available? Fairy Dash, I can't imagine I'd be so close to returning home only to let something like grubins stand in my way. Also, I'm not trying to be pushy, but the longer I'm stuck here, the harder and harder it's going to be to leave. Not to mention I think my stony heart has become contagious and is spreading to other parts of my body. Sadness is the heaviest thing I've ever lugged around, and I just don't think people are designed to carry all this weight.

Very truly yours,

Pippa North

PS: The question of how I arrived here is more complicated than you'd think. What's not complicated, however, is how you and I met. That was purely the Winds of Wanderly. And that's why I'm not giving up on you, Fairy Dash. How could I?

Oliver's heart sank. All his life, he'd been the unlucky recipient of an endless barrage of orders and insults; sometimes he engaged in a slightly one-sided conversation with the wooden rowboat *Syd*, but he'd never really had anyone just plain talk to him. Not like Pippa did, anyways. Pippa seemed . . . nice. And Oliver was doing something horrible to her. Early on it was easy enough to blame the mix-up on the Winds of Wanderly. After all, Pippa herself agreed that the Winds were the ones responsible for delivering the letters in the first place. But the Winds of Wanderly weren't the ones pretending to be a fairy godmother; the Winds of Wanderly weren't the ones writing dishonest letters; the Winds of Wanderly weren't the ones who'd tried to take advantage of someone else's sadness.

That was all Oliver.

What had he done?

Oliver looked down at the letter, held loosely in his hands. And then he had an idea. If the Winds of Wanderly could dive into a place like the Swinging Swamp, they should have no problem twirling into the Merry Meadow. Oliver couldn't grant Pippa's wish, but there were plenty of other fairy godmothers, real ones, who could. Oliver knew the significance of time, the crushing weight of each passing second. He couldn't give Pippa back what she had already lost, but at least she wouldn't have to wait any longer.

Oliver reached beneath his cape and pulled out a sheet of paper and a pencil. He bent his head low and wrote the letter he should have written in the first place. And when he was done, he slid down the hill and marched near to the paddock where Master Von Hollow's herd of horses shuffled their muddy noses through the swamp moss.

Oliver gasped. Up close the horses looked almost more skeletal than they had before. Oliver initially hoped an act of sabotage might keep him from becoming homeless, along with possibly preventing a mutiny on Triumph Mountain, but if it also meant saving the lives of the horses, it simply had to be the right thing to do.

Oliver rose to his feet. He was surprised to feel the Winds of Wanderly rise along with him. They ruffled their fingers through his scruffy hair, and for once, the reminder of his absent hat didn't make him cringe but instead pause. Who would have ever imagined he could accomplish so much without one?

As Oliver creaked the paddock gate open and approached the frail horses, the only things that gleamed in the starless night sky were the beady, interested eyes of Master Von Hollow's murder of crows.

ELEVEN

# A Missing Goat

On that very same night, way up high on the peak of Triumph Mountain, the unthinkable was happening. A record-breaking stretch of perfectly fair weather had been broken, and not by a bit of cloud cover, a sparse patch of fog, or a slight chill to the air. It was raining. Pouring, actually.

I know that we just came from Oliver's harrowing ordeal by which he found himself still utterly hatless, strapped with a lingering piglet's tail, and trying to stall a suspected magician's takeover, but through the years the Triumphants—as you have now seen firsthand—had become very . . . delicate. Indeed, in all of the Chancellor's arranging, finagling, negotiating, scheming, and strong-arming to remove every single obstacle from the life of a Triumphant, this was the devastating result: the Triumphants of Wanderly had never been weaker. And whether the

Chancellor had expected this or not, who could really know?

Alas, the rain was proving a challenge for even Mistress Peabody to pretend away. At dinnertime she had invoked an energetic four-string quartet to drown out the relentless *pitter-patter*. Every time a deep rumble of thunder rolled across the land, she giggled anxiously and said, "My, I'm hungry tonight," as if it were nothing more than a stomach growl. When sudden flashes of lightning ripped across the normally perfect sky, fracturing it into pieces, she glanced up at the flickering candlelit chandeliers and said in a high-pitched voice, "The candles certainly are . . . bright tonight."

The other children, except for Bernard and Prudence Bumble, who looked curiously smug, as if they were sitting on some sort of secret,[27] pushed their food around on their plates and took turns sighing anxiously. It was Viola who finally broke the facade.

"Mistwiss Peabody," she called out in her three-year-old voice while looking anxiously toward the window. "Why's sky crying?"

All the other Triumphants turned expectantly to face Mistress Peabody, but they shouldn't have hoped for much. "The sky is not crying!" Mistress Peabody huffed. "Why, it is perfectly

---

27. At this point, I'm sure I don't have to point out the obvious, but I promised you from the beginning I would do what I could to ease you through the traumatic parts. And so, I shall offer it up for consideration as to whether you think Bernard and Prudence Bumble could ever have a *good* sort of secret.

pleasant. It—it is the same sky that hangs over Triumph Mountain every night. A perfect sky for a perfect mountain for perfect children!" she screamed at them.

Viola trembled in her throne.

Mistress Peabody did too. And then she swept abruptly up, executed the jerkiest sashay Pippa had seen from her, and called out over her shoulder, "I shall see you all in the morning for another gloriously bright and sunny day!"

The string quartet followed closely on her heels, and the Triumphant children were left with nothing but the steady drum of rain and a basket of umbrellas Maisy had quietly placed beside the door when no one else but Pippa was looking. After dinner, on their way up to bed, every single one of the Triumphants had stooped down to take one of those umbrellas and carried them warily to their dormitories as if wielding swords.

And so, even though Pippa had survived many a day and night of rain back in Ink Hollow, and even though Castle Cressida seemed quite proud that it hadn't sprung a single leak, given the ominous mood of the castle's inhabitants, Pippa was hardly surprised at the urgent knocking that erupted in the dead of night when everyone was supposed to be fast asleep.

"Pippa! Pippa, it's me!" Ernest said in a loud whisper.

Pippa rolled quickly out of bed—or rather as quickly as one can when climbing down a tower of eight mattresses—hastily stuck her arms into her soft, royal blue sleeping robe, and padded toward the door. She opened it the merest crack and poked her head out.

She gasped out loud. Ernest stood with his shoulders slumped and a piece of paper dangling from his right hand. His hair, which was usually quite tidy, was sticking up in every which direction. His face was splotchy, his nose was runny, and the moisture coming from his eyes was making the lenses of his eyeglasses foggy.

"Ernest, what is it?" Pippa asked, stepping fully out of the dormitory and closing the door behind her. "What's happened? Are you all right?"

But Ernest merely lifted the crinkled paper in Pippa's direction. She read aloud: You're a joke, your goat is too. Leonardo's gone, and now you're blue. Maybe you'll find him, maybe you'll crumble. But this ought to teach you, for messing with BUMBLE. Signed, Prudence and Bernard

Pippa shook her head. "I—I don't understand. What does this mean? What have they done? A loyal companion can't just disappear!"

Ernest winced. "It can if you leave the gate wide open. And that's what Bernard said he and Prudence did. About one hour before it started to . . . rain. And all because Leonardo knocked Prudence into that mud puddle."

As if on cue, a deep rumble of thunder shook the ground beneath them, and a bright flash of lightning illuminated the dark hallway.

A panicked look flashed across Ernest's face. "Pippa, no one knows what to do in the rain on Triumph Mountain! I—I—I bet Leonardo doesn't even know what the stuff is! He's probably slipped and fallen somewhere; he's probably lying on a pile of soggy leaves, shivering and cold and alone!"

Pippa resisted the temptation to despair. It certainly did seem cold and wet and scary in that moment, but just because something felt a certain way didn't mean that it was true, and despairing hardly seemed to be what Ernest needed most.

Pippa glanced behind her at the long row of umbrellas the girls had lined up outside their dormitory before falling, fitfully, to sleep. Pippa still wasn't entertaining any real thought that she actually was Triumphant material, but you didn't need to be a hero to know how to hold an umbrella. She bent down and plucked two of the umbrellas off the floor. She held one out to Ernest and tucked the other beneath her arm.

"Are you ready, Ernest?" she asked.

Ernest eyed the umbrella. "Ready for what?" he asked.

"To go find Leonardo, of course. When something's lost, you have to go and find it."

Ernest's jaw dropped. "Even when it's raining?" he asked.

Pippa and Ernest both looked toward the window, where the dark world swayed and shook mere feet away. Pippa couldn't stop the shiver that ran down her spine. "Maybe especially when it's raining," she said.

"And Mistress Peabody? If she catches us, surely she'll—"

"Ernest, according to Mistress Peabody, there is no rainstorm. How can we get in trouble for running about in something that doesn't exist?"

Ernest almost smiled. Almost. Then he took a step closer to Pippa, held up his umbrella, and asked, "How do these things work anyways?"

After a brief introduction to the wonders of umbrellas, Pippa and Ernest slipped out the doors of Peabody's Academy for the Triumphant, never once imagining that they weren't the only ones sneaking about on such a dark and stormy night.

After about twenty minutes of sloshing around an unusually muddy Triumph Mountain, Pippa realized her skills with the umbrella weren't very handy, after all. Because when rain persists in coming down that hard and at that angle, there's really no stopping it from soaking everything in its path. In short, Pippa and Ernest were a soggy mess.

To make matters worse, after stopping by the Loyal Companions' Barn to see if Leonardo had perhaps found his way back home on his own (he hadn't), Pippa decided it would be a good idea to take Ferdinand along with them. Even if the little solitary flame that sprang up from time to time on Ferdinand's mane wasn't enough to scare off any villains, it was just the right amount of light to help Pippa and Ernest find their way.

What Pippa hadn't counted on was how agonizingly *slow* Ferdinand was.

"Um, Pippa, are you coming?" Ernest asked a few feet ahead.

"Yes, I'm . . ." Pippa let out an exasperated sigh. She gritted her teeth and gave a hearty tug on Ferdinand's lead rope. "Right behind you!"

But Ferdinand plopped suddenly down in the soupy mud. As if he were bored, he stretched his neck to the side, curled back his lips, and snatched up a generous mouthful of grass.

"Ferdinand!" Pippa admonished. "This is not a hero's behavior, let me tell you that!"

Ernest jogged back to Pippa's side. "Remember, Pippa, your loyal companion is supposed to be a mirror."

"Are you trying to tell me that *I* behave like this?" Pippa said. "Ferdinand's acting like no one else exists in this world except for him!"

"I think Ferdinand's problem is that he doesn't know who he is yet," Ernest said softly. "He's acting like any horse would act, because he doesn't know that he's a fire horse."

Pippa felt her cheeks grow warm. She stared down at the lead rope in her hands. "Well, whatever it is he's doing, it's not helpful right now. Light or no light, I think we're better off getting along without him. We've really only got one more place to search, so I'm going to tie him up here, if you don't mind."

Ernest, however, wasn't paying any attention to what Pippa was doing with Ferdinand. He looked instead in the direction of the forest that Pippa had gestured at. The one that lay just to the left of Castle Cressida and was marked with a somewhat ominous sign that read: "Triumphant Training Forest . . . Beware!"

Ernest's face paled. He shook his head from side to side. "Oh, uh, Pippa, we don't actually go in there. Like ever."

"But it says Triumphant *Training* Forest. How can you train in a place that you never visit?"

"That's just it. The sign's old. The forest is too. And super creepy. I mean, I've never actually been in it, but sometimes it makes noises. Mistress Peabody said that Triumphants are much more civilized these days, and that it would be silly to send us into such a barbaric place."

"By civilized, is she referring to the way she's taught you all how to politely say 'Stop,' as if that's supposed to work?"

"I, um . . ." Ernest frowned. "That sort of hurt my feelings, Pippa."

Pippa's shoulders sagged. "Oh, Ernest, I'm sorry. I didn't mean for it to. I think I just get . . . angry sometimes."

"Angry?" Ernest asked. "But why do you care what Mistress Peabody is teaching us? You're still waiting to hear back from your fairy godmother, remember?"

"I don't know how I can help it. Mistress Peabody's so-called training isn't helping you, it's hurting you." Seeing Ernest's blank expression, Pippa went on, "Ernest, villains are villains for a reason. They're dangerous."

"I guess so," Ernest said. "But a villain would never actually hurt us. It's against the rules."

"But what if they break the rules, Ernest? What then? All it takes is one villain to do something . . . unthinkable." Pippa sucked up a breath. "In fact, I think we came awfully close to that happening when Ms. Bonecrusher came to visit."

Ernest's jaw dropped. And then he lowered his eyes. "How come I never thought about any of this stuff?" he said softly.

"Because you're brave," Pippa answered without hesitation. "But you still need a good teacher."

Ernest looked nervously in the direction of the Triumphant Training Forest. "So you really want to go in there?" he asked.

"Don't you think we ought to at least try?"

Ernest swallowed. He reached into the deep pockets of his robe and pulled his umbrella back out. He held it solemnly in front of him. "For Leonardo," he said, and then looked expectantly in Pippa's direction.

"Oh!" Pippa exclaimed. She fumbled around in her pocket until she found her umbrella too. She laid it across Ernest's and echoed just as solemnly, "For Leonardo."

And as the two of them ventured closer to the forest, slicing their umbrellas through the air, Pippa couldn't help thinking that she could almost, maybe, imagine more scenarios like this—adventuring side by side with Ernest, scouring the woods for a lost soul—and that maybe the greatest thing about being a hero had nothing to do with the rewards and perks lavished by the Chancellor, but in simply doing what was right.

Pippa's and Ernest's umbrella slicing slowed a bit when

they approached the border of the forest, where the tree roots slithered across the ground like snakes and the withered leaves shuffled to and fro like restless ghosts. Red eyes blinked at them from the shadows.

"Um, Ernest, do we know what sort of creature those eyes belong to?" Pippa whispered.

"That would be bats," Ernest whispered back. "Shall we tell ourselves they're really just like cute, flying puppies?"

"Yes, let's do that," Pippa said. And then a moment later, she asked, "Did that help you at all?"

"Nope, not at all," Ernest said. "Let's get Leonardo and get out of here." He threw back his head and shouted at the top of his lungs, "LEONARDO! LEO-NAR-DOOOOO!"

The bats did not seem to appreciate the disturbance of their quiet solitude. Nearly one hundred pairs of red eyes flew open, and when the first bat lifted off a tree branch, all the rest followed. Hundreds of bats swarmed through the air. The sharp prick of their wings tangled up in Pippa's ponytail, and when she raised her hands to shield her face, their warm bodies beat against her arms.

Beside her, Ernest yelped, "Not puppies! Not puppies! Definitely *not* puppies!" And although Pippa tried to grab hold of Ernest's hand, it proved nearly impossible. She found herself stumbling forward alone. The bats' squeaking drowned everything else out. And when the flock finally began to thin, when only a few could be heard flapping their wings to catch up,

Pippa couldn't see Ernest anywhere. Despite entering the forest to find Leonardo, all Pippa had managed to do was lose Ernest.

"Ernest?" she cried. "Ernest?"

But nobody answered.

Trembling, Pippa lifted her umbrella. She held it out in front of her and began to traipse slowly through the forest. She scrambled over a thick fallen log and gasped when she sank her foot into a mud puddle that squished up and over her ankle. The hem of her once plush but now sopping royal blue robe caught on a scraggly branch, and her teeth chattered so violently it was giving her a headache. The forest was so much different without Ernest by her side, so much less welcoming. And, for the first time, Pippa found herself longing not just for home but even for Castle Cressida.

"Oh, honestly, Gulliver, it's nothing but a spit of rain!" A man's voice rolled toward Pippa.

Pippa froze. She hadn't expected anyone else to be in the forest! It was the Triumphant Training Forest after all, and according to Ernest it was properly abandoned. Not to mention, it was the dead of night. All the Triumphants were sleeping, and surely no one else had an authorized permit for this hour. A cold wave of fear washed over Pippa as she saw the approach of two extraordinarily tall and skinny shadows. With nothing left to do, she dove beneath the nearest fallen tree trunk and tried very, very hard not to think of how many spiders loved to make their homes in piles of wood.

"If you had endured the sort of rainstorm I endured two weeks ago, you might have a different opinion," the man, Gulliver, replied. "And this rain reeks of swamp life. You don't think the Swinging Swamp will follow us, do you, Victor?"

"Follow us? You mean on its little legs?" Victor paused for a moment and then exploded, "Of course it won't follow us, you numbskull! Now either hurry up so that we can get the stage area measured or tell me excellent things about myself."

"Maybe you can tell me excellent things about myself," Gulliver mumbled to himself.

"What was that?" Victor snapped.

It was quiet for a full five seconds before Gulliver replied in a falsely cheery voice, "Nobody can make things disappear the way you can, Master Von Hollow."

Victor Von Hollow didn't seem to detect the note of insincerity. "Who, me?" he said with a chuckle.

Pippa held her breath and pressed her body deep into the log as the two men stomped by. Once they had passed, she lifted her head up the tiniest smidge. She realized instantly why their shadows had looked so tall and skinny—they were wearing very tall and skinny hats. They were magicians! But Pippa couldn't imagine what business a magician had on Triumph Mountain. Magicians weren't in the same category as witches, but they certainly weren't known for doing *good* things. Although her first thought was that Mistress Peabody should be alerted right away, her immediate and sinking second thought was that Mistress

Peabody wouldn't do a single thing because she would refuse to believe it. How could anyone ever do any real hero's work if they couldn't see the real problems that needed fixing?

Pippa was so distraught over it all that when a voice whispered softly into her ear, "Hi, Pippa," she yelped out loud, delivered a swift elbow jab, and whirled around only to see Ernest's round face wincing in pain.

"What was that?" Victor Von Hollow called out sharply.

There was no time for apologies. Pippa yanked on Ernest's shoulders and pulled him down beneath the log with her. Her heart thumped so wildly, she was certain Ernest could hear it too.

"Hmph, probably some sort of little forest creature," Gulliver said.

But Victor Von Hollow traipsed *nearer* to the log that Pippa and Ernest were hiding under.

"Since when do forest creatures sound like little girls?"

"Who are they?" Ernest whispered in distress.

"Shhh!" Pippa insisted.

"Beats me," Gulliver said. "But since when do those scaredy-cat Triumphants roam around a dark forest in the middle of a rainy night?"

*Scaredy-cat Triumphants?* Pippa was certain that was a first. Unless it was the sort of conclusion that lots of citizens were coming to, but no one dared say out loud.

"Oh, look at that," Victor Von Hollow said. "You've dropped your umbrella, Gulliver." And before Pippa and Ernest could breathe a word, before Gulliver had time to exclaim that he didn't bring an umbrella, Victor Von Hollow swung his head down beneath the log, wrapped his spindly fingers around Ernest's umbrella, and gave it a mighty yank, never mind that Ernest was still attached to it.

Ernest and Victor Von Hollow took one look at each other and screamed. Victor Von Hollow tossed Ernest and his umbrella to the side while Pippa rolled hastily out from beneath the log, ready to run.

"Come on!" she shouted.

But Victor Von Hollow brought his fingers to the brim of his hat and a snarling black panther appeared in Pippa and Ernest's path. Ernest's eyes widened. He grabbed ahold of Pippa's hand and spun her in the opposite direction. Victor Von Hollow, however, was too quick. A trio of cobra snakes hissed menacingly at them.

The second magician, Gulliver, pressed out of the shadows, and Pippa's breath caught in her throat. It was Council member Slickabee! The same magician who had escorted her to the Triumphant examination and was (somewhat) present on the day of the Loyal Companions Ceremony, though he had wandered away with his notebook before the big reveal. Victor Von Hollow hardly seemed like the sort of company a Council member should keep, but Pippa was more focused on not being recognized. Fortunately, her mud-streaked face, along with Council member Slickabee's tendency toward self-absorption, proved a perfect disguise.

The gravity of the situation seemed to hit Pippa and Ernest at the same time. They exchanged terrified glances. When the trio of hissing cobras slithered a bit too close for comfort, the only recourse they had were the umbrellas, which now seemed rather silly.

Pippa opened her umbrella first, and Ernest immediately followed suit. She held it out like a shield, but that hardly seemed to deter the cobras. Without any warning at all, one lunged straight for Pippa! Though she danced backward, she held her umbrella steady. The snake collided against it and disappeared in a puff of green smoke.

Pippa's jaw dropped.

Ernest's did too. And then, with his cheeks flushed, he stepped boldly toward the next cobra and exclaimed, "Come meet my magic umbrella!" And that cobra disappeared in a second puff of green smoke.

"Oh, pooh," Victor Von Hollow said as if sorely disappointed. He touched his fingers to the brim of his hat and nearly a dozen more cobra snakes appeared. By this time, however, Pippa and Ernest knew how to make short work of them.

Victor Von Hollow frowned. "Gulliver, grab hold of those two ruffians!" he commanded.

Not wanting to wait around for that, Pippa and Ernest

sprang up and prepared to sprint away, but they were once again a hair too late. Council member Slickabee plucked them up by the collars of their soggy robes. He dangled Pippa and Ernest in front of Victor Von Hollow.

"If you ask me, babysitting shrieking children hasn't a thing to do with staging a showcase," Council member Slickabee said with a pout.

"No one asked you, and you'd do well to hold your tongue!" Victor Von Hollow hissed.

But Council member Slickabee shrugged. "You don't know Griselda the way I do. You could spell out the whole plan, and it wouldn't matter. She'd never believe a word of it, and especially not from a couple of kids."

Pippa shifted uncomfortably. If the magicians had a secret plan Mistress Peabody wouldn't want to believe a word of, it must be an especially rotten one.

Suddenly, the loud neigh of a horse weaved through the forest. Pippa recognized it immediately as coming from Ferdinand. Did he know she and Ernest were in danger? Was he coming to rescue them? The way fire horses were known to do?

Pippa's heart quickened unexpectedly with hope, exactly the hope that came from having a loyal companion.

Council member Slickabee's head snapped up. "Did I just hear a horse?" he asked.

"Impossible," Victor Von Hollow said.

But the sound came again, and this time louder.

While still dangling Pippa and Ernest off the ground, Council member Slickabee began to fidget in place. "I thought you said there weren't any fire horses on Triumph Mountain anymore," he said to Victor Von Hollow a bit accusingly.

Ernest piped up, "Nobody *thought* fire horses were on Triumph Mountain anymore, but recently a new herd was discovered."

Pippa's eyebrow shot up. She didn't know if one fire horse constituted an entire herd but judging by the aghast expression on Victor Von Hollow's face, Ernest was on to something.

And all around them, the ground began to shake. The forest took the thunder of Ferdinand's hooves and tossed it back and forth against the massive trunks of the trees for added effect. It sounded, indeed, like an entire herd was on its way.

Council member Slickabee promptly dropped Pippa and Ernest into the mud. He brought his fingertips to the brim of his hat and exclaimed, "It's been a pleasure, Victor. But I have a Council position to think about, as well as a life—my own, of course—to preserve. I'm sure you'll understand." And in the blink of an eye, he disappeared off Triumph Mountain.

Victor Von Hollow's eyes came to rest on Pippa and Ernest. He glared at them and then, in a chilling tone, he said, "I never forget a face," as if he planned to see them sometime in the future, maybe soon, and that when he did, things were not likely to go well for them.

Still, he brought his fingertips to the brim of his hat, and he too disappeared.

Ernest and Pippa were again all alone. And not a moment later, Ferdinand came tearing through the underbrush, looking as muddy and bedraggled as ever, with two meager flames blazing on his mane.

But that hardly mattered.

In that moment, Ferdinand was exactly the horse she and Ernest needed.

And in Pippa's eyes, he couldn't have possibly looked more magnificent.

Perhaps Ferdinand wasn't so bad after all.

But perhaps magicians were far worse than she'd ever imagined.

## TWELVE

# SAVED BY A SINKHOLE

In the dormitory of Razzle's School for Meddlesome Boys, sleep had never been a restful activity for Oliver. But on that night, instead of merely sleeping with one eye open, he lay fully awake, hands balled into fists at his sides and boots fully laced up in case he needed to make a run for it.

After breaking into Headmaster Razzle's office and setting Master Von Hollow's horses free, Oliver was practically oozing guilt out of his pores. But when he had snuck back into school no one had been waiting to seize him. No one had even been waiting to question him. Everything seemed as "normal" as it ever had.

Oliver rolled up onto his hands and looked out toward the window, expecting to see nothing more than a bit of swamp fog or perhaps a few swarms of gnats. Instead he saw something sparkling. Oliver blinked. The Swinging Swamp was not known for sparkling; if it had been, the magicians might not have spent so many years trying to find a way out.

The sparkle, however, was looming larger, or perhaps it was moving closer, and before Oliver knew it, a fluffy doughnut came streaking through the window and right onto his lap.

Oliver grabbed hungrily for the doughnut, but the moment he touched his finger to it, it exploded into a sugary cloud and transformed into a letter. Oliver's jaw dropped. The only person he was expecting a letter from was a fairy godmother, but he never imagined he'd hear back so quickly.

Trying to see by the murky swamp light, Oliver pressed his face so close to the letter that it touched the tip of his nose. Curiously, the letter smelled as delicious as it had looked. He read hurriedly:

> Dear Oliver,
>
> I'd be lying if I said your letter wasn't the best one I've ever received.
>
> However, I'd also be lying if I didn't let you know that your letter is the first one I've ever received. I hope your heart's not sinking right now. I may be brand-new to fairy godmothering, but I feel as if I've been ready for ages.
>
> And so, if you're willing, I'm willing. I would like nothing more than to help your friend find her

way home. Note: I know you didn't use the word "friend," but only a friend would make a wish on someone else's behalf, so friend it is. As far as first-time wishes go, "fix-it" wishes are the easiest and least controversial—meaning no special Council authorizations required—to grant.

So let's do this! Let's meet this Wednesday at sunset on the South Peak of Triumph Mountain. I hope the Triumph Mountain part's not too inconvenient, but work obligations are keeping me indefinitely away from the Merry Meadow. Triumph Mountain really is lovely this time of year (always, in fact), and I think you'll agree the extra miles are totally worth it.

Well, I guess that's it. I'm so excited I could scream! I'm not quite sure what I'm going to do with myself until Wednesday. Twiddle my thumbs, count stars, or maybe bake a cake. It's always a good time for cake, don't you think?

Thanks for trusting me, Oliver. Every fairy godmother has to have her first assignment sometime, and for the Winds of Wanderly to have delivered mine feels just about perfect.

Bibbidi Bobbidi Boo (sorry, I've always wanted to write that),

Fairy Margaret

PS: I understand there's a possibility that given your friend's circumstances, she may not be able to travel. That's okay. You can pick up the granted wish and deliver it to her. Also, you never told me your friend's name. If you get the chance before Wednesday, can you send it to me? It would speed along the granting process. Thanks.

Oliver slowly lowered the letter.

When he'd decided to find a real fairy godmother for Pippa, one who could do the things he couldn't, he thought that would be the end of it. He didn't anticipate there being *more* problems.

Fairy Margaret seemed nice enough. And it really didn't bother him that she was a newbie fairy godmother—he knew firsthand what it was like to wait on magic—but one very glaring issue remained: How was either he or Pippa going to get to Triumph Mountain?

Pippa's whole problem was that she was stuck. Oliver's was that he didn't want to leave. He feared that the moment he set even a pinkie toe outside the Swinging Swamp, it would be all too easy for the magicians to shut him out forever. Not to mention—how would he even get to Triumph Mountain? He'd never gone anywhere without *Syd*, but there weren't any waterways that could take him that far.

Oliver sighed. He folded up Fairy Margaret's letter and

slipped it in his pocket. He felt like every time he took one step forward, he went scuttling back about twenty.

"OLIVER!" a voice suddenly boomed down the hallway.

Oliver gulped. That did not sound good. It was loud enough even to stir the other magician boys awake. And then, from outside the dormitory window came a sudden explosion of cawing. It was followed by the sharp tapping of beaks against the glass and a flurry of black feathers, as Master Von Hollow's murder of crows fought for a prime viewing spot.

Oliver couldn't imagine what Master Von Hollow's crows would find interesting about a roomful of bleary-eyed boys, unless—

The door to the boys' dormitory blasted open. It was Master Von Hollow! He stood poised in the doorframe with his face twisted into the most gruesome scowl Oliver had ever seen. While the other boys straightened quickly to attention, Oliver wanted to hide under his bed.

Just behind Master Von Hollow, another door opened up and Headmaster Razzle emerged stumbling down the hallway. His hat was askew as if he'd hastily plunked it on his head, and he was still clad in his pajama shirt and pants, which looked quite rumpled.

"Victor?" Headmaster Razzle questioned. "What is it? What is going on here?"

Master Von Hollow lifted a shaking finger in Oliver's

direction. "He tried to ruin us all! He tried to ruin everything!"

"Who—Oliver?" Headmaster Razzle asked. "I find that hard to believe. Oliver is annoying, but he isn't capable. Why for the past three or ten days, he's been locked in the dungeon as a piglet."

"Well, it wasn't a piglet that snuck onto my property and opened the gate for my herd of horses. I've been chasing the dumb beasts around all night! If even one of them had been lost it would have been disastrous." Master Von Hollow stormed at Oliver. He picked him up by the collar of his nightshirt and began shaking him violently to and fro. "Why? Why did you do it, boy? Did someone put you up to this?"

The murder of crows tapped eagerly on the window, as if there were no greater pleasure than tattling on others. Oliver was certain they were the most hateful creatures in the swamp (which was saying a lot).

"Now wait just a minute, Victor. Let the boy speak," Headmaster Razzle said, a hint of panic in his eye.

Master Von Hollow snorted in disgust before releasing his grip on Oliver so that he dropped to the floor with a heavy *thud*.

Oliver's heart pounded in his ears. He didn't know how he could deny the accusations, but admitting to Master Von Hollow and Headmaster Razzle that he'd tried to sabotage the showcase would be the end of him for sure.

Master Von Hollow's gaze swept impatiently around the room. A few of the younger magician boys cowered beneath their blankets, but Nicholas and Duncan nodded importantly while shooting looks of disdain in Oliver's direction for good measure. "You all live with the rat," Master Von Hollow said, gesturing at Oliver. "Have you noticed any suspicious behavior from him lately?"

One by one the boys shrugged. Until Theodore, the seven-year-old who had recently received his magician's hat and was still trying desperately to impress Master Von Hollow, piped up, "Oliver's been sneaking letters. He thinks no one can see him reading late at night or early in the morning, but I peeked over his shoulder and saw it myself."

Oliver's rock heart sank to the pit of his stomach.

"Letters?" Master Von Hollow said sharply, whipping toward Oliver. "Letters from whom? Who could you possibly be exchanging letters with?"

"I have never seen letters such as these!" Headmaster Razzle said. "How long has this practice been going on? The post doesn't even delve into the swamp more than three times a year."

Sensing that he was on to something, Theodore began to bounce up and down. He jabbed his finger in the air, pointing toward Oliver's mattress. "He keeps 'em under there. Yeah, I'm sure of it!"

Master Von Hollow crossed the room in one giant leap. He

tossed Oliver's mattress toward the ceiling, and just as Theodore had said, the two letters Oliver had received from Pippa lay neatly folded. Master Von Hollow shot a venomous look in Oliver's direction. He snatched the top letter and quickly scanned the contents.

"Pippa North?" Master Von Hollow said with his mouth agape. He shook his head. He looked at Headmaster Razzle with a bewildered expression. "I—I can scarcely believe it. I don't know how it's possible, but he . . . somehow, Oliver has been writing to a *Triumphant* girl. And he's been posing as a fairy godmother!"

The boys began to shift about on their beds, sneaking curious glances at Oliver and whispering among themselves.

Oliver cried out, "It-it's not what you think. First of all, I didn't get the letter from the post. It was delivered by the Winds of Wanderly. And Pippa can't be a Triumphant, because all she wants is to get home to her family—and I never meant to hurt her!"

"Oh, because you have the magic required to grant her wish? Is that right?" Master Von Hollow said, voice dripping with sarcasm.

Oliver's shoulders slumped. It sounded so awful coming from Master Von Hollow. "No, I don't. And I was wrong to do what I did. I just thought that if she gave me some grubins in return—"

"In return for nothing?" Headmaster Razzle interjected.

Oliver nodded miserably. "In return for nothing, that I

might be able to use those grubins to help me get a spot in the showcase."

Master Von Hollow's eyes widened. For a moment, Oliver thought he might possibly understand. But then he crinkled his nose. "Not everyone is cut out to be a magician, Oliver. I'm afraid the more you try, the more you prove to us that we should have tossed you out long ago."

Oliver felt his chin begin to tremble. Tears pricked at the corners of his eyes, and a wave of panic rose in his chest. Surely this was it. The moment he'd done everything to avoid. The moment Oliver would lose the only home he'd ever known. He could scarcely breathe.

But a sudden poof signified the arrival of a third magician in the dormitory. Holding his own letter in hand, Council member Slickabee was hardly a welcome addition. He took one look at the somber faces in the room, rattled the paper in the air, and exclaimed, "So I take it you've already heard?"

"Heard about what?" Master Von Hollow barked back.

Headmaster Razzle, meanwhile, stared at Oliver with a bewildered expression. "Say," he began slowly, "if Helga's curse wore off enough for you to sneak over to Master Von Hollow's mansion and tamper with his horses, did you happen to make a pit stop in my office along the way? Were you the one who smeared muck all over my desk, and what business did you have in there?"

Council member Slickabee gasped. "Break into your office?" he said before whirling around to Master Von Hollow. "Tamper with *your* horses? Is this what those Triumphants meant about a new herd?"

Master Von Hollow let out an exasperated sigh. "You mustn't believe everything you hear, Gulliver. Anyhow, my horses are back where they belong—no thanks to you, *Oliver*." Master Von Hollow sent a nasty look in Oliver's direction before turning back to Council member Slickabee. "Now why have you so rudely interrupted us?"

"Helga Hookeye," Council member Slickabee said with his eyes narrowed. "She's submitted an official complaint to the Council for suspicious behavior in the Swinging Swamp, specifically incessant hoarding of the Black Wreath!"

"But Helga's a witch!" Headmaster Razzle exclaimed. "Witches don't care if people break the rules! Witches love when people break the rules!"

"Yes, but Helga is a witch desperate to tangle with the Triumphants," Council member Slickabee said. "She'd do anything to get on the Council's good side, and apparently, it's working. The Chancellor is already putting together a task force to come investigate the Swinging Swamp!"

"No!" Headmaster Razzle said. "It can't be! He—he simply mustn't. Oh, we're so close! We've waited so long to get out of this place and out of this humiliating role! We've—"

"Enough!" Master Von Hollow bellowed. "Nothing of the

kind is going to happen. In fact, as I believe the saying goes, we can kill two birds with one stone." Master Von Hollow turned to Oliver with an eerie smile. "You don't belong here, Oliver. And in the past twenty-four hours you've made some absurd decisions. But perhaps it is not too late for you to be of some use to our cause. We shall avoid the Chancellor's inquiry by turning you in to the Council on charges of harassing a Triumphant and"—Master Von Hollow paused and licked his lips—"hoarding the Black Wreath."

"But that wasn't me; that was you!" Oliver burst out.

"To the contrary, I'm sure there are at least a dozen witnesses at the Twisted Goblet who would attest to your meeting with Helga. People might not notice you, Oliver, but they notice piglets."

"But I was only there because you sent me!"

"And you think anyone will believe a bitter eleven-year-old—the oldest boy never to have received his hat—over the most distinguished magician in the entire swamp?"

Council member Slickabee cleared his throat. "Although it is up for debate whether owning a mansion or holding a seat on the Council is actually *more* distinguished. . . ."

Oliver stared glumly down at his toes and muttered, "But Pippa's not a Triump—"

"Silence!" Master Von Hollow chided. "Gulliver, what are the names of the two newest students admitted to Peabody's Academy for the Triumphant?"

Council member Slickabee slipped his hat off his head. "Um, let's see here. Wait, just one second, it's on the tip of my tongue. . . . Uh, oh yes! Another Bumble boy and—surprise, surprise—*my* nominee, Pippa North. Though I still don't know exactly why they picked her, to be honest. Anyhow, why do you ask?"

Oliver's feet swayed beneath him. He couldn't imagine why the magicians would lie about Pippa being a Triumphant, but neither could he imagine why Pippa would lie to him. He'd felt so bad about ruining Pippa's plans, but was she, meanwhile, ruining Oliver's? It took Oliver only a half second to realize that couldn't possibly be true. Pippa didn't even know Oliver the hatless magician existed—if she was lying to anybody, she was lying to Fairy Dash. What a mess.

"Do you see, Oliver?" Master Von Hollow went on. "Everything you touch ends in disaster. Well, now you'll be the Chancellor's problem, and he can decide what to do with you." He turned to Council member Slickabee. "Gulliver, do you have those handy cuffs Council members tote about? You know, the ones that zap treasonous citizens to the Capital for questioning?"

Oliver took a step backward. He glanced frantically toward the window, wondering how much of a running start he would need to break through it, but while he was calculating, the ground beneath them began to shake. Then it began to quake. And one of those nasty sinkholes that plagued the Swinging

Swamp opened up right under the dormitory of Razzle's School for Meddlesome Boys!

The meddlesome—whoops, I mean the *magician*—boys all screamed. The superior looks fell right off Nicholas's and Duncan's faces as they leaped away from their beds, which were the first things to tumble into the exceptionally large hole.

"My school!" Headmaster Razzle cried. "Oh, it has happened! This horrid swamp has finally sunk to a new low!"

Council member Slickabee shook out the folds of his Council cloak as if preparing to conveniently pop right out of the chaos, but Master Van Hollow caught him on the shoulder with a snarl.

"You mustn't always disappear when things get messy, Gulliver!" Master Von Hollow hissed.

All the while, the ground surrounding the sinkhole continued to split into an intricate network of cracks. The walls and the ceiling groaned at the disturbance, and Oliver wondered if the entire school would cave in.

He also knew that maybe, for once in his life, he had been dealt a rare hand of luck. And so he didn't squander a moment. When Master Von Hollow turned to deal with one of the littlest magicians, who had attached himself to his leg and was wailing and smearing his nose all along Master Von Hollow's fine pants, Oliver crept toward the door.

He scooted right past Headmaster Razzle, who was busy bringing his fingertips to his hat and casting illusion after illusion as if it were possible to intimidate a sinkhole. It wasn't, of course, but it proved surprisingly helpful to Oliver as he ducked alongside a growling grizzly bear and made it to the door entirely undetected.

Oliver bolted through the doorway and sprinted down the hall. Even though he heard the others calling after him, he didn't stop until he burst through the school's front doors and gulped in breath after breath of muggy air. Then he continued his escape down the wobbly sand hill, leaping spectacularly off the boat dock and landing on *Syd*'s middle bench. *Syd* shimmied a greeting, but the knot in Oliver's throat was so large it was hard to talk.

After eleven years of trying desperately to fit in, Oliver realized at last that he'd been trying to hold on to a home that he never had in the first place. Oliver wasn't going to be homeless, Oliver already was homeless. And he had been for years.

Oliver hadn't a clue where he was going to go. He still had that appointment with Fairy Margaret, of course, but he was hardly feeling eager to help Pippa after finding out she'd (sort of) lied to him. Of all places, she had to be on Triumph Mountain. How could she possibly want to leave a place like that?

Suddenly, Oliver gasped.

Pippa was on *Triumph Mountain*. How did he miss it? Why didn't it hit him immediately? In less than a few days' time, the magicians were going to perform their ill-fated showcase on Triumph Mountain on the night of the Triumphant Fall Picnic.

Pippa *and* her family were going to be in the audience. What if something terrible happened to them? If Pippa wanted to have any real chance of getting home, wasn't it more important than ever that it happen now?

Oliver couldn't see any way out of his doom, but maybe not all was lost. Maybe one person could still find their way home. Even if it didn't get to be him.

Oliver couldn't believe he was actually considering it, but he could think of only one way to make it to his appointment with Fairy Dash and secure Pippa's wish. He'd have to go back to the Creeping Corridor and, more specifically, the Twisted Goblet.

Oliver briefly shut his eyes and imagined the row of broomsticks leaning brashly against the cabin wall. A row of broomsticks no one in Wanderly would dare to touch, except perhaps a boy with nothing left to lose. When he opened his eyes, his chin was set.

He reached down and gave *Syd* a small pat. "Are you ready, buddy?" he asked.

Reader, I'm hardly certain that I am.

THIRTEEN

# DUELING FAIRY GODMOTHERS

$\mathcal{M}$istress Peabody and the Triumphant students were gathered together in the dining hall for breakfast. The sun poured gloriously through the windows, which was a stark contrast to the epic rainstorm a mere two nights ago and the still-pouting faces of Bernard and Prudence Bumble. Indeed, despite their worst intentions, when a frazzled Pippa and Ernest had returned to Castle Cressida after their chilling magician encounter, they discovered Ernest's beloved loyal companion, Leonardo, safe and sound, cheerfully scraping his buck teeth along Castle Cressida's famed golden steps. Remarkably, despite all the very many other ways in which Castle Cressida seemed to be fragile, its paint was apparently goat proof.

Pippa looked up when the dining hall door swung open, revealing the largest cake she had ever seen. It was at least four feet tall, attached to a skinny pair of legs, and must have been extravagant even according to Triumphant standards based on the stunned looks on the other students' faces. When the cake scurried forward and slid onto the buffet table, Pippa was relieved to see that the legs didn't actually belong to the cake but rather to a sparkly-eyed, flush-faced Maisy. When Mistress Peabody wasn't looking, Maisy sent Pippa a little wave and a flash of a bright smile. Pippa marveled at how even her hair seemed to have an extra spring to it. Regrettably, Maisy didn't stick around for long, but shuffled out almost as quickly as she had shuffled in.

With a slight nod to the cake, Mistress Peabody rose gracefully out of her chair and delicately cleared her throat. Seeing how composed she was made Pippa feel squirmy inside. Surely Mistress Peabody wouldn't be acting in such a manner if she knew that two wily magicians had been traipsing around Triumph Mountain just two nights ago and speaking suspiciously about a secret plan. But as much as she hated to admit it, Pippa also knew that Council member Slickabee was right: even if Pippa and Ernest told Mistress Peabody everything, she'd never believe them, and she'd most likely punish them. Accordingly, they had decided to keep quiet, but that hadn't done a thing to relieve Pippa's fears.

Mistress Peabody turned her dazzling smile up to full wattage. "Students, you may have heard the saying that good news comes in threes, perhaps especially when you are a Triumphant!

And so, without further ado, I am pleased to inform you that today we will be taking a . . . field trip!"

A chorus of cheers erupted from the Triumphants. Some even began to applaud. Mistress Peabody executed several deep curtsies, and for the first time all morning, Prudence's expression brightened a hair. "Will there be reporters from the *Wanderly Whistle*?" she asked, likely hoping to redeem herself after the humiliating incident with Leonardo. "Will there be adoring fans and a chance to practice our waving technique?"

"Yes, yes, and yes!" Mistress Peabody said, eyes shining. "We will be traveling to the Crowne Stadium to attend the Triumphant-Dragon Duel. The Chancellor has even set aside a special cheering section for the students of Peabody's Academy for the Triumphant!"

"Ooooh, caramel corn and butter toffee pecans!" one of the younger boys, Simon, exclaimed.

Anastasia beamed and added, "Pink cotton candy and Fizzoops!"[28]

As the Triumphants began to chatter and babble excitedly, Pippa leaned over to Ernest. "Is it just me or has everyone missed that Mistress Peabody just said the word 'dragon'? I'm

---

28. In case there is nothing akin to Fizzoops in your kingdom, simply imagine the bubbliest of soda pops tied in with an always delightful and blissfully *temporary* "oops." As in, "oops" your nose turned blue or "oops" your hair's standing on end or "oops" you can't keep from bursting into song, all brought to you by the wizards of Emerald Hills.

not sure I *want* to see a real dragon."

"Don't worry, Pippa," Ernest said. "I've been to tons of these things, and I've never once been scared. You're gonna love it!"

"Are they, um, miniature dragons, then?" Pippa asked hopefully.

Ernest grinned. "Nope, full grown and full toothed. But the Triumphants usually have the dragon under complete control before anyone's even taken their seats. Sometimes the dragons are so wiped, they start snoring!"

Pippa felt the tiny hairs on the back of her neck prickle the way they did whenever she encountered a glaring inconsistency. Since she had arrived at Peabody's Academy for the Triumphant, it seemed to be happening often. "Ernest," Pippa mused, "does it really count as a duel if no one sees it?"

"Well, sure it . . . does," Ernest said, his voice trailing off. He frowned. "It is sort of strange, isn't it?"

"And not very heroic, if you ask me," Pippa tossed in.

"Even though the Triumphant always wins?"

Pippa shrugged. "I don't think winning has nearly as much to do with being a hero as the Chancellor says. I think one of the bravest things a hero can do is be willing to lose."

Ernest nodded thoughtfully while Mistress Peabody clapped her hands to regain the chattering students' attention. "Now for my second bit of good news! Since all of our Triumphant students have been matched with their loyal companions, it's time to celebrate with our Annual Fall Picnic Extravaganza! There will be games, food, fun, *oodles* of reporters to capture every shining moment, and of course . . . prizes! Plus"—Mistress Peabody paused and looked significantly around the room—"this year we have invited some very special guests. But do not ask me who, because it is a surprise, and I shall not breathe a word of it—not a single word!" she finished with a giggle.

Even though the other students oohed and aahed, Pippa wasn't impressed. The last special guest to show up at Castle Cressida, Ms. Bonecrusher, nearly had her way with them. Even if the Chancellor himself showed up, Pippa didn't know if she actually wanted to meet him. Indeed, the only people's names who Pippa hoped to hear were Mother and Father, Charlie, Jane, Louisa, Miles, Artie, Finn, and baby Rose. The Norths.

Pippa swallowed back the knot in her throat. She wondered how long she could be away from home before her family— out of sheer necessity—began to slowly fill in the hole she'd left behind. Had Jane taken over helping their mother with the cooking at dinnertime? Who was folding her father's holey socks? Did anyone remember that Rose liked to be sung "Twinkle, Twinkle, Little Star" five times before she was put down for her afternoon nap? Or was it possible they were all getting along just fine without her? Maybe even better?

"Pardon me, Mistress Peabody," Prudence said with a small, expectant smile. "But you said you had *three* bits of good news. And that was only two."

"Right you are, Prudence!" Mistress Peabody said. She whipped out that morning's edition of the *Wanderly Whistle*, and there, on the front page, was a picture of Pippa from the day of her first official training session with Ferdinand. Pippa's jaw gaped. Prudence's smile fell flat. Mistress Peabody exclaimed, "My news has to do with none other than Bettina!"

Without missing a beat, at least a dozen Triumphants corrected, "Pippa!"

"Ah yes," Mistress Peabody said, shaking her head. "I'm not sure why I still have such difficulty with that. Anyhow, the Chancellor—yes, *the* Chancellor—was so smitten with the idea of the fire horse returning to Triumph Mountain that he has chosen to honor Ferdinand with a visit to the Capital!"

Pippa's pulse began to race. A wave of heat washed over her. She couldn't think of anything worse than sending Ferdinand off to the Capital. "But, Mistress Peabody," Pippa began, "you saw what happened with Ms. Banks the other day. Ferdinand was terrified at the sight of her hat! Who knows what might set him off in a place as crowded as the Capital?"

Mistress Peabody waved her hand through the air. "Nonsense! That visit went smashing."

Pippa was at a loss. Mistress Peabody seemed fully incapable of seeing or remembering anything at all as less than smashing. Even still, Pippa couldn't give up. "And—and he's terribly skinny. He's only just starting to fill out a little bit.

And what about his flames? I've never once seen him ignite anything more than a flicker or two."

Mistress Peabody raised her eyebrow. "And that's not enough for you?"

"Of course it's enough for me, but I'm afraid it won't be enough for the Chancellor. The—the paintings of the fire horses—they always show them as being larger-than-life and Ferdinand's . . . not."

"Are you saying you have concerns about accepting the Chancellor's invitation?"

Relieved that Mistress Peabody seemed to be coming around, Pippa bobbed her head up and down. "Yes, that's exactly what I'm saying."

But Mistress Peabody didn't bob her head in return. Instead, her eyes narrowed. "Are you also saying you believe the Chancellor is incapable of appreciating the significance of a symbol as meaningful and heroic as a fire horse? Tell me, Pippa, what kind of ruler do you think we have?"

The room grew suddenly very quiet. All the Triumphants turned to stare at Pippa.

Pippa took a deep breath. She answered carefully, "I'm just worried about Ferdinand is all. Aren't Triumphants supposed to be concerned about their loyal companions?"

Mistress Peabody's dazzling smile returned, but it left Pippa feeling cold inside. Nothing about Mistress Peabody was ever truly genuine. "Yes, of course they are, dear. If it would make you feel better, you can stay with Ferdinand until his escort arrives—"

"Could I go with him?" Pippa blurted out.

"To the Capital?" Mistress Peabody said, and then, almost immediately, "No! That would hardly be appropriate. One does not simply invite themselves to an appointment with the Chancellor. Now are you going to stay behind or not? It really would be a shame to miss a trip to a place as lovely as the Crowne Stadium."

Pippa was hardly torn. Based on Ernest's comments, the Triumphant-Dragon Duel sounded as heroic as the agendas governing school villain visits. Pippa couldn't see much value in that. But above all else was Ferdinand. Pippa had never wanted a loyal companion, and she certainly never thought she could become attached to one, but neither could she keep from reliving that moment when Ferdinand stormed into the Triumphant Training Forest to rescue her and Ernest. Pippa might not be able to keep Ferdinand away from the Chancellor, but at least she could send him off the way a true loyal companion should.

"I'd like to stay behind, ma'am," Pippa said at the exact same time that a terrible groan erupted from Ernest's direction. Pippa and the rest of the Triumphants looked over to where Ernest was seated with Maisy's extravagant cake in front of him. Or at least Maisy's extravagant cake *used* to be in front of him. All that remained on the platter was a pile of messy crumbs, a few smudges of frosting, and Ernest rocking himself to and fro with an anguished look on his face.

Hours later, Ernest's stomachache still hadn't subsided, but that was hardly the worst of it. Pippa and Ernest stood shoulder to shoulder in front of Ferdinand's empty paddock. Their eyes were glued to the back of the Quill member's carriage as it jostled along the road, dipped below the hill, and slipped, finally, out of sight.

For the time being, Ferdinand was gone.

Pippa's lower lip quivered. "Ferdinand looked so scared, Ernest. I—do you think he's going to be okay? Do you think I should have done something more?"

"Against an officer of the Quill?" Ernest shook his head. "The Chancellor doesn't pick those guys on accident, Pippa. You couldn't have done anything to stop him, at least not without getting into serious trouble. Ferdinand would have tried to protect you, and then who knows what they would have done to him? You did everything you could, Pippa."

Pippa's chest squeezed tight. The ends of her ponytail lifted gently in the breeze. "I hope so," she said quietly.

She dipped her hand into her pocket and fished out one of Maisy's butterscotch candies. Even though Maisy's butterscotches had the uncanny ability to make her rock heart feel the smallest bit lighter, it wasn't nearly the same as having Maisy's company. Of course, as soon as the Triumphants left for their field trip, Pippa and Ernest had run, slightly doubled over in Ernest's case, to the kitchen to fill Maisy in. But, strangely, she wasn't there. Pippa didn't think she had any real reason to worry—especially considering Maisy's radiant mood that morning in the dining hall—but Maisy hadn't mentioned anything about having somewhere to be, and the day felt hopelessly gloomy.

Pippa held out a butterscotch candy in Ernest's direction. "You want one?" she asked.

Ernest winced. "Ugh! Candy, Pippa? I don't think my stomach's going to be back to normal for a week. I didn't think it was possible to get enough of Maisy's baking, but now I know the cold, hard truth."

"But why did you have to eat the entire cake, Ernest?"

"That's easy," Ernest said. "It was the best way I could think of to stay behind with you. It's not like I could just ask to be excused from something like the Triumphant-Dragon Duel! But nobody—especially Mistress Peabody—likes a sick Triumphant. The scary part is, Maisy's baking is so good, eating an entire cake, especially one that huge, was a lot easier than it should have been."

Pippa stared at Ernest in disbelief. She shook her head. "Ernest, you didn't have to—"

"I know," Ernest said shyly. "But I wanted to. It's actually pretty nice to have somewhere you really want to be instead of just always going where you're told."

Pippa's eyes glistened. For all the hard things that had happened since she'd left Ink Hollow, there were some good things too. Meeting Ernest was perhaps the brightest of them all. Pippa looked hard at Ernest. "Thank you," she said.

Ernest smiled and leaned gently back on the rail of the paddock when a loud *RIBBIT* burst forth at his feet. He yelped and shot straight up in the air, landing on top of the paddock gate. Perched beneath Ernest, planted on the delicate green grass, was the ugliest, wartiest, largest toad Pippa had ever seen. The toad blinked unbecomingly. It let out a small, unceremonious belch. It looked from Ernest to Pippa and back again.

Still clinging to the paddock gate, Ernest whispered loudly, "What do you think it wants?"

"I think it's a toad. I don't think it wants anything. I also don't think it understands words," Pippa whispered just as loudly.

The grass around the toad suddenly began to bend and ripple. Pippa's breath caught in her throat, and she lifted her head in time to see the Winds of Wanderly swirl near.

"Uh, Pippa . . ." Ernest began warily.

And then to Ernest's utter horror and Pippa's delight, the offensive toad exploded into a cloud of green dust. Almost immediately, the Winds of Wanderly lifted the dust up and transformed it into a letter. The Winds didn't linger but paused just long enough to brush gently against Pippa's cheek and tickle Ernest beneath his chin. Despite his bulging eyes, Ernest couldn't keep a few peals of laughter from spilling out.

When everything grew still and quiet, he finally managed to stutter, "D-did that really just happen? Were those the *real* Winds of Wanderly? And why did the toad have to explode?"

"That wasn't a real toad, Ernest," Pippa said. "I'm not sure why my fairy godmother's letters arrive like that, but her last one blew in as a bright green dragonfly. And as far as those being the real Winds of Wanderly . . . well, can you possibly imagine they were anything else?"

"No," Ernest said softly. But a moment later he furrowed his brow and said, "I am sort of curious about that letter though. If you ask me, ugly toads and buzzing dragonflies don't exactly scream 'fairy godmother.'"

Pippa, who had tried not to think too hard on the matter, didn't respond. Instead, she brought the letter near and read:

*Dear Pippa,*

*I received your last request to reduce the price of your wish, and guess what? Today just so happens to be Free Wishing Day. It's sort of a new thing here in the Merry Meadow, and we don't really like to advertise it. Still, based on what you said regarding those cockroaches, it sounds like you really need it.*

*If you're up for it, and if your rock heart hasn't slowed*

*you down completely (because I've heard sometimes that happens), I'll meet you at the South Peak of Triumph Mountain on Wednesday at sunset. Also, if you're wondering how I know you're stuck on Triumph Mountain, just remember that you SHOULDN'T KEEP SECRETS from a fairy godmother. On that note: don't be late! I'm pretty sure granting a wish for a Triumphant is against a bunch of the Chancellor's rules, but I won't tell if you won't.*

*Bibbidi Bobbidi Boo,*

*Fairy Dash*

Pippa's hand trembled. She lowered the letter and looked toward Ernest, but his eyes were glued to the toes of his shoes.

"Ernest, can you believe it?" Pippa said. "I—I never imagined the price of my wish would go from an impossible one hundred grubins to . . . free. Ernest, this means that—"

"You're leaving," Ernest said flatly.

As if all of Triumph Mountain were listening in, over Ernest's shoulder Pippa saw a green vine sprout up from the ground and wrap itself around the west wall of Castle Cressida. Castle Cressida sagged unwittingly beneath its weight.

"Now everything's going to go back to normal," Ernest said, kicking the toe of his shoe through the grass. "And since knowing you, I've decided that I don't really know if I like our normal anymore."

"What don't you like about it?" Pippa asked carefully. Normally Pippa wouldn't have had any problem laying out the very many concerns *she* had, but saddling Ernest with that, knowing she might not be around to help anymore, hardly seemed right.

"Do you think *any* of it is real?" Ernest burst out, his eyes searching Pippa.

"Yes," Pippa said solemnly. And then, "I think you're real."

Ernest let out a little sigh. "Well, of course I'm real. That's not exactly what I meant—"

"I know what you meant, Ernest. And I meant what I said too. You belong here at Peabody's Academy for the Triumphant because you're a *real* hero."

"I almost believe you," Ernest whispered. "And maybe that's why I really, really don't want you to go. Are you sure you can't stay? Even just a little while longer?"

For as much time as Pippa had spent dreaming about leaving Triumph Mountain, she'd never once considered that it wouldn't be easy. She laid her hand gently on Ernest's shoulder. "As much as you belong here, Ernest," she began, "I belong with my family. I can't imagine Free Wishing Day comes around more than once a year, and I'm afraid if I don't go now, I might never find my way back home." Pippa paused. Her eyes lingered on Ferdinand's empty paddock. "I do have one favor to ask though." When Ernest straightened up, she continued, "If—I mean *when*—Ferdinand gets back from the Capital, can you keep an eye on him for me? I know he's a fire horse, but he . . .

needs something. I haven't figured out exactly what yet, but I don't think it's something he can do on his own."

Ernest was silent for a moment, but then he nodded his head. "I don't think any of us were meant to do things alone," he said, and then he pushed away from Ferdinand's paddock and walked briskly through the grass.

He didn't stop to look back at Pippa.

"Where are you going, Ernest?" Pippa called out. "Aren't . . . aren't you going to say goodbye?"

Ernest, however, tilted his head toward the sky. "I'm headed to the South Peak, of course. It's nearly sunset now, and you heard that fairy lady. You're not supposed to be late."

"Wait, you're coming with me?" Pippa exclaimed, running to catch up with him.

"Pippa, I ate a four-foot-tall cake so I could stick around here with you. If I gave up my last chance to say goodbye, that'd just be plain dumb," Ernest said.

"I don't think I'll ever meet anyone else quite like you, Ernest," Pippa said. "I never dreamed it would take coming all the way up to Triumph Mountain to find a best friend, but now I can never say it wasn't worth it."

Ernest slid his glasses up along the bridge of his nose. "A best friend?" he echoed. "No one's ever said that about me before. But, Pippa"—he paused—"can people still be best friends if they never see each other?"

"I think that's what the 'best' is there for. It beats all, even things like distance—and authorized roles." But Pippa was hardly confident. If Mistress Peabody didn't want the Triumphants to befriend the Triumphant staff, what would she think about Ernest being friends with a commoner? Though Pippa had always been fairly content in her role as a commoner before, lately the flaws of the system felt unbearable.

Ernest, however, smiled bravely. "Beats all," he repeated. "I like the sound of that."

Fifteen minutes later, Pippa and Ernest scrambled up the last rocky ledge and emerged onto the flat plateau of the South Peak. The sun hung low in the sky, just about to slip beneath the surface of the perfectly tranquil Sapphire Sea. Pippa looked anxiously around, but she didn't see any sign of Fairy Dash.

Her stomach flip-flopped. She'd been so worried about Ernest, she'd felt so surprisingly torn about having others to leave behind as well—Maisy, Anastasia, Viola, Ferdinand, and even Castle Cressida—that she hadn't stopped to wonder if Fairy Dash's offer was the real deal.

What if Fairy Dash didn't show up?

Did Pippa *really* know that much about Fairy Dash other than, as Ernest pointed out, the peculiar manner in which her letters arrived? And now that Fairy Dash knew about her Triumphant status, was it possible she'd use it against Pippa? Pippa had trusted the Winds of Wanderly not to lead her astray, but did she really have a good reason other than what she assumed to be true about them? Pippa felt a hard prick of doubt deep in the center of her chest. She'd never questioned the Winds of Wanderly before, but maybe that was a mistake.

Pippa jumped at a rustling sound a few feet ahead. She smoothed a hand over her ponytail. She took a deep breath and prepared to meet Fairy Dash, when—

"Pippa?" Maisy said, popping out from behind the trunk of a nearby tree. "What are you and Ernest doing up here?"

At the sight of Maisy, Ernest grabbed ahold of his stomach and groaned again. Maisy frowned. "Oh no, Ernest! Do you have a stomachache? And here I was, planning to make you a fresh batch of lemon bars for dessert tonight," she said sweetly.

Poor Ernest turned a terrible shade of green but managed to say, "Thank you, Maisy. D-don't mind me. I'm sure I'll feel better by tonight."

Certain that Ernest was eager to change the subject, and a bit overcome with emotion, Pippa threw her arms around Maisy and said, "Something miraculous has happened, Maisy! I was so worried I wouldn't get to say goodbye to you, but you're here, and your timing couldn't be more perfect."

Maisy's eyes widened. She looked quickly in Ernest's direction, but he nodded glumly. "Wh-what do you mean, goodbye?"

"I received another letter from Fairy Dash. She's decided to grant my wish for free. And she's coming here. Right now—this very instant!"

Before Maisy could answer, however, Ernest jabbed his finger toward the horizon. "Uh, Maisy? Pippa? Not to interrupt, but what is THAT?" he cried, voice rising.

Pippa and Maisy both looked toward the setting sun. Shielding her eyes, Pippa drew in a sharp breath. "It looks like a . . . a . . . witch? You don't think Ms. Bonecrusher's come back to finish what she started, do you?"

Maisy, who had hastily drawn her wooden spoon, lowered it just slightly. "I can't imagine that's Ms. Bonecrusher. She seemed to be a pretty experienced witch, and, um, well, *look*," she said.

Look, indeed. The witch zipping toward them didn't seem to have an ounce of control over her broomstick. She zigzagged up, down, and all around. She flew in three complete circles, and when she finally broke out of the dizzying cycle, her broomstick forged ahead while she remained upside down!

"Wow," Ernest said, tilting his head to the side. "I guess I never realized how hard it is to ride a broomstick. Most witches make it look so easy. I almost feel a little sorry for this one."

"Well, I wouldn't feel too sorry for her, Ernest," Pippa said. "Mistress Peabody wouldn't have scheduled an authorized witch visit for the day of a field trip, and we're here all alone!"

"Um," Maisy began with her eyes still glued to the sky, "don't all witches wear hats and pointy boots? This one seems to be missing hers, and she's wearing a curiously short cape."

"Maisy, does that really seem like what we should be focusing on right now?" Ernest asked in a squeaky voice.

Maisy opened her mouth to reply but froze. As the witch drew near, they could hear her shouting from atop her broomstick. Though it was nothing more than a frantic "AHHHHHH" it was clear enough to tell that the witch was not a witch at all but rather a boy.

Maisy, Ernest, and Pippa stood and gawked just long enough to miss their chance to run. The boy's broomstick hurtled toward Triumph Mountain, but just as it was about to (crash) land, it launched him through the air with a mighty *thwack* of its bristles. The boy bounced and rolled a short distance before finally stumbling to his feet, his short cape flipped clean over his head. He wrestled mightily with the fabric before managing to uncover a thoroughly mussed-up head of hair and a shy half smile.

"One of you wouldn't happen to be Fairy Margaret, would you?" he said.

Pippa crossed her arms. "There's no Fairy Margaret here—"

"Pippa—" Maisy interjected.

"Hold on, Maisy, he could be dangerous," Pippa said, before turning back to the witch boy. "Fairy Dash is on her way, unless of course, you've wickedly intercepted her and now you're here to explain yourself?"

"Pippa—" Maisy said again.

The boy licked his lips. "No intercepting necessary, wicked or otherwise. But I did come to explain myself. You're . . . Pippa, right?" Though Pippa's expression was guarded, she nodded her head. A look of agony washed over the boy's face, and he awkwardly bent to one knee. "I owe you an apology. A big one. I'm your fairy godmother, otherwise known as . . . Olivanderella Dash. People have always called me Oliver though."

Ernest shook his head. "Wait a second. Didn't you just arrive on a broomstick? Fairy godmothers don't travel by broomstick!" And then Ernest turned to Maisy and Pippa and whispered, "We can totally still run."

But Pippa felt like she had cement blocks strapped to her feet. *This* was her fairy godmother? *This* was Olivanderella Dash? *This* was her one and only source of hope? A boy named Oliver?

Pippa was having great difficulty stringing her words together. "Did you—why would—where is—"

"PIPPA!" Maisy interrupted for a third time but in a voice louder than Pippa had ever heard her use before. Everyone turned to stare. Maisy sheepishly tucked a strand of hair behind her ears and inched forward the slightest bit. "Um, I was just trying to say that, if it's any help at all, Fairy Margaret *is* here. And she's me."

"*Fairy* Margaret?" Pippa asked.

"But your name's Maisy," Ernest cried in distress. "And you bake things. You don't . . . grant wishes. Unless . . ." Ernest blinked. He reached up and pinched his arm. "Do you think eating that giant cake affected more than just my stomach? Am I *imagining* all this?" he asked, voice rising.

Maisy lowered her eyes. "I would have told you both sooner,

but I didn't know if it was actually true. Not until I received a letter from Oliver. I've been waiting for my call to duty ever since my granny disappeared. That was over three years ago." She gulped. "And Maisy's short for Margaret."[29]

Pippa felt terrible. Had she truly been so wrapped up in her own problems, in her own heartache over missing her family, that she'd never thought to ask Maisy about herself? Her family, and her hopes and dreams? Pippa suddenly wanted to know everything. Alas, it was Oliver's turn to be confused.

"Wait," Oliver said, rising back up. "You two already know each other?" And then he turned to Maisy. "If you're friends with Pippa, why did she send me a letter in the first place? Why didn't she just ask you to help her get home?"

Maisy shook her head, confused, and then a look of realization washed over her face. "Oh no," she said. "Oh no. Oh no. Oh no!"

"What is it, Maisy? What's wrong?" Pippa asked.

"*You're* the friend Oliver wrote about in his letter," she said to Pippa.

Pippa glanced in Oliver's direction. "No offense, but I'd say 'friend' is a rather strong word. Especially since I haven't any clue why he's here or why he pretended to be my fairy god-mother, which seems pretty low, if you ask me."

Maisy paced back and forth. "He's here because he tried to

---

29. Perhaps Maisy's true identity comes as no surprise to you; perhaps you spotted the magic in Maisy from the first moment you met her. In which case, I applaud you. Observing tiny details is written into my job description, and even *I* failed to see this one coming.

fix it. He tried to send a letter to a real fairy godmother on your behalf, and he got . . . me."

"But you told me you *are* a real fairy godmother!" Oliver cried.

Ernest massaged his temples. "So confused, so confused, so confused," he muttered to himself.

"I thought this would be an easy first wish to grant—but this is a wish of the highest order! Pippa is here because another fairy godmother officially changed her role from commoner to Triumphant," Maisy explained to Oliver. "I told you in the letter I'm a newbie. I can't undo another fairy godmother's magic, and I certainly can't change someone's role without Council authorization! If I could have, I would have done so a long time ago."

Pippa lifted her head. "You would have?"

"Of course I would have. But I'm afraid this is now just a waste of everyone's time. I—I thought this was really my official call into the guild." She slipped her hand into her pocket and pulled out her trusty wooden spoon with a sad smile. "I guess I ought to just stick to what I'm good at, hmm?"

Pippa had a word or two to say about that, but Ernest spoke up first. He looked warily at Oliver. "I might really regret asking this question, but if you're not a witch, and you're not a fairy godmother . . . what are you?"

Oliver sucked in a rattling breath. "I'm supposed to be a magician."

"But then where's your hat?" Maisy said automatically.

"Exactly," Oliver said, pressing his eyes shut.

Maisy, Pippa, and Ernest exchanged glances. They had clearly struck a nerve, but was Oliver someone who deserved their sympathy? Pippa hadn't read a single story where trusting a magician brought about any good, not to mention her own misadventures with the two magicians in the Triumphant Training Forest a mere two nights ago.

"Oliver, if you planned a meeting for Maisy and me, why are you here too?" Pippa asked. "That broomstick ride didn't exactly look easy."

"Because there's something else I have to tell you. Something that no one else except the magicians know." Oliver took a deep breath. "The magicians are planning to do something on Triumph Mountain. Something that might harm the Triumphants and upset the roles in Wanderly." Oliver looked directly at Pippa. "And after reading the things you wrote about your family, about how much they mean to you, I knew at the very least I had to warn you."

Pippa's knees buckled. Upon receiving Fairy Dash's—or rather Oliver Dash's—frog letter, she had rushed to the South Peak, certain she was mere moments away from being reunited with her family. But so far nothing was turning out the way she'd hoped, and Oliver's grave tone frightened her.

"What does my family have to do with anything?" she asked, her voice low.

"The magicians are coming to Triumph Mountain on the

night of the Fall Picnic. And your families"—Oliver paused and looked at Ernest and Pippa—"are the special guests."

Pippa gasped. Here? Her family would actually be here? On Triumph Mountain? With *her*? But if Oliver was right, that also meant the magicians would be too.

A shiver went down Pippa's spine. She had suspected that the two magicians in the Triumphant Training Forest had a secret plan, but she never expected anything of this magnitude. Not to mention, the picnic was scheduled to take place in four days. They barely had any time! Pippa wanted to cry and cheer all at the same time because out of all the news she had received in the past two weeks, this was simultaneously the best and the very, very *worst*.

# FOURTEEN

# A Red Hot Rescue

The vast sky stretched overhead as far as Oliver could see. The salty scent of the Sapphire Sea swirled through his lungs, and the last rays of the sinking sun set everything aglow. Oliver could hardly believe he was no longer in the murky depths of the Swinging Swamp.

How strange it was that the one thing he had been so afraid of—leaving the swamp behind—had happened and he was *kind* of okay. True, the broomstick he'd swiped had tried to get rid of him on three separate occasions and nearly bucked him into a terribly jagged ravine, but that was hardly surprising considering the broomstick's wicked upbringing. And true, he was a bit flustered having had to explain himself in front of Pippa, Fairy Margaret—who maybe wasn't a fairy after all—and a boy named Ernest who didn't seem to care much for Oliver, but at least Oliver had done it. He'd delivered the terrible news, and now he could get on with . . . well, whatever there was for him to get on with.

Oliver looked over his shoulder for the naughty broomstick. He found it lying a few feet away in a pouting heap, and set off after it. Pippa followed along behind him.

"Oliver, you told us when the magicians are planning to arrive, but you haven't told us *what* exactly they're going to do. How could they possibly do something as drastic as upset the roles in Wanderly? Isn't that something only the Chancellor can do? Aren't the magicians sort of . . ."

"It's all right. You can say it," Oliver said. "It's the whole reason why all this has happened in the first place. I believe the word you're looking for is 'insignificant.'"

Pippa frowned. "That's not my opinion, but I'm afraid it is the Chancellor's."

"And that's what the magicians want to change. They're tired of being shoved out of the spotlight. They want to force the Chancellor, and everyone else, to see them differently. I don't know much, except Master Von Hollow's going to perform his showcase here, in front of an audience of Triumphants and their families, and the magicians have been packing up their belongings for weeks."

Ernest slid his glasses up along the bridge of his nose. "Um, what is a 'showcase' exactly?"

"A magic show," Oliver replied quickly.

"Ugh, magician magic!" Ernest said, wrinkling his nose. "I do *not* like those illusions! If Pippa and I didn't have the magic umbrellas Maisy passed out the night of the rainstorm, we would have been toast!"

"Umbrellas *I* passed out?" Maisy echoed. And then, with a hint of sparkle returning to her eyes, "Magic?"

Oliver frowned. "Magicians were here on Triumph Mountain?"

"I don't think they meant to be found," Pippa said. "Ernest and I bumped into them when we were out past bedtime searching for Ernest's lost goat. Some of the things they were talking about fit right in with what you're saying, Oliver. But with the picnic being only four days away, I haven't a clue how we're supposed to prepare for such a thing! Mistress Peabody never thinks anything can go wrong, and she'd never let us call off such a showy event."

Ernest's shoulders slumped. "Not to mention, the one thing that did manage to scare off those two magicians is on his way to the Chancellor as we speak."

Oliver bit his lip. He was trying very hard not to get tangled up in any of the Triumphants' problems. He had a terrible track record as a problem solver. Plus, it was one thing to warn Pippa, to tell her the truth to try to make up for his dishonesty, but wouldn't it be another thing to actively work *against* the magicians? Still, he couldn't help asking one more question.

"Who did you send away to the Chancellor?" Oliver asked.

Pippa swallowed hard. "My loyal companion, Ferdinand. He's a fire horse."

"Whoa," Oliver breathed out. "A real one? I—I didn't think those even existed anymore."

"Nobody did," Ernest said with a proud look in Pippa's direction. "It's been ages since a Triumphant was matched with a fire horse."

Oliver paused. He looked at Pippa. He'd clung to the Swinging Swamp for years without a hat, and Pippa had a *fire horse*? "You'd think that might be a sign that you're right where you're supposed to be," he said softly.

Pippa's eyes glistened. "I know. I get it. And I actually really like Ferdinand. But I already have a home. A home that I never wanted to leave behind."

"Maybe it's possible to have more than one home though. Maybe finding a new one doesn't always mean leaving the other behind. Maybe if it does, that can be okay too." Oliver's voice was thick. He shook his head. "I—I don't really know what I'm trying to say. . . ."

Suddenly, Pippa straightened up. "Oliver, you're a magician—"

"Actually"—Oliver pointed to his hatless head—"I'm not sure anyone else would agree with you on that."

But Pippa shook her head. "I think what *you* have to say about yourself means a whole lot more than some old hat."

*Some old hat?* Despite the peculiarity of the situation, Oliver almost smiled. He was certain he'd never once heard anyone refer to a magician's hat like that, and he was suddenly very glad to know Pippa.

"You also pulled a terrible trick on me that dashed every single hope I had of making my way back home," she said, hands planted firmly on her hips. "But now something more important has come up: saving Triumph Mountain and keeping our families safe." Pippa's expression softened just a bit. "And despite all those concerns I just listed, I still have a good feeling about you. Plus, you have a broomstick."

Beside Pippa, Ernest coughed. "A good *feeling*? Pippa, I'm not so sure that's the most reliable measure. Not to mention, did you see the way he flew in on that broomstick? Um, no offense," Ernest finished with a quick sideways glance in Oliver's direction.

"Ernest, I come from a family of ten," Pippa said. "That's ten people with ten very different personalities. I've become very good at judging people's intentions."

"Maybe so," Maisy said warily. "But that doesn't speak to the broomstick. I mean, it's sort of a miracle Oliver got here in one piece."

Pippa looked around matter-of-factly. "Yes, but does anyone see any other way off Triumph Mountain?"

Oliver would have jumped in sooner, but he was having great difficulty swallowing. He couldn't believe where this was headed. Pippa wanted *Oliver* to take her somewhere? On a witch's broomstick? He was a fugitive magician! He didn't have a clue what he planned to do next, but at the very least he knew he should remain out of sight. If he was caught with a runaway Triumphant, wouldn't he be in even *more* trouble? Then again, if Pippa was with him, he also wouldn't be alone. In all of his worrying over being kicked out of the Swinging Swamp, the alone part had seemed inescapable.

Oliver drew in a sharp breath. "You want me to take you back home, don't you?"

"Don't be ridiculous, Oliver. Unless my role is officially changed back to a commoner, I *can't* go home. I'd be accused of acting outside my role. And the last thing I need is a Council detention." Pippa paused. She lifted her chin in the air. Oliver didn't know much about girls, but they certainly seemed brave. "I need you to help me get Ferdinand back. We need him here on Triumph Mountain. I have a feeling we're going to need all of our loyal companions, but Ferdinand especially."

"But didn't you just say he's with the Chancellor?" Oliver asked.

"He's on his *way* to the Chancellor, accompanied by an officer of the Quill," Pippa explained. "If we hurry—and from the stories I've read, speed's not a problem for a broomstick—we can stop the carriage and free Ferdinand!"

With a determined nod, Maisy hustled toward the broomstick. "All right, then," she said. "Everybody pile on!"

"I—oh—loop the loops? Nosedives?" Ernest muttered. Nevertheless, he dragged his feet behind Maisy. "Why did today have to be *cake* day?"

Oliver, however, threw his hands up. "Wait!" he cried. "Just because something's the only option doesn't mean it's a good one." Oliver gestured at the broomstick. "I still don't know how to fly that thing, and I nearly met my End three separate times on the way here! Not to mention it's a *witch's* broomstick. Witches' broomsticks are meant to be ridden solo, and there's no way it can carry all four of us."

"But two of us can fit," Pippa said matter-of-factly. "Surely two kids are the same as one plump witch. Anyhow, you can't go without me. Ferdinand's flames might burn you."

"Are you even sure Ferdinand's flames won't burn *you*, Pippa?" Ernest asked gently.

Pippa frowned. "No, but I think I have to trust that they won't. I think that's part of having a loyal companion. So," Pippa said, turning to Oliver, "are you ready?"

Oliver wanted to tell Pippa that it sounded flat-out impossible. Then again, she was also the very same girl who, when whisked away to Peabody's Academy for the Triumphant, sent a letter to a fairy godmother via the Winds of Wanderly. Oliver didn't imagine there was anything Pippa wasn't willing to try when her family was involved. But that didn't mean he had to put himself at risk.

Oliver looked at Pippa. "You're asking me to take you on my broomstick, track down your fire horse, and free him from an officer of the Quill? What reason do I have for saying yes?"

"None," Pippa said. "And I bet most people would say no. I'm only asking because most people wouldn't have come here in the first place. But you did."

For most of Oliver's life he had felt like he never really had a choice. Things just happened to him. Things outside his control. But in this moment the choice was very clear: he could decide whether he wanted to keep going down an obviously risky path with Pippa or move safely ahead on his own.

But was anything *really* guaranteed to be safe? What did it mean to be safe anyhow?

"Okay," he heard someone say.

Pippa's eyes widened. A small smile tugged at the corners of her lips, and she plopped onto the broomstick, directly behind Oliver. That's when Oliver realized it had been him. *He* was the one who had said okay. And as Maisy wrung her hands, Ernest's jaw gaped, and the broomstick spat out an array of angry sparks, Pippa and Oliver lifted off Triumph Mountain, speeding away by the light of the stars just beginning to twinkle and shine.

It almost seems as if everything is going to be okay, doesn't it?

Oliver hadn't a clue if his stolen broomstick was trying to impress Pippa because she was a Triumphant or if it had merely succumbed to the humiliation of hauling around two kids, but so far it hadn't once tried to toss them off. And when it began to twist into a downward spiral of swizzles, a slight admonition from Pippa was all it took for it to start behaving again. The broomstick's tracking skills were also second to none. This was both 100 percent helpful and 100 percent scary, as Oliver began to wonder precisely how long it might take a witch to relocate her stolen broomstick by using another. This, of course, would also mean locating Oliver, and he couldn't imagine said witch would be very happy about what he'd done. But that was another problem for another day. At least he hoped.

"Are there any other magicians like you in the Swinging Swamp, Oliver?" Pippa asked.

Oliver shifted a bit uncomfortably. "Like me, how?" he said. But he was already certain the answer was no. If he had been anything like the other magicians, he never would have found himself in the position he was in.

"Ones who think what the magicians are planning is wrong."

"Oh." Oliver paused. "Did I *say* that I thought it was wrong?"

"You didn't have to. The very fact that you're trying to stop them says it all."

Oliver felt a wave of heat creep across his cheeks. He didn't want Pippa to think he was some kind of hero. If he had happened to secure a spot as Master Von Hollow's assistant the way he'd set out to, wouldn't Oliver have been *leading* the charge?

He shivered, wondering how he could have so easily wound up on a path that was beginning to seem more and more wrong.

Oliver's rock heart lightened the smallest bit. Though he could hardly believe it, maybe, possibly, some good had come of him never receiving his hat. Maybe it had helped him to see more clearly.

"It's not what you're thinking, Pippa. I would be like all the other magicians if they had let me. But they didn't; they kicked me out. I'm not even allowed to go back to the Swinging Swamp."

Pippa gasped. "Oliver, that—that's horrible. And it's all just because you don't have your hat?"

"Well, that and about a dozen other things I did wrong over the past two weeks. That's what got me writing to you in the first place. I asked you for the grubins because I wanted to be chosen as an assistant in Master Von Hollow's showcase—"

"You mean the one he's going to perform on the night of the picnic? You were going to be . . . a part of that?" Pippa asked, aghast.

Oliver nodded miserably. "At the time I had no idea it wasn't going to be held in the Swinging Swamp. I just knew that a role like that would help me get my hat. But I . . . didn't get it. I mean, I missed the auditions because I . . . well, after that I tried to sabotage the showcase because—"

"Because once you found out it was going to be on Triumph Mountain you knew it was wrong?" Pippa asked.

"Not quite," Oliver said sheepishly. "I wasn't trying to stop it, just postpone it. It wasn't until I found out *you* were on Triumph Mountain that I started to look at things . . . differently. Well, that and almost getting shipped off for a Council detention."

"For a *what*?" Pippa exclaimed. The broomstick must have been eavesdropping too because it shuddered dramatically, and Oliver gripped the handle tighter. "Oliver, you're a—fugitive? Why didn't you say anything? Do you know where we're headed right now?"

"Uh, I thought we were going to free your fire horse . . . Freddy, was it?"

"Ferdinand," Pippa corrected. "But what's important here is the officer of the Quill part. If he suspects who you are, he could haul *you* away!"

"Yep," Oliver said.

Pippa was beside herself. "But—but . . . Oliver, we're talking about a detention. I don't think I've heard of anyone ever being released from a detention."

"Honestly, Pippa, I'm not sure where I'm supposed to go anyway." They were the worst words Oliver could think of. The words that had been haunting him. The words that scared him. An admission that maybe there really was no place for him at all.

Pippa pressed her lips together. "Oliver, our lives are supposed to look like what we see in the storybooks, but have you ever read a story with an accidental character?"

"Um . . . no?" Oliver said, slightly puzzled.

"Right! A character can't write themselves. Someone else had to think of them; someone had to include them; a character never happens by mistake."

Oliver's eyes widened. The last time he'd heard the word "mistake," he had been sitting in Headmaster Razzle's office, and it was in reference to him.

Pippa tumbled on, "I don't think it's all that different in Wanderly. Oliver, just by being here, you already belong. From the first moment you opened up your eyes, you became a part of something bigger—there's a spot that only you were meant to fill. And even if your story is turning out differently than what you expected, maybe it's the Chancellor who's wrong. Maybe instead of trying to make our stories look like someone else's, instead we should see where our stories take us."

Oliver felt everything inside him squeeze tight.

Could all of that really be true?

But before he could respond, beneath them, the stolen broomstick froze. It began to twitch and wiggle. It skipped a few feet back as if winding up for something *big*.

"I think it's found Ferdinand," Oliver said. "Pippa, quick! You'd better hold—"

Oliver didn't have time to finish his sentence before the

broomstick made a nauseatingly sharp nosedive into the forest below. Tree boughs and tree trunks zipped by in a blur until the steady drum of horse hooves could be heard along with the deep hum of a man's voice. The broomstick jerked upward so that Pippa and Oliver slid right off the end and into a very prickly bush.

"It's dark out here," Pippa whispered.

"Are you scared?" Oliver asked with a shiver.

"No, I'm glad. It'll make what we're about to do easier." Pippa bent down and began scooping up dirt in both hands. She smeared dirt first on her cheeks and then on her chin. She reached up and tore a hole in the collar of her shirt and snagged the hem of her sleeves.

"What are you doing?" Oliver asked.

"Getting into character," she said with a grin. Before Oliver could wiggle away, she dipped her fingertip in the dirt and smeared a long, thick line across his forehead.

"Ugh!" Oliver said. "That's messy even by swamp standards."

Pippa raised her eyebrow. "Would you rather be recognized?" When Oliver shook his head, she continued, "Anyhow, here's the plan. I'll do my best to distract the officer while you sneak around back and undo the latch on Ferdinand's trailer. If we get separated, meet back here." Pippa reached for her now frayed sleeve and tore free a strip of fabric. She hastily tied it around one of the bush's branches.

"O-okay," Oliver said a bit uncertainly.

Pippa, however, was already making her way toward the dirt road. The carriage jostled closer, and she ran out in front of it. She waved her arms wildly to and fro, but the officer didn't stop, nor did he bother to pull up the reins and slow the horses.

"Outta the way!" he shouted.

"Please! Please stop, sir!" Pippa cried.

"OUTTA THE WAY!" the officer shouted again, but this time much louder.

Oliver anxiously ruffled his hair with his hands. This was madness! Oliver should have known Pippa wouldn't back down, but he hadn't anticipated the officer being just as stubborn. Officers of the Quill weren't supposed to run over young girls, but this was only Oliver's first day outside the Swinging Swamp. What did Oliver know, really?[30]

"STOP!" Pippa insisted.

Oliver couldn't tell whether the officer actually obliged or if his horses just had more sense than he did. Either way, the carriage slowed to a crawl, and the officer cracked his whip hard at the ground near Pippa's feet.

"I've got precious cargo, kid, and yer slowing me down!" the officer roared.

---

30. Oliver's intuition was spot-on. Officers of the Quill were most definitely *not* supposed to run over young girls. But it is hard to expect much from one whose job description was perhaps best described as a professional bully.

As Oliver was wondering what Pippa was going to do next, she turned and looked pointedly in his direction. The desperate "what are you waiting for?" look written on her face caused his knees to buckle. Oliver hadn't expected his part to come so quickly, and he was a mess of nerves! Still, Pippa was depending on him, and he couldn't let her down.

Oliver slipped toward the carriage. He heard the sound of the fire horse breathing and the heavy stamp of its hooves against the metal floor. Great big beads of sweat began to roll down Oliver's forehead as he envisioned a mane of flames scorching his skin.

"MOVE!" the officer barked at Pippa. Oliver heard the terrible crack of the whip again, and he knew he had to hurry. There simply wasn't time to be afraid.

Oliver took a deep breath, yanked on the latch with all his might, and swung the trailer door open. It let out an impossibly shrill creak! With a terrifying grunt, the officer leaped free of the driver's seat and tore around the back of the carriage.

"GO!" Pippa shouted. "RUN!"

Though Oliver didn't need to be told twice, Ferdinand seemed like he was half-awake. He also seemed awfully . . . small. So small that Oliver wondered fleetingly if he and Pippa had freed the right horse. But no horse deserved to be stuck with an officer of the Quill. Resolute, Oliver reached out and slapped Ferdinand on the backside the way he'd read about in storybooks. Reading, I'm delighted to report, hadn't steered him wrong, because Ferdinand reared to life!

He also, unfortunately, streaked right *past* Oliver and left him completely vulnerable to the fuming officer. Oliver, having narrowly escaped so many attempted pranks at Razzle's School for Meddlesome Boys, expertly ran a tight circle around the officer until the officer was hopelessly dizzy. By the time Oliver reached the designated meeting spot, the grumbling and disoriented officer had crawled back into the driver's seat and cracked his whip against the backs of the two horses that were far less fortunate than Ferdinand.

Oliver let out the breath he was holding and looked up at the sound of crunching leaves. It was Pippa, and she was holding tight to Ferdinand's lead rope. Her face glowed warm by the light of three flames that flickered on Ferdinand's mane and two that flickered on his tail. Though Ferdinand wasn't anything at all like what Oliver had pictured, though he almost looked like he'd fit right in with Master Von Hollow's herd of sorry-looking horses, Oliver wasn't a bit disappointed.

Pippa lifted her bare hand. She sucked up a tiny breath, pressed her eyes shut, and began combing her hand through Ferdinand's mane.

"Watch out!" Oliver cried.

But Pippa didn't jerk her hand away. Instead, she opened her eyes and grinned. "He's never had this many flames at one time.

I think Ferdinand's getting stronger, Oliver! And look—" Pippa cupped a flame in her hand. "We trust each other. His flames don't hurt. If I want to, I can even ride him!"

Oliver reached for the stolen broomstick. It huffed rudely at him. "Well, at least you won't have to put up with this rascal on the trip back to Triumph Mountain. You'll probably be glad to be rid of it."

Pippa lowered her eyes. "Not really, because that means you'll be leaving too. Anyhow, I'm not going back to Triumph Mountain right away. I'm going to the Capital first."

"The Capital? Pippa, we just rescued Ferdinand so he wouldn't have to go to the Capital!"

"Yes, but I'm sure I can hide him somewhere."

"It can't be that easy to hide a horse that's on *fire*!"

Pippa's face fell. "I know, but I just keep thinking that we're going to need help on the night of the picnic, that even if we have one solid, experienced Triumphant on our side, it might make all the difference. And the only person that could be is Ms. Bravo."

"Ms. Bravo the giant tamer?" Oliver asked. "Even I've heard of her."

Suddenly, Oliver's heart began to thump.

And his palms began to sweat.

He had already come to terms with the fact that soon Pippa would have to go, and he would be back to trying to figure out what to do next, but was it possible that this was his next step? With only four days remaining before the picnic, Pippa couldn't do everything that needed to be done. At least not all by herself. And then wouldn't Oliver's warning—and everything that followed after it—have been for nothing?

Oliver's voice trembled. "I can't ride Ferdinand back to Triumph Mountain, and if no one listened to me at Razzle's School for Meddlesome Boys, I can't imagine they'd listen to me at Peabody's Academy for the Triumphant, but. . . I think I can go to the Capital for you. If you want me to, I mean."

Pippa vehemently shook her head. "I can't ask you to do that, Oliver. Especially knowing that you're wanted for a Council detention. If anyone suspects anything, they'll seize you right there. It's too risky!"

"Going unnoticed is one of the things I'm best at. It's actually kind of nice to think that it might come in handy." Oliver paused. "Ms. Bravo's not, um, super tall or anything, is she?"

"You mean because of the giants?" Pippa asked. Oliver nodded, and she continued, "Not in the slightest. I'm pretty sure that's why her loyal companion's got wings." Pippa peeked in Oliver's direction. "You're, um, really serious about this, aren't you?"

"Dead," Oliver said with a nod.

Pippa winced. "Can we maybe not say the word 'dead'? Also, you have to promise that once you get to the Capital, if anything at all seems too dangerous, you'll get out of there as quickly as you can."

Oliver nodded, and Pippa quietly led Ferdinand over to a tree stump. She climbed on top of it, swinging her leg up and over Ferdinand's back. When she landed a bit sideways, Ferdinand whinnied and danced back and forth on his hooves. Pippa's eyes grew wide. For a moment, Oliver thought she might leap off, but instead she gritted her teeth and wrapped her fingers more tightly around Ferdinand's flaming mane.

"Easy boy," she said while stroking his side. "Nice and easy." After a moment she looked at Oliver. "You know, when you showed up on Triumph Mountain and said you were my fairy godmother, my confidence in the Winds of Wanderly nearly hit the bottom. But that's because I was forgetting what makes the Winds of Wanderly so grand. The Winds aren't like us. They do things we can't understand, they see things we can't know, and Oliver, I can't imagine there was any fairy godmother in all of Wanderly I needed more than you."

Oliver couldn't help looking away. "But you didn't get home to your family," he said.

"I haven't given up on that. But maybe what I really needed was to see that the story's not all about me. With what the magicians might be planning, it's not just my family at stake, Oliver. It's everyone's."

With that, Pippa dug her heels into Ferdinand's sides. She

rode off into the dark night. And no matter what she said, nothing would convince Oliver that Pippa wasn't a Triumphant through and through. Now if only he could apply that same confidence to the mission he had just signed up for.

# FIFTEEN

# Triumphant Training 101

The very next morning, a mere three days before the Annual
Fall Picnic, Pippa, Maisy, and Ernest sat in the dining hall
at Peabody's Academy for the Triumphant all squished into the
same giant throne. Even though it was eight thirty and the smells
of Maisy's decadent breakfast buffet were wafting through the
halls, all the other students, along with Mistress Peabody, were
fast asleep. Ernest said that field trips were so unusual, and
effort was so rarely expended atop Triumph Mountain, that
students often slept for an entire *day* after an event like the
Triumphant-Dragon Duel.

Pippa was just relieved that when she and Ferdinand galloped up to Castle Cressida's front lawn late the night before,
she had managed to send Ferdinand off to a place where no one
would dare to look for him: the Triumphant Training Forest.

Never mind that she had spent the remainder of the night worrying over how Oliver was faring at the Capital, she had also come upon a startling, however obvious, realization. Pippa was in a school full of Triumphants in training. Supposedly, Wanderly's next generation of heroes. Perhaps if they put forth just a little bit of effort, perhaps even if Ms. Bravo didn't come to their rescue, they could teach themselves the techniques necessary to keep the magicians at bay.

But all of that had seemed much more doable while half-asleep.

And before Pippa took even another breath, there was something that had to come first.

"Maisy," Pippa began. "Was your granny a . . . fairy godmother too?"

Maisy's face paled. She looked down at her hands folded carefully in her lap. Finally, with her voice trembling, she answered, "Yes. But if you're wondering whether she taught me anything—"

"No," Pippa said, shaking her head. "I don't care about that, Maisy. I just want to know more about you. I only wish I would have asked sooner."

Ernest cleared his throat as if maybe there was a *slightly* better time for this, but he slumped right back into the throne at a pointed look from Pippa.

"All right, then," Maisy said, trying unsuccessfully to tuck her hair behind her ears. "Well, um, you said it. Gran was—*is*—a fairy godmother, and also the one who raised me. Like every fairy, she got her start in the Merry Meadow, but when the Chancellor announced that fairy godmothers were forbidden to grant anyone's wishes but a commoner's, she fled to Triumph Mountain. She said it was ridiculous to think that a hero didn't need help from time to time, and when they did, she wanted to be there to provide it. But one day the Quill . . . came for her."

Maisy paused, her face grim. "She—she made me run out into the forest, and I hid. She made me promise that if she didn't return in a week that I would knock on the door of Castle Cressida and ask for a job in the kitchen, but all I really wish is that I wouldn't have left her that day. Granny said I could never tell anyone who I really am, but it's all I think about. I want to keep doing the work that Granny started. And when I get my magic, I want to free her first of all. . . ." Maisy's voice trailed off. "I guess now you know why that letter from Oliver got me so excited. I thought it was my call to duty. I thought it was time for me to be a fairy godmother."

As Maisy ducked her head to dab at her eyes, Pippa laid her hand gently on Maisy's arm. "Maisy, what makes you so certain that it's *not* time? Just think, your granny left the Merry Meadow to help Triumphants, and you're right here with us, inside Castle Cressida."

"Yeah, but I'm not doing anything to make a difference!"

"But maybe not all magic works instantly. Maybe some

transformations take time," Pippa said. "Especially the lasting ones."

Maisy frowned. She dipped her hand into her apron pocket and pulled out her wooden cooking spoon. "Does it sound dumb that, for once, I'd just like to twirl a magic wand in the air and have magic—*real* magic—fly off it?"

Ernest gasped. "Oh my goodness, I knew something wasn't normal about those lemon bars!"

Maisy put her hands on her hips. "Ernest, you always said those lemon bars were your favorites."

"Yes," Ernest said with a wide-eyed glance at Maisy's cooking spoon, "but that was before I knew why they tasted so good. Maisy, you're not just a good baker, you're a *magical* baker!"

"Ernest, that's genius!" Pippa cried. She whirled around to face Maisy. "That's why your butterscotch candies always make me feel better; that's why those cockroaches from the Chest of Unnecessaries followed the scent from your spoon. You've been wielding a magic wand all this time, and you didn't even know it! Maisy, what if you already *are* the fairy godmother you want to be? What if you have been for a long time?"

"But—but that's impossible . . . isn't it?" Maisy asked.

"Well, it *is* Wanderly," Ernest said. "Impossible things happen here all the time."

"True," Maisy said, taking a deep breath. "But even if I am somehow performing magic, I haven't been officially authorized by the Council."

Pippa shrugged. "So maybe there are some things you can't do—but there are plenty of other things you can," she finished with a grin.

Maisy leaped suddenly out of the throne. She gazed upon her trusty wooden spoon, her eyes shining. "I never imagined. I never would have thought. Magic in something so ordinary!" Maisy turned to run out of the dining hall, but then whirled back around. "I hope you don't mind my running off, but I have about one million ideas for new recipes. And all of them have very much to do with defending Triumph Mountain against a group of sneaky magicians."

Ernest let out a whoop. "Now this is something I can firmly get behind!" he said before a slight shadow fell across his face. "Just, maybe . . . no cakes. It's still a little too soon for cakes."

Marveling that Maisy would return to the very same kitchen but with a completely new perspective, Pippa couldn't have been happier for her friend. But she also had a big task ahead of her.

Turning toward Ernest, Pippa said, "We've only got three days until the magicians' showcase. If the other students sleep all day, that'll leave us with just two. We've got to get them up, Ernest."

Ernest frowned, but then his eyes lit up. "I think I've got an idea! Say, where do you want everybody to meet?"

Pippa thought for a moment. She glanced down at the two trunks of training supplies she'd cobbled together earlier that morning when she'd first told Maisy and Ernest about her plan.

She certainly didn't have any business teaching Triumphant classes, but for the time being she would have to set all that aside and just go with it.

Pippa's head snapped up when the curtains in the dining hall began to wriggle in unison. The warm glow of a fire spontaneously ignited in the hearth, and the walls of Castle Cressida began to twitch. Pippa's eyes were drawn up toward the tightly wound tapestries near the ceiling—the ones Pippa had been certain held secrets. They began to flutter as if being stirred awake, and in one sudden whirling gust, they all flew open.

Pippa and Ernest gasped.

The tapestries were exquisite.

And they all featured the same thing: Triumphants side by side with their loyal companions. Pippa had never seen so many bright, bold, and joyous images. One girl was sailing across a murky river on the back of a grinning crocodile. One boy was nestled in the curve of an enormous elephant's trunk. Another girl was leaping across a treacherous ravine with a very dapper grasshopper leaping jubilantly alongside her. It was exactly what Pippa needed to see.

"Thank you, Castle Cressida," she said softly. She turned to Ernest. "We shall be meeting at the Loyal Companions' Barn."

Without missing a beat, Ernest threw back his head and shouted, "AWARD CEREMONY AT THE LOYAL COMPANIONS' BARN IN FIVE MINUTES! AWARD CEREMONY!"

"Wait? An award ceremony? An award ceremony for what?" Pippa asked.

"Doesn't matter," Ernest said, moving out toward Castle Cressida's main entry. "Prize winning is a way of life on Triumph Mountain. It's what we're best at. Some kids' drawers are stuffed so full of prizes they can't even properly shut them."

Pippa followed along behind him. "But you didn't even say what it was for. Is it meaningful to win a prize for, say, Best Garden, if you don't even tend a garden?"

Ernest shrugged. "Sure, why not? Anyways, I'd give it one, two, three—"

Ernest was interrupted by the sound of a door banging open and a fast and furious pounding of footsteps. The Triumphants streamed down the staircase. Some skipped two and three stairs at a time, others were still pulling on their royal-blue-and-gold-striped socks, and at least two or three of the younger ones hadn't even fully opened their eyes. Prudence Bumble was nearly dragging a very sleepy-looking Bernard down the hallway.

"Come on, Bernard!" she said in a low voice. "These are the sorts of things you can't be late for!"

It wasn't long, however, before she gave up on Bernard, relinquishing his hand and pushing several Triumphants out of the way until she was at the very front of the pack. When she spied Pippa and Ernest waiting in the entryway of Castle Cressida, her eyes narrowed.

"Why did you get to make the announcement, Ernest? And

why are the both of you already up and dressed? Where's Mistress Peabody?" Prudence demanded.

Pippa felt her pulse race. She couldn't imagine she would ever win Prudence over to any plan she'd come up with, but she couldn't have Prudence disband the whole operation before it even had a chance to begin.

"Ernest and I didn't go to the Dragon Duel, remember? Yesterday was just another ordinary day for us." Pippa's breath caught in her throat, because zipping around on a wicked witch's broomstick with a fugitive magician was hardly what she'd call "normal." "And Mistress Peabody's already at the Loyal Companions' Barn."

"Oh yes, you and Ernest were left behind," Prudence said. "That's too bad for you because it was the most exciting Dragon Duel yet."

Ernest perked up. "Really? Was the dragon especially ferocious? Did this one breathe fire? Did you, um, *see* the duel?"

Prudence leaned forward. She lowered her voice dramatically. "Not a single moment. How could we when the dragon was so wickedly sneaky? The dragon tried to lure Triumphant Victoria Golden in by playing dead!"

"It would have been sort of nice to see it move though. Even just once," Connor, one of the older boys, said. "I got so bored of eating candied walnuts I think I spent most of the duel counting the number of people in the audience wearing a hat."

"Five hundred and forty-nine," Anastasia piped up. "At least in the section we were sitting in. And it's funny how a dragon starts to look like a craggy mountain when it doesn't move for such a long time. I almost forgot it was there."

"Well, it was lucky for us Ms. Golden stuck it out. With a creature that big, imagine what could have gone wrong if she hadn't?" Prudence said with a shiver.

The still-sleepy Triumphant children managed to chime in with a half-hearted chorus of "Yep" and "Sure thing," before Pippa interrupted, "Thanks for, um, filling us in, but it's probably not a good idea to keep Mistress Peabody waiting."

A reinvigorated Prudence surged through the door while the other Triumphant children followed along behind her. As the group charged across the lawn, Pippa and Ernest—laden with the two large trunks of training supplies—lagged just slightly behind. Pippa's heart quickened when she saw that Castle Cressida had already managed to toss off yesterday's predatory vine. Pippa didn't know when she had become so invested in Castle Cressida's apparent comeback, except that it seemed important somehow, as if in Castle Cressida making a comeback, other things on Triumph Mountain could make a comeback too.

The Triumphants continued their trek, sliding down the hill and racing across the peaceful valley until they skidded to a breathless halt in front of the barn doors. They looked from left to right. The loyal companions mulling about in the outside paddocks—including Bob, who trilled obnoxiously—looked curiously in their direction.

Prudence marched purposefully toward the barn door. She wrapped her hand around the metal handle and gave it a good tug. It opened with a loud creak, but other than the shuffling and snuffling sound of the animals, all was quiet. She leaned her head all the way in and then whirled around with an accusatory look in Pippa's direction.

"Mistress Peabody isn't here!" she said with a toss of her head.

Pippa's breath rattled in her chest. This was it. This was where she—the most reluctant Triumphant of them all—tried to motivate a group of chronic winners to prepare for the riskiest, and perhaps most important, event of their lives.

"You're right, Prudence. Mistress Peabody wasn't actually the one who wanted us to meet here," she began. "It was me."

The Triumphants began to whisper among themselves. Prudence crossed her arms hard against her chest, and Viola asked, "Pippa give prizes? Prizes in there?" She pointed to the two big trunks sandwiched between Pippa and Ernest.

"No," Pippa said regretfully, "I don't have any prizes to give. But I do have something to share that's much more important."

Bernard, who was finally awake by that time, said, "Ha! My father says to always keep your eye on the prize. If you're telling me there aren't any prizes here, then I'm going back to bed!"

Bernard whirled around on his heel but froze when Pippa said, "How about your role as a hero? How about your family? Do those matter as much as a prize?" Pippa swallowed and continued on, "I know this is going to be hard to believe, but

I found out that the magicians of the Swinging Swamp are planning to do something terrible here on the night of the Fall Picnic. Even worse, I found out that the special guests Mistress Peabody's been keeping a secret are our families!"

Though most of the Triumphants' faces were awash with confusion, concern, and even a little bit of fear, Prudence Bumble laughed. Loudly.

"The magicians? The magicians of the *Swinging Swamp*? Are you kidding us, Pippa? Everyone knows they're a bunch of washed-up wannabes! The magicians of the Swinging Swamp can't even control their overgrown population of toads. I don't know where you heard something so ridiculous, but honestly, who cares?"

Pippa shook her head. "Everyone thinks they're a joke because that's how the Chancellor treats them. But they've got magic, Prudence. Real magic. And they're not afraid to use it." Pippa paused and glanced in Ernest's direction. "The other night Ernest and I snuck out of Castle Cressida in search of Leonardo. We went looking for him in the Triumphant Training Forest"— Pippa paused as a few Triumphants shuddered—"and we bumped into two magicians who were staking the place out—"

"D-did they show you their permit, Pippa? Don't those with villainous tendencies have to have a permit to be on Triumph Mountain?" Anastasia whispered.

"They didn't have a permit, and they didn't care. That's what I'm trying to tell you. We've all grown so dependent on the

Chancellor's rules to keep us safe, but if the citizens of Wanderly stop following the rules, everything could fall apart."

"But we're heroes! Nobody can defeat a Triumphant!" nine-year-old Simon proudly exclaimed.

Pippa drew in a sharp breath. She spoke carefully and deliberately. "Are we?" she said. "Are we *really*?"

Her words settled heavily on each of their shoulders. No one in all of Wanderly had ever dared to say such a thing.[31]

Prudence's eyes narrowed. "If the magicians are so dangerous, what exactly are they planning to do on the night of the picnic?"

"I'm not sure," Pippa said. "But isn't it better to be safe than sorry?"

Prudence scoffed. "Safe? But you just said that we're not *real* heroes. If that's true, then why call all of us out here if we're so helpless?"

"Because I don't think we have to be. I know we only have three days. I know that's not much time. But I still think there's a reason why we're here. And I think if we practice, and"—Pippa paused and looked right at Prudence—"if we work together, I think we can protect Triumph Mountain."

Standing beside Prudence, Bernard wrinkled his nose.

---

31. I bet there are all sorts of rules against a book choosing a favorite part, but I simply cannot help it. It is this one. Right here. Because of all the things the Triumphants were so desperately in need of, truth was perhaps the most important of them all. And Pippa saw it clearly.

"Practice?" he said as if the word itself left a bad taste in his mouth. "Practice what?"

But Prudence had already linked her arm through his. She tugged Bernard backward in the direction of Castle Cressida. "*We're* not going to practice anything. Pippa is a homesick commoner without an ounce of sense. Just because she wants to make a fool of herself at the Fall Picnic in front of our families and perhaps even the Chancellor himself, doesn't mean we need to join the spectacle. Keep at it though, Pippa. You might find your way out of here after all—in the form of a Council detention!"

Several of the other Triumphants gasped. And as if Pippa already had a sentence hanging over her head, at least half of them hurried to catch up with Bernard and Prudence, some brushing by Pippa with wary glances and others not bothering to make eye contact at all.

Once they were gone, Pippa turned to those remaining. She forced a smile onto her face. Pippa wasn't an overly smiley person, but she figured Ms. Bravo would smile at a moment like this, and that was the only real hero she had as an example. Almost as soon as the thought entered her mind, however, Pippa knew it wasn't true. In fact, she had grown up surrounded by heroes.

For the past eleven years, hadn't her mother swept her into the warm fortress of her arms and kissed away nearly every single one of her tears? Hadn't her father rushed to her side when dark thoughts invaded her dreams at night and replaced them with words that burned bright like lanterns? Hadn't the triplets' antics chased away the sort of boredom that could leave every day feeling utterly the same? Hadn't Louisa and Jane forced her to stop and muse over things as fanciful as fiery sunsets and roses in bloom only to walk away full of quiet wonder? Hadn't industrious Charlie, with both pockets and plans full of cogs, fastenings, and springs, helped her appreciate order and the essential role of each very small thing in the workings of the very large things? And hadn't baby Rose, who had little more to offer than her cries and the occasional coo, taught Pippa that sometimes it's in the act of sacrifice that love flourishes the most?

And for the first time since arriving at Peabody's Academy for the Triumphant, Pippa could almost imagine a place for herself. The Chancellor held heroes out to be the ones with the grandest and the most victories, but maybe it was possible to be a hero in the small things too. Maybe that even mattered just as much. And if that were true, perhaps the number of heroes and happy endings in Wanderly weren't nearly so limited as the Chancellor claimed. Maybe a happy ending could be found by anyone who knew how to look for it. Wouldn't that be something?

Pippa looked carefully at the six remaining Triumphants: curious Viola, cautious Anastasia, enthusiastic Simon, forthright Connor, contemplative Winnie, and Ernest. Always Ernest. He nodded at her encouragingly.

Though her hands were shaking a bit, Pippa bent toward the

two trunks at her feet and flipped them open. One trunk was filled to the brim with umbrellas. The other was overflowing with tomatoes. "I suppose before we get started, I ought to pass out the materials I brought. Come and help yourself. There's plenty."

The Triumphants shuffled closer, a bit uncertainly. They reached into the trunks and gingerly began picking at the items. Simon grabbed hold of a tomato and brought it closer for inspection. He squeezed it so hard, however, that it popped out of his grasp and crashed onto the ground in a juicy explosion.

"Whoops!" he exclaimed, quickly stuffing his hands behind his back, because Mistress Peabody often impressed on the children the importance of keeping a pristine appearance.

But Pippa clapped her hands. "Great job, Simon! You've already discovered one of the tomato's best features. They're super messy."

"Wait, we want messy?" Anastasia said with a raise of her eyebrow.

"Yes. One of the things the magicians hate most about where they live is how messy it is. So I figure if they experience the same mess, and maybe worse, here on Triumph Mountain, they won't want anything to do with us. Also, and I speak from experience because I have triplet brothers back home, it's really hard to see when someone lobs food at your face. So if you find yourself in a pinch and a magician's coming right for you, aim for the eyes!"

The other Triumphants began to nod slowly, and Winnie, a quiet teenager who Pippa often saw reading stories to the younger Triumphants, cleared her throat. "You said earlier the magicians have magic they're not afraid to use—"

Upon hearing Winnie's words, Viola sprinted wide-eyed toward Pippa, and Pippa scooped her up and into her arms. The little girl wrapped her arms tightly around Pippa's neck, and in a rush Pippa remembered what it felt like to take care of someone again. It was strange how much easier it was to be brave for someone else and not just for herself.

Winnie's face flushed. "I'm sorry, Viola. I didn't mean to scare you. I just want to be the most prepared that we can be. Is that okay with you?" When Viola nodded, Winnie met Pippa's gaze and continued, "So what kind of magic is it, exactly?"

"Illusions," Pippa said definitively. "Magicians can also make themselves and objects that fit within their hats vanish, but we don't need to worry about either of those things. The illusions are pretty awful, though. In a blink of an eye, magicians can make the scariest creatures you can imagine appear. But that's where these come in." Pippa reached down and snatched up an umbrella. She twirled it in the air with a grin. "Magic umbrellas."

Connor eyed the umbrella skeptically. "Wait, aren't those the same umbrellas left out for us in the dining hall during the rainstorm?"

"Yes—and the very same umbrellas that Ernest and I used to

destroy the illusions the magicians cast at us in the Triumphant Training Forest."

"You saw magicians' illusions and got *chased* by them, Pippa?" Anastasia said with her hand against her heart.

"That's how I know this works. You simply position it like a shield." Pippa pushed on the umbrella. It opened with a flourish while the other Triumphants took a few shuffling steps back. "Jab and . . . presto! Magic."

"But I thought Triumphants weren't supposed to have magic?" Simon said, tilting his head to the side. "I thought that stuff was just for witches, wizards, magicians, and fairy godmothers."

"In Wanderly, when magic makes up its mind, I don't suppose it's something anyone can stop. Not even the Chancellor." Pippa took a deep breath before continuing, "The tomatoes and umbrellas should help, but our best training will come from our loyal companions."

Before the words were even out of Pippa's mouth, Anastasia began wringing her hands, tears glistened in her eyes.

"What is it, Anastasia?" Pippa asked. "What's wrong?"

Anastasia shook her head miserably. "I don't want Whisper to hear me."

Pippa looked around for Anastasia's loyal companion marmoset but didn't see him anywhere. "I think Whisper's in the barn. Did something happen to him?"

"No, but surely something will!" she wailed. "Oh, Pippa, he's not like your fire horse. He's not designed for things like battles and magic and scary magicians. He-he'll probably go and hide. I always worried one day something like this might happen."

Pippa thought back to the first day she met Ferdinand—at the time he certainly hadn't looked like he was designed for any of the things Anastasia listed either. But that was because Pippa just hadn't seen him yet for what he really was and what he was becoming.

"What if this is what Whisper's been waiting for?" Pippa began. "What if Whisper wants you to see what he and you are both capable of? The Chancellor tries to make us all fit into the same mold of hero, but it's the differences that make us stronger. Whisper doesn't need to be like Ferdinand. He just needs to be like Whisper."

"But Whisper's so quiet," Anastasia said, brow furrowed.

"That's good for moving about undetected," Pippa said with a nod. "Maybe he can help us pass along important messages."

Anastasia looked right at Pippa. "But he gets scared and hides in the trees sometimes!"

"Perfect," Pippa said. "He can spy on the magicians. He'll have a top-level view of everything and can help us strategize."

Anastasia's expression was thoughtful. "That's what you *really* think about Whisper?" she asked. "You're not . . . disappointed in him?"

Pippa locked eyes with Anastasia. "Never."

Beside Anastasia, Simon piped up, "My turn! My turn! Tell

me what you think Rocky can do in the battle!" he said.

While Pippa set about thinking of the very many attributes of a loyal companion tortoise, the rest of the Triumphants gathered close to one another, for once thinking about and discovering not all that they were supposed to be but what they maybe already were. And a short distance behind them, perched on the tallest point of Triumph Mountain, Castle Cressida swelled with pride. The tops of its spires very nearly tickled the bellies of the marshmallow clouds, in the way they did once a long, long time ago.

# THE MOST WANTED MAGICIAN IN ALL OF WANDERLY

Merely a few broomstick sprints away from the place where the thick green forests of Wanderly gave way to the gravel roads leading into the kingdom's Capital, Oliver froze at the shrill sound of a witch's cackle.

He would have gladly pretended that he was just being paranoid, except the stolen broomstick beneath him skidded to a sudden halt. It flipped decidedly around. And before Oliver could sputter a word, it zipped away from the Capital and toward the witch's cackle!

Oliver jabbed his feet wildly in the air. He leaned all the way to one side, hoping to throw the broomstick off balance so that it would be forced to turn around. But the broomstick forged ahead without batting a single bristle. The only moment it slowed even a smidge was when the cackling witch burst through a patch of dense foliage and soared into view.

Oliver nearly fell off the broomstick.

Even from a distance, he would recognize that witch anywhere.

Any wicked witch would have been bad news, but did it really have to be Helga Hookeye? The witch with the plethora of potions, namely, the Black Wreath? The witch who had mercilessly turned Oliver into a piglet and caused him to miss the auditions for Master Von Hollow's showcase?

Out of all the broomsticks Oliver could have snatched from the Twisted Goblet, why did he have to choose hers?

Helga barreled closer. If she recognized Oliver as her erstwhile pork dinner, she didn't let on. She only seemed to have eyes for her missing broomstick. "Oh, Creeeeep-er!" Helga shrieked. "Creeep-er!"

Beneath Oliver, the broomstick heaved a tiny sigh before continuing in Helga's direction but with slightly less oomph.

Oliver's pulse quickened. If there was one thing he knew how to recognize it was weary reluctance. How many times had *he* been ordered around with not one other choice except obedience? Perhaps here now was a chance for the both of them.

Oliver leaned down toward the broomstick. "Please," he said urgently. "We can't go that way! Do you know what will happen to me if we do? Not to mention, *Creeper*? Is that really what your witch calls you? Do you actually like that name?"

The broomstick halted. It almost seemed to be thinking.

Oliver barreled on while he had the chance. "Look, you don't have to go back to Helga if you don't want to. I know that's what you're used to, but if you'd like, you can stay with me instead."

The broomstick recoiled as if it found that proposition the most offensive of all. And then it promptly resumed its forward progress.

"Wait!" Oliver cried. "You're right. That would never work, would it? You like magic stuff. Well, wicked stuff, really, and I don't think I'm great at either of those. But maybe if you help me get to the Capital, maybe after that I can . . . set you free?"

At the sound of the word "free," the broomstick fluttered. Helga, meanwhile, zoomed closer. She cackled loud enough to rustle the leaves on the trees. To Oliver's horror, she lifted her finger in the air and pointed right at him.

"She's close enough to do magic now!" Oliver cried. "You have to decide! Do you want to stay with Helga or do you trust me to set you free?"

But the broomstick continued to hover in place. A spray of crackling sparks flew off Helga's fingers, first to Oliver's right and then to his left, and all Oliver could do was duck.

Panicked, Oliver resorted to knocking on the broomstick's handle. "Hello? Hello, down there? Can you please move? Even a few feet would help because—AHHH!"

Helga nosed her broomstick mere inches from Oliver and grabbed him by the shoulder! Oliver still didn't know how he survived his first encounter with Helga, and it seemed terribly unfair to have a second go-around with her. As if reading Oliver's mind, a flash of recognition ignited in Helga's eyes.

"My piglet!" she exclaimed. "You're the little pip-squeak who caused me all that trouble and left me with a hankering for pork chops!" She rubbed her hands together like a giddy child. "Ooooh, looks like it's my lucky day!"

With that, Helga sprang entirely free of the broomstick she was riding—and leaped onto Oliver's.

But the weight was too much for the conflicted broomstick. It creaked and it groaned in agony. It began to spiral wildly downward. Oliver and Helga slid off, barely snatching the handle by their fingertips, swinging through the air below the broom. Helga made nasty faces at Oliver while Oliver tried, unsuccessfully, not to look down at the ground.

"The broomstick's not strong enough for the both of us!" Oliver cried.

"That's right! And that's why you're gettin' off!" Helga thrust her witchy boot at Oliver with all her might. The impact of her kick broke Oliver's grip on the broomstick. He tumbled wildly through the air, clawing at anything he could find, but the only thing he managed to grab ahold of was the strap on Helga's witchy knapsack.

Helga hissed her displeasure. But, fortunately for Oliver, absent releasing her grip on the broom's handle, there wasn't a thing she could do except try to bump Oliver off with an awkward swinging motion of her hips. Oliver knew the strap wouldn't hold for long. He reached up his free hand and blindly set to rummaging about inside the knapsack, hoping to find something useful. But with each potion Oliver pulled free, his hopes sank. Stench of Ogre Feet, Excessively Long Hair Growth, and Apple Redux weren't what he had in mind.

*Riiiiiip!* The knapsack handle hung from Helga's shoulder by a single thread. It was ready to break at any moment, and Helga was trying to hurry it along by grating her pointy teeth against it. Oliver grabbed one last potion but didn't have time to read the label before the strap snapped in two. With a celebratory cackle from Helga, Oliver plummeted helplessly toward the ground, arms swimming through the air.

Its load suddenly lightened, the broomstick bucked wildly about. Helga tried to whack it into submission, but the broomstick managed to toss her off into the sharp and pokey branches of a nearby tree.

The broomstick plunged toward a still falling Oliver. It swept beneath him. It rescued him with mere inches to spare, and with an *oof* and a wild twirl, together the two of them soared past a cursing, spitting Helga.

"Come back here, you dumb piece of wood! Come back here, you little pork ball! Give me back my potion!"

But Oliver and the broomstick kept right on going. Oliver didn't even pause to read the label of the potion he'd stuffed into his pocket but kept his eyes on the horizon, determined to put as much distance between him and Helga as possible. When the last shrill notes of her shrieking faded into the distance, Oliver bent toward the broomstick and said, "Thanks for what you did back there, Creep—"

Oliver paused. Despite their rather rocky start, it hardly seemed polite to call the broomstick *Creeper*. So, he instead cleared his throat and said brightly, "Say, did you ever think about getting a new name?"

Still gliding along, the broomstick perked up with mild interest.

"All right, then," Oliver said. "How about Tom?"

The broomstick hacked its displeasure.

"Whoa. Okay, not Tom. Maybe you're looking for something more . . . epic. How about Champion?"

But the broomstick didn't seem to like that either, shaking its handle vigorously from side to side.

Oliver frowned. "I guess it is a bit braggy, but I didn't think you'd mind that sort of thing. Um, well, you're used to being around witches. Maybe you want something with teeth. How about *Nightmare*?"

The broomstick rolled to a stop, which Oliver had the distinct sense was akin to an eye roll. "You certainly are picky," Oliver muttered. But when he looked around for inspiration, he thought about where the broomstick had come from and where it might want to go. "Forrest," Oliver breathed out. "How about Forrest?"

And the broomstick shivered down to its very last bristle.

"Forrest, it is," Oliver said. "And before you know it, that's exactly where you'll be. Or anywhere else you want to go, actually. But first we've got to make it in and out of the Capital. I'll take you inside with me, but you have to promise no flying."

The broomstick jerked his handle in indignation, but Oliver insisted, "I mean it. If a citizen spots a boy flying on a broomstick, the Quill will be questioning us in half a second. Once we get through those gates, you've got one job and one job only: do what your ordinary comrades do."

Forrest tilted his handle questioningly in the air, and Oliver couldn't suppress a grin. "Sweep, of course!"

Without missing a beat, Forrest promptly dove fifteen heart-pounding feet through the air.

"Hey!" Oliver cried. "You didn't even give me any warning!"

Forrest gleefully did it *again*.

Oliver wondered why making a deal with a wicked witch's broomstick had seemed like such a good idea in the first place. Maybe he ought to have given Helga her broomstick back when he had the chance.

Only a few minutes later, Oliver and Forrest swept into the steady stream of traffic pouring through the gated entry of the Capital.

It was busier and more bustling than anything Oliver had

imagined. Citizens of all shapes, sizes, and roles could be found. Commoners plodded forward by foot and by cart. A few witches zoomed by on broomsticks; one wizard could be seen puttering about high in the sky, fully powered by boot;[32] and a trio of rosy-cheeked fairy godmothers soared through the air with their wands lifted high. There were, of course, no magicians popping in or out while holding tight to the brims of their hats, because they had been boycotting the Chancellor's offensive list of "suggested nuisance activities" for quite some time and refused to be coerced into completing even one of them. The Chancellor, of course, hadn't yet seemed to notice the magicians' absence.

Just inside the gates was a prominent sign with four golden arrows pointing in different directions. The first pointed toward the "Official Library."[33] The second pointed toward "Council Business." The third pointed toward "The Hub." And the final had been left, curiously, blank.

Oliver peered down the unmarked road. Unlike the rest of Wanderly Square, where everything was lovely and tidy, the

---

32. The wizards of Wanderly varied in a great many ways, but the one thing they all shared in common was a wholehearted devotion to the art of cobblery, or rather, magical shoe-making. If shoes seem a bit boring for your taste, perhaps you have never heard of ruby slippers or seven-league boots?

33. In Wanderly there was regrettably one library for the entire kingdom, to ensure that only Chancellor-approved titles were in circulation. I have heard rumors that some citizens maintained underground, entirely unapproved secret libraries—but if anyone asks, you did not hear it from me.

unmarked road led down a path overgrown with thorny weeds and vines. An arch of trees grew across the top of it, making it look like a dark tunnel. Oliver spied a few ominous-looking iron fences in the distance. He pressed his lips grimly together, wondering if that's where the Council detentions took place.

Oliver's stomach let out a sudden and noisy growl. He realized for the first time how woefully little he'd had to eat since he first fled the Swinging Swamp. Though he wanted very much to follow the arrow pointing at "Council Business," for surely that was where Ms. Bravo's office could be found, he didn't think it would help to faint from hunger along the way.

So he turned instead toward the Hub, where the bulk of the crowd was headed. Of all the very many reasons to visit Wanderly Square, the Hub was by far the most popular. If Pigglesticks set the standard for all marketplaces, the Hub was its ambitious little sister. Though the Hub was smaller in size, it wasn't lacking in variety. With only the Creeping Corridor for reference, Oliver could hardly believe his eyes when he sailed past Fairy Dearest's Powders, Perfumes, and Wishing Candles situated right *beside* Wickedly Humorous Jokes and Pranks, where a witch cackled to herself while laying out sticky tape along the store's entrance to "delight" potential customers. Oliver moved farther down the street toward Wizard Dibbin's Bootery—which, if he had time, he would have *really* liked to pop into—Common Patty's Uncommon

Stitchery, and a shop that sounded exactly like what Oliver needed: Witch Wendy's Chocolate Brewery.

By this point you probably assumed Oliver had had it up to there with witches, which wouldn't be wrong, but he was also starving. He doubted he would make it out to the Capital again soon and figured he oughtn't to miss out on the one skill that a small percentage of witches in Wanderly were revered for: candy making. Indeed, some of these witches had even built entire *houses* out of such goodies, but those were strictly off-limits for eating.

The crowd pressed tight against Oliver's back as he and Forrest veered toward the creaking wooden steps of Witch Wendy's cabin. Forrest's handle jerked, but Oliver bent close and whispered, "Don't worry. I'm not going back on our deal. I know it looks like a witch's cabin, but we're nowhere near the Dead Tree Forest."

Forrest must have deemed that explanation acceptable because he settled back into Oliver's hand. When they climbed the steps to Witch Wendy's, however, they drew up short. A line of customers twisted around and around the cobwebbed posts of the front porch. Judging by the customers' dejected posture and the children's pouting faces, Oliver had a feeling they'd been waiting for a long time.

Oliver sighed. As delicious as Witch Wendy's drinking chocolate smelled, he didn't really have the luxury of time. The Annual Fall Picnic was in less than three days. He'd told Pippa he was going to find Ms. Bravo, and he needed to figure out how to do so without revealing his own identity. He—

Oliver froze.

He took a step backward.

And then another.

He gripped Forrest so tightly, Forrest's bristles made a wheezing sound.

Oliver couldn't believe his eyes. Nailed to the post in front of him was a Wanted poster. The face staring back at him was his own, albeit with a fierce-looking set of eyebrows. Written above his portrait were the words:

*Wanted by the Quill. Magician Oliver Dash. Armed and dangerous. Report any and all information. Reward for capture is 1,000 grubins.*

One thousand grubins? For *Oliver*?

Forrest, meanwhile, was doing all he could to wriggle out of Oliver's suffocating grip. Despite their earlier "no flying" agreement, Forrest must have grown a bit desperate for air because his bristles let loose a little spark and he, ever so slowly, began to rise up.

"No!" Oliver whispered, trying to tug Forrest firmly back down. "Now would be the worst time to fly. We've got to get out of here!"

Oliver turned and pushed through the crowd. He mumbled, "Excuse me," to an elderly couple debating whether the Chancellor sported a set of false teeth, but Oliver somehow managed to trip over the man's cane and go bumping down Witch Wendy's steps. When he'd thumped to the bottom, he glanced up and saw that his Wanted poster wasn't just nailed to Witch Wendy's establishment. There was an identical poster nailed to every shop on the entire block!

A few customers rushed forward to help Oliver up and ask if he was okay, but he merely nodded, kept his eyes low, and merged into the swiftly moving crowd. Before long, a group of citizens began to point and shout. Several others skidded to a halt, looking curiously around. Oliver hoped not curiously enough to notice that standing beside them was a fugitive magician wanted by the Quill! A moment later, however, the random shouts and excited chattering turned into one very distinct and fervent chant: "Ms. Bra-vo! Ms. Bra-vo! Ms. Bra-vo!"

Oliver's knees buckled.

The crowd parted to make way for her.

Ms. Bravo? Here—right here?

*Yes.*

Ms. Bravo's smile was bright; her hair was tightly curled; her clothes were bold and colorful; and her loyal companion, Dynamite, was sweeping through the air and posing for the crowd of fans growing by the second. Pippa was right, Ms. Bravo wasn't tall by giant proportions, but her presence was so enormous that she might as well have been.

Still, approaching a Triumphant had to be better than approaching a wicked witch. If Oliver had marched up to Helga Hookeye at the Twisted Goblet, surely he could find the courage to make his way toward Ms. Bravo, especially because Pippa was counting on him. But Oliver had barely inched forward when something caused him to freeze.

It was his face. Staring back at him from where it was posted in more than a dozen different directions. What was Oliver thinking? The moment he stepped into Ms. Bravo's spotlight, he would be found out for sure! Even if he waited and tried to catch Ms. Bravo on her way back to her office, the Council district of the city would be teeming with officers of the Quill. Officers who—with a reward of 1,000 grubins at stake—would probably tear one another apart trying to be the first to seize Oliver.

Pippa had told him to turn back if it was too dangerous, but the sinking weight of disappointment was almost more than he could bear.

"Thank you, thank you, everyone!" Ms. Bravo boomed in a warm voice. "Lovely to see you, but I'm afraid I only have a short break before I must return to Council headquarters. I will, however, be at the Official Library for a meet and greet tonight and hope to see you all there!"

With that, she trotted briskly up the steps of Witch Wendy's and straight to the front of the line. Oliver stared after her for a moment before turning glumly in the direction of a dark alley. He hoped he could find a way back to the main gates while avoiding the crowds, but he had just squeezed into the narrow passageway when Forrest leaped out of his hand and whacked him hard on the backside.

"Ouch!" Oliver said. "What did you do that for?"

Forrest jabbed his bristles in the direction of Ms. Bravo.

"Yeah, I know that's who we came to see, but I can't now. Not with those Wanted posters everywhere."

Forrest simply shrugged.

"So what?" Oliver cried. "I didn't say 'so what' when Helga came looking for you. You could have been stuck with her forever, but at least I'm trying to set you free!"

Forrest gave a little huff before rising pointedly off the ground. Oliver clamped onto his bristles, but Forrest continued to rise, and soon Oliver's feet were dangling off the ground. "You are not holding up your end of the bargain," Oliver said in between breaths. "If someone looks down this alley, it is *not* going to go well for us!"

But as he hung there, Oliver realized how very much Forrest *had* done for him, and his grip loosened. His feet landed on the ground with a soft thud, and he stared down at his hands. Forrest peeked curiously over his shoulder.

"It's much easier to be wicked than I imagined," Oliver said quietly. "You took me to Triumph Mountain, helped Pippa and me set her fire horse free, and got me all the way here. Every step of the way, I've forced you to do what I want." Oliver sighed. "I really did plan to set you free after I spoke with Ms. Bravo, but now that's not going to happen. And just because I'm stuck, doesn't mean you have to be."

Oliver reached for Forrest. His eyes fell on the gold band that encircled every witch's broomstick and necessitated servitude. His trembling fingers worked to unwind the screws holding the band in place while Forrest held absolutely, breathlessly still. When the band finally clattered to the ground, Oliver sighed. "Thank you, Forrest. I should have said that a long time ago."

Without so much as a goodbye swish, Forrest zipped through the alleyway and burst into the main walkway. Right away he began sparking and cavorting, charming delighted oohs and aahs from the crowd. Oliver thrust his hands in his pockets and tried to ignore the familiar ache of loneliness. He supposed Forrest was merely celebrating his newfound freedom, but as more and more citizens flocked toward the dazzling broomstick, as Witch Wendy's front porch nearly emptied and the line fizzled out, Oliver understood what was really going on. Forrest was creating a distraction. Forrest was helping Oliver—not because he was compelled to, but because he wanted to.

Oliver felt suddenly brave enough to charge a castle! Wanted posters or not, this was by far the best chance Oliver was going to get to talk to Ms. Bravo and convince her to help Pippa and the Triumphants. Buoyed by Forrest's confidence in him, Oliver raced out of the dark alley. He hopped up the steps of Witch

Wendy's two at a time, and he pushed through the swinging door. It was darker and cozier than Oliver imagined; Witch Wendy must have specialized only in chocolate because there were no signs of brightly colored gumdrops or lollipops here. Unfortunately, there was no sign of Ms. Bravo either. Behind the counter, however, Oliver spotted a closed wooden door with a crudely scratched sign that read: *Private! He, he!*

Oliver gulped. Poking around behind a witch's closed doors didn't exactly seem smart, but Forrest couldn't keep the crowd's attention forever.

Decided, Oliver darted behind the counter, wrapped his hand around the doorknob, and twisted it open.

He was surprised to find the room beyond wasn't quite a room at all, but a broom closet.[34] And in it sat none other than Ms. Bravo, all by herself at a lone wooden table.

On the wall behind Ms. Bravo hung a variety of slightly crooked witchy portraits—all of whom glared energetically at Oliver—and to her right a fat orange and gray cat snored in the lap of a raggedy armchair. Candles flickered from a chandelier overhead, and the aroma wafting from Ms. Bravo's cup of drinking chocolate made Oliver's stomach growl yet again.

Oliver clicked the door shut behind him and locked it.

---

34. It may be helpful to note that witches' broom closets are not the tiny, pocket-size spaces you are used to, but more of the walk-in variety. Considering (a) some witches have multiple brooms, and (b) even one broom needs enough room to stretch its bristles.

He turned to face Ms. Bravo. "Hello," he said. He tried to act as if his heart wasn't pounding in his ears.

Ms. Bravo blinked. "Is it not Thursday?" she asked.

Of all the very many questions that she *could* have asked, Oliver thought that was a fairly good start. "Yes," he answered.

"Curious," she mused. "Witch Wendy always reserves this space for me on Thursday mornings, but I suppose there's room enough. Would you care to sit down?" she asked, as gracious as gracious could be.

"Um, sure," Oliver said, hoping Ms. Bravo wouldn't notice the trembling of his hands as he pulled out the chair. He took a deep breath, preparing to tell Ms. Bravo everything he'd shared with Pippa, but Ms. Bravo spoke first.

"Am I correct in assuming you are about eleven?" she asked with a small, tight smile.

"Ye-es," Oliver said.

"I thought so. You see, I am quite good friends with an eleven-year-old, and I could tell right away that you're about the same age. Perhaps you know her?" Ms. Bravo asked, her eyes wide.

Oliver didn't want to be rude by pointing out that Wanderly was a fairly large kingdom full of lots of eleven-year-old boys and girls, so instead he shifted a bit uncomfortably and said, "Yeah, maybe."

Ms. Bravo continued, "Recently something terrible happened

to my eleven-year-old friend. Do you mind if I share it with you?"

From the tone of her voice, Oliver could tell she was going to tell him whether he wanted to hear or not, and it struck him anew that he was sitting in the same room as a woman who voluntarily woke up sleeping *giants*. She probably wasn't used to listening to anybody, much less a kid.

And when Ms. Bravo said his name, his last small bit of hope was dashed.

"You see, *Oliver*, my friend Pippa was tricked by a lying, scheming, failing magician boy. A boy now wanted by the Council for multiple offenses. So here I am wondering what you could possibly hope to achieve by locking us in the closet of Witch Wendy's?"

Ms. Bravo brought the cup of drinking chocolate to her lips and took a long, deep sip.

"Ms. Bravo, please. I can explain about all of it, but the only thing that actually matters right now is Pippa—"

"Don't you dare try to fool me, Oliver. Whatever you got away with in the Swinging Swamp, you're in the Capital now!"

"Just let me explain, Ms. Bravo. Only a fool would come here in my situation, but I did it for Pippa. Because she asked me to. Ms. Bravo, it's not me that's threatening anybody—I don't even have my hat," he said, gesturing at his head. "It's the magicians. They're planning to do something terrible on Triumph

Mountain during the Triumphants' Annual Fall Picnic. And Pippa's afraid because her family will be there."

A look of surprise flashed across Ms. Bravo's face. "But that doesn't make any sense! The magicians are a bunch of ne'er-do-wells. They don't have any business in a place like Triumph Mountain. What do they have to gain from such a preposterous stunt?"

"Ms. Bravo, I could try to explain what they're thinking, but none of that will change the fact that it's going to happen in less than three days! And from what Pippa says"—Oliver gulped; he spoke cautiously, knowing what he was about to say was probably the last thing Ms. Bravo wanted to hear from an outsider—"the Triumphants aren't exactly . . . prepared. That's why she sent me to you. She was certain you'd help."

An unexpected wave of relief washed over Oliver.

He'd done it.

He'd said it.

He hadn't a clue what would follow, but simply completing the task felt important.

Ms. Bravo drummed her fingers on the table. Her eyebrows furrowed as if deep in thought, and when her eyes came to rest on Oliver's ridiculously short cape, she pursed her lips. "And the charge that you've been hiding large quantities of a particularly vile potion called the Black Wreath? What did you intend to use it for, Oliver?"

Oliver vehemently shook his head. "I didn't intend to use it for anything, because I never had the potion in the first place! The one who had the potion was . . ." Oliver bit his lip. Master Von Hollow hated him. Master Von Hollow was the one who had gotten Oliver sentenced to a Council detention in the first place. Oliver hardly owed him any loyalty. "Master Von Hollow was the one ordering the Black Wreath. He didn't want anybody to know, so he blamed it on me."

Quick as a whip, Ms. Bravo leaned over and tugged hard on Oliver's cape. Slipping from Oliver's shirt pocket, falling onto the table with a soft *clink*, and rolling right into Ms. Bravo's open hands was the nearly forgotten vial of Helga's potion. Oliver was aghast. Now was pretty much the worst time to finally learn what sort of potion he'd managed to swipe from Helga's knapsack.

Ms. Bravo's eyes roved across the crudely written label. "The Black Wreath," she announced. She locked eyes with Oliver. "Well, isn't this interesting?"

A sudden and loud thumping exploded against the door. Ms. Bravo plunked the potion back onto the table, and the midnight black liquid swirled and gleamed in its vial.

"Ms. Bravo! Are you all right in there? It's the Quill! Open up! Open this door right now!" a voice shouted.

Ms. Bravo and Oliver locked eyes.

A witchy voice, presumably Witch Wendy's, shrieked, "I've got your back, Yolanda! I always smell the kiddies, and when that boy walked into your private chamber, you betcha I called the Quill lickety-split!"

"I know this looks bad," Oliver whispered. "So, so bad. But you have to believe me!"

A shadow flickered across Ms. Bravo's face. "What kind of a magician tells on his own kind?"

Oliver gulped. He didn't have time to explain that he wasn't *actually* a magician, so instead he answered, "The kind that cares about Wanderly." And then, remembering Pippa's words, remembering what he desperately wanted to be true, he added, "The kind that calls Wanderly home."

The door began to creak and groan beneath the heavy sole of an officer of the Quill's boot.

"Hey, easy on the decor there, fella!" Witch Wendy chided.

Not a moment later, the door burst open. A large officer with a square head and block shoulders wrapped one hand around Oliver's neck. He lifted Oliver right off the ground, jostling the table and causing the little vial of Black Wreath to roll toward Oliver. Oliver didn't know why, perhaps merely out of instinct, but he wrapped his fingers tightly around it, and as the officer swung him toward the door, with his feet kicking and causing a hearty commotion, he slipped the vial back beneath his cape and no one saw.

On his way out, Oliver tried to catch Ms. Bravo's eyes one last time, but she had settled comfortably into her seat. She brought her cup of steaming drinking chocolate near to her lips, as if all that time she'd merely been waiting for Oliver to leave so she could resume her midmorning snack.

Oliver had failed, in every sense of the word, but even worse than that was how foolish he felt for ever believing it could have turned out any different.

SEVENTEEN

# DOWN IN THE DUMPS

Change was afoot at Castle Cressida.

In the dining hall, the unveiled tapestries of Triumphants and loyal companions past fluttered cheerfully from the rafters. Outside, the golden steps gleamed in the afternoon sunlight. And underfoot, the very ground upon which Castle Cressida stood had taken to periodic bouts of quaking.

At first, Pippa had been quite alarmed. She wondered if Castle Cressida had grown so dilapidated that it was breaking apart at the seams. But now she had come to quite the opposite opinion. Castle Cressida wasn't falling apart; it was coming to *life*. And she couldn't help thinking that it was in direct response to the Triumphants'—at least a small group of them—making an effort to become the heroes they were always meant to be.

After a long and typically useless morning of instruction from

Mistress Peabody (the day's subject had been twofold: "The Art of the Perfect Wave" and "Strengthening Your Strut"), the Triumphants finished their lunch buffet and were entering their daily period of rest. Though on most days the hours between one o'clock and four thirty seemed to stretch endlessly on, Pippa was glad for it today. She and Ernest had already scheduled another training session for their small group of mobilizing Triumphants at two o'clock sharp. But first, she was on her way to the kitchen to see Maisy. If Pippa had delighted in Maisy's chocolate chip cookies, cinnamon rolls, and butterscotch candies beforehand, she could only imagine how delicious (and magical) her newest creations would be.

Pippa had made it only halfway down the hallway, however, when a loud whinny rolled in from the nearest window. Pippa's stomach flip-flopped. There was only one horse who currently called Triumph Mountain home, and that was Ferdinand. But as far as anyone else knew, Ferdinand wasn't supposed to be there. Ferdinand was supposed to be in the care of the Quill, as far away as the Capital, and awaiting an interrogation, er, visit with the Chancellor—*not* stowed safely away in the Triumphant Training Forest.

Pippa rushed to the window and, sure enough, spotted Ferdinand prancing about in plain sight just beyond Castle Cressida's famed golden steps! Pippa didn't hesitate. She sprinted down the hall and burst through Castle Cressida's front door. She even remembered to close the door behind her. But I regret to inform you, she did not stop to look back at the window where she'd just been standing. And she did not see the other Triumphant girl stepping up to the glass or the way her fingernails scraped against the paint on the windowsill as her eyes narrowed, taking in the sight of Pippa and her fire horse.

All Pippa saw was Ferdinand.

Ferdinand veritably danced around her. He snorted and bobbed his head up and down. He buried his nose beneath the folds of her cloak as if searching for a snack. Pippa could scarcely believe her eyes.

"Ferdinand, what has happened to you?" she said in a whisper.

For he looked like a different horse. Though he was still small in stature, Pippa could no longer count every single one of Ferdinand's bones. His golden coat shone beneath the brilliance of the sun, and there wasn't a speck of mud to be found on him. His once gnarled mane and tail were now silky, full, and illuminated by a soft glow. Though Pippa could still see a shadow of the sadness Ferdinand carried on his shoulders since the day they met, its weight seemed to have lifted—just enough for a bit of happiness to exist alongside it, allowing Ferdinand to proudly raise his head once again.

Pippa ushered Ferdinand back toward the Triumphant Training Forest, where they took cover beneath the dense foliage. She stroked the velvety fur on Ferdinand's neck, deep in thought. The day before, Viola had learned that, like her loyal companion beaver, she wasn't just good at making brick castles, she was a creative problem solver and determined to boot. Simon had marveled over how his loyal companion tortoise wasn't just slow and stubborn, but also steadfast, resolute, and solid as a rock. And Ernest had decided that all the reasons that students such as the Bumbles turned their noses up at Leonardo—his strong aroma, his balding front knees, his bucky front teeth, his overall "un-Triumphantness"—were the very same reasons why Leonardo's presence on Triumph Mountain was so important: he was proof that there wasn't just one mold for a hero.

Pippa took a deep breath. She looked into Ferdinand's eyes framed by his long, soft eyelashes. "If you're my mirror, Ferdinand, what are you telling me?" she asked.

Ferdinand merely blinked. But when he did, Pippa caught sight of a reflection in his gaze. And she gasped when she saw her mother's eyes looking back at her. A choked whisper spilled out of her. "Mother?"

And then again, her voice rising, "Mother?"

It was not, of course, Pippa's mother's eyes that were looking back at her. They were nothing more than her own, a mere copy of the original, but the reminder made Pippa miss her mother so desperately and so suddenly that she began to cry. And as if she were making up for all the very many days that she had been gone, as if she were calling out about all the things that, for once, her mother had not been there to fix, as if she finally realized what it meant to call the name of someone you love and have them *answer*, Pippa whispered again, "Mother?"

But everything was silent.

Pippa collapsed, sobbing, against Ferdinand's warm body. She stayed that way until he began nosing through her hair and tickling her cheek with his soft whiskers. She pulled ever so gently away. And when she looked into his eyes her reflection hadn't changed, but her heart lifted the smallest bit. Her mother still wasn't *there*, but she hadn't disappeared either. There were pieces of her in Pippa. And maybe that's how it was with all of them. Mother, Father, Charlie, Jane, Louisa, the triplets, and Rose all inextricably stitched into her, a part of her. Always.

Pippa stroked Ferdinand's nose. "You are alone and so am I. But we don't have to be lost, do we? We know who we are, because we know where we're from, and nothing will ever change that." Pippa paused. She frowned. "Oh, Ferdinand, I'm so scared of what's to come! All I wanted was to leave Triumph Mountain, but I'd stay here forever if only it would keep my family away from the picnic."

As if in answer, the trees around them began to whisper. The dirt and dust on the ground rose up as if infused with magic. And the Winds of Wanderly swept into the Triumphant Training Forest. Ferdinand's mane and tail streamed gloriously behind him, his nostrils flared, and in the face of the Winds, he bowed his head ever so slightly. Pippa's breath caught in her throat as a bright green shiny beetle buzzed near and then burst into a cloud of metallic green dust. The Winds quickly sifted it into a letter and laid it gently down at her feet. By the time Pippa bent to pick it up, the Winds were already gone.

Pippa's hand began to tremble. The only person she had ever exchanged letters with via the Winds of Wanderly, or otherwise, was Oliver. Once he reached Ms. Bravo at the Capital she had assumed she would see them both in person.

She brought the letter near and read:

> *Dear Pippa,*
>
> *Wow. I didn't realize how nice it would be to sit down and write you a letter without pretending to be a fairy godmother. Sort of like you're my actual friend. Considering the way things started out between us, and my track record when it comes to friends (I have zero unless you count rowboats), it's the last thing I expected to happen.*
>
> *I do, however, have some bad news. The worst news actually.*
>
> *I found Ms. Bravo, but she didn't believe a single word I had to say. Part of that was probably because of the Wanted posters plastered all over the Capital with my picture and a reward of 1,000 grubins! Can you even believe it, Pippa? One thousand grubins for ME, an eleven-year-old hatless magician. I guess the Council thought my list of suspected offenses was a big deal because I've seen witches wanted for half that amount.*

*Don't feel bad about trusting Ms. Bravo, though. You're right. She really likes you. I think that's why she was so suspicious of me. Well, that and the fact that I got caught toting around a vial of an ultra-wicked potion called the Black Wreath. I snagged it completely by accident while escaping from the witch whose broomstick I stole (yep, she found me), and I completely forgot I had it. Once Ms. Bravo found it on me, and the Quill came to take me away, there just wasn't time to explain. I guess that witch got her revenge after all.*

*Now I'm here, in the Den for Traitorous Individuals, waiting for a hearing on my Council detention. The Den Master said waiting could take anywhere from three days to seven and one-half years, but honestly maybe that's all right. It's not like anyone's ever gone to a hearing and been found innocent, which means it's only downhill from here.*

*Pippa, if you knew me better, you probably would have known this letter was coming. I normally fail at everything. But I'm not used to failing when other people are counting on me. I don't think anyone's ever done that before.*

*This will also probably be my last letter. My current holding cell's one of the only ones with a small crack in the ceiling, but I can't imagine the Winds of Wanderly squeeze into this place often. I think I'm lucky they've even arrived to deliver this letter.*

*So I hope you find another way to get help from Ms. Bravo. I hope you and Ferdinand knock the magicians' socks, or should I say hats, off. I hope Maisy can now officially step into the role of your fairy godmother. And I hope that whatever happens on the night of the Fall Picnic, nobody gets hurt.*

*I'm scared for us both, Pippa. But I guess that's why this was all worth it in the first place. Heroes are worth trying to save, even if it means we lose everything else.*

*Bye for now,*
*Oliver*

Pippa lowered Oliver's letter. She swallowed back the knot in her throat. Oliver had been captured. Oliver was in a holding cell for a Council detention, and soon his fate would be determined by a whole list of suspected offenses. How could she have let him go to the Capital? Maybe there really was something to the Chancellor's roles. Maybe by sending a non-Triumphant to do Triumphant work, Pippa had endangered Oliver, and for what?

For herself. For her family.

Pippa hung her head. She still didn't know much about what it really meant to be a hero, but she was learning more and more about what being a hero wasn't. It wasn't all about winning, and it wasn't only thinking about yourself. Heroes considered others. Pippa had wanted to save her own family so desperately that she hadn't thought about what was really at stake for Oliver.

"How can I help you now, Oliver?" Pippa whispered, looking off into the distance. "What can I possibly do?"

Pippa jumped at the sound of a twig snapping, and at least *twelve* flames on Ferdinand's mane ignited. The flames snarled and crackled, whipping around Ferdinand's face.

Pippa frowned. "What is it, boy?" she asked. "What's upset you?"

"Surely it isn't me, is it? Animals and children *love* me," Mistress Peabody's voice rang out as she moved artfully past a row of bushes. She was flanked by none other than everyone's favorite Bumbles, Prudence and Bernard.[35] Pippa's gaze fell to where Mistress Peabody was clutching a halter and lead rope so tightly that her knuckles were white.

"Don't feel too badly about Ferdinand's naughty behavior, Pippa. Not all loyal companions are well behaved when they first arrive. It seems even a fire horse is no exception."

Pippa frowned. "Naughty behavior? But Ferdinand hasn't done anything wrong."

---

35. I jest. We all know there's no such thing as a "favorite" Bumble. This, of course, is not to say that things cannot change. At times, things even change very quickly. But the Bumbles' behavior in our story so far has been undesirable to say the least, and I'm afraid it is not about to get any better.

"I beg your pardon, Pippa, but you don't think it's wrong to run away from an officer of the Chancellor? I received the report just this morning that Ferdinand was on his way to the most important appointment of his life when he slipped out the back of the officer's carriage and galloped away."

"He—he did?" Pippa said.

"Of course he did! He's standing right next to you, isn't he? I was just beginning to wonder where he might have run off to, but, thanks to Prudence's timely reporting, it is no longer a mystery and perhaps this story can still get its happy ending." Mistress Peabody thrust the rope in Pippa's direction. "Now go and tie him up, dear."

Beside Mistress Peabody, Prudence fumed. "But, Mistress Peabody, I *told* you that—"

"Quiet!" Mistress Peabody interrupted. "Let us give Pippa a chance to do what Triumphants do best. First and foremost, we must always honor the Chancellor, and because he has put me in charge of this academy, that means you must honor *me*." As if it were as easy as all that, as if there were not a single thing more to be said about the matter, Mistress Peabody's grave tone lightened. "Come now, if we secure Ferdinand and send him back on his way, the Chancellor may hardly notice that he was late."

Pippa bit her lip. Beside her, Ferdinand continued to flame. He had come so far. He and Pippa had grown to trust one another, and maybe, just maybe, they really were meant to be companions for life. Pippa couldn't imagine trying to defend Triumph Mountain against the magicians without him. But above all, Triumph Mountain was Ferdinand's home—if he went off to see the Chancellor, what if he never found his way back? Pippa couldn't let what happened to her happen to Ferdinand too.

Pippa took a few unsteady steps in Mistress Peabody's direction. She wrapped her fingers around the rope Mistress Peabody dangled in front of her. But when she walked back to Ferdinand, she didn't coo at him or rub her hand softly along his neck to settle him down. Instead she jerked her arm high in the air and brought the rope crashing down as if it were a whip. It made a loud and unsettling *crack* against the ground, and Ferdinand started. He reared up on his hind legs and danced backward. He eyed Pippa with a look of wild confusion.

"Git!" Pippa forced herself to shout. "Go on, Ferdinand, git!" And then beneath her breath, "I'm sorry. . . ."

With one more crack of the rope, Ferdinand bolted. He streaked through the Triumphant Training Forest in a blaze of light. Pippa stood and watched until the bleak shadows of the forest crawled back into place. When she finally turned around, Mistress Peabody's jaw was agape.

"I don't understand it. My instructions couldn't have been more clear. I told you to—"

"Do what Triumphants do best," Pippa finished for her.

"And I always understood that to mean doing the right thing." Pippa took a deep breath. She hadn't planned on telling Mistress Peabody, but now she didn't see how it could be avoided. "Mistress Peabody, I have something important to tell you. I recently learned that on the night of our Fall Picnic an unauthorized visitor is planning to arrive."

A peculiar shade of green rolled across Mistress Peabody's face. She tried to wag her finger playfully at Pippa, but everything about her was tense. "Oh, now, don't you go trying to find a way to spoil the surprise. I won't tell you who our guests are, but I did get advance permission, and they are very much authorized, let me tell you."

"I'm not talking about our families, Mistress Peabody," Pippa said, and Mistress Peabody gasped. "I'm talking about the *magicians*! They're planning to—"

"LA-LA-LA-LA-LA." Mistress Peabody closed her eyes and shouted while sticking her fingers in her ears. Her actions were so outlandish, so juvenile, so unnerving for a grown-up Triumphant in charge of an entire academy of Triumphants that even Bernard and Prudence exchanged bewildered glances.

When Mistress Peabody finally quieted down, an unsettling smile spread across her face. She reached into her pocket, and with trembling hands, she pulled forth a small spool of translucent thread. Though Pippa had never used such a thing before, she knew right away what it was: magician's thread.

Mistress Peabody cleared her throat. "It appears, Prudence, that you are right. We do have a rabble-rouser in our midst. We mustn't stand for such a thing, and especially not two nights before a momentous occasion. An occasion when Castle Cressida will be practically spilling over with important people. Indeed, haven't I always said, appearances are everything? And so, without further ado"—Mistress Peabody turned to face Prudence and Bernard—"I shall now give the two of you a chance to do what Triumphants do best. Tie Pippa up and take her to the dungeon. That is where she will stay until the picnic is complete."

"No!" Pippa cried. "No, you mustn't!" But Mistress Peabody grabbed ahold of her. Despite the daintiness of her dance moves, Mistress Peabody was frighteningly strong. And as Bernard and Prudence scurried near and all too eagerly wound the thread around and around Pippa's wrists and ankles as if they weren't doing something heinous, Mistress Peabody never once loosened her grip.

Until that day, Pippa hadn't known Castle Cressida had a dungeon.

Most respectable castles were in possession of a dungeon, but it wasn't the sort of thing Mistress Peabody liked to advertise. Indeed, it begged the question of who should be put in the dungeon, and that becomes difficult to explain when one insists one has zero enemies.

As far as dungeons went, however, Castle Cressida's wasn't all that bad. True, it was buried two stories underground. Its rickety staircase was supported by one broken and splintered handrail, and it emptied out into two narrow rows of nine lonely cells. But, for Pippa's sake, Castle Cressida seemed intent on putting its best face forward. This included trying to keep its dank dripping to a minimum, periodically sending forth gusty drafts to fan the candlelit sconces ever brighter, and keeping its resident spiders tucked discreetly into the shadows.

Pippa sighed. She glanced down at her feet. Though Mistress Peabody had ordered Bernard and Prudence to remove the magician's thread around her wrists, it remained very much intact around her ankles.[36] The magician's thread wasn't wrapped around too tightly, but it was enough to keep her from running, hopping, or climbing.

Pippa shuffled slowly over to the corner of her cell. She leaned her back against the wall and slid down into a sitting position. For perhaps the first time in her life, Pippa did not feel like thinking. If Pippa were to spend time thinking, she would inevitably think about her family and how soon they would be traveling to Triumph Mountain. She would think about magicians and secret plans, and then, of course, she would think

---

36. Mistress Peabody, of course, *couldn't* untie Pippa herself because she wasn't the one who placed the thread on in the first place. She was strong, but unbreakable is still unbreakable. I've even heard a rumor that, when properly applied, magician's thread can bind a dragon's wings together.

of Oliver trapped in a dungeon of his own. Pippa was certain things had never been more wrong. Had it really all started with an unusual rainstorm that had driven a Council member magician, of all people, to knock on her family's door? Was this what the Winds of Wanderly had envisioned when they had sent her letter scuttling into Oliver's hands? Was there still time for anything to be set right or would it all remain utterly broken?

Pippa started at the sound of the dungeon door creaking open, followed by a heavy *thud-thud* of footsteps. A shadowy figure emerged at the bottom of the stairs. Pippa was primed to let loose a healthy scream, but not a moment later, the shadow untangled itself into Viola, Anastasia, Simon, Connor, Willa, Maisy, and Ernest. They rushed to crowd around Pippa's cell.

Pippa let out a cry of delight. "But how did you know where to find me?"

Before anyone could answer, Viola pushed her tiny arm through the iron bars. She slipped her hand into Pippa's and asked, "Pippa scared?"

Pippa smiled. "Not anymore, Viola. I couldn't be, with all of you here."

Ernest slid his glasses up along the bridge of his nose. "It was Bernard and Prudence who told us. Well, not Prudence really, but Bernard. He showed up in the dining hall bragging about how you got exactly the punishment you deserved and that Mistress Peabody chose him to—to . . ." Ernest's voice trailed off.

He wiped his nose. "It's not true, is it, Pippa? He didn't actually put magician's thread on you, did he?"

"I wish I could say no," Pippa said. "But honestly, that's not even the worst of it. The worst is that Mistress Peabody is planning to keep me in here until after the picnic—"

Anastasia gasped. "But your family, Pippa! How can she do such a thing?"

The dungeon grew very, very quiet.

Simon was the first to speak. "Well," he began, looking tentatively around. "Considering we're all here, and the picnic's not getting any further away, I wonder if we ought to use this time to . . . practice?"

"Practice?" Pippa echoed. "But, Simon, I'm stuck in here. I can't even move my feet. And Mistress Peabody's not planning to do anything about that until after the picnic is over."

"But *we're* not locked in a cell. We can still help defend Triumph Mountain." Simon swallowed hard and looked right at Pippa. His voice wavered. "Don't you think we can do it?"

"Of course I think you can do it!" Pippa exclaimed. "I just didn't know how I could ask you to do something dangerous if I'm not right there with you."

From the back of the group, Maisy squeezed forward with her cooking spoon held high. "Don't speak too soon, Pippa," she said. "If I get my way, you'll be out of this cell as soon as tonight!"

The Triumphants cheered heartily, but the afternoon's danger had proven all too real to Pippa, and she wanted the others to know exactly what they might be walking into.

"The picnic's not going to be like anything you've ever practiced in Mistress Peabody's classroom," she continued. "It's going to be real. Ernest and I experienced it for ourselves on the night of the rainstorm. If Ferdinand hadn't found us . . . I'm not sure what would have happened."

Anastasia hiccupped. "But if the danger's real, and we win, does that mean we'll be real heroes?"

"No." Pippa shook her head. "You'll be real heroes at the start. You'll be heroes for showing up, no matter what happens."

"Even if we're . . . scared?" Anastasia asked.

"Courage wouldn't mean very much if you weren't," Pippa said.

Ernest nodded in hearty agreement while stooping down for a basket overflowing with stuffed animals.

"What's that, Ernest?" Pippa asked, gesturing at the basket.

"I borrowed these from the Castle Toy Shoppe to help us with illusion training," he reported proudly. "I thought it'd be nice to have a real target, and maybe when the magicians throw out their worst, we'll think of these instead. What do you think, Pippa?"

Only Ernest could come up with the idea of substituting a snarling panther with an endearing teddy bear. Pippa loved it.

With a smile tugging at the corners of her lips, she said, "I guess practice is on, then," and Ernest hurried off to set up stuffed animals in every dark and dreary corner.

Viola trailed after him, jumping up every few steps until she managed to snatch a pink teddy bear out of the basket and press it adoringly to her cheek. The other Triumphants reached eagerly for their umbrellas. They took turns opening them up like shields, spinning them through the air, and dancing right up to every stuffed gorilla, elephant, and kangaroo they could find, while shouting out "Take that!" and "Not at *our* castle!"

Meanwhile, Pippa looked to where Maisy had since dropped to her knees and was eye to eye with the lock on Pippa's cell. She stared fiercely at it, whirled her spoon in the air for the umpteenth time, and then—when nothing happened—gave it a hearty whop.

She looked up at Pippa, crestfallen. "I don't seem to know what to do if there's not sugar involved," she said.

"You'll think of something, Maisy. Don't worry," Pippa said.

But Maisy shook her head. She rose to her feet and reached into her pocket. She pulled out a sheet of paper and pressed it into Pippa's hand.

"What's this?" Pippa asked.

Tears glistened in Maisy's eyes. "Plan B."

"Plan B for what, Maisy?"

"Helping you," Maisy said. "Pippa, my granny was right.

Even the best Triumphants need help sometimes. But right now, with my spoon not working the way I want it to, we don't have time to sit and wait. You need *magic*. And as far as I see it, your best chance for that is to write a letter."

Pippa's shoulders slumped. "But isn't that how this whole mess started? With letters? With letters that went to all the wrong people in all the wrong places?"

Maisy's gaze swept around the room. She looked at Ernest, his cheeks flushed from exertion, pumping his fists in the air as he led the other Triumphants. She looked at Anastasia, her face set in grim determination as she snuck up on a stuffed rabbit, umbrella fully extended. Maisy tucked her wooden spoon securely back into her pocket and squeezed Pippa's hand through the iron bars. "It's hard to say where any of us would be without those letters, isn't it?"

Through welling tears of her own, Pippa nodded in understanding.

It was funny how sometimes what you most needed to see could be right in front of your eyes, and you still might almost miss it. So much had happened. And even if Pippa and her friends weren't exactly where they wanted to be, they were so far from where they used to be, and who was to say that wouldn't continue so long as she didn't give up hope?

"Thank you, Maisy," Pippa whispered.

She reached into her pocket for a pencil. She settled on the ground and paused thoughtfully before scrawling the name of the one person who still might be able to fix things and, at the very least, was used to solving giant-size problems.

Dear Ms. Bravo . . .

EIGHTEEN

# A Hat Worth Waiting For

Buried in a mountainside in the Capital of Wanderly, within the Den of Traitorous Individuals, Oliver sat in a cell of his own. He stared at the small gap in the arrangement of boulders that served as the ceiling. And he listened.

He did not hear the *swoosh* of the Winds of Wanderly.

He hadn't since he sent his last letter to Pippa.

And he was beginning to wonder if he would ever hear the Winds again. It was funny how you could be mad at losing something you never expected to have in the first place. But Oliver had almost come to depend on the Winds of Wanderly, and he didn't know if that made him very foolish or very wise.

Oliver leaned back against the rock wall. It was the morning of the Fall Picnic, and he couldn't believe he was indefinitely stuck. The Den of Traitorous Individuals was terribly uncomfortable to be sure, but that wasn't the worst part about it. The worst part was how the cells were lined up all in a row; how the cells were close enough that, at times, Oliver could even hear the soft wheeze of the other citizens' *breathing*, and yet no one spoke to one another. It was as if they were all alone.

Oliver had tried several times.

He'd announced his name. He'd announced his age. He even tried asking people whereabouts in Wanderly they were from, but after thirty-six attempts (he'd counted), only two people had bothered to answer him back, and they both mumbled the same thing: "I am loyal to the Council."

Oliver had tried to politely point out that the Council couldn't actually hear them, so perhaps a simple hello wouldn't hurt, but so far nothing had worked.

So, the quiet had dragged on.

And at night when it was time for sleep, the quiet became *louder*.

It filled every square inch of physical space, and when it tired of that, it crawled into Oliver's mind, leaving no room for thoughts of his own.

The quiet was the sort of enemy Oliver had never expected. And he began to wonder if perhaps the Chancellor was smarter than he seemed. If all the very many strings he tied around the citizens of Wanderly had never been put in place to control the endings but only to control the people.

The thought frightened Oliver.

What if sitting all around him weren't citizens who were disobedient but just miscast? What if the one who was tampering with the real story of Wanderly was actually the Chancellor?

Oliver jumped at the heavy clang of the Den's entry gate. The prison guard who had served their breakfast had left an hour or so ago, and Oliver hadn't expected to see anyone until dinnertime. He tilted his head to the side and listened to the approaching footsteps.

But it wasn't just one set of footsteps, it was two.

The footsteps drew nearer to Oliver's cell.

Oliver's pulse quickened. There were lots of cells. Surely the footsteps were approaching one of the cells near Oliver, and not actually Oliver's. Certainly they hadn't come for Oliver already, had they?

*They had.*

The Den Master rattled the bars of Oliver's cell. In the light of his torch, shadows leaped wildly about. Oliver's chest squeezed so tight he thought he might burst.

"Someone's come for you," the Den Master growled. He slipped a long, tarnished key inside the lock on Oliver's cell. With a slight twist of the key, the lock burst open, and the Den Master jerked his head for Oliver to come forth.

But Oliver's feet were stuck.

He couldn't quite see the stranger standing just outside the circle of torchlight, but he appeared to be dressed all in black. Was it a Council member? Another officer of the Quill? Oliver swayed uselessly from side to side until the Den Master picked him up by the collar and tossed him out of the cell.

Oliver fell onto his knees. He could feel the scrape and burn of his skin against the stone, but then a hand reached out to help him up.

A hand that was dripping in gemstones. And Oliver's blood ran cold.

He looked up.

"Master Von Hollow?" Oliver whispered, hoarse.

Master Von Hollow pulled Oliver to his feet, and Oliver was able to make out the all-too-familiar silhouette of his magician's hat.

"Hello, Oliver," Master Von Hollow crooned. "Happy to see me?"

"But what—I thought—you said . . ." Oliver was at a loss for words. Master Von Hollow had been the one who turned him in for a Council detention. Why would he come back now?

"Shhhhh . . ." Master Von Hollow admonished. "We needn't bore this, er, *gentleman* with the piddly details of our visit now, hmmm? Let us wait until we can get a bit of fresh air." Master Von Hollow turned toward the Den Master. He offered up his most charming smile. "Would you please direct us back to the entrance? This place is a bit of a maze."

But the Den Master did not look charmed. His eyes gleamed hungrily. "How many more grubins you got?"

The smile slipped off Master Von Hollow's face. He thrust

his nose in the air. "Plenty," he said, eyes flashing. And he tossed two grubins into the air, leaving the Den Master to drop to his knees and grapple about in the darkness. Once he found them, the Den Master straightened back up with a snarl, shouldered past Master Von Hollow and Oliver, and led them through the twisting network of dark tunnels.

The other prisoners remained as quiet as they had during Oliver's stay. No one asked where he was going. No one wished him luck. No one bothered to say goodbye. And now that Oliver was being plucked out, now that he was being given a temporary reprieve, even if it was at the hands of Master Von Hollow, Oliver became convinced he could never go back to that ruthless quiet again.

They made their tenth turn and came upon a door with bright light glowing around the edges. Oliver's pulse quickened as the Den Master cracked it open. He placed a hand on Master Von Hollow's and Oliver's backs and shoved them both through with a grunt.

"Excuse *you*," Master Von Hollow hissed. He carefully dusted off his cape where the Den Master had touched it, but the Den Master didn't seem to notice.

"Fifteen minutes," the Den Master said, and he slammed the door shut, leaving Oliver and Master Von Hollow alone.

Oliver stumbled forward a few steps. He blinked his eyes. After so many hours in his cell, the sunlight was too bright to take in.

"Has it been a rough few days, Oliver?" Master Von Hollow asked with mock concern. "I've heard a few rather interesting reports regarding your recent activities." He bent close enough that Oliver could smell his sharp, minty breath. "For starters, did you really steal Helga Hookeye's broomstick? She was livid, you know. Telling anybody who would listen about it and then some. Even with your hat, I'd suggest keeping your distance from her. She's quite volatile."

Oliver froze. "With my hat?" he echoed. "But, Master Von Hollow, I was kicked out of the Swinging Swamp precisely because I *don't* have my hat. And now I'm stuck here waiting for a hearing on my Council detention. I think it's safe to say that any chance I had of getting a hat is gone."

"Frankly, I'm a bit surprised at you, Oliver. True, you had an abysmally disappointing start, but it wasn't for lack of effort. Are you really going to give up now? Now that I've come to deliver this?" Master Von Hollow asked.

His eyes gleamed as he pulled his right hand out from behind his back. Oliver gasped. There, dangling from Master Von Hollow's hand, was a hat. A perfectly sized, perfectly round, perfectly jaunty hat. And Oliver knew in an instant that it was his. It had to be. The hat he had been waiting for as long as he could remember. The hat he had nearly given up on.

With his fingers twitching, Oliver lunged for the hat, but Master Von Hollow snapped it backward. "Not so fast, Oliver.

Your hat may have finally arrived, but is it my fault your actions prevented you from being present to receive it? Surely you won't be surprised to learn that many of us have concerns."

But Oliver couldn't stop staring at his hat. Oliver had dreamed about his hat every night for years, and he was determined to fish out every last detail surrounding its arrival. "How did you find it? Was it on top of my pillow? Does anyone know precisely what time it arrived?" he asked in a rush.

Master Von Hollow clamped a hand on Oliver's shoulder. "You are not listening to me, Oliver," he said. "And I am not handing this hat over until you do."

Oliver's jaw gaped. "But it's *my* hat, Master Von Hollow. It's not yours. You can't keep it from me. That—that's not how hats work."

"Is that so? To the contrary, it looks like I am the one in possession of the hat, and a hat alone won't make you one of us. So, if you would like your hat, you'll need to prove you can be trusted. Lucky for you, I'm not asking for much. Indeed it's something you've proven to be quite good at. I need you to write a letter to your friend . . . Pippa."

Oliver's knees buckled. "Pippa? Why would you want me to write a letter to her? You said that we could get in big trouble with the Chancellor for doing that!"

"Yes, Oliver, but all of that's in the past. In just a few short hours, the Chancellor will have much, much bigger problems than a few little rule violations. You've established a nice connection with the girl, and now it's time to make good use of that."

"But what do you want from Pippa?"

Master Von Hollow reached beneath the thick fold of his cape and pulled forth a copy of the *Wanderly Whistle*. A photograph of Pippa was splashed across the front page. Just beyond her, a bit hazy and in the background, was the outline of Ferdinand. Master Von Hollow jabbed his fingernail so hard into the newspaper that he punctured a small hole in it. "That. I want that," Master Von Hollow said with a growl. "It's the only one missing from my herd, and the only thing that could possibly stand in the way of our new role and our new home."

"Your herd?" Oliver began. "They can't be—"

"Of course they're fire horses! I caught them myself! And it's been simply abominable to sit on this achievement and not have a soul to brag about it to. But now you know. Just like you ought to know that tonight's showcase won't be taking place in the Swinging Swamp." Master Von Hollow paused, and Oliver tried to look surprised, as if he hadn't already found out that information and been busy sharing it with Pippa. "It will be taking place on Triumph Mountain—which we will be making our new home. At last, no more Swinging Swamp for us!"

Oliver blinked. He tried to sift through the very many thoughts competing for his attention. A letter to Pippa. A home for magicians atop Triumph Mountain—that was certainly news to him. Ferdinand's herd being imprisoned in the Swinging Swamp right beneath all their noses! But the thought that soared above all the rest was the one that sat in Master Von Hollow's hand: Oliver's hat.

Oliver could scarcely believe it had happened. After so much waiting and dreaming and hoping; after so much heartache; after coming to terms with a seemingly inescapable sentence of loneliness, the one thing he'd always wanted, the one thing that guaranteed he would belong, had finally arrived.

How could he turn his back on it now?

As if reading Oliver's mind, Master Von Hollow twirled the hat through the air. "It's practically yours, Oliver. You just need to write one little letter. You need to arrange for Pippa and her fire horse—that's very important; you mustn't forget that part—to meet you on the South Peak of Triumph Mountain before sunset." Oliver opened his mouth to speak, but Master Von Hollow hurriedly pressed on, "Don't tell me you want all your friends to remain stuck in the smelly old swamp forever? Don't you want to make a new life for yourself atop Triumph Mountain? A new life as a *real* magician?"

Oliver, however, found himself stuck on the word "friends." Oliver had never had any friends in the Swinging Swamp. Oliver knew boys who wrote nasty names for him on the walls; Oliver knew boys who chased him into sinkholes just for a laugh; Oliver knew boys who smeared slug slime on him while he was asleep; Oliver didn't have a single memory of anything even closely resembling friendship.

But Oliver did have Pippa. And maybe there was still a way to help her and secure his hat.

Oliver reached for the paper and pencil Master Von Hollow held out toward him. And even though he trembled all over, he wrote the message Master Von Hollow commanded him to. Because no one had ever said being a real magician required keeping company with other magicians. Just as soon as he had his hat, wouldn't he be able to perform the same tricks as the rest of the magicians? Like vanish away wherever he wanted?

And that was precisely the first trick Oliver planned to do. Then he could warn Pippa not to believe a single word of the letter. He would explain that he had only done it to get his hat, that it turned out he really was a magician after all, and that now—armed with magic—he could finally give Pippa the kind of help she would need at the Fall Picnic. He could almost imagine the expression on her face!

Master Von Hollow grabbed for the letter, but Oliver whipped it backward. "My hat, first," he insisted.

"Oh yes, of course," Master Von Hollow said. "A deal's a deal, isn't it?"

Oliver felt his entire body tingle as Master Von Hollow placed the hat in his hands. He lifted the hat in the air and carefully placed it atop his head. He wasn't at all surprised to find it was a perfect fit. Oliver's heart filled to bursting. A small gasp escaped his lips, and he brought his fingers to the brim as he had practiced so many, many times before. Preparing to vanish away to Triumph Mountain, he closed his eyes, gave a nod of his head, and—

Didn't budge an inch.

A cruel peal of laughter rolled toward him.

Master Von Hollow rocked back and forth on his heels, clutching his belly. He laughed so hard and so loud, he could barely find the breath to speak. "You actually thought it was real, didn't you?" he said, gasping for air and waving his hands about. "Oh, Oliver, you're so pathetic, you're very near Tragical. In fact, I'd be careful if I were you. The Chancellor might send you to Tragic Mountain!"

Oliver felt hot tears pricking at his eyes. He shook his head. He refused to listen to Master Von Hollow. He couldn't have been tricked! He couldn't have been so stupid! Perhaps he had to warm up a bit. He suddenly remembered Theodore and his bevy of mushrooms back in the dormitory. In retrospect, those mushrooms hardly seemed laughable. He brought his shaking fingertips to the brim of his hat to conjure an illusion of something, *anything*, but, again, nothing happened.

"Well, if you like it all that much, Oliver, you ought to at least get yourself another. I got it on clearance at a clothing shop in

Pigglesticks. It doesn't have a single magical stitch. But, as fun as this has been, I've got much work to do. I've got a fire horse to get rid of and a showcase to begin warming up for. Tonight will be quite the event. I like to think of it as opening night for us and closing night for the Triumphants. Ta-ta, Oliver."

But Oliver wasn't about to let Master Von Hollow go. He ran at him. He wrapped his arms around Master Von Hollow's waist and tackled him to the ground. "Give me back that letter!" Oliver cried, rifling through Master Von Hollow's pockets.

But Master Von Hollow had every advantage in the world. He wrinkled his nose at Oliver in disgust, and with a simple flick of his wrist, he brought his fingers to the brim of his hat and vanished. Oliver's arms wrapped around empty air, and he fell hard against the dirt.

For a moment, he didn't move.

He thought long and hard about perhaps never bothering to move again, but the touch of a hand on his shoulder made him flinch. Certain it was the Den Master, Oliver whirled around, but he found himself staring into the small, bright eyes of Ms. Bravo.

She wore a hooded cloak that concealed her tightly curled hair, and her loyal companion, Dynamite, perched on her shoulder.

"Quickly," she whispered. "We must go."

Oliver's eyes widened. "Are you taking me to my hearing for a Council detention?"

Before she could answer, the door to the Den of Traitorous Individuals creaked open. Without bothering to thrust his head into the blazing morning sunlight, the Den Master barked, "Hey! It's been seventeen minutes. You're two minutes over time. Pay up or get back inside!"

Ms. Bravo set her jaw determinedly. She beckoned Oliver closer, toward the cover of the trees. "We mustn't linger," she insisted. "You—you must trust me the way I failed to trust you."

"But what made you change your mind about me?" Oliver asked.

"Let's just say I received a letter," Ms. Bravo said.

Oliver's eyes widened. "Pippa?" he whispered. When Ms. Bravo nodded, his face fell. "Ms. Bravo, we've got to get to Triumph Mountain. I-I've done something terrible. We've got to get to Pippa before Master Von Hollow does!"

"And we shall," Ms. Bravo said, shaking out the folds of the brilliant purple Council cloak she'd hidden beneath her plain one. "But first we must make a few brief stops."

"A few brief stops?" Oliver echoed. "Ms. Bravo, I don't think you understand!"

But Ms. Bravo's face was stern. "I didn't become Wanderly's number one Triumphant by a bit of poor planning. Despite what the Chancellor says, only a fool doesn't know how to ask for help, and surely at least one or two Triumphants is up for the task. I'm afraid you'll have to come along for the flight, unless you see another way out of your predicament?"

Oliver hesitated. Although the idea of him making house visits to Wanderly's Triumphants was nothing short of ridiculous, Ms. Bravo was right. He had no other options. "No, ma'am," he said softly. "But please, let's hurry. For Pippa's sake, we *must* hurry."

"Yes, yes, of course," Ms. Bravo said with the unwavering confidence of someone who has never once failed at anything. And as she placed her hand firmly on Oliver's shoulder, as she twirled her purple Council cloak through the air, as she, Dynamite, and Oliver disappeared in the blink of an eye, Oliver could only hope that today wouldn't be the day her confidence was, for once, ill-placed.

# NINETEEN

# THE WORST MAGIC TRICK OF ALL

*P*ippa didn't know exactly what she expected the day of the Annual Fall Picnic to be like, but she certainly hadn't imagined she would be bored. Ernest and the other Triumphants had determined to spend the bulk of the day training at the Loyal Companions' Barn; the other Triumphants, the ones who insisted that Pippa was bananas, were busy decorating for the big event; and Maisy had stayed up through all hours of the night trying to perfect a promising new recipe. All alone in the dungeon, Pippa found it hard not to feel both useless and a bit forgotten.

And so, when a pounding erupted from the dungeon stairs, Pippa scrambled to her feet as quickly as she could given the magician's thread still tied around her ankles. She waited with eager anticipation as Maisy tore through the dungeon and nearly crashed against the iron bars of her cell. Her eyes were glistening, and her cheeks were red with exertion.

"Pippa," she said, in between breaths and waving an envelope wildly about. "Your letter—it worked! You've already received a letter back. It took everything I had not to tear it open at the sight!"

She thrust it through the bars, and Pippa pulled it close. "How did it arrive, Maisy? What did the Winds bring this time? I imagine it must have been something grand, considering it's from Ms. Bravo!"

At that, Maisy stopped bouncing about. She hesitated before answering, "You know, I didn't think of it until now, but I don't know if the Winds of Wanderly delivered this letter. Unless the Winds have taken to ringing doorbells, because that's what got me to the front door. When I opened it, the letter was sitting there on Castle Cressida's front steps looking just like you'd expect a letter to look."

Pippa unfolded the paper and began to shake her head. "It—it's not from Ms. Bravo. She . . . maybe she's not on her way to rescue us like I hoped."

"Not yet. But it doesn't mean she still won't," Maisy said. She stood on tiptoe to peer closer. "If it's not from Ms. Bravo, who is it from?"

Pippa read aloud:

*Dear Pippa,*
*You're never going to believe it. My luck has changed.*

*I found a way out of the Den of Traitorous Individuals, and I'm coming to see you. I have something very important to talk to you about. Meet me at the South Peak of Triumph Mountain this afternoon. And, whatever you do, don't forget to bring Ferdinand.*

*See you,*
*Oliver*

"Wait, Oliver has managed to escape from his Council detention?" Maisy cried. "Oh, Pippa, this is wonderful, wonderful news! Isn't this—" Maisy stopped abruptly. She looked at Pippa. "Um, Pippa, why don't you look happy? This *is* wonderful news, isn't it?"

"Certainly Oliver being free is wonderful news, but this letter is—strange. It's so . . . short. It's possible he may have just been in a hurry, but even a note or two about how he managed to escape would be nice. Not to mention, how can he possibly get here so quickly? I can't imagine they let him keep a wicked witch's broomstick in his dungeon cell. And I just—" Pippa frowned. "Well, can we trust a letter that wasn't delivered by the Winds of Wanderly?"

"Maybe it was delivered by the Winds of Wanderly, and we just missed all the special effects? Anyhow, you can trust Oliver, can't you?"

Pippa's eyes lit up. "Yes, that's true, isn't it? I guess I'm just a bit paranoid. But there is, um, one other problem. How am

I supposed to meet Oliver this afternoon when Mistress Peabody's keeping me locked up until the picnic is over?"

Maisy grinned. "That may be the very best part of all this. I think I have a solution to that." She took a deep breath and called out, "Prudence? You can come down now."

Pippa's jaw dropped. "Prudence?" she whispered. "Did you just say *Prudence*?"

"That's exactly what she said." Prudence's voice snaked down the dungeon stairs as she emerged into the dim, flickering candlelight. "And don't think for a second that I'm here to help you."

"Gee, why would I think that?" Pippa asked, shooting an incredulous look in Maisy's direction. Maisy gulped nervously.

"I'm here," Prudence said, drawing closer, "because at breakfast this morning, a terrible thought came into my mind. And no matter what I do, that terrible thought won't go away. In fact, I think it's getting worse."

Pippa frowned. It was strange to think that the people who cause terrible thoughts for others might suffer from the same malady themselves.

"A terrible thought about what?" Pippa asked.

Prudence looked right at Pippa. "*You*," she said unequivocally.

Pippa's stomach flip-flopped. "Me? But what can I possibly do to you? I'm stuck here in this dungeon cell until after the picnic!"

"Exactly! And won't others wonder where you are? The surprise Triumphant nominee who was assigned a fire horse? It will be all of three seconds before people start whispering and gossiping and soon all sorts of rumors will be circulating, and they'll all say one thing: that you're a total joke!"

Pippa took a deep breath. She looked down at the magician's thread Prudence had helped tie around her ankles. "It's sort of hard to see why you'd care what anyone else thinks about me, Prudence."

"Ha! I don't care what anyone thinks about *you*, I care what they think about my sister!" She leaned so close to Pippa's cell that her cheeks squished against the iron bars. "Bettina was supposed to be here, Pippa! You were the one who stole her spot—"

"But I never wanted to be here! I just want to be with my—"

"Don't say it!" Prudence shrieked. "Your family may be nothing but warm hugs and kisses, but not all families are like that."

"But—but you're a . . . Triumphant. Your family is full of Triumphants! Shouldn't that mean you're all happy?"

A rare look of sadness flickered in Prudence's eyes. But then she gritted her teeth. "I'm just trying to survive. Bettina is too. And I'm not going to let you humiliate her more than you already have." She reached into the pocket of her cloak and pulled forth a rusty old skeleton key. She thrust it into the lock and twisted it. The door to Pippa's cell popped open.

Pippa blinked. "You convinced Mistress Peabody to let me go?"

"Of course I didn't. But just because my raccoon's not a fire horse doesn't mean he's any less of a loyal companion. Bandit's the best thief on Triumph Mountain. Getting this key away from Mistress Peabody was a piece of cake. Now." Prudence nodded at Pippa's ankles. "Sit down so I can remove that too."

Prudence worked quickly. She unwound the magician's thread and stuck it in her pocket. When she finished, she looked at Pippa. "Stay out of sight until the picnic. Don't let Mistress Peabody see you. Once the picnic begins, she won't want to make a scene, so you'll be safe to come out then and"—she paused and narrowed her eyes—"you'd better."

"There's nothing in all of Wanderly that will keep me away from that picnic," Pippa said emphatically. And then, softly, "I really am sorry about Bettina. . . ."

But Prudence had already spun on her heel and marched toward the dungeon steps. When she was gone, Pippa turned to Maisy. "I guess your baking *was* enough to get me out of the dungeon, Maisy. How did you do it?"

"This morning I served up a batch of Happiness Hotcakes. I figured the deepest sort of courage comes from fighting for the things that bring us the most joy. I was hoping the Triumphants would tap into that once the picnic's underway."

"That's genius," Pippa said. "But it must not have worked quite right for Prudence. Thinking about Bettina didn't seem to make her happy at all."

"Unless her happy and her sad are all mixed up," Maisy said with a sigh. "You'd better get on your way though. Prudence was right about one thing—you can't let Mistress Peabody see you, and you've got an important meeting with Oliver. Maybe he'll have news about Ms. Bravo or maybe it's something even grander, like the magicians changing their plans altogether!"

Although that sounded a little too good to be true, Pippa forced a smile, determined to hope for the best.

Pippa didn't have to look hard to find Ferdinand. The moment she stepped into the Triumphant Training Forest, he plunged out of the bushes and dipped his nose into the crook of her arm, nearly bowling her over. His mane glowed with a soft golden light, and he blinked his big brown eyes at her.

Pippa wrapped her arms around his neck. "I'm so glad you're all right, Ferdinand. I'm so glad Mistress Peabody didn't call the Quill to come back for you. I hope I didn't frighten you the other day, but it was all I could think of to keep you safe."

Ferdinand nickered as if he understood her words, and then he gently lowered himself to the ground so that Pippa could climb onto his back. Pippa took a deep breath and grabbed hold of Ferdinand's flickering mane. Even though she'd touched it before and not been burned, she was still relieved when she felt nothing but a soothing warmth against her hands.

"We're not going far, Ferdinand," Pippa said. "In less than two hours' time Triumph Mountain is going to be crawling with magicians—and our families! We'll have enough to do then, but first we're going to the South Peak to meet Oliver."

Pippa clucked her tongue and squeezed her legs around Ferdinand's belly. He surged forward with more speed than Pippa remembered from the night she and Oliver rescued him. Her ponytail streamed behind her, the trees and sights around them zipped by in a blur, and she gulped in the fresh mountain air. If they weren't coming up on such a monumental night, Pippa might consider riding Ferdinand to be one of the greatest thrills of her life.

But before she knew it, the South Peak was flattening out. They were drawing near to the very same plateau where Pippa had first met Oliver and discovered she had never been writing to a fairy godmother at all, but a magician. She only hoped the topic of today's conversation wouldn't be quite so unsettling.

Pippa pulled Ferdinand to a stop. He snorted and tossed his head, as Pippa slid carefully off his back. She didn't see Oliver anywhere, but maybe that wasn't surprising considering his transportation complications. Pippa squinted and looked toward the horizon, wondering if she should be expecting him by broomstick again.

She never saw the tall, skinny man with the tall hat slip up behind her.

"Hello, Pippa." His voice slithered toward her.

Pippa whirled around. It was Master Von Hollow, the magician she and Ernest had bumped into in the Triumphant Training Forest. The one whose showcase was scheduled for that very evening, and the one who Oliver said was the nastiest magician in the Swinging Swamp.

Ferdinand took one look at Master Von Hollow's hat and let out a piercing whinny. He pranced backward. He reared up on his hind legs twice in a row. He strained hard against his halter, and his eyes rolled wildly back in his head. Pippa could barely hold on to him.

"Your hat!" Pippa said through a grimace. She tried desperately to dig her heels into the springy grass for leverage. "If you don't take off your hat, I can't guarantee he won't trample you!"

The magician's smirk faded just a little as he eyed Ferdinand. He reluctantly took off his hat and cast an accusing glare at Pippa. "What have you done to him?" he asked. "He looks so . . . so . . . *healthy.*"

But Pippa hardly thought it was wise to engage in conversation with a magician. She took a running leap at Ferdinand and had nearly managed to swing her leg up and over his back when Master Von Hollow said, "Aren't you going to ask about Oliver?"

Pippa hesitated. She looked over her shoulder. "What do you know about Oliver?"

Master Von Hollow drummed his fingertips on the hat he held against his chest. "I know lots of things about Oliver. For instance, I know Oliver has received his magician's hat. Just today, in fact. Aren't you happy for him, Pippa? *We* certainly are."

Pippa frowned. Oliver said he wasn't like any of the other magicians; he couldn't possibly be working with them. Not when he had stolen a broomstick solely to warn Pippa, helped free Ferdinand, and risked his life going to the Capital to find Ms. Bravo. Oliver definitely hadn't had a hat during any of that, but even if one had arrived, that wouldn't really change anything, would it? Oliver wasn't the sort to switch sides, was he?

Master Von Hollow and Pippa both whirled around at the sound of something thrashing through the underbrush. Footsteps pounded against the hillside, and Oliver burst onto the plateau. His face was covered in sweat.

"Pippa!" he shouted. "Pippa, you've got to go!"

Master Von Hollow licked his lips. He swept closer to Pippa, and Pippa leaned closer to Ferdinand. "Oliver! I didn't realize I'd get the pleasure of your company. Did you come to assist with our little arrangement?" Master Von Hollow asked.

"Arrangement? What arrangement?" Pippa's eyes darted toward Oliver. "Oliver, what is he talking about? And is it true? Did you really get your hat?"

But Oliver didn't answer. "You've got to leave, Pippa. *Now!*"

Master Von Hollow huffed. "Oh, I do wish you'd stop saying that, Oliver. You're not even trying to help out now, are you?"

Hearing the urgency in Oliver's voice, Pippa tried again to mount Ferdinand, but Master Von Hollow was too quick. He tossed his hat back on his head and with a flick of his wrist a trio of snarling tigers surrounded Pippa and Ferdinand. Pippa yelped out loud and Ferdinand began pummeling his hooves out in front of him. In his panic, one of his high-powered kicks just barely missed Pippa.

"It's all right, Pippa," Oliver shouted above the commotion. "A magician's illusion can't actually hurt you! It feeds off your fears, but if you touch it, it will disappear."

"But I—I don't have my magic umbrella!" Pippa cried.

"Magic umbrella?" Master Von Hollow echoed. And he brought his fingertips to the brim of his hat and conjured two more tigers.

"Just touch it, Pippa!" Oliver begged.

Pippa's heart pounded. The illusions looked so real! She knew she had to do something, but could she trust Oliver? Was it just another trick to capture Pippa and Ferdinand both?

She turned at a sudden flash of movement coming from Master Von Hollow's direction. The edges of his cape swirled to and fro as he rummaged about for something. When he pulled his hand loose, he held a small glass vial with a wooden stopper.

"NO!" Oliver screamed from the other side of the tigers. He rushed forth and began batting his hands against them, but they didn't disappear, and he couldn't get past them.

"If all you have to do is touch them, why isn't it working for you?" Pippa cried.

"Because they're feeding off *your* fears. It has to be you, Pippa. And it has to be now! Master Von Hollow's got the Black Wreath!"

Pippa's heart sank as she watched Master Von Hollow pour the potion onto the brim of his hat.

"Watch, Oliver," Master Von Hollow said. "Watch and see what a real magician can do. The impossible, that's what! Now I shall fit this fire horse inside my hat and make it disappear. If you think that's impressive—just imagine what's in store for tonight!"

With both hands gripping the edge of his hat, Master Von Hollow closed his eyes. Pippa gasped as a wreath of black smoke began to snake, wind, and twist away from the hat's brim. Everything inside the wreath began to spin about. Faster and faster and faster. Pippa tried to push Ferdinand out of the way, but he was frozen in place and the wreath of black smoke was growing thicker.

"Get out, Pippa! Get out of the way!" Oliver shouted. "The potion's extending the brim of his hat. Pippa, he's going to make you disappear!"

"I hardly meant for the girl to go too," Master Von Hollow said, "but the more the merrier, hmm?"

Oliver didn't appear to be listening. His eyes were fixed on Pippa as he took a running leap, soaring clear over the backs of the still-prowling tigers. He stretched out his arms as if he meant to push Pippa out of the way and knock her outside the smoky radius of Master Von Hollow's hat.

But his timing was a half second off, and the moment he pushed into the wreath was the precise moment it sent Pippa,

Ferdinand, and now Oliver hurtling away from Triumph Mountain and into a place so sticky, humid, and odious that Pippa knew without asking where they were: the Swinging Swamp.

Pippa lifted her head with a groan. Her right cheek was buried in sticky mud, and some of it even clumped her eyelashes together. She heard the high-pitched whinny of a horse and called out in alarm, "Ferdinand? Ferdinand, is that you?"

Beside her, Oliver answered softly, "It's not Ferdinand, Pippa. Just look."

Pippa forced herself upright and gasped. They had landed inside a gated paddock and Ferdinand was surrounded by a cluster of nearly two dozen horses. They snorted and snuffled and nuzzled against him. They bobbed their heads and stamped their hooves and became so tangled up with one another that Ferdinand was hard to distinguish. Anyone else would have mistaken the horses as ordinary—less than, even—but Pippa knew in an instant what they really were.

"This is where the fire horses have all gone to?" Pippa whispered. "Master Von Hollow has been keeping them all here, hidden in the Swinging Swamp? No wonder Ferdinand was terrified of hats. It was at the hand of a hat that he's watched everything he loves . . . disappear."

Pippa blinked back tears. With so much going wrong, it seemed monumental to have something go right. Ferdinand had found what he was missing. This was what Ferdinand had needed help with, and now they'd done it. Ferdinand hardly seemed to care that he'd been dropped into the least desirable location in all of Wanderly or that the other fire horses seemed to be in an even weaker state than he'd been when he and Pippa first met: Ferdinand and his herd were at last *together*.

Pippa could only imagine what that felt like.

Oliver turned from watching Ferdinand. His head hung low. "I'm sorry I messed up so badly, Pippa. If I wouldn't have written that letter, you never would have gone to the South Peak, and then you and Ferdinand would be safe on Triumph Mountain."

"Why did you do it, Oliver? Is it because of what Master Von Hollow said? Because you got your hat? And, um, where is it?"

"Master Von Hollow wouldn't give me my hat until I wrote you the letter, and I figured it would be a piece of cake to fix. As soon as I put my hat on my head, I was just going to vanish away to Triumph Mountain and tell you all about it."

"And then?" Pippa implored.

"And then Master Von Hollow gave me the hat all right, but it wasn't real. It was a fake." Oliver's expression was pained. "I don't know why I keep hoping my hat's going to come. I don't know why I can't just accept that I'm never going to be a magician!"

"'Never' is a strong word, Oliver. And I don't think there's anything wrong with hoping for something, but I think it's important to consider why you want it." Pippa took a deep breath. "Why do you really want to be a magician, Oliver?"

Oliver looked down at the ground. He shrugged his shoulders. "Before, it was because I didn't want to be kicked out of the swamp. But yesterday, aside from getting out of the Den of Traitorous Individuals, it was because I wanted to help you. I thought it would make me . . . better."

"Magic can do a lot of things," Pippa said. "But it doesn't make a person better. That comes from inside. Oliver, in these past few weeks I'm not sure anyone has helped me more than you. And all without a drop of magic. You just need to be you. Oliver. That is, and will always be, enough."

Oliver swiped at his eyes with the back of his hand. "Just Oliver, huh?"

"Just Oliver," Pippa said. A moment later she peeked behind his back and asked, "You're not hiding that broomstick of yours anywhere, are you? That would really come in handy right about now."

"I didn't return to Triumph Mountain by broomstick, Pippa," Oliver said quietly. "I came by Council cloak."

Pippa's head snapped up. "Ms. Bravo came for you?"

"Only because of your letter. We would have made it to Triumph Mountain sooner, but she wanted to bring help."

"So that means our families will be okay? Back on Triumph Mountain there are Triumphants waiting to protect them?" Pippa asked, her voice rising hopefully.

But Oliver was quiet.

"Oliver?" Pippa asked.

Oliver shook his head. "No one wanted to come, Pippa."

"But—but we're talking about Triumphants! This is what they do. This is what—" Pippa froze when the ground began to tremble. All around them, the mud began to split apart and blasts of green fog hissed up from the depths. Ferdinand and his herd jittered nervously to and fro with their ears pinned back.

"Oliver, please tell me this is normal for the Swinging Swamp," Pippa said.

But Oliver's face had gone pale. "It's normal, but it's not any good. It's a sinkhole, and it looks like this time it's after Master Von Hollow's land."

"Oliver, the horses!" Pippa cried. "We've got to open the gates; we've got to get them out."

Oliver sprinted toward the gate, but when he reached his hand out to pull on the latch, he froze. His face was stricken. "Master Von Hollow's put a lock on it! It—it didn't used to have a lock on it, but now he's put one there because of *me*."

"I don't understand," Pippa said, shaking her head.

"Remember?" Oliver said weakly. "I tried to sabotage his showcase by freeing the horses."

"But the horses are still here," Pippa cried.

Oliver's voice rose. "I know; it didn't work. I tried to warn you, Pippa. The things I do don't usually work out."

A cold wave of fear washed over Pippa. She turned from Oliver and looked hard at Ferdinand, wondering how much experience he had with jumping. But even if he managed, she didn't know if the other horses would—they looked so weak and sickly. Now that they had been reunited, Ferdinand would never leave them behind, and she could never ask him to.

Pippa threw her arms out for balance as another violent tremor rumbled through the Swinging Swamp. In its wake, Oliver straightened up with an unusual glint in his eye and a determined tilt of his chin.

"I'll be right back!" he called out over his shoulder as he quickly scaled the fence and sprinted up the hillside. Pippa barely had time to blink when he disappeared into the thick cover of trees, leaving Pippa all alone with the trapped horses.

Despite the humidity of the swamp, Pippa shivered. She felt so far away from Triumph Mountain. She felt so far away from her family. Even if a miracle occurred and they managed to get Ferdinand and his herd out of the paddock, they were at least a full day's travel away from Triumph Mountain. Master Von Hollow's showcase would be long over by then. Surely nothing Oliver had in mind would be able to fix that.

When Oliver reappeared at the top of the hill, Pippa blinked. He held something in his hands. Something he clutched tight against his stomach. It almost looked like . . . a hat?

"Oliver, what are you doing with that? Where did you get

that?" Pippa asked as he ran closer and climbed back into the paddock.

"Master Von Hollow's rock garden. He keeps them there for decoration."

"He dresses up rocks in hats?" Pippa exclaimed. "That's maybe the strangest thing I've ever heard. I also don't understand how that hat is going to help us."

Oliver reached beneath the fabric of his short cape and into his shirt pocket. He pulled forth a small vial with a wooden stopper in it. It must have been the one he'd accidentally swiped from Helga Hookeye. The dark liquid inside swirled like midnight sky. "Because I've got this. And with both of these, I can do the same trick that Master Von Hollow did. I can send us all back to Triumph Mountain. You, me, Ferdinand, and his herd."

Pippa's stomach flip-flopped. "Have you ever tried anything like this before? And if getting a hat was as easy as stealing one from a rock, why didn't you do it earlier?"

"Because . . . well." Oliver paused. His cheeks flushed a hint of pink, as if maybe he wasn't being completely honest. "I never took one because everybody would know I stole it. A hat's only meaningful if it's your own. Otherwise anyone could be a magician, right?"

"I guess," Pippa said. She had a fair amount more to say about it, but a particularly large jolt jiggled the swamp. Several of the cracks in the ground merged into one sizable hole. Pippa watched as rocks and swamp goo slid down into the hungry earth.

"Come on!" Oliver cried, tugging on Pippa's wrist and positioning them in the center of the herd. His hands trembled violently and beads of sweat rolled down his face. He looked hard at Pippa. "Sometimes tricks like these can have a strange effect on a magician. But no matter what you see, you mustn't doubt in the magic. Magic is sensitive to that sort of thing, and if you interfere, something might go wrong. Also, it's possible we might not all end up in the same place, but I'll try my best."

Pippa shook her head. "But we will be on Triumph Mountain, right? And what sort of strange things are you talking about, Oliver? I didn't see anything strange happen to Master Von Hollow!"

"You have to trust me, Pippa. You have to let me play my part, so that you can play yours. Even if the Chancellor's been terribly wrong about everything else, that may be the only thing he's gotten right: a storybook kingdom is all about working together. Commoner or Triumphant, our actions affect one another. They change the story. Pippa, let's tell a good story."

With her chin trembling, Pippa nodded. In one continuous motion, Oliver planted the hat firmly on his head and poured the infamous Black Wreath all along its brim. Pippa waited warily, but in less than half a second the same twisting, winding snake of black smoke swirled away from Oliver's hat. It began to huff and puff and push its way beyond Pippa and Oliver. Inside the wreath of smoke, a racing wind began to howl, and Pippa's fingertips tingled in anticipation of the magic. The smoke continued to crawl along the fractured swamp floor, but it barely covered half of Ferdinand's herd. In a panic, Ferdinand began to run in and out of the wreath. Pippa realized that the diameter of the hat wasn't only coming up short, but it also wasn't as strong as it had been on top of Triumph Mountain. What if it couldn't send them as far either?

Pippa tugged on Oliver's arm. "Oliver, the wreath's not big enough! We've got to make it bigger!"

Oliver, however, was completely silent. His eyes were closed and his skin was a pasty shade of gray.

"Oliver!" Pippa shouted, shaking him harder. "Oliver, are you all right?"

But Pippa might as well have been alone. Oliver wasn't responding. Pippa had never been so terrified. The sudden *crackle* and *pop* reminded Pippa that the wreath wasn't going to last forever. Whether she was ready or not, it was going to take them somewhere, and it was going to do it soon. Oliver had told Pippa not to interfere in the magic, he had told her not to doubt it, and so Pippa closed her eyes and thought of the most magical thing she knew. If the real, true magic of Wanderly was in working together, then perhaps nothing could be so powerful as the thing that had brought her and Oliver together from the start, the one that could be in all places at once, the one to whom nothing had ever been lost.

*Swoosh!*

Pippa's heart soared.

*Swish!*

The Winds of Wanderly had come just as she'd believed they would.

And as they dipped into the paddock, as they fanned out and pushed hard against the boundaries of the black wreath of smoke until it stretched around every single last one of the horses, the smoke transformed. It began to sparkle and shine. It paled to a lovely shade of soft blue, and Pippa couldn't keep from shouting, "We've done it, Oliver! Together, we've done it!"

But when she reached for Oliver's hand, all she felt was stone.

Cold, hard stone.

And when she looked up into his face, his pasty complexion had deepened to solid gray.

"No!" she choked out. "No, no, no!" she insisted as she realized all at once what Oliver had really meant when he'd said rock garden.

As the ring of sparkling blue light closed around them for good, as the Swinging Swamp faded away and they tumbled back toward Triumph Mountain, Pippa threw her arms around Oliver's lifeless form and wept.

# TWENTY

# TAKE A BOW

When Pippa crashed onto the peak of Triumph Mountain, her arms were still wrapped around Oliver. She lifted her tearstained face away and collapsed on the ground beside him. Pippa had never been so near to tragedy. She had read about it in storybooks, certainly, but in the warmth of the North family home, wrapped up in her mother's arms with the constant chatter and squealing of her siblings filling the empty spaces, it had seemed like the sort of thing that didn't—couldn't—really happen.

But Oliver really had turned into stone.[37]

---

37. For once, I am a bit out of words. I never know quite how to handle this part of the story—Triumphant books simply aren't well equipped for sadness. And so, I suppose I simply wanted to let you know that I am still here . . . and I am very glad that you are too.

Pippa was sure she'd never seen a more frightening sight in all her life.

His heart was supposed to be beating. His lungs were supposed to be breathing. Wanderly had a place for Oliver, so how could he just be gone? And if Pippa was really a Triumphant, how could she have let this happen?

"I never would have let you do it, Oliver. Why didn't you tell me what that hat might do to you?" Pippa cried. And then, remembering some of the last words that Oliver had said to her, "How did you think this could ever turn out to be a good story?"

But Oliver, of course, didn't answer. And as Pippa sat beneath the sky, as the late afternoon turned into the early evening, she realized for the first time that she and Oliver were all alone. Ferdinand and his herd weren't with them. And Pippa didn't have a clue if they had made it to Triumph Mountain at all.

A strange chorus of whooping, hooting, screaming, and crying rolled suddenly toward her. Bright fireworks soared up to the sky and exploded in glittering bursts. Master Von Hollow's showcase, it seemed, was about to get started. And whatever it was he and the magicians had been planning to upend Wanderly and change their destiny was under way.

Pippa glanced back at Oliver. "You made a way for me, Oliver, but I haven't a clue what to do with it now. You shouldn't have believed in me like this. I'm not cut out for this! And all I've ever wanted was to go back to my old, ordinary life. But now you're gone and so is Ferdinand. What am I supposed to do?"

And as Pippa's heart reeled, two small words escaped.

*Show up.*

Hadn't she told Anastasia that they would be heroes just for showing up? Hadn't she told Ernest that one of the bravest things a hero could do was be willing to lose? Even if Oliver's confidence was unfounded, he'd given up everything to bring Pippa back to Triumph Mountain; couldn't Pippa at least try to do what he'd thought she could? Did anyone ever gain anything without trying? And, in this instance, if no one tried to defend Triumph Mountain against the magicians, the Triumphants could lose everything.

Pippa set her jaw. She forced herself up and onto her feet. She gently pushed Oliver's cold, stone form back toward the trees where he would be sheltered, and she let her hand linger on his shoulder.

"It won't be for nothing, Oliver," she said, her voice trembling. "And when we've won, I'll find help. Surely with so much magic in Wanderly, there must be some way we can bring you back."

But Pippa knew it was a stretch. She knew that in Wanderly, people were born and people died in much the way they did in an ordinary kingdom, and as far as she knew no one had ever once been brought back to life.

With her heart aching, Pippa spun around and ran for the manicured front lawn of Castle Cressida. She leaped over perfectly round boulders and fallen logs adorned with colorful mushrooms. It was hard to imagine that on a mountain so pristine, in a place that hadn't known any real hardship for decades, an entire swamp full of magicians was about to change that forever.

When the three towers of Castle Cressida came more fully into view, Pippa prepared to step away from the cover of the trees, but something hard hit her on the side of the head.

"Ouch!" she cried. But she kept going. When something hit her on the other side of the head, she twitched in annoyance, but nevertheless kept moving. It wasn't until she heard a loud whisper of "Pippa! Pippa!" that she drew to a skidding halt and looked around.

The bushes around her began to *move*. And jumping out from behind them were her friends!

Three-year-old Viola, with leaves tangled in her hair, flew so hard at Pippa that they both nearly tumbled to the ground. Anastasia, Simon, Connor, and Willa rushed in close, all talking at the same time. Maisy threw her arms around Pippa, her face fraught with worry, while Ernest slipped his finger beneath the lens of his glasses because, it appeared, something was causing his eyes to water. Their loyal companions stepped out of the shadows and clustered around them.

"Pippa! Oh, Pippa!" Viola cried out, holding fiercely to Pippa's leg while her beaver, Choo-Choo, scurried about piling up sticks in his arms. "The gagicians are here, and they so, so bad!"

Pippa swallowed hard and looked to Maisy. "But you are all

safe? How did you end up out here?"

"Maisy saved us, Pippa," Anastasia piped up as her marmoset, Whisper, peered over her shoulder. "Those magicians came banging on the castle door, and Maisy tried to get us all to follow her down to the staff's quarters. The six of us got up and followed her, of course, but none of the other kids did. Mistress Peabody stuck her fingers in her ears while Ms. Bravo tried to talk some sense into her. . . ." Anastasia paused, wringing her hands together. "Oh, Pippa, I don't think it worked one bit because the magicians have got all the Triumphants, our families, and even Ms. Bravo seated on the front lawn as an audience. Every single one of them's tied up with magician's thread!"

Pippa's heart sank. She knew the perils of magician's thread all too well. Tied with the unbreakable material, the Triumphants and their families were the very definition of a captive audience. Pippa tried not to think about Master Von Hollow's Black Wreath potion. She tried not to think about whether he had enough stashed away that he might be able to make an entire audience . . . disappear. But to where? Where would he send them? What did he think it would take for the Chancellor to surrender and give the magicians the role they wanted?

"Does everyone have their magic umbrellas?" Pippa asked.

The Triumphants pulled them out from behind their backs. Pippa bit her lip, remembering what Oliver had shared with her about the illusions and how they fed off fear. Not wanting the Triumphants to lose their confidence, she simply said,

"Now, remember, the umbrella's magic works best if you actually manage to touch the magician's illusion. So let's make that the goal. Touching the illusions, so that they'll disappear."

The Triumphants nodded and Ernest's goat, Leonardo, bleated enthusiastically. Maisy stepped forward with a basket in her arms.

"I've got the tomatoes, Pippa. I've been treating this batch to be extra juicy and extra explosive, with a sprinkle of humiliating."

"Well done, Maisy," Pippa said. "Everybody take as many as you can possibly carry."

As the Triumphants busied themselves making room in pockets and makeshift pockets, Maisy bent near and whispered to Pippa, "Where's Ferdinand, and what happened to Oliver? Did he have something valuable to share?"

At the mention of Oliver, Pippa felt her eyes fill with tears. "It was a trap, Maisy. Master Von Hollow sent us to the Swinging Swamp, where he's been keeping all the fire horses prisoner."

Maisy gasped. "Ferdinand's family?"

"Yes, and I—we—tried to bring them all back, but something went wrong. So many, many things went wrong." Pippa hung her head miserably. "I haven't a clue where Ferdinand and his herd have gone."

Maisy sucked in a breath. "And . . . Oliver?"

Pippa was silent. She choked back a sob, and Maisy clutched the hem of her apron so tightly that her knuckles turned white.

Ernest drew up alongside them, and Pippa quickly turned her head so he couldn't see her distress.

"We're all ready, Pippa," Ernest said. "We managed to load up on all the tomatoes. But other than pelting the magicians with them, do we, um, have any more specific sort of plan?"

Pippa swallowed back the knot in her throat. "Yes," she answered. "Everyone needs to help me get to Master Von Hollow. It's his showcase. He's the one in charge, and he's the one who needs to be stopped."

Right away, Willa stepped forward. In her quiet, calm voice she said, "Let me be the one to do it, Pippa."

"You?" Simon cried from where he was sitting on his tortoise. "But you're not really the fighting type—your favorite thing to do is tell stories!"

"Simon," Pippa began, "sometimes telling a story is the bravest thing that can be done."

Simon peeked in Willa's direction before lowering his eyes. "I'm sorry, Willa," he said. "I didn't mean it like that."

Willa placed a hand on Simon's shoulder. "It's all right," she said. "And anyhow, I only volunteered because I'm the oldest."

"Which is why you have to stay behind," Pippa said with a firm nod. "Master Von Hollow has a potion that he can't be allowed to use. If I get it away from him, then we might be able to save the other students and our families. If I don't . . ." Pippa gulped and looked at Willa. "Then you might be leading whoever is able off Triumph Mountain in search of help."

Anastasia cleared her throat. "Speaking of families, Pippa. I—I think I saw yours. I mean, I know I did. I don't think anyone else here has a family that big. Or three brothers who all look the same."

Pippa's heart caught in her throat. "Were they hurt? Did they look okay?"

"More than okay. In fact, they were all taking such good care of one another they didn't seem to have much time to panic. It was a real calming influence on everyone else too, even Bernard Benedict Bumble the Fourth, who your dad was unlucky enough to be sitting next to. Anyways, as I was watching them, I couldn't help thinking that maybe you've been training for this longer than you think."

Pippa lifted her head the smallest bit. She tried to keep her voice steady. "Thank you, Anastasia."

And then she turned to face the group. "It doesn't matter how many scheduled duels a kingdom's heroes attend if they aren't available for a true emergency. This is what the magicians of the Swinging Swamp are counting on, and this will be our greatest advantage. They're not expecting any opposition, so we need to make a big entrance. We need to rattle them. We need them to think that we're just the start and that bigger and more powerful backup is on its way. Do you think you can do that?"

Anastasia was the first to hold her umbrella out in front of her. Viola followed her lead, and then soon Simon, Connor, and Willa joined in. Maisy proudly held out her wooden cooking spoon, and then Ernest and Pippa laid their umbrellas on top.

"For Wanderly," Ernest said.

"For Wanderly!" the group repeated together.[38]

And with their loyal companions at their sides, they sprinted forward at top speed. When they burst through the trees, Pippa spotted Master Von Hollow immediately. He was perched on a makeshift stage elevated two feet off the ground and surrounded by nearly two dozen magicians. He waved his hands and arms through the air in a grandiose gesture before bringing his fingers to the brim of his hat and conjuring an illusion of rats. Enough rats to cover the entire stage, rats piled one on top of the other and spilling into the screaming audience while Master Von Hollow laughed.

The others must have seen it too, because they all slowed down, but only for a moment. Anastasia drew her magic umbrella out and opened it up as a preventative measure. Willa and Connor followed suit while Maisy proudly twirled her wooden spoon through the air. The Triumphants and their loyal companions forged ahead.

"Are you all scared?" Master Von Hollow boomed to the squirming audience. "Are you hoping that someone will come and *save* you? Imagine that, Triumphants cowering atop Triumph Mountain! But just wait, as you shall soon see, you can always count on a magician to have a dazzling trick up his sleeve!"

---

38. FOR WANDERLY!—Whoops, did I write that out loud?

Master Von Hollow tapped quickly on his hat and every single one of the squeaking rats vanished. With only a short distance left to go, Leonardo fixed his eyes on Master Von Hollow and bared his buck teeth. He let out the loudest bleat Pippa had ever heard from him. Master Von Hollow wheeled around at the intrusion and stomped his foot on the stage.

"What is this?" he hissed. His head snapped toward one of the magicians positioned below him. "Razzle! Did you forget to tie up some of the students? Did these manage to slip away from you?"

And then one cry that nearly brought Pippa to her knees.

"Pippa!" her triplet brother Artie shouted. And then, with the other triplets joining him, "Pippa! Pippa! Pippa!"

Master Von Hollow heard it too. *"Pippa?"* he roared.

Pippa felt as if a spotlight had been thrust upon her. The magicians glared, the audience gaped, and her friends tensed. Fortunately, Ernest lifted his chin and boomed, "The tomatoes!"

The Triumphants didn't hesitate. They plunged their hands into their pockets. They began hurling tomatoes through the air, and Pippa gasped as Viola's first launch landed *splat* on a magician's face! The magician yelped. He brought his hands to his face and frantically began swiping at the tomato goo, but it just made a bigger mess. The magician next to him pointed and snickered until Simon landed a juicy one on his shoulder, and he began to run around in circles shouting, "I'm bleeding! I'm bleeding!"

The audience of Triumphants and their families did something entirely unexpected, something a bit miraculous: they began to laugh. And as tomato after tomato soared through the air, a chant began to gain momentum, until it reached an unmistakable crescendo and rained down on the stunned ears of the magicians.

"Boo! Boo! BOO!" the audience shouted.[39]

From atop the stage, Master Von Hollow seethed. He shook his head from side to side, and Pippa could see his lips form the word "No." Surely this wasn't what Master Von Hollow had been practicing for all those many late nights; surely this wasn't the new role that he'd had in mind for himself. Master Von Hollow was watching it all slip through his fingers, which made him, unfortunately, very, very desperate.

Master Von Hollow lifted a trembling finger in the direction of Pippa and her friends. "Seize them!" Master Von Hollow shouted to the magicians covered in tomato juice. "Seize them! SEIZE THEM!"

Pippa's heart pounded. It was happening. This was it. A handful of Triumphant students were about to engage in direct magic-to-hand combat with full-grown magicians! Pippa watched as Viola and Choo-Choo darted ahead of the group.

---

39. Obviously this was not the sort of "BOO!" your little brother shouts at you from a dark corner; this was the sort of "BOO!" that is an intense expression of an audience's displeasure. As such, being the showmen that they were, there was no greater poison to a magician as that one three-letter word.

They were both so small, no one noticed them, and when Choo-Choo began laying the sticks he'd been gathering in front of the magicians' feet, several of them tripped and tumbled to the ground! Simon stood on top of his stalwart tortoise while his tortoise snapped stealthily at the magicians' ankles and capes, sending several of them away howling. Perhaps most successful of all, however, were Anastasia and Whisper, who had reluctantly untangled his arms from around her neck and leaped into the fray of magicians. He hopped effortlessly from one shoulder to the next, dutifully snatching the magicians' hats off their heads and tossing them into the air.

"Argh!" a magician screamed. "My hat's gone! Who took my hat?"

"It was the monkey!" another shouted back.

"The only monkey I see here is *you*!" the magician hollered.

The missing hats caused a ruckus as the magicians poked around, plucked a hat up, examined it, and were forced to toss it back over their shoulders if it was not their own. All the while, Pippa stole closer to the stage. Pippa slipped undetected from one pocket of magicians to the next until she had very nearly reached Master Von Hollow. She heard the magician called Razzle shout out, "Nicholas! Duncan! Do it now! Show us what you've been working on! Show us what the next generation of magicians can do!"

Pippa winced, thinking of Oliver. He should have been the next generation of magicians. The one time he'd donned a true magician's hat, he'd worked a magic far greater than any of them would ever manage. These were the very magicians who had cast so much doubt into Oliver's heart; these were the very magicians that had rejected him; and these were *not* going to be the magicians that conquered Triumph Mountain.

Pippa climbed quietly onto the stage just as Nicholas and Duncan's illusion burst out from the trees. Suddenly, the entire front lawn of Castle Cressida burned with light. Firelight. Nicholas and Duncan had conjured a dragon! The audience erupted into screams. Pippa's friends froze in their tracks. And a slow, sickening smile spread across Master Von Hollow's face.

"Excellent!" the magician named Razzle shouted, though there was even a tremor to his voice.

"Fear not, ladies and gentlemen!" Master Von Hollow shouted. "I can take you away from this ferocious, fire-breathing dragon in the blink of an eye! It will be the greatest disappearing act of my entire career."

Master Von Hollow reached beneath the fold of his cape. He emerged with a swirling vial of the Black Wreath potion—a vial nearly three times the size of the one he'd poured onto the brim of his hat when he made Pippa, Oliver, and Ferdinand disappear.

Pippa took a deep breath and sprang up from where she lay hidden in the shadows. She didn't have any plan other than to tackle Master Von Hollow with all her might and hope it was enough to send the Black Wreath hurtling out of his grip. But as she lunged in Master Von Hollow's direction, he whipped around to face her. He quickly stuffed the vial of the Black Wreath beneath his lapel and caught Pippa by the shoulders.

"HELP!" Pippa shouted desperately. But no one could hear her over the screaming of the audience as the dragon prowled about the lawn, and Pippa's friends shuffled bravely toward it with their umbrellas drawn.

"Honestly, Pippa, this is starting to get *very* annoying," Master Von Hollow growled into her ear. And in his eyes Pippa could see a reflection of fire.

Pippa whipped her head around and there, on the front lawn of Castle Cressida, the shrubs were *burning*.

"But . . . how can that be?" she said, aghast. "I—I thought an illusion couldn't hurt us. I thought they weren't real!"

"Of course they're real, because fear is real," Master Von Hollow said, his tone chilling. "And the amount of fear a creature like this generates in an audience this large is nearly impossible to overcome. It would take something ridiculously brave to destroy it, and I hear that's very difficult to find up here." Master Von Hollow licked his lips. "But just in case, let's seal the deal, shall we? I would like you to join me onstage now as my assistant. This will be a clear signal to the Triumphants that they have no choice but to do as I say!"

Pippa was horrified. "No," she choked out, struggling to free herself from his grip. But when a familiar cry rose up from the crowd, Pippa's heart sank. It was Rose. Baby Rose. Her sister was being held up in the air by the magician known as Razzle, and Rose just so happened to be hat-size.

"Razzle can make her disappear even without a potion," Master Von Hollow said. "And I'm sure you don't want to see her separated from her mummy now, do you?"

And he was right. Pippa could see her mother standing alongside her father. Their faces were stricken, but they were bound so tightly by the magician's thread that when Pippa's father attempted to lunge at Razzle, he crashed helplessly against the ground. Razzle dipped a wailing Baby Rose lower into his hat.

"No!" Pippa begged. "No, you mustn't!"

Even among all the shouting, even with the dragon setting the lawn ablaze, Pippa could pick out the anguished cries of her family. With tears streaming down her cheeks, she fell down to her knees. It was more than she could bear. And she found herself wondering if perhaps she should accept Master Von Hollow's offer. Perhaps if she agreed to be his assistant, it might spare some of his wrath against not only Rose but others too. Regardless, she had to do something.

Pippa drew in a shaky breath. She tried to stand. But then a sound rolled out over Triumph Mountain. A sound that was not the fire-breathing dragon.

It was Castle Cressida. This time Castle Cressida wasn't settling into its foundation and causing the ground to rumble, but puffing itself up, soaring, reaching, striving, until in one loud burst a deafening blare of trumpets exploded over the landscape.

Pippa marveled.

Castle Cressida *did* have a warning system; it had just gone so long without any real reason to sound its cry that it had forgotten it even existed at all. But on that night it remembered. On that night Castle Cressida did precisely what it was built to do, and on that night, because of Oliver's sacrifice, Castle Cressida's call was answered.

The outline of a flaming mane and tail emerged from the Triumphant Training Forest.

"Ferdinand!" Pippa cried out. She could scarcely believe it! Ferdinand was here; Ferdinand hadn't gone scuttling off to some unknown location but had made it to Triumph Mountain. Oliver had managed to save not just Pippa . . . but Ferdinand too. And Ferdinand's timing couldn't have been better.

What Pippa wasn't at all prepared to see, however, was *another* mane and tail bursting into flame fifteen feet away from Ferdinand. And then five feet away . . . another mane and tail caught fire. And another, and another, and another, until Ferdinand and his entire herd stood poised at the edge of the forest in all of their flaming glory. Pippa gasped for breath. She was certain she'd never seen anything so beautiful. And she knew now why no one had ever thought to represent the fire horses as being small in stature. When they were together as they were meant to be, when they were planted on the soil they were meant to defend and in the presence of true heroes, their flames combined to create one enormous aura of light.

Beside Pippa, a strange choking noise erupted from Master Von Hollow's throat.

But he didn't have time to say a word before the fire horses charged. They galloped full speed across the front lawn of Castle Cressida. Castle Cressida puffed another deafening round of trumpet blasts, and the audience all cheered. At the sight of the fire horses blazing past, Pippa's friends raised their umbrellas up to the sky and began to jump up and down in celebration. The entire mountain held its breath as the fire horses barreled headfirst into the dragon, and it disappeared in a giant blast of crackling red smoke that reached all the way to the sky.

Before the smoke had time to clear, Pippa struck Master Von Hollow's vial of the Black Wreath. It tumbled free of his jacket and shattered on the floor with a sizzling *hissssssss*. And Master Von Hollow did exactly the sort of thing a villain like Master Von Hollow would: he abandoned his fellow magicians. He brought his fingertips to the brim of his hat and—

This time, quite surprisingly, it was Council member Slickabee who stopped Master Von Hollow. He knocked Master Von Hollow's hat right off his head! It tumbled off the stage and rolled at the feet of the other magicians, who were busy doing precisely what Master Von Hollow had attempted to do, but with greater success: disappear.

"You clumsy fool! What is wrong with you, Gulliver?" Master Von Hollow shrieked.

But Council member Slickabee merely clasped his hand

around Master Von Hollow's wrist. "I spent years working my way into a Council position. And right now it seems like staying in one is my best option. The tides have turned rather quickly, Victor. And it seems I have no other choice but to sentence you to a Council detention on account of treason."

Council member Slickabee tilted his head and shouted at the magician named Razzle, who had sheepishly placed baby Rose back in Pippa's mother's arms, "You're not going anywhere, Razzle! You've got an entire audience full of people that you and only you can untie. If you do so satisfactorily, I'll make note of that to the Council. Oh, and I'll take your hat too, please."

A very flustered-looking Magician Razzle tossed his hat toward the stage while Master Von Hollow huffed. "You won't be able to get away with this, Gulliver! You were a part of every planning committee; you were an indispensable part of the plan!"

"Yes, I was," Council member Slickabee said, "and wasn't I the perfect undercover agent? At least that's the way it looks anyhow, and we all know there's nothing more important to the Chancellor than a neat and tidy appearance. It's much easier to place the blame on one rogue mastermind than an entire swamp full of magicians, isn't it? Who's the most distinguished magician now, hmm?"

Before long, the majority of Triumphants and their families had been untied and the magician's thread handily wound up and collected by Ms. Bravo. Castle Cressida's front lawn was awash with a chorus of victorious whooping, joyous greeting, and deep sighs of relief. Pippa stood on tiptoe, certain it shouldn't be that hard to pick out a family of nine even among the large crowd, but when she felt a warm hand on her back she knew in an instant she had been found.

Pippa felt her feet lift right off the ground as her father's arms wrapped tight around her, and he spun her in the air, much to the triplets' delight. As she twirled, Pippa felt the heavy weight of all those days away from home slip right off her shoulders. Pippa's father set her down and the North family simply drew near, pressed near, and surrounded her. Tears streamed down Pippa's face, because in the entire kingdom of Wanderly there was only one Mother and one Father, only one Charlie, Jane, and Louisa, only one Artie, Miles, and Finn, and certainly only one baby Rose. The North family. They were hers and she was theirs, and at last, they were back together.

Artie tugged on Pippa's hand. "Why Pippa sad?" he asked, looking up at her. "Pippa a hero!" At which Miles and Finn joined in, chanting enthusiastically, "Pippa a hero! Pippa a hero!"

"I'm not sad, Artie," Pippa said, smiling through her tears. "In fact, I'm quite certain I'm the happiest I've ever been."

To her right, Louisa's shoulders slumped a bit. "Is that because you're a Triumphant? Triumphants always get the happiest endings, right?"

Pippa squeezed Louisa's hand. "Not at all. It's because I already had the happiest ending I could ever imagine—being with all of you—and I was afraid I'd lost you forever."

Louisa's eyes widened. "Us? You think we're the best thing in Wanderly?" She glanced down at the triplets, who had already grown a bit bored with the reunion and had dropped down to search for interesting things like slugs and beetles in the grass.

Louisa wrinkled her nose, and Pippa giggled. "You'd be surprised what life is really like up here on Triumph Mountain. And how there's no place like home."

Pippa's oldest brother, Charlie, tugged on her ponytail, while Jane slipped her arm through Pippa's. Rose gurgled and blew little bubbles and didn't make even a hint of a protest though she was likely awfully hungry (because, indeed, she was always hungry). Pippa's mother kissed Pippa fiercely on the top of her head.

"Nothing was the same without you, absolutely nothing," she said.

"Really?" Pippa asked in a small voice. "I figured with nine of you left, it'd be easy to sort of, you know, fill in the gap. . . ."

Jane snorted. "Ha! Gap? More like gaping ravine. I never realized all that you did to help Mother, Pippa. If she asked me one more time to fold Father's socks—" Jane stopped abruptly at the impeccable arch of their mother's eyebrow. She cleared her throat. "As I was saying, if Mother asked me one more time to fold Father's socks, I would have been happy to do it."

Pippa's mother nodded approvingly, and then gently cupped Pippa's cheek in her hand. "But if you hadn't been here at

Peabody's Academy for the Triumphant, I'm not sure anything would have been the same for the entire kingdom. I want you back in Ink Hollow more than anything, Pippa, but I think it's also important you know that family is one of those things that cannot be lost. No matter where you go."

Pippa bit her lip. "I—I think I know that now. I felt it, when I was here and so far away. But there's nothing like having a hug every now and again, is there?"

"Nothing at all," Pippa's mother agreed, and she pressed Pippa so close against her chest that Pippa could hear her heart beating, and everything at last seemed right with the world, except for one thing.

"Mother," Pippa said, pulling gently away, "there is something I need to do. Would you mind if I excused myself for a bit?"

Pippa's mother squeezed her shoulder while Jane and Louisa began strolling toward the glittering front steps, pointing and gushing and oohing over "just how lovely everything is!" much to Castle Cressida's delight.

"Don't worry about us," Pippa's mother said. "We should have more than enough to do."

Without another word, Pippa ran toward Ms. Bravo, who was busy reassuring the Triumphant families that the situation hadn't been nearly so dangerous as it appeared. One of them was a woman who bore the same exact nose as Prudence and a scowl to match. "Hmph! I suppose there *was* something to that

Pippa girl, then, wasn't there?" she said pointedly. Ms. Bravo looked more than a bit relieved when Pippa touched her gently on the arm.

"Ms. Bravo," Pippa whispered. "I need your help with something. It-it's important."

"Certainly," Ms. Bravo said. She excused herself from the crowd and followed Pippa, who sped up to a slow jog. A short distance away, Maisy and Ernest spotted them and hurried to catch up.

"Where are you going, Pippa?" Maisy asked. "Is something the matter?"

Pippa swallowed back the knot in her throat because something very much was the matter, but she also had the faintest, smallest twinge of hope, and she didn't want to do anything to squelch it. "Come on," she said, and she ran faster until they all four skidded to a halt in front of the statue of Oliver.

Sheltered beneath the trees, with the hat he'd spent a lifetime longing for perched on his head, with Triumph Mountain as it should be, he almost looked content. Pippa's chest squeezed tight. She looked over at Ms. Bravo, whose eyes glistened with tears.

"So he used the Black Wreath after all," she said softly. "It's amazing what something dark can do when someone is bent on using it for good." Ms. Bravo's shoulders collapsed. "Oh, Pippa, I am so, so . . . sorry."

Pippa's heart skipped a beat. Ms. Bravo was a Triumphant.

Ms. Bravo had always been the one she could count on. Of course she was sorry, but wasn't there something she could do?

"You can't bring him back?" Pippa asked. "You can't unfreeze him or reverse the effects or do anything at all?"

"I'm a Triumphant, Pippa. I'm just like you. I haven't any magic, and even if I did, I'm not sure that's the way magic works, even in Wanderly."

"Excuse me, pardon me," Maisy said, brushing in front of them and drawing near to Oliver. With her lips pressed determinedly together, she buried her ear against his chest. And her face lit up. Her eyes sparkled, and her cheeks flushed a perfect shade of rosy.

"I hear his heartbeat!" she exclaimed. "It's faint, but I can hear it. If his heart's beating, that means there's still a chance." She whirled around to face Ms. Bravo, gesturing excitedly. "Ms. Bravo, as the resident fairy godmother in training at Peabody's Academy for the Triumphant, I am quite certain this is nothing more than a very sophisticated sleeping curse. But in order to wake him, I will need to undo magic that's already been set in place. That will require Council authorization." Maisy paused. She took a deep breath. "Do I have your permission?"

Ms. Bravo looked to Pippa with a questioning expression. "Fairy godmother in training?"

Pippa nodded. "We couldn't have done any of this without her, Ms. Bravo. Please let her try. She's been waiting a long time for this."

"But she doesn't even have a wand!" Ms. Bravo said.

Maisy proudly held up her wooden spoon. "You'd be surprised what this can do, Ms. Bravo."

With Ernest, Maisy, and Pippa watching her expectantly, Ms. Bravo let out a sigh and nodded her head. "I never imagined I'd be surrounded by so many precocious children," she muttered.

Maisy, meanwhile, began walking circles around Oliver. She removed the hat from the top of his head. She waved her spoon up, down, and all around, and then came to stand just in front of him. She closed her eyes; she laid her wooden spoon on his shoulder; and when she did, everything around them began to stir. The Winds of Wanderly rolled near. They slipped through the leaves on the trees, they rustled the folds of their capes, they playfully skipped over the tops of their heads. And then, as Oliver began to stir awake beneath Maisy's magic, the Winds swept over him, gently blowing away the layers of crumbling stone and scattering it through the air like nothing more than a bit of harmless dust.

Oliver opened his eyes.

Maisy squealed.

Ms. Bravo gasped.

And Pippa rushed at Oliver, nearly knocking him to the ground. "You're alive! Oh, Oliver, you're alive!" At the same time, Ms. Bravo asked incredulously, "Do you mind if I take a look at that cooking spoon of yours?"

Oliver meanwhile looked down at his hands. He wriggled his

fingers. He brought them to the top of his head and, feeling the absence of a hat, he looked down at where Maisy had placed it beside him. His face broke into a wide grin. "Would it be weird to say that for the rest of my life, I hope I never ever have to wear a hat again?"

"Not weird in the slightest! Isn't that what I've been trying to tell you all this time?" Pippa asked.

Oliver looked right at Pippa. "I'd have to say that depends."

"Depends on what?" Pippa asked.

"On whether you finally believe me that you're a real hero."

Ernest slid his glasses up along the bridge of his nose and cleared his throat. "I would just like to take this moment to say that I was the one who said it first. I'm claiming full responsibility for Pippa's hero status."

Ms. Bravo snorted. "Let's not forget our manners, children. Wasn't *I* the one who chose Pippa at the examination for admittance to Peabody's Academy for the Triumphant?"[40]

Pippa was thoroughly mortified. "I am not hearing this conversation. I cannot believe this is a conversation that anyone is having."

"In all seriousness, though, Pippa, great things were accomplished today on this mountain. By each one of you." Ms. Bravo

---

40. For as lovely as it is to have been the very first one to see the potential in Pippa, it is also no small thing to be the last. I may not have seen much in Pippa from the start, but I stand fully corrected. And I shall spend all the rest of my days (which are quite a lot when you're a book) being her staunchest supporter.

paused. She looked directly at Oliver, Maisy, Ernest, and finally, Pippa. "I know all you've ever wanted to do was go home, but I do hope you'll consider what it would mean to the kingdom if you stayed. Not to mention, I promise to establish regular family visiting hours immediately, among quite a great many other things that need serious attention."

Pippa looked down at her feet. She'd spent so many hours imagining her feet running away, running home, and never once returning. How could so much have changed in so little time? How could she really, seriously, be considering that she belonged at a place like Peabody's Academy for the Triumphant? But maybe, on this day, she just needed to take a single step. Maybe she could handle that.

Pippa swallowed, and a shy smile curved on her lips. "I wonder if we should return to the castle now? I hear an outstanding feast has been prepared, and we wouldn't want to miss out."

"Especially not with so very much to celebrate," Maisy said, while leaning into Pippa and laying her head on her shoulder. Oliver quickly scooped up the magician's hat that lay at his feet. He ran to the edge of Triumph Mountain, and tossed it jubilantly over the side, where it was swept up by the Sapphire Sea, never to harm anyone ever again. Despite all of the magicians' planning, despite their desire to be rid of Oliver in time for their new beginning on Triumph Mountain, it turned out he was the only one who belonged there after all.

As Ms. Bravo led the way toward a radiant Castle Cressida,

her loyal companion, Dynamite, swooped overhead like a banner. Pippa, Ernest, Maisy, and Oliver locked arms with one another, and the Winds of Wanderly swirled behind, tossing emerald strands of grass in the air like confetti because at long last, the wait was over. The Triumphants of Wanderly had returned.

# Bravo!

I knew the moment you picked me up that you would make it this far.

But that doesn't make me any less proud.

I know this is not the traditionally Triumphant tale you assumed you were picking up, that it is full of stumbles, mishaps, and setbacks, but in the telling of Pippa's real story, I have come to the rather shocking conclusion that this is what makes it so grand.[41] Not because I enjoy airing the Triumphants' dirty laundry (I am a Triumphant book, don't forget), but because a very, very good ending is ever so much more satisfying when it is born out of very, very difficult circumstances.

It is precisely in Pippa's being the "least" Triumphant that she has proved to be one of the greatest, and I remain convinced that eliminating some of her and her friends' more obvious disappointments would be, instead, a tragedy.

---

41. Beware! I've heard rumors that, in the Chancellor-authorized version circulating throughout Wanderly, Pippa hasn't a drop of homesickness, Ferdinand arrives fully engulfed in flames, and Oliver's name isn't mentioned even once. Can you imagine?

Because a hero's tale is not simply a means of rote record keeping, or a personal trophy to brag about, but a means of inspiring others to action. And if there is one thing I have come to learn it is that, whether in your world or in mine, there will always be a need for heroes.

If you have not figured it out by now, I am looking at YOU.

Are you surprised?

You shouldn't be. I sensed it in you the moment you first flipped through my pages or I wouldn't have bothered to tell you this story at all.

If being a hero is not the sort of role you have ever imagined for yourself, let me assure you: I am not the sort that tends to be wrong. I am patient, however, and if you simply turn back to the page where our story first began, I would be more than happy to tell it to you all over again.[42]

Though it is terribly bittersweet to part with a reader such as yourself, I have stories that must be shared, and I'm certain you have work that must be done. Isn't that always the way with heroes? And however small or big that work happens to be, however far or near it happens to take you—I am certain that it will be extraordinary.

Perhaps I shall even hear all about it in a book one day.

---

42. Indeed, we all need a bit of reminding from time to time, heroes included.

# Acknowledgments

In the Kingdom of Wanderly, everything is always better together, and it couldn't be more true of writing a book. My deepest thanks to my literary agent, Molly O'Neill, whose support, kindness, and knack for asking the perfect questions helped me find the heart of Pippa and Oliver's story when I needed it most. I will forever be grateful that you pulled me (and Birdie!) out of the slush pile years ago.

Thank you to my magical editor, Stephanie Stein. I mentioned before that you just might be a fairy godmother, and now I am ever more convinced of it! Thank you for loving Wanderly and all of its citizens the way that I do, for being so patient as I dug deeper on draft after draft (after draft), and for continually lighting my way. I have learned so much from you.

My sincere thanks to the entire team at HarperCollins for allowing me one more adventure in Wanderly. Wanderly truly found its perfect match in cover designer Jessie Gang and illustrator Melissa Manwill. Your talent amazes me, and the cover exceeded my greatest hopes (again). Thank you to copy editors Jon Howard and Stephanie Evans. Thank you to Erica Sussman for believing in Wanderly early on. Thank you to Vaishali Nayak and Jacquelynn Burke for working to put this book into the hands of the readers who will love it most. Thank you to Kristen Eckhardt for overseeing production from beginning to end. Thank you to Almeda Beynon for bringing this book to life through the audio edition. And thank you to Louisa Currigan for so expertly connecting all the dots. I wish I could give a heaping platter of Maisy's magical lemon bars to you all!

Thank you to the amazing team at Root Literary Agency and their tireless efforts every day on behalf of authors and, of course, readers. Special thanks to Heather Baror for helping Birdie, and now Pippa, find her way into children's hands around the globe.

Thank you to authors Jessica Day George and Liesl Shurtliff. Not only have you written some of my most favorite books, but I am still pinching myself over your kind support of Wanderly. Liesl, thank you especially for your generous encouragement and advice along the way.

Special thanks to bookseller extraordinaire Alexandra Uhl for always making me feel so welcome at A Whale of a Tale (the loveliest bookstore!) and for being a dear friend of Wanderly.

For Mom, Dad, and Ryan—this book is all about family, both the family that we are born into and the family that we find along the way. Thank you for giving me the most loving start. I love you all so much. Mom, my fellow bookworm, sharing this journey with you has been an extraspecial gift.

And thank you to my loves Jerad, Ellie, and Violet. Jerad, my heart found its home the day I met you, and you are my hero in the truest sense of the word. Ellie and Violet, you make every day magical and being your mama will always be the greatest role I could ever hope for. Without the three of you—your love, your patience, and your sacrifice—this book simply wouldn't exist. I love you all dearly.

Finally, to each reader, blogger, teacher, librarian, and bookseller who has so kindly taken the time to read or recommend my books, I am deeply honored and humbled. I hope now, and always, you will find within the pages of Wanderly what I hoped from the very start: a friend you can count on.

# Another Fairy-Tale Adventure Awaits

**KEEP READING FOR A SNEAK PEEK!**

## ONE

# UNHAPPY BIRTHDAY

itches aren't the celebrating sort.

But birthdays, as you well know, are different.

Not even a witch forgets her birthday.

And so, on September 5, as she had been doing for seventy or eighty or who really knows how many years, Agnes Prunella Crunch settled into her familiar rocking chair. She pulled the rickety table with the oozing slice of mud pie on it a bit closer.[1] She scratched her favorite wart at the tip of her exceptionally large nose. She kicked off her smelly, striped socks and wriggled her bony toes in front of the cauldron that emitted a puff of

---

1. Mud pie was Agnes's favorite. Lest you nod eagerly because you love it too, let me inform you that Agnes's mud pie was not the sort you order in a restaurant. It was not even the sandy sort you might make on the playground. It was the real deal. Real, stinking, goopy mud with a few juicy worms tossed in for good measure.

green smoke every now and again.

It was time.

*Oh yes.* Agnes nodded. *It was time.*

Agnes tilted in her rocking chair. Agnes tilted so far she might have tipped right out had she not spent years teaching her rocking chair to float. She wrapped her fingers around the cover of a ginormous book and hoisted the book up off the floor and onto the squishy lump of her belly with a soft grunt. She eyeballed the cover. It gleamed back.

*The Book of Evil Deeds,* it hissed.

At least that's what it would have done if Agnes or any other witch worth her salt had written it.[2] In fact, if it had been Agnes, she would have thrown in a few additional perks like a front cover nasty enough to chomp off whole fingertips when properly slammed, or pages guaranteed to deliver paper cuts every single time. Imagine that!

But as the only book in all of Wanderly written just for witches, Agnes considered it better than nothing. And it did say "evil" on the front cover, which practically guaranteed that even if the other 2,793 pages had been filled with spells ranging from the embarrassingly easy (how to light your cauldron without a match) to the utterly useless (how to polish your witchy boots in

---

2. But this, of course, was impossible. Like every book in Wanderly, *The Book of Evil Deeds* was penned by a carefully trained scribe and personally inspected by Wanderly's infamous ruler, the Chancellor. This was likely why most witches tossed *The Book of Evil Deeds* out with yesterday's dinner carcass.

a snap), the last spell, the final spell, simply *had* to deliver.

Especially on, of all days, Agnes's birthday.

Agnes wriggled her fingers; she squiggled her nose; she inhaled a deep, raspy breath. She turned the page and . . . her floating rocking chair crashed down against the dusty floorboards with a jarring thud. Her eyes darted back and forth across the scrawling script. She began clawing at the bottom corner of the page to see if another page had become stuck, and perhaps this wasn't really the last page after all?

But it was.

And it contained one measly spell.

One measly, awful spell titled "**How to Transform Your Hair to Slime Green.**"

Hair?! The last page of *The Book of Evil Deeds* was reserved for a hairstyle? Day in and day out, week after week, year after year, Agnes had dutifully completed thousands of banal spells to arrive at nothing more than a hairstyle?

Agnes didn't need a new hairstyle! Over the years, she had honed her ratty strands to a nearly perfect shade of purple and didn't see any good reason to change it. Not to mention slime green was last popular over a century ago. What Agnes really needed—what Agnes wanted more than anything—was to find some way to make witching fun again!

It is a terrible thing to feel that one has wasted years. It is a more terrible thing to feel that one hasn't any plan for the days to come. So, Agnes did what any respectably infuriated witch would do: she slammed *The Book of Evil Deeds* shut. She growled at it. She tossed it down toward her witchy foot and gave it a sharp, swift kick.

At well over two thousand pages long, however, the book kicked back.[3] Even worse, as it careened off Agnes's now throbbing big toe and boomeranged about the room, it finally landed—*squish!*—atop Agnes's mud pie.

Agnes's birthday was going from bad to cursed!

Oh sure, there had been a few bright spots, like that morning's visit to Fairy Fifi's Woodland Boutique, where Agnes enchanted the entire stock of ball gowns to dance the ogre's shuffle instead of the waltz, but even that wasn't what it used to be. It was a perfectly evil curse. It should have been glorious! It should have been thrilling! Fairy Fifi's resulting scream had been a record-breaking eleven! But all Agnes felt was utterly and completely . . . bored.

At this point you may be jumping up and down in your seat, wondering why Agnes doesn't just try something new? Perhaps apply those top-notch potion-making skills to becoming a scientist. Maybe adapt those impressive broomstick acrobatics to life as a trapeze artist. Or do something completely wild like become a schoolteacher. This would be the perfect sort of advice if Agnes hadn't happened to live in the kingdom of Wanderly.

In the kingdom of Wanderly, stories ruled all, and the

---

3. Fear not, dear reader! Books rarely lash out of their own accord and instead use their hefty weight merely for defensive purposes.

citizens were required to live "by the book." You tell me how many witches you've seen waltz through a storybook in a frilly pink dress while humming a merry tune with a bunny rabbit underfoot? Considering Agnes would rather eat her smelly sock than do any of those things, that doesn't seem significant, but it was. Very much so. Because Agnes wasn't supposed to do *anything* other than what some storybook witch had already done. But what if not all witches were the same? What if Agnes were different? What if Agnes had an idea that no storybook witch ever had? Whether by accident or by calculated avoidance, those were the sorts of questions the Chancellor never bothered to answer.

Which meant Agnes was stuck.

Stuck on a rotten birthday, in a haunted cabin, all alone.

To be fair, the haunted part wasn't all that bad. Yes, the shelves on the walls sagged with jars full of hopelessly witchy things: rolling eyeballs, venomous snake fangs, and frog legs that still twitched. Yes, the ceiling was enchanted so that, no matter what time of day, it looked to be the unsettling hour of just past midnight, and, okay, fine, the black cauldron that bubbled endlessly over the hearth was guilty of throwing out a sharp crackle of lightning and a deep rumble of thunder from time to time. Still, somehow, Agnes's cabin oozed with its own sort of coziness.

Coziness, however, couldn't answer prickly questions. Coziness couldn't dole out appropriately wicked advice. Coziness couldn't solve the fact that Agnes didn't have anyone to talk to. Of course, Agnes didn't want another witch's company for some sappy, chatty-chat sort of reason. Blech! Agnes just wanted to find out if there were any other witches who were similarly stuck. If there were any other witches who had fallen into a bit of a slump. If there was some easy fix Agnes just hadn't thought of yet.

But that was never going to happen for the simple fact that in Wanderly—unless for the purposes of hissing, cursing, or plotting—witches didn't talk to one another. Ever.

Indeed, it was one of the ten governing provisions of the Witches' Manifesto that all witches were bound to. Lately, Agnes found herself wishing she'd never signed the thing, but when it was presented decades ago, the provisions had seemed ridiculously straightforward.[4] The brand-spanking-new cauldron and year's worth of bewitching dust the Chancellor tossed in as a signing bonus hadn't hurt, either.

But how to get around that aggravating rule now?

---

4. For example, what witch in her right mind would ever giggle instead of cackle? And if a witch couldn't commit at least three evil deeds a year, was she even a witch at all?